About the Author

Maria Johnson (pen name) is an author based in North West England. She has published two historical fiction novels, 'The Boy from the Snow' in January 2018 and the sequel 'The Veiled Wolf' in May 2019. They tell the story of Daniel, a warrior in Celtic Northwest England in 590AD. Maria has also a stand-alone fantasy novel for adults and older children, Lottie's Locket, published in November 2020. Along with writing, Maria also loves reading, swimming, walking, spending time with friends and a good cup of coffee. You can find out more about Maria and her books at mariajohnsonauthor.com

The Reckoning of Rheged

Maria Johnson

The Reckoning of Rheged

Olympia Publishers
London

www.olympiapublishers.com
OLYMPIA PAPERBACK EDITION

A CIP catalogue record for this title is
available from the British Library.

ISBN: 978-1-80074-491-2

First Published in 2023

Olympia Publishers
Tallis House
2 Tallis Street
London
EC4Y 0AB

Printed in Great Britain

Acknowledgements

"For the Christian Indie Writers Podcast and community — for the support and prayer, wisdom and inspiration, love and laughter."

"Be Thou my Breastplate, my Sword for the fight;
be Thou my whole Armor, be Thou my true Might;
be Thou my soul's Shelter, be Thou my strong Tower,
O raise Thou me heavenward, great Power of my power."

Map designed by Beth Baguley
Find more of her work available at:
LawandDraw Facebook Page
LawandDraw Instagram Page
LawandDraw Etsy Shop

Stratchclyde
Caer Liguali̇d
Bernicia
North
Rheged
Caer Liguali̇d Road
Klumeck Road
Klumeck
Great Lake
Gaeson
South
Rheged

Glossary of Royalty

Royals of Rheged

Caer Ligualid

King Urien — former King of Caer Ligualid, and Supreme Royal of Rheged. Deceased 590 AD.

King Owain — eldest son of King Urien. King of Caer Ligualid and Supreme Ruler of Rheged.

Queen Penarwen — married to King Owain.

Prince Elffin — son of King Owain and Queen Penarwen. Next in line to inherit the throne.

Prince Rhun — son of King Urien. Third in line to inherit the Caer Ligualid throne.

Princess Morfudd — daughter of King Urien.

Prince Elffin — son of King Urien. Deceased 593 AD.

Prince Rhiwallen — son of King Urien.

Prince Pasgent — son of King Urien. Married to Princess Lynette.

Prince Gilroy — son of Prince Pasgent and Princess Lynette.

Klumeck

King Cedric — former King of Klumeck, deceased 592 AD. Married to Princess Angharad, deceased 570 AD.

Princess Imogen —sister of King Cedric, deceased 570 AD. Married to Lord Adair, deceased 570 AD.

King Bryce — royal title of Daniel. King of Klumeck. Son of Princess Imogen and Lord Adair. Married to Queen Evelyn of Gaeson.

Princess Lynette — royal title of Sarah. Daughter of Princess Imogen and Lord Adair. Married to Prince Pasgent.

Princess Imogen — daughter of Queen Evelyn and King Bryce. Next in line to inherit the kingdoms of Gaeson and Klumeck.

Gaeson

King Reghan — Former King of Gaeson, deceased 590 AD.
Queen Evelyn — Queen of Gaeson, married to King Bryce.

Other kingdoms

King Lot — King of Gododdin.
Princess Thaney — Princess of Gododdin, daughter of King Lot.
King Ethelfrith — King of Bernicia, a once-Briton kingdom dispossessed by the Angles.
King Morgant — dispossessed king of Bernicia, now allied to King Ethelfrith and the Angles.

Part One

Chapter One

"There." Prince Pasgent hunkered back down beside me. "Looks like we've found them at last." There was a thread of humour in his voice, but his eyes remained sober in the afternoon light.

Slowly, I lifted myself to my knees and dared to glance over the ridge. At once I saw them. Dozens of tents sat scattered across the field below. Soldiers clad in Bernician armour walked about the camp as canvas flapped in the breeze. Others were clustered in groups, talking, playing games, or tending to camp duties.

"At least a hundred," I guessed quietly. "Probably double that." Grass blades rubbed against my hands as I inched closer, keeping my body low.

"Aye. Look." My brother-in-law risked raising his arm to point. "There he stands, in the middle of it all." I followed his gaze, already knowing exactly who he was referring to.

"King Morgant." It took all my military training to speak his name evenly. His armour, grander and brighter than the rest of his troops, easily marked him out, as did the velvet red cloak swishing behind him. My gaze flickered down the hill.

"I've seen you shoot." Pasgent murmured words that were only meant for me. "You would be well hidden from view. It would be so easy for you to slip down there."

"Aye, that it would," I agreed. Why was he tempting me? Surely, he could tell how I longed to skid down the slope to pierce him with my arrow. My bow called to me, daring me to succumb. My fingers itched to brush against the feathers atop my arrows.

Yet at what cost? Even if my aim proved true, the Bernicians would know of our presence. We only had twenty or so soldiers with us. Their horses were within easy reach. We had left our horses some distance away, knowing we would be quieter without them. By the time we got to them, there was little chance any of Pasgent's troop would survive.

"No," I said finally, only a little louder. "His Majesty King Owain told us to report on King Morgant's movements. Nothing more."

"You're right, of course." His words were reluctant, almost disappointed. "Besides," he muttered, as a smirk crossed his face, "I doubt my brother would be pleased if we brought war to our door early."

"Indeed." The retribution of King Ethelfrith of Bernicia would be swift. "Well, King Morgant certainly is on the move," I said. I felt suddenly lighter, almost liberated. It was as if I had looked out onto the abyss, but then turned back.

"Aye. Come on, let's head back." My brother-in-law patted my shoulder, then grinned. "After all, I might be meeting my son today."

"It could be a girl, you know," I pointed out. Prince Pasgent, the youngest brother of King Owain, had married my sister Sarah just over a year ago.

"I think not, though I should be honoured if we did." Pasgent's voice was quiet as we trod away from danger. His troop of soldiers followed our movements, boots almost noiseless as we retreated.

"Aye, your family do have a pattern of sons." My voice was not so quiet now we were part way down the hill, heading to where the horses were tethered. Prince Pasgent chuckled.

Soon we came to the horses and I swung up onto Epos, my faithful friend. I bent forward to pat her mane. I could not help then but cast a longing glance back up the hill. On the other side of it, at the end of my arrow, lay justice and vengeance. It was difficult to walk away from such an opportunity. What if there was never another chance to end his life?

"We ride for Caer Ligualid," Prince Pasgent called. His soldiers were already clambering atop their horses. Pasgent nudged his steed closer to me for a moment.

"We did the right thing, Daniel," he muttered. "King Morgant will meet his fate in the end, without us being responsible for us all being slaughtered." I smiled wryly.

"I know." My hands tightened the reins, then I glanced to him. "I await your lead." Technically as a king I outranked him, but these were his soldiers, not mine. I was here as his guest. Prince Pasgent flashed me a grin, tightened his grip on the reins and steered his horse back to the safety of Rheged lands. He set off at a gentle trot, heading back to our capital kingdom, Caer Ligualid.

I rode almost parallel to my brother-in-law. Prince Pasgent was more fair-haired than the rest of his siblings, with slightly softer features. He was perhaps a year younger than Sarah, with some ruddiness to his face still. There was an ease and levity to him that made him more pleasant company, perhaps, than the rest of his family. Not for the first time, I could see why Sarah had accepted the proposal of marriage from him.

It was the Year of our Lord 596AD, over four years since my sister had moved to Caer Ligualid. This was shortly after the death of King Cedric, our uncle. He had been the king of Klumeck, which six years ago had fallen to Bernicia, only days after Sarah and I had learned the truth of our royal blood.

I had inherited the dispossessed kingdom after our uncle's death, but Sarah resided with the people of Klumeck. Some citizens had chosen to move to Gaeson lands, where I remained with my wife Queen Evelyn and our daughter, Imogen.

It was two years after Sarah moved to Caer Ligualid that Sarah began mentioning Pasgent more in her letters. At first it was little more than a passing mention, but Evelyn and I suspected they had begun a courtship. When Sarah wrote to tell us they were betrothed, we were not surprised. The wedding the year before had been a joyous occasion for all, an alliance that not only spoke of their love, but further tied the bonds between the peoples of Rheged.

Once we were far away enough that King Morgant's troops wouldn't hear the horses, we broke into a gallop. Soon we were back into the boundaries of Rheged and the land swirled past, a blur of trees adorned with leaves of gold and russet, blazing in the afternoon sun.

"I do wish they had quarrelled for longer, about who would wear the crown after King Hussa," Prince Pasgent called a little darkly, over the din of hooves. He could be changeable like that; one moment full of cheer, the next sober.

"Aye," was all I said. The last time I had seen King Hussa was when he had granted me the opportunity to finally confront the Wolf, the Bernician spy Aldred, who had infiltrated Gaeson years earlier. He had been one of the foremost advisors of King Reghan, Evelyn's late father. The Wolf had even served Evelyn for a year or two before finally being revealed as a treacherous snake. It had been Aldred that had sowed the seeds of distrust between Evelyn's late father and King Cedric, my uncle.

Over twenty-five years ago, at the order of King Reghan, who had been poisoned so long by Aldred's twisted advice and driven by his own paranoia and greed, Aldred had snuck into Klumeck one fateful night. There he murdered my parents, my aunt and her unborn child in their beds. King Cedric, barely surviving the attack himself, had sent Sarah and me away in a carriage, where we had ended up in the woods outside Gaeson.

The revelation of the Wolf had nearly torn my marriage apart, for I also discovered then that she had known what kind of foul company she had in her court. She spent the first two years of her reign longing to expose him, but Aldred had threatened he would unleash a scheme that would kill me and half of Rheged. We reconciled after being kidnapped by the Wolf, but then escaping him by falling off a cliff into a lake.

King Hussa died only a year after my final fight with the Wolf. I had been a little disappointed that I would not be facing him myself in battle. After his death in 593AD, his cousin, King Ethelfrith, had ascended the throne. It had not been a clean succession, however, for King Hussa's son, Prince Hering, believed that he should be king instead.

Indeed, much of the peace we had enjoyed for the last four years was owed to the feud between King Ethelfrith and Prince Hering. The young prince had attempted to take the throne last summer, but he had been soundly beaten.

Prince Hering had survived, but barely. I had heard he had travelled further north in Bernician lands where he could lick his wounds and try to rally others to fight his cause. Sadly, without Prince Hering to distract him, King Ethelfrith had once more fixed his eyes upon Rheged.

"I cannot understand King Morgant!" Prince Pasgent shouted over the galloping. "At times he seems completely within King Ethelfrith's circle, but then at other times…" His bitter voice trailed away.

"He's nothing but a foul snake," I called back. My words were calm, but I was once more trying to keep my blood from boiling. "He's a king without a people, just using Bernicia for his own gain. That's why he made the deal with King Hussa." Pasgent only nodded, his eyes darkening again.

King Morgant had once been king of Bernicia, but after the kingdom fell to the invading Angles, he had retreated and resided for some years in Strathclyde, a Briton kingdom much further to the north. Inexplicably, though the enemies had taken over his kingdom and assumed the name 'Bernicia' for themselves, King Morgant had made a deal with King Hussa and had long worked against Rheged.

He was originally an ally, though no one had ever really trusted him. He had fought with us as one of the Confederation of Kings at the siege of Ynys Metcaut over six years ago, along with King Urien, King Gwollag and King Rhydderch. However, this was when he betrayed Rheged and ordered the assassination of King Urien, Prince Pasgent's father, during the battle.

That was why I knew Pasgent had also yearned for me to fly an arrow into King Morgant's skull, for he sought justice and revenge just as much as I did. In the past four years, we had learnt what we had always suspected — that the Wolf had been working for King Morgant all along. So, it was this traitor who had orchestrated the deaths of half my kin and the murder of King Urien. I often wondered where the war might stand now if the mighty Ruler of Rheged had not died that day.

My mood lifted considerably then, as Caer Ligualid came into view, its three spires shining in the afternoon. Despite my dark thoughts, I smiled at the sight of it.

"Home again," Prince Pasgent said. Then he grinned, all traces of his sombreness vanishing. "So, you think Sarah will have given birth yet?"

"No," I answered, chuckling. "Sarah will be waiting for you to be home, first, if she has anything to do with it." Indeed, it seemed that my sister's birth pains had not yet begun, for as we slowed our horses to a trot as we came to the portcullis, I saw Sarah stood near the avenue of trees just outside the main courtyard.

My face cracked into a grin, for she was watching my daughter, Imogen. Little Immy ran in and out of the trees, the russet leaves gleaming and casting dappled light in the early evening sunshine.

The strands of her honeylike hair billowed about her, glowing gold as the sun kissed the top of her head. My daughter's skin was pale but healthy. Tiny freckles that had speckled her arms and cheeks had begun to fade again now that high summer had passed. Her eyes were as blue and as fathomless as the ocean, full of life and twinkling whenever she smiled.

Imogen had quite different features to us. She did not have my slightly round chin, nor Evelyn's eyes. Rather than my auburn hair or Evelyn's raven locks, Imogen's hair glowed bright in the sun. Her natural mother was Morwenna, a castle maid in Gaeson, who had fallen pregnant out of wedlock.

We did not know who Imogen's natural father was, only that he was one of the soldiers in Gaeson's army. However, what little I knew of his character I did not like. He had left Gaeson after only a brief affair with Morwenna. As far as we knew, he did not even know that the child existed.

A few weeks later Morwenna went to Leigh, the surgeon, who had diagnosed her as being with child. Rather than face dismissal, scandal and poverty, word was spread that Morwenna had contracted a contagious disease. She isolated herself in part of the castle when her pregnancy began to show. After the child was born, Leigh declared Morwenna 'cured' and she returned to work as before.

The timing of the situation had suited Evelyn and me well, for the discovery of Morwenna's pregnancy coincided with the revelation that my wife was not able to bear us a child. We adopted Imogen, naming her after the mother who had borne me. From the first moment I first saw Immy and held her in my arms, I knew I could not love my daughter an iota more than if had she come from my own blood and bone.

From time to time in Gaeson, I saw Morwenna when she thought herself unseen, just for a moment. She would look up from her task of lighting a fire or sweeping a corridor. Her eye would linger over Imogen, desperate to catch a glimpse of the child she had birthed. I felt much sympathy for Morwenna. Though she had agreed to Leigh's proposal with much relief, there was a sadness there, also. I knew that in a better, kinder world, Morwenna would have loved Imogen well.

I grinned again as I watched my little child run. Imogen's notes of gentle laughter wafted up into the air as she giggled. She often shrieked with joy at the smallest thing that might please her, clapping her hands at the most normal occurrence. More than once of late, I had started to gently rebuke her; to tell her that as a royal, she should perhaps act with a little more decorum. These rebukes were sparingly given, however, for she was not yet five. What little girl should not be able to run and laugh with such joy?

"Father!" Imogen cried, as suddenly she saw me. She pelted towards me and I barely had time to swing down from Epos before she crashed into me.

"Easy, Imogen." It was only a half-hearted attempt at a rebuke as I swooped her up into my arms. "You must remember to slow down a little."

"Sorry, Father." Imogen beamed a smile in my arms, not looking the slightest bit apologetic. "Hello, Uncle Pasgent."

"Hello, my dear." He winked at her before his eyes roved to his wife. "It looks like your little cousin isn't quite ready to meet us yet," he said. Imogen chuckled, shaking her head.

"I hope she hasn't been too tiring," I called to Sarah as she approached. My sister's eyes were warm and full of good humour, but then I noticed the tiredness in them. She walked slowly, her stomach swelled full with child.

"She's been fine." Sarah moved her hands behind her long skirts, placing them on the small of her back. She smiled at us in the afternoon sun. "Evelyn is still talking to King Owain."

"Still?" My eyebrows rose. Then again, I told myself, this was no surprise. Discussing the politics between our kingdoms could take them until sunrise. My wife had been trained for royalty her whole life, but I was rather less used to council meetings and dealing with disputes at court.

We had arrived in Caer Ligualid only yesterday, to be in time for Sarah to give birth to her child. It was not the best timing that, today of all days, King Owain had ordered his brother to lead a patrol to track King Morgant's movements. The relief was all too plain in Pasgent's face that he had not missed the birth of their first child. I smiled at the thought of it. Whilst Imogen was all my heart desired, Sarah's child ensured our bloodline would continue.

"We need to report to Owain." At this, Pasgent's voice cooled, his face hardening. Sarah's smile faded, already understanding we had indeed seen King Morgant.

"Come on, Immy," I said brightly, hoping that my daughter had not picked up on the change in atmosphere. "You can tell me all about your day."

I should have liked to spend the rest of the remaining daylight talking with my child, but soon I found myself next to Prince Pasgent in the ornate throne chamber, so splendid it made Evelyn's hall in Gaeson look almost plain. King Owain sat on his throne, looking as sombre as his father ever had done. My wife flashed me a brief smile as she came to stand beside us.

"We saw him, my king." Pasgent's voice was dark as he began. "Dozens of tents, apparently over a hundred men. We could have struck down King Morgant then," he pointed out, "but did not want to risk an early war."

"Quite right." King Owain gave a nod. He listened as my brother-in-law gave details about the layout of the camp.

"Enough for now," King Owain then said, a little heavily. He sighed. "Then it is as we thought. War cannot be far away." Suddenly he smiled — but it seemed to take a lot of effort.

"However, it is not at our gates yet. Tonight, we feast. Princess Lynette is to give birth at any moment," he said, using Sarah's formal title, the name our parents in Klumeck had given her. "That is all." We inclined our heads and departed the hall. Evelyn stuck a hand under my arm. It was time to prepare for the grand dinner King Owain had ordered.

"I thought she was unwell," I muttered in surprise about two hours later, stood in the biggest banquet hall. King Owain had entered the exquisite chamber with Queen Penarwen on his arm.

"So did I. Perhaps she has recovered?" Evelyn murmured, a slight frown on her features. I did notice Queen Penarwen looked a little pale, with lines of worry etched into her face. Her countenance brightened, however, as she approached us. Her ornate gown gave her the impression of gliding.

"Ah, Queen Evelyn, King Bryce." In the moments before she reached us, I noticed she took care with her steps. Either she was more well than I thought, or she was avoiding showing her illness.

“Your Majesty, Queen Penarwen.” I bent in a half-bow in a formal greeting as Evelyn curtsied beside me. It was the first time we were seeing her in Caer Ligualid, as dinner upon our arrival the previous night had been a far simpler affair.

“I am pleased you could be here for the birth.” Her eyes sparkled as she spoke. “How is your child? She is not long four now, if I’m not mistaken. Ah, Elffin,” she added then, as a lanky lad approached. “You have met my eldest, I’m sure.”

“Once, or twice,” Evelyn said, smiling as she nodded. I thought I vaguely remembered him, from a handful of previous visits to Caer Ligualid.

“Your Highness, Prince Elffin.” I inclined my head to him. In my peripheral vision, though Queen Penarwen kept her casual smile, she put her hand on her son’s arm. Was that relief in her eyes, that she could lean on him?

Prince Elffin nodded to us but said nothing. I studied the young prince briefly. He looked no more than perhaps eighteen. His features were sharp, but his cheeks and eyes were still ruddy with youth.

“This is King Bryce of Klumeck and Queen Evelyn of Gaeson.” Queen Penarwen introduced us regally, her tone forcefully bright and only a little sharper. Her words both raised awareness of and ignored his rudeness.

“It is an honour to meet you both, Your Majesties.” Prince Elffin spoke solemnly, bowing his head a little more. Before we could talk any further, King Owain coughed loudly.

“Let us begin the feast,” King Owain began simply. As we made our way to the grand tables, I hid a smile. Being a king of few words could have its advantage. A royal who did not drone on was far more relatable to the people they ruled.

Evelyn and I sat opposite each other at one end of the table, with Sarah and Pasgent immediately beside us. Sat the other side of Pasgent and Sarah were Prince Elffin and Queen Penarwen. The other side of them were the extended royal family; King Owain’s other siblings and their children.

King Urien had been father of six children in total. After King Owain, there was his sister Princess Morfudd, who was not present tonight — she had married a royal in Strathclyde about a decade earlier. Then there had been Prince Elffin. He had died four years before, also at the hand of King Morgant.

Prince Rhun was second in line to the throne, after the young Prince Elffin. Following Prince Rhun was Prince Rhiwallen and finally the youngest brother, my sister's husband Prince Pasgent. Beyond them, at the end of the table, were a few officials.

As my gaze flickered across the party, I felt a wave of sadness. In all these occasions, I was keenly aware that King Cedric was missing. My eyes met Sarah's briefly. Though neither of us said a word, I could tell she also missed our uncle's presence.

"Tell me of King Morgant, if you would, Uncle," Prince Elffin suddenly called to Pasgent, rather loudly. "How lies the land? Did you see him?" His voice was urgent.

Pasgent took a mouthful of wine before answering, then glanced to King Owain. The Ruler of Rheged regarded his son for a moment.

"Prince Pasgent and King Bryce have already given me their report." His voice was gruff, using my formal, royal name as he tore off a hunk of bread. "It's not the most pleasant topic of conversation for dinner, but I'll not deny you your interest, lad." He turned back to his plate.

"Aye, we found his camp today," Pasgent said. Elffin nodded rapidly, his food forgotten. "King Morgant was there. He still seems to be loyal to King Ethelfrith." I helped myself to some roasted vegetables from a platter nearby.

"I still cannot understand why King Morgant would betray us." Elffin's words were bitter as he reached for his goblet of wine. "Why would he make peace with those that invaded him? That tore the kingdom away from his hands?" He set his cup down and finally began to eat.

"Perhaps he is just using Bernicia for his own gain." It was the same answer I had given Pasgent earlier, on the ride back to Caer Ligualid. "Perhaps he plans to destroy them from within, one day, as he has tried to do with Rheged." I thought briefly of the Wolf here as I took another mouthful of wine.

"That does seem his way. It seems as though he is determined to destroy the royals of Rheged, piece by piece." Pasgent's speech was a little muffled by the beef he chewed. "First our father, then Elffin," he added, swallowing. We never did really trust him." he added, shaking his head. "King Cedric warned us not to as well, if I'm not mistaken."

"Aye," I answered. My uncle's warning had come at the first meeting between royals of Caer Ligualid, Gaeson and Klumeck for twenty-two years. The royal representatives had not met since the war had broken out between the late King Reghan and my late uncle. The meeting was only the day after King Urien had marched against Gaeson with King Cedric and Prince Owain, only to be met with Gaeson's complete surrender. Sarah should also have been present, but I had not had the chance to tell her of her true identity.

During the meeting, King Urien had spoken of the Confederation of Kings, an alliance between himself, King Gwollag (King Urien's cousin), King Rhydderch and King Morgant. My uncle had said that whilst the two former kings could be trusted, he was deeply suspicious of King Morgant. King Urien had overruled him, saying that without King Morgant's aid, we had no way of stopping Bernicia.

"A house does seem to be as easily broken inside as outside," Evelyn said here. Her voice was casual, but I knew she was thinking of her father, whose deceit and greed had nearly caused Gaeson's ruin. That was without the mention of the Wolf, who had manipulated King Reghan for so long.

"Here could be our chance, then, with him right on the edge of the border," Prince Elffin said, glancing to King Owain. "What do you plan to do, Father?" The king watched his son impatiently.

"Nothing, for now. We are still gathering our forces and making our alliance with Gododdin," King Owain replied. Gododdin was a vast Briton kingdom near Strathclyde, to the north of Rheged. "If we were to slay King Morgant, the retribution from King Ethelfrith would be swift. We do not want to start this war a moment before we have to," King Owain concluded.

"He is right there, though," Prince Elffin protested immediately. "We do not know if we will get another opportunity—"

"Enough!" King Owain slapped the table. We all turned surprised gazes to the king. "That is enough." His voice was lower, but no less cold. "King Bryce and Prince Pasgent did the right thing in not attacking King Morgant today. There is more to ruling a kingdom than vengeance, boy."

The king's words seemed unnecessarily harsh. I noticed how Prince Elffin stared back at his father stonily, almost impertinently. There seemed to be some bad blood between them. Perhaps that was why the king had been so easily vexed.

The awkwardness lingered over our dining. We waited, but King Owain merely grabbed another beef pie from his plate, taking another enormous bite. Rich gravy dribbled down his chin.

We too resumed eating, following the king's suit. Yet nobody spoke. Prince Elffin's nostrils were still flaring. The quiet was filled only with knives scraping against meat and plates and food rolling in mouths. I could hardly remember when such noises were so pronounced.

Eventually the plates from the main meal were removed. Then smaller plates arrived, bearing cakes made with honey. Goblets of wine were refilled, but still the silence was continued. It was with relief that King Owain promptly put down his knife. Wordlessly, he stood and departed the dining hall.

"If you'll excuse me, I might partake in a breath of air for a moment." Sarah's words came politely, whilst servants hastily cleared away plates and knives.

"I believe I shall join her," I said, getting to my feet. It would be a relief to leave the chamber and I was concerned for my sister's wellbeing. I paused to pour myself a measure of mead into a fresh goblet and filled one with water for Sarah before following in her footsteps.

I found her in one of the palace gardens. She glanced my way as I approached, a knowing smirk across her face. She must have guessed I would follow her. My sister rested against a low wall, with one hand resting lightly above the swelling of her stomach.

"Thank you, Daniel." Sarah accepted the water and took a drink, whilst I tasted my own honeyed tonic. She was viewing the garden; my own gaze followed. Though the sweet, earthy scent of fallen leaves filled my nostrils, only a dim outline of the garden could be seen.

"It grows darker quicker now," my sister said. Her thoughts mirrored my own, for dusk had already faded into night. The garden was only lit by the sparse beacons set high upon the nearby walls.

"Aye, winter will not be far away." I took another sip of mead. "Is all well with King Owain?" I asked now. "I was surprised at his harshness to Prince Elffin."

"I believe he is well. Prince Elffin does not always understand the larger perspective and talk of King Morgant vexes us all." Sarah's voice turned bitter. I nodded. After all, King Morgant had killed her kin at the hands of the Wolf, as well as mine.

"In truth, King Owain is almost too well. He is being well entertained at court." Her eyes, flickering in the light from the beacons, hardened.

"Is this entertainment of particular tastes?" I asked vaguely. My sister raised her eyebrows, drawing her mouth into a thin line. Clearly, she did not approve. Perhaps this was the reason for the bad blood between King Owain and Prince Elffin?

"I was surprised to see Queen Penarwen, given her illness." I said, after sipping the mead again. Sarah nodded knowingly.

"Aye, it is a rare occurrence these days." There was more than a little sarcasm in her voice. Then she sighed. "I do not wish to speak against King Owain. He is my brother-in-law."

"Here you are." The new voice was Evelyn's, as she came to join us, a goblet in her hand. "What are you discussing so intently?"

"How the nights come in quicker these days," I replied, mostly truthfully. If my sister did not wish to discuss King Owain, I would not press the subject further. "Winter will soon be here."

"Indeed." Evelyn's mouth curled. "You need not tell me what else you are scheming." Her eyes narrowed in mock indignation. I smirked. "How are you tonight, Sarah?" she asked my sister.

"As well as I can be, waiting for it to begin." My sister placed a hand on her stomach again. "The surgeon here says it is any day now."

"Aye, it must be so distressing for you." Evelyn frowned in concern. "Perhaps you should retire early? King Owain would not mind. You must get some rest if you can."

"I think I will." Sarah gave us a brave smile, but I saw the stress in her features and the tiredness in her eyes. My heart tightened. "Perhaps you can tell Pasgent I've retired."

"Of course." I touched her hand briefly. I watched her depart as my brow furrowed further. I knew childbirth was a common occurrence, that women had survived since the beginning of creation, but that did not make such any easier. I wished I could remove the pain about to befall her.

"Your Majesties?" We turned to see a castle servant bow at the entrance to the small garden. I recognised her as Imogen's maid. "I am sorry to disturb you, my lord and lady." She dipped her head as she crossed over to us. "The princess has woken and seems a little distressed. I was wondering—"

"Of course, I'll go." I finished my mead in a swift gulp. "King Owain may still wish to talk to you," I added. My wife gave me a wry smile — I could tell she'd had her fill of politics for today. She took the empty cup of mead from me, her fingers brushing against mine for a moment.

The grand corridors of Caer Ligualid were quiet. I stretched my arms on over my head a moment as I walked. I was mostly sober, but the tiniest waves of the wine and the mead lapped pleasantly around my head. Unbidden, the day's patrol and discovering King Morgant thrust itself into my mind. I tried to push it away as I went to attend to my daughter.

"Hello, love." I opened the door to Immy's chamber expecting tears, but distressed was not quite the word. She was sat up in bed, frowning, but her eyes were dry. She gave me her usual bright smile as she saw me. "Why are you still awake? Did you have a bad dream?"

"Not really, Father." Her frown burrowed deeper. Clearly, it was deep thinking about something that kept her up. I sat on the edge of the bed and raised my eyebrows, waiting.

"Mother said we were to see Aunt Sarah because she is about to have a baby." Imogen was almost talking to herself, but then she glanced my way. "Is that why her stomach is so big now?"

"Aye." I kept my tone low and gentle, hoping it would help ease her back to sleep. "Come on, lie down." My daughter dutifully obeyed. I pulled the covers back up to her chin.

"Mother's stomach was not big like that, was it?" My hands stilled as I reached for the blanket, turning back to Imogen. Ah, was this what she was wondering about? She stared at the ceiling, her head slightly tilted.

"No, love." I left the blanket for now. One of my hands reached for hers. "Do you remember what the word adoption means?"

Evelyn and I had decided long ago we would always be truthful about Imogen's origins, talking of it freely and explaining things as she came to enquire about them. I understood why my parents had hidden it from me for what might happen should King Reghan discover it, but it had made the truth about my identity no less painful to swallow. I had not wanted that distress to come to her one day.

"Aye, Father." The frown eased slightly. "It means you and Mother chose me to be in your family," she murmured, repeating the truth she was only just beginning to grasp.

"That's right." I nodded. "You are not linked to us by blood, but every baby does come from a woman's body. It grows in a place called her womb, near her stomach. That's why Aunt Sarah's stomach looks so big." Imogen gave a slow nod, but confusion still lined her features a little.

"So, where did I come from, then?" A smile tugged at my features. I was pleased with her logic. At only four, she had worked out she had come from somewhere.

Then I hesitated. The hour was late, and Evelyn was not here. Should I leave the conversation about Morwenna for another time? The topic was obviously keeping Imogen awake, though. Would she be wondering about it all night long? If I mentioned Morwenna, would she wish to meet her? Would Imogen even consider that she belonged to her now, rather than to Evelyn and me?

"The woman who grew you in her womb, like Aunt Sarah is doing with her baby, is a lady who lives in Gaeson. She works at the castle," I said eventually. No matter how much I might wish to cling to her, I knew Imogen deserved to know the truth. I saw the obvious question in Immy's face, of why she was with us, rather than her birth mother.

"Not every woman is able to take care of a child in the way she might like to. Your birth mother was young and alone, without much money or people that could help her. While she was carrying you, your mother and I dearly wanted a child of our own. So, once you were born, we chose you to be in our family." I swallowed hard. Had I said too much? Too little? Had I just made things more confusing?

"The important thing you must remember, Immy," I added, a little urgently, "is that your mother and I love you very much. You are our daughter, in every way that matters." My heart lightened considerably to see her face brighten into a smile.

"Aye, Father." Her expression was much cleared. The conversation seemed to have solved something for her. I reached again for the blanket.

"It's late now, Imogen." I placed the blanket on top of the sheets and bent to kiss her forehead. "Go to sleep." I stood, hoping this was the end of the matter for one night. I blew out the candle on the bedside table, casting us into near darkness.

"Father?" A sleepy voice reached my ears, as I reached the chamber door. I turned back to her dim outline. "The lady, what's her name? The lady who…?"

"The lady who gave birth to you?" I guessed softly, as she trailed away. Why was there a strange feeling in my throat? Perhaps I felt if I said Morwenna's name, it could never be unsaid. Immy's natural mother would go from being abstract to a real person with a real name.

"Her name is Morwenna." For who was I to judge what truth could or could not be shared? Imogen deserved to know the truth of her bloodline, just as Sarah and I had done.

"Morwenna." Imogen repeated the name slowly, as if tasting it. "Goodnight, Father," she added, her tone much brighter. I listened to her breathing, hearing her fall asleep before I had even quitted her chamber. I smiled, my hand still on the door. I hoped my daughter would always be this safe and content. That she would always slip into slumber this quickly.

"Goodnight, my love." I made my way back to the banquet hall. As I walked along the corridor, I had the ridiculous notion that Imogen could be dreaming about Morwenna. Was she imagining what her birth mother could look like? I hoped that no matter what interest Imogen had in Morwenna, even if she met her, our relationship with Immy would not change. That she would remain mine and Evelyn's child, just as she always had been, from the moment I first held her in my arms.

Chapter Two

"Your Majesties!" A call at the door, followed by a rather sharp knock, woke us. I rolled to sit up in bed, yawning.

"It must be far from dawn," Evelyn groaned, still half full of sleep. The knock came again. She rose to sit also, rubbing her eyes. I heaved myself out of bed, pulled on my trousers and went to the door.

"Sorry to disturb, Your Majesties." The castle guard's voice was quick as I opened the door a crack. "King Owain bids you come. It is Princess Lynette, sire. The child is coming."

"Of course!" In my recently woken state, I had almost forgotten this could be why the guard was knocking on our door. "A moment," I muttered distractedly. I shut the door again to throw on my robe, to see Evelyn had done the same. She fastened the sash around her waist and quickly tied her hair. I shoved my feet into my indoor shoes.

The two of us hurried through the castle after the guard. I was concerned for Sarah, yet elated at the prospect of new birth. We came to a small hall near Sarah's chamber. Pasgent was pacing about the room.

"I pray all will be well, brother," I said, going straight over to my brother-in-law and clasping his arm. "Any further news?" Pasgent shook his head.

"There is nothing to do but wait." He folded his arms, then unfolded them again. "It is difficult to see her in such pain, but to be so helpless."

"I'm sure." Evelyn gave him a reassuring smile. "It will not be long now." Pasgent only nodded, running a frustrated hand through his hair. Then abruptly he turned, heading for the large jug of wine. As he poured a generous amount into his goblet, I suspected it was not his first measure.

"Easy." I grinned as he turned back to me. "You do not want to meet your child drunk." Pasgent managed a small smile.

"Just to help me be calm, Daniel." He gestured the goblet in our direction before taking a quick swig. I was tempted to join him.

"Mother?" Evelyn and I both turned to see our daughter, her face crumpled with fear and tears, running into the chamber, her maid right behind her.

"My apologies, your Majesties, Your Highness." It was the same maid as before, looking further flustered. "I think Her Highness had a nightmare. I tried to calm her, but she kept asking for you."

"It is no trouble." Evelyn gave the servant a smile, to let her know she had not failed in her duties in the slightest. "You are relieved, I will take her to bed later." The maid bent to curtsey and then left the chamber, looking grateful indeed.

I went to the wine, but only poured myself a small amount. I turned back to see Evelyn comforting our daughter. I frowned. It was such a change from a few hours ago. Had our conversation about Morwenna given her the nightmare?

"Did you have a bad dream, darling?" I came to sit near them, goblet in hand. Imogen nodded, bringing a curled fist to her mouth to suck. I smiled tenderly, watching her. Earlier I had been impressed with her logic, but now she seemed younger than ever. "What was it about?" I asked gently.

"I don't remember now." Imogen rubbed her eyes and sniffed. "Everybody's still awake?" she said in a small voice, lowering her hands again. "What's going on? Where's Aunt Sarah?" She glanced to Pasgent, who had hardly noticed his niece's troubled state. Not that I minded, for my brother-in-law was much preoccupied at present.

"Aunt Sarah is having her baby." Evelyn's arms shifted, still comfortably wrapped around Imogen's body. "It's exciting, isn't it?" Our daughter only nodded. She was still shaking off the dream.

"Forgive the intrusion, Your Majesties." It was a voice I knew well. I turned to see the short stature of Taliesin stood in the doorway, bowing grandly to us. His eyes were as sharp as ever. "His Majesty King Owain wished the birth to be recorded." He dipped his head to us again.

Taliesin had been the bard, poet and chronicler to the late King Urien. He now did the same to King Owain. I had often felt uneasy about this man, but he had also safeguarded the evidence needed to expose Aldred as the Wolf.

"I am sure we will inform you when it is time." Prince Pasgent's voice was curt. I hid a smirk. My brother-in-law's disdain implied I was not the only one who found the bard wearying.

"The King wished me to record the exact moment," Taliesin replied, his voice only a little cooler. "It is his wish." Pasgent stilled again, gaze narrow, but he nodded.

"I, of course, wish you every prayer for Princess Lynette's birth." Taliesin turned on the spot as Pasgent once more resumed his pacing. The bard's gaze swept around the chamber, stopping abruptly when his eyes came to Imogen.

"Ah, the little princess. May I offer my respect? I have yet to make her acquaintance." Before I could reply, the bard had crossed the hall. He stopped in front of Imogen and performed another sweeping bow in front of Evelyn and Imogen. I hid a sigh, for his pomp was one of the most vexing things about him.

"The princess is young and beautiful; I sense great wisdom in her eyes already." Evelyn inclined her head, a courteous smile on her features.

"Thank you," she answered, giving him a silent nod. Taliesin's eyes were alit with interest. I sighed, wondering how many unwanted words he would spill about meeting our daughter.

"She had a nightmare," I said abruptly, hoping Taliesin would have enough tact to leave Imogen alone.

"Aye, my lord." The bard's voice was soft. "A common occurrence in children, I'm sure. Her Highness does seem a little distressed still." I bit my tongue to stop myself saying that was probably because he was hovering so near to my daughter.

Taliesin opened his mouth to speak further, but no words came out. Instead, the bard took a sharp intake of his breath, eyes frozen wide.

"There is great strength in her." Taliesin's words were rasped when he eventually spoke them, in a voice that didn't seem quite his own.

"Mark me, this child will rise like the dawn," he continued rapidly. "Her heart and body are strong. She will forge new alliances, giving new hope to Rheged. The day will come when she does battle on blood-soaked fields, next to a river." Immy stirred in her mother's arms, gazing back uncertainly at Taliesin. I opened my mouth to object.

"Princess Imogen may yet turn the tide against Bernicia." The words tumbled out of him quicker still. "She will bring peace and hope to our people." His voice grew louder, more intense. "However, this is only if she overcomes the danger, the great harm that may come sooner than she knows—"

"Enough!" My single harsh word cut across him. Taliesin blinked and jerked his gaze back to mine, stricken. "Of what do you speak?" The poet only blinked further, uncertainty all about him. It was as if he had just broken away from a spell.

"Leave us." Evelyn's tone was equally firm. "You unsettle our daughter." He blinked and glanced to Evelyn. Imogen's distress was plain, angering me further. She was only just calm, after her nightmare.

"I… uh, forgive me, Your Majesty." Taliesin dipped his head as a little colour returned to his cheeks. "It was a prophecy I just told, my lady." Though his composure had returned, his expression was sombre, with none of his usual pomp. I had not seen him look so solemn since King Urien's funeral.

"I have the sight, passed down from my fathers," the poet continued. His gaze focused again on Imogen. "This is no ordinary child, Your Majesties. My visions are hardly ever wrong." His conclusion was flat, almost dark.

"She is our daughter, there is nothing ordinary about that." Evelyn's voice was firm. "I must ask you to take your leave of our company."

"Of course, Your Majesties." Taliesin stepped backwards quickly. "No offence was meant. I shall await the royal birth from elsewhere." He gave a final bow before abruptly heading to the other side of the small hall.

"What a lot of nonsense!" I said immediately, making no effort to lower my voice. I cared not whether Taliesin had heard me.

"Indeed." Evelyn frowned. I wondered if my queen was just as unnerved by the encounter as I was. Still, sitting down next to my wife and child, I tried to put the strange conversation behind me. I was about to become an uncle. I smiled broadly at the thought. Evelyn returned my smile.

"It cannot be long now—" My wife halted her speech as the surgeon burst through the doors. Prince Pasgent ran over to him. There were a few hushed words before he turned back to us, beaming.

"It is done!" Pasgent announced. "Princess Lynette is well! We have a healthy baby boy. I bid you remain here a few minutes, then you may come meet him."

As the last word left his mouth, he hesitated as if looking dazed. Then he almost crashed into the door in the haste to get to Sarah's chamber. I chuckled, remembering that feeling well. I hardly knew what to do with myself when Imogen was born.

"Can we go through now?" Immy asked at once, full of gleeful impatience, wriggling on her mother's knee. Evelyn gave a gentle laugh.

"Soon, Immy. Uncle Pasgent said a few minutes, remember? The baby will be bathed," Evelyn said. "Aunt Sarah will want to catch her breath and Uncle Pasgent will want to meet his new child properly, without all of us crowding around."

"Aye, Mother," Imogen replied dully. Immy therefore cast her eyes to the frayed tapestry rug and spent the next few minutes in relative silence, swinging her legs and fidgeting with her hands. She was almost sitting on them when Pasgent came back into the chamber.

"Come on, then." Evelyn stood, taking our daughter's hands. "Good timing, for you were about to wear right through my knees with all your wriggling." Immy giggled. "Also, the longer you wait, the longer you are out of bed." The three of us headed for Sarah's chamber.

"Daniel, Evelyn." Despite the pain and tiredness in the redness of her cheeks, her joy was clear. "Ah, Imogen, I see you are here as well. I am glad of it. Come," she invited simply, "meet our son."

"Well done, sister," I told Sarah warmly, as we crossed the chamber. "His hair!" I said, stopping short. My sister's hair was a chestnut brown. My own colour was a dark auburn, like an autumn leaf, slightly more brown than red. The same colour had been atop our uncle King Cedric's hair.

My nephew's hair was something else entirely. There was not much of it, but the babe's tufts of hair were stark crimson, almost as vivid as the sun before it dips below the horizon. It was a colour I had only seen before in my dreams.

"It's from our mother, is it not?" Sarah asked eagerly. Her eyes were lit in anticipation, desperate for a deeper connection with the woman she had never known. While I possessed a few fleeting images, my dear sister had been too young to remember our birth parents.

"Aye. Even more vivid than our uncle's," I said hoarsely, my throat gripped tight. It was as if our mother and King Cedric were here amongst us. As if they too had witnessed the birth.

"This is Gilroy," Sarah introduced. I smiled wide. The meaning of my nephew's name was not lost on me. It literally meant 'serves the red-haired one'. "In memory of them both," she said softly. Her hand touched her son's crimson tufts, then her gaze moved deliberately to Imogen.

I understood at once. This day, we had truly preserved the royal family line. The blood flowing through her son and my daughter bearing our mother's name. I nodded slowly, at a loss for words. I stepped closer and Sarah saw the unspoken question in my eyes. With a slight smile, my sister passed her newly born son to me.

"Hello, Gilroy." My voice was a murmur as I gazed at my nephew's face. Beneath the clumps of red were orbs of endless blue, bright and deep at the same time. It should have been impossible, but they seemed remarkably like Imogen's eyes.

"Welcome to the world, little lad," I greeted softly. Gilroy had a little puffiness around his cheeks, with ten tiny fingers and perfectly formed nails stretching out from his cloths. I reflected that he had Sarah's eyes, but perhaps Pasgent's strong chin. I sensed Evelyn come closer to me.

"Come, Immy." I turned to them both, lowering the precious bundle of the babe in my arms. "Meet your cousin." My heart tightened a moment, then, realising she was probably the same age I would have been in meeting my cousin, had my aunt and her unborn child lived. Would I have greeted my kin in a similar way, had they not departed before seeing any of this world?

"Careful, now." My warning was gentle as Imogen lifted her hands to the babe. Immediately, then, I saw my instructions had not been necessary. She touched Gilroy's head delicately, as if he were an egg and the slightest pressure from her fingers could crack him.

"Hello, Gilroy." Imogen's whisper was just as gentle, perceiving well the beautiful mystery of this moment. He began to stir a little. Imogen watched quietly, transfixed by the sight of her new cousin, as I passed my nephew back to Sarah. He soon became peaceful in her arms again. Pasgent bent his head, smiling at his wife and son.

"Come, Imogen." Evelyn spoke low. "It is far past your bedtime." The three of us retreated slowly from the chamber, as Sarah and Pasgent retreated to their new world of mother, father and son.

***

"Did Imogen go back to sleep all right?" I asked Evelyn, as she came to join me. She had taken Imogen back to bed and we were standing in the same part of the palace garden as five or six hours before. The sky had paled considerably, but it would still be some time before dawn came.

"Aye." Evelyn leant back against a pillar. "Let's hope the nightmare does not return." She wore a slight look of concern as she passed me a goblet of wine.

"Thank you." I took a sip of the wine. "I meant to tell you earlier, but you were already asleep," I said. "When the maid came the first time, she wasn't really distressed. She had questions."

"Oh?" As Evelyn took a drink of wine, a thin dribble of it trailed down her chin. On impulse, I reached to stem the red remnant with my thumb. She bent her head to briefly press it against my touch.

"Yes?" Evelyn prompted, her mouth lifting into a smirk while she waited. The sudden intimate moment was stilled, rather than broken. I dropped my hand. "She had questions?"

"Imogen asked about Morwenna tonight," I admitted. "I think her thoughts about it kept her awake." Evelyn's eyes widened slightly, then her expression settled as she nodded.

"She's old enough to begin growing an interest. Perhaps Sarah being with child has sparked her curiosity." She took another drink of wine. "We expected this at some point."

"Aye. I thought of delaying her questions until we could talk to her together, but she looked like she would have been up all night, thinking about it otherwise. Immy… may want to meet Morwenna," I told her. My wife gave a slow nod to the side of her head.

"That is only natural. Right, too. We can arrange a meeting, perhaps, when we are back in Gaeson." It was my turn to nod. "To be honest, there's another matter that troubles me more." Evelyn sighed as her frown grew.

“Taliesin’s prophecy, as he called it,” I guessed quietly. “Taliesin is a bard,” I said flatly. “He weaves words for a living.”

“I know.” She sipped her wine. “I found it… unsettling. Even a poet as legendary as him should not use such dark words about one so young. ‘Blood-soaked fields’,” she repeated, shaking her head.

“Aye. I’ll talk to him,” I promised. Evelyn leaned further against the low wall. “I keep thinking about Gilroy,” I mused, as his features came again to mind. “His hair…”

“Your mother,” she murmured. I nodded. I knew my wife would understand. Her hand reached to run through my hair. “It is brighter than yours.”

“The colouring from my father darkened my hair a bit. Sarah’s is even more like his, from what I remember of him.” I frowned. Was I forgetting my father, Adair the hand of Klumeck, in all this talk of my mother and my uncle?

“Gilroy’s hair is as bright as my mother’s ever was.” The words rasped from my throat into the night air. “All these years, I’ve wondered how much of it was my imagination. Then, to see it on top of my nephew’s head…”

“It makes the memory more real.” My wife’s voice was quiet as her fingers curled around my hand. For a moment we simply stood there together, quietly in the grey light.

“Thank you, for always understanding.” I squeezed her hand gently. My wife shifted a little closer, resting her head upon my shoulder. I felt the curve of her smile against my neck.

“You’re welcome.” Evelyn pulled away and my skin prickled in the wake of her touch. “That is marriage, my boy from the snow.”

“Aye.” I bent my head and pressed a kiss to her forehead. My fingers ran through a curl of her hair, loose from her tightly wound raven locks.

Gilroy came to mind again, then turned to the image of my mother. I was years away, remembering my mother’s features. Her vivid hair, the musical notes of her smile. Then, suddenly, her face transformed into Enid, the woman who had raised me in Gaeson. I swallowed hard as guilt shot through me.

“Daniel?” Evelyn murmured the question softly. I glanced up from where my gaze had fallen to the stone slabs bordering the palace garden.

"What is it?"

"I'm not sure," I admitted finally, looking to the floor again. "I suddenly thought of my mother in Gaeson…" I folded my arms.

"Enid will always be your mother," Evelyn said, "but you knew so little of your parents in Klumeck. It's a life you can barely remember. Gilroy has brought the memory of her closer to you, that's all. It isn't wrong for you to think of her." Her hand reached for mine again. "It's almost like you are haunted by what you cannot fully remember."

"I suppose, except haunting implies fear," I pointed out. "When I think of my mother, my life in Klumeck, I feel elated and safe, as if she is where I truly belong. Sometimes, I probably desire to remember her more than I should." My gaze fell to the paved slabs again.

"Sometimes, I'm ashamed I should think of her, rather than my mother in Gaeson. I also feel guilty that I can remember her, whereas Sarah does not."

"I see how Sarah yearns to have the fleeting memories that you have. I saw the brightness in her eyes, thinking that Gilroy's hair came from your mother," Evelyn said. "Thinking of your birth mother does not mean you love Enid any less," she added, as her hand roved along my back.

"Neither is it your fault that Sarah doesn't remember Klumeck," she continued. "I am sure she does not resent you for it. You have nothing to feel guilty or shameful for."

"Thank you." A smile flickered across my face. I stood and stretched, lifting my arms above my head. "Come," I said, "we should retire while we can."

"Aye," Evelyn said, raising a hand to stifle a yawn. "We need to be as rested as we can, for the royal banquet tomorrow."

"As if I could forget." King Owain had ordered a feast every night for a week in celebration for Gilroy's birth, starting the day he was born. Seven days of mingling with nobles. I rubbed my tired face. "I think I'd rather be stabbed by my own blade."

"It won't be as painful as that, surely." She chuckled, walking back to our chambers. A wry grin crossed my face. Despite all the effortless grace my queen displayed, I knew she had no more time for these lavish ceremonies than I did. She pressed a quick kiss to my stubbled cheek. We went back to our chamber, to get what little rest we could before the first feast began the next evening.

***

Hiding a sigh of relief, I finally slipped away from the latest group of nobles. I was used to the far smaller receptions in Gaeson, which I had attended since discovering my royal blood and hosted with Evelyn since our marriage. I had thought the banquets at home luxurious, but those were almost plain compared with the feasts here.

This was the fifth night of such indulgence. A sea of mingling nobles and officials glided around King Owain in endless waves. Officially the week-long feasts were to celebrate Gilroy, but it really seemed another way to fawn over the Supreme Ruler of Rheged. Thankfully, Sarah had been excused from the first three evenings, to recover a little in peace, away from the pomp and parade from the king's court.

From what I could tell from my reluctant conversations with court members, they just wished to revel in the air of each other's company and discuss their fine accomplishments. It was over six years since my royal blood had been discovered, yet to this day I still found this duty just as odious. I suddenly rather envied my nephew, peacefully asleep in his chamber, away from all of this.

"Evening, Daniel," Sarah greeted from beside me. "Enjoying yourself?" I smirked. I knew my sister took as much pleasure in these affairs as I did.

"Aye, of course." I didn't bother to disguise my sarcasm. "At least the wine is good." Sarah chuckled as I lifted my goblet to my mouth again, savouring the warm, slightly spiced flavour while I surveyed the scene before us.

There were at least two-hundred nobles and officials milling around the banquet hall. The ornate chamber was vast but warm, illuminated by lit candles hung around the walls. In the near corner, only a little way off from us, sat a minstrel band. There were harps, lyres and a small, handheld drum. Accompanying them were a few singers who swayed as they sang, then leapt around as the tempo reached its peak.

"I'm trying to decide whether I'm a fan of this music, or not," Sarah said. "Their clashing seems deliberate, but I'm not sure whether it works." I nodded, frowning slightly as I listened. The instruments gradually built up again into a cacophony. At the point where it was almost unpleasant, suddenly they harmonised back into a melody, both beautiful and haunting.

"I'm pleased to see you looking so well, sister," I told her, after another sip of wine. "You seem much recovered." I knew childbirth was no easy thing.

"Aye, thank you." Sarah gave me a quick smile. "I only wish Gilroy was sleeping more," she said, a thread of worry now entering her tone. "He has a minor sickness that disrupts his slumber. The physician says it's nothing serious and that it will pass soon enough. I'm sure he's right, but..."

"It is natural to be concerned." I hid my guilt that I had almost envied him earlier. Obviously, he was not quite as peaceful as I had thought. "I expect you miss Leigh," I suggested. "His care of patients has always been his strength."

"Aye," Sarah agreed at once, with stronger feeling than I had anticipated. "The surgeons here are rather more... clinical." I nodded again as her eyes roved around the banquet hall. "Evelyn certainly seems at home here." She gave a nod to where our queen was talking to yet another group of nobles.

"She was raised for this," I said simply. I took another swig of wine. "Whereas over six years later I still feel like a stranger in these grand halls. The court at Gaeson was enough to get used to, but here..."

"It's like another world." Sarah gave a short sigh. "Sometimes I do feel very far away from the baker's daughter," she said wryly, "who cared for your mother and managed your house." I glanced to my sister. I reflected that Sarah's life had probably changed more than mine had. Though my function in Gaeson's army was quite different, at least it was familiar.

"It is good for you to be here, Daniel." Sarah took a small sip of wine. "It is good for Klumeck to have their king, at least for a while." My sister sighed, but she was not being self-pitying.

"You are doing a fine place in my stead," I said. "King Owain has oft told me how much the Klumeck citizens here love your presence among them."

“That’s kind, but I fear I will never do as well as their king.” I looked from the grand chamber to my sister again. The warm candlelight reflected against the soft red of her gown. The amber hue almost made her dress look alight. Sarah looked away, tucking the usual stray hair behind her ear.

“What would you have me do?” I asked quietly. “They are welcome to move to Gaeson, but they seem to be content in their lives here.” This had been the compromise Evelyn and I had come to, in the wake of King Cedric’s death. Though I had inherited Klumeck from my uncle, my marriage to Gaeson’s queen prevented me from moving to Caer Ligualid.

Therefore, the people of Klumeck were welcome to move to Gaeson and its surrounding villages if they wished. Many had done so, but most remained here in Caer Ligualid. Sarah had decided to reside here, among our people.

“I know, Daniel.” She met my gaze again. “I know those who wished to move to Gaeson have done so. Those who live in Caer Ligualid are content. As am I, truly.” Her smile became brighter.

“I am glad to live in this fair city with our people. I dearly love Pasgent and already cherish Gilroy. I just wish I had been better prepared. Sometimes I feel I am about to be revealed for the small baker’s daughter that I am and shown the door.”

“Nobody would ever call you small,” I said, touching her arm. “You have always been strong, wise and loyal, long before we knew the truth about our birth. You are doing your task splendidly, Sarah. The main reason I do not worry so much about our people here is because you are leading them in my stead. They all love you dearly, as do I.”

“Thank you.” Her warm smile was sincere. I hoped she believed me. Then, suddenly, as her gaze moved beyond me to the hall, her smile vanished. Her mouth drew in a thin line as she stiffened.

“What is it?” I half-turned around. My eyes swept along the grand chamber, full of nobles and their refined talk. The scene seemed usual enough to me.

“Nothing.” Sarah’s voice came quick. Instantly, I knew it was anything but nothing. “It is only that King Owain looks very engaged at present.” Her words hardened.

I looked back again. A small group of nobles in conversation suddenly moved, looking like they were heading to refill their goblets. I saw King Owain had been behind them. It took me only a moment to understand Sarah's meaning. Caer Ligualid's king was talking animatedly to a tall, slender woman, her hair dark. Even at this distance, there seemed to be an intimate connection between them. Perhaps it was the way he regarded her, or the way she tilted back her head as she laughed.

"You're not imagining it." Sarah's voice was flat. I glanced to my sister. I suddenly remembered the conversation a few nights ago, about King Owain being well entertained. What with Sarah giving birth, Taliesin's so-called prophecy and my thoughts about my mother, I had almost forgotten.

"Who is she?" My gaze was drawn back to King Owain as I spoke. Just then, the woman tilted back her head again. King Owain stepped closer, taking her wrist as he whispered something in her ear.

My eyes widened. The court officials and nobles floated past them, inclining their heads but somehow averting their gaze. It was a clever balance between paying him honour, but not directly looking his way. It was enough to tell me the whole of his court knew.

"She is Princess Thaney," Sarah answered at length. My gaze flickered to my sister and back again to see the king and the princess now stood apart. "She is the daughter of King Lot."

"Truly?" My eyes widened again. King Lot ruled the kingdom of Gododdin, a kingdom far to the north, with one edge bordering upon Bernicia. The land had been attacked many times, but so far, they had survived with the aid of Strathclyde, their neighbouring kingdom. They were another ally in the war against Bernicia. I could only hope King Owain's affair with his daughter would not jeopardise our alliance with them.

"Does Her Majesty Queen Penarwen know?" Sarah only nodded. When I looked back at her, I saw her gaze had narrowed further. "You've known for a while," I guessed.

"Aye." Her voice was still flat. "Two weeks before Gilroy was born, I was taking a walk in one of the gardens, before I came upon them. Their conversation was… most intimate," she said hesitantly. "I walked away. I only told Pasgent," she continued. "We kept the matter to ourselves." I nodded. I could well imagine my sister's feet crunching on the soft-stoned path between flowers and bushes, before she abruptly changed course.

"I suppose it is not our place to intervene." I took another mouthful of wine. "What a family you have married into." I chuckled and shook my head. "Just think, should he be alive today, the mighty King Urien would be your father-in-law."

"Daniel!" Sarah gave me a playful punch on the arm, almost making me spill my wine. "Aye, that thought came to me when Pasgent and I wed. A terrifying prospect." She smiled wryly. "Though, he was always very protective of his kin."

"Aye. He was a ruthless man, but I believe he was a good one." I took another drink of wine, noticing my goblet was almost empty. "Yours is a strong union for Rheged. I believe Gilroy is the first royal to be from all three kingdoms," I reflected. "Klumeck and Caer Ligualid blood, yet his mother also hails from Gaeson."

"Related to Gaeson by marriage, as well," Sarah agreed. "Then there's Imogen, who currently stands to inherit both Klumeck and Gaeson. Hopefully, it makes our stand against Bernicia all the stronger." Sarah's eyes darkened as she lowered her goblet.

"What you and Pasgent saw on your patrol," she murmured, concern etched onto her face. "I do worry what world Gilroy has been born into. War is coming, isn't it?"

"I'm afraid so. As surely as the dawn." I finished the dregs in my goblet. "I am grateful Imogen's life has been marked by peace, so far," I told her. "We will do everything we can, to ensure the pain of battle does not touch their lives."

"I know." Sarah sighed. "We must fight, for the sake of Imogen and Gilroy and our people." I nodded. Together we watched the nobles mingling. Thoughts of King Owain's affair slipped from my mind. How much longer would Caer Ligualid enjoy such finery? How long before the final reckoning of Rheged came to our fair city's gates?

"Well, as much as I cannot tear myself away…" Sarah smirked, then covered her mouth as she yawned. "I think I shall look in on Gilroy and retire."

"Of course. Sleep well." I touched my sister's hand briefly as she left. In her wake, I glanced down at my empty goblet. Common sense told me I should take no more wine, but I had another hour or so in the company of splendid strangers and now I no longer had talking with Sarah to avoid them. I therefore took a new goblet from a passing servant before more of the dreaded mingling came my way.

***

"Sarah and I were saying how effortless you are in these occasions." It was two hours later when Evelyn and I were finally able to leave the chamber. I was more than relieved to finally leave the hall, long grown stuffy with guests and wine. "You are the epitome of grace, my love."

"Thank you." My queen smiled as she tucked her hand further into my arm. "I've had a lifetime of practising. It doesn't mean I'm not as delighted as you are when they are over." I chuckled.

"Your speech was a little slurred then, my husband." I glanced at her to see her grinning. "Might I suppose you have had more than your fair share of wine this evening?"

"A little." My answer was vague, partly because I'd lost track of how many goblets I'd consumed. I returned her grin, feeling a little sheepish. "In truth, I'm not sure how else I would get through these fine occasions." It was her turn to laugh.

"I can empathise." She let go of my arm as we entered my chamber, then stretched her arms above her head. "The conversation was not as pleasant as the other evenings," Evelyn said now, sitting down on the bed to remove her elegant indoor shoes. "The talk turned often to war."

"Aye, Sarah and I spoke about that, too." I sighed as Evelyn now rose from the bed, undoing her ornate curls, each lock coming to cascade prettily about her shoulders. "It vexes me that we seem to be doing nothing, just waiting for King Ethelfrith or King Morgant to make his move." I went to the table on the other side of the chamber to pour water into our goblets.

"Did you see Prince Elffin tonight?" I passed her a goblet. "I'm not sure I saw him, but the chamber was so full."

"I saw him once, early on." I took a long drink of the refreshing water. It helped to clear my head a little. "I think he slipped away as soon as he could. He knew his father would be engaged," she added flatly. "He wouldn't be missed."

"So, you saw it too." My voice was thoughtful as I sat on the bed, thinking back to the moment Sarah and I had witnessed.

"The whole chamber saw it," Evelyn said now. "They just pretended not to notice." I nodded, remembering the way the nobles had glided around them.

"It must be difficult for the lad, to see his father behave like that in front of his mother." I stood to strip down to my nightshirt, then moved back the bedsheets. "Perhaps I should try to befriend him."

"A good idea," Evelyn agreed, coming to lie down beside me. I stared up at the dim ceiling. The effects of the wine lapped around my mind, making the darkened ceiling spin ever so slightly.

"Maybe have a little less wine tomorrow," she suggested gently, smirking. I cracked a grin and then turned my head to blow out the candle, leaving us in darkness. "After all, we have two more of these fine evenings ahead of us."

"A wonderful thought." She chuckled at my sarcasm. I turned to kiss her. "Goodnight, my love." I settled back against the pillow, thinking again of Prince Elffin and how the lad might want to talk to someone. With that thought I drifted into slumber, lulled by the wine and the lateness of the hour.

Chapter Three

My boots thudded on the loose gravel path, strewn with vibrant leaves. The fresh autumn chill was most invigorating. It helped to clear my head after supping a little too much wine the previous evening. I was heading to find Prince Elffin, as I heard he normally practised his swordplay after breakfast. Sure enough, as I headed towards the small inner courtyard he used for training, he came into view.

As I approached him, I saw how well Prince Elffin handled his blade. He leapt forwards and back, slashing left and right, practising his strikes and parries. I folded my arms casually as I watched him. The young prince was the next in line to the throne. Only eighteen, I reflected. If when the war came and the worst happened, would the lad be ready?

"Something I can help you with, King Bryce?" He stopped practising with his blade to regard me. I smiled, taking a step forward. I hadn't tried to disguise my footsteps, but Elffin was so engrossed with his training I had thought myself unnoticed. It was a good sign he was aware of my presence.

"Prince Elffin." I bent my head to him in a formal greeting. "I was taking a walk about the grounds. The morning is fair, is it not?" Elffin gave a curt nod of his head in return. His words had been civil enough, but his features were guarded.

"I did not mean to spy on you," I said, as he walked over. His features were ruddy, with black hair and slight stubble on his chin. I saw his resemblance to Pasgent, except perhaps his darker hair. "Your skill with a blade is fine indeed. Have you been in any battles?"

"Not a true battle, no." His voice was still a little stiff, but it warmed much with my compliment. "I was there when Bernicia marched against Caer Ligualid, but I had a guard of soldiers at all times. I spent most of the battle guarding my people deeper within the castle walls, but hardly any of the enemy reached that far. For which I'm grateful, of course," he added quickly.

"Indeed. Since then, there has been relative peace." Elffin nodded. His gaze flickered down to his blade, turning it this way and that. "Do you find it restless?" Often the young recruits in Gaeson grew idle, wishing far too often for a battle too soon.

"I do wish to prove myself, eventually." Elffin met my eyes square on, as if my question had been a challenge. Perhaps it had, unintentionally. "I wish to serve Caer Ligualid well. However, I would be a fool if I wished to speed the coming of war, when so many lives will fall."

"Well said." I gave him another smile, impressed with his mature answer. His youthful features, but sharpness beyond his years, reminded me of Ewan, a soldier in Gaeson, when I first met him in recruitment training.

"I have heard you are a great warrior in battle." His gaze moved abruptly from the tip of his blade to me. Prince Elffin's features were sure and steady, his eyes alight with sudden interest. I noticed the hazel in them seemed to take after Queen Penarwen's colouring.

"Is that so?" I cracked a grin. "I suppose my skill has grown over the years. I've been fortunate in the war thus far, but I'm sure I would have fallen long ago, without the help of my friends." I had lost count long ago of how many times John and Aife had spared me from harm or even death in battle.

Elffin bent his head to the side a moment, as he considered this. Then, suddenly, a wry smile crossed his features. It was the first smile I had seen cross his face since coming to Caer Ligualid.

"Come on, then," he challenged. "Let's see how much fortune you really need. Let's use these." He picked up two wooden swords at his feet. "I would hate to accidentally decapitate the king of Klumeck." I laughed as he threw one wooden blade to me.

"Aye, I doubt your mother would approve if I hurt the future king of all Rheged." Elffin chuckled, then the humour faded from his face. His posture was completely alert. His fingers flexed on the hilt of the wooden sword. I was impressed. Prince Elffin may be yet to charge through a battleground, but the warrior in him was evident. Already, only from his stance, I had no doubt he would be ready, when the time came.

I bid my time, walking slowly around the inner courtyard, across cobbles still damp in the morning dew. We circled each other, but neither of us lunged. Our mouths curled, as we realised we were both using the same tactic. I could already tell besting Prince Elffin would be no easy task.

A crow squawked from somewhere overhead, but I kept my gaze on my opponent. The two of us were enclosed in our game of waiting. A little humour, almost a cockiness, entered the young prince's eyes. At this, I decided to make the first move. If nothing else, I wanted to see how he would react.

Abruptly I leapt forward, crossing the space between us with my wooden blade brandished high. I just caught Prince Elffin's wry smile before he darted to the side, raising his blade to parry me easily. Our swords broke apart as I spun to my left, then brought it down again. Swiftly we practised the ancient dance. I was used to metal clanging, but instead the air filled with the dull thuds of wooden blades.

"You fight well," I told him, leaping back after his latest successful parry. Just for a moment, a true smile broke across his features. I thought how well it suited him.

His features then sharply changed as I leapt forward again. The heir of Caer Ligualid successfully parried me once more. As he did, I spied a weakness. I feigned a strike, then as he moved to parry, I span to the right and brought the wooden blade down to a gap at his side.

"I am struck!" Elffin half-laughed, half-grimaced as he lowered his sword, moving to rub his side. "You are an excellent warrior," he said, slightly panting.

"Thank you. You will likely have a bruise there." I chuckled, glad we had fought with wooden blades. "Watch your left side as you parry," I said. "You would leave a gap in your armour exposed. Perhaps turn a little," I added, demonstrating the movement, "as you bring your sword down."

"I will try to remember that." Prince Elffin nodded, straightening again. "My father told me you were there, that day, when my grandfather died."

"Aye, I was there. I saw King Urien fall." In my mind's eye, the scene flashed before me again. Aife trying to shoot the assassin, before being severely injured. "I tried to save his life," I told him quietly, "but he was too far away. I'm sorry I could not get there in time, Elffin." Even six years later, my words were laced with regret.

"The fault was not yours," he told me. "That traitor, King Morgant, was responsible." I saw his eyes harden. How many of us boiled with rage with the thought of our enemy?

"You were there, too, when King Cedric died, were you not?" he asked suddenly. Then his face slackened, as he crossed the space between us. "I'm sorry, I meant no disrespect…"

"It's all right." I gave him a small smile as I patted his shoulder. "Aye, I was there too. Like with your grandfather, I saw it happen, but I was too far away. It seems I am always a little too late," I reflected, only a little sadly.

"You were not too late in killing Aldred," Elffin pointed out. I shot him a quick smile, but this quickly faded, as I remembered plunging my blade into the Wolf.

"That was not without cost." We made our way together from the training courtyard back to the main castle. "That villain threatened slaughter throughout Rheged, saying nothing of the poison he poured within my marriage. It nearly drove my wife and I apart." Elffin nodded, but his features stiffened. I realised this time it was me who had been tactless.

"I'm sorry, Elffin," I said. He turned me, his eyes still hardened. "Perhaps your parents still love one another?" I suggested. From the way I had seen King Owain hold Princess Thaney, I was unsure, but I wanted to try to comfort him.

"Not likely." The young prince sniffed. "I saw their love fade when I was a child," he said with a sigh. "Besides, my father has other interests at present." His sarcastic words cut through the air.

"The whole of Rheged probably knows what he is up to with Princess Thaney of Gododdin," he told me now, folding his arms. "The whole of his court sees what is going on, they just ignore it. You saw it, didn't you?" he asked sharply.

"Aye, I did." I hid my surprise at his tone. It was understandable for him to have such anger and disapproval about his father. However, Prince Elffin was probably the only one in all Rheged who could speak about King Owain this way, without fear of being beheaded. Prince Elffin smirked again.

"Being so candid is a perk of being an heir," he muttered, as we fell into step together. We walked about the castle grounds, without a particular destination in mind. I hoped a friendship between us was beginning to form. More than ever, I felt like he might need to talk about his father. As the early morning sunshine cast its light on the path before us, I wondered how I would begin to approach the topic. Then we rounded the corner.

"Oh." I pulled myself up automatically as I spotted them, taking a quick step back around the curved wall. A bird squawked from somewhere, disturbed by my movement.

"What is it?" Elffin asked at once. I hesitated. The bird — it was a robin — landed on the path in front of us. It swivelled its beak in my direction, almost as if admonishing me for rudeness. It flapped its wings once, most indignantly, before suddenly taking off again. "Well?" Elffin prompted.

"It is your father." I could think of no way not to tell him and he deserved to know the truth. "He is with company." The prince's eyes narrowed. No further explanation was needed.

"I wish to see," he said, through gritted teeth, features already livid. Reluctantly, I stepped aside. Elffin took a step forward, to peer around the castle wall. A moment later I dared to join him.

I exhaled sharply through my nostrils at the sight. The king of Caer Ligualid stood behind a tree, one of several neatly lining the path. He leant against the trunk, only partially visible. Princess Thaney was in his arms, in the throes of their passionate embrace. They moulded their mouths together as if the world would end tomorrow.

Prince Elffin said nothing. He didn't have to — the rage was palpable with each breath. I could not say I blamed him. How would I react if I saw my father amidst an affair, all the while my mother grew more ill by the day? For in the last few days, it had become known that Queen Penarwen had taken a turn for the worse. She had clearly been putting on a brave face at the banquets, hiding how ill she really was.

My gaze flickered up to the windows. I was relieved that all the wooden doors were shut. At least the cold weather meant they were likely to be unseen. Perhaps that was why they were so bold, but there was nothing to stop anyone coming upon them, as we had done.

Did King Owain simply not care who might see them? I knew he was Supreme Ruler of Rheged, but surely that entailed being a wise leader who inspired people, rather than the selfish freedom to do anything he chose. I stared hard at them, almost willing them to look up and see that they were being watched.

"How dare he!" Elffin hissed beside me. "I can hardly believe my father would do this. I thought him a good man." His words were laced with hurt, almost despairing.

"Wait, Elffin!" My hand was already on his arm, my voice urgent. At once the lad swung back at me, furious. The ire in his features reminded me of his grandfather.

"You dare!" His voice rose. "You may be a king and Aunt Sarah's brother," he growled, throwing my hand off him. "However, you are not the heir to Caer Ligualid." Prince Elffin's eyes narrowed, his voice entirely cold. "It is beyond impertinent to try to stop me. If you think I will stand back and let my father carry on like this, while my mother lies ill in bed…"

"Don't be so hasty, lad!" I reached for his arm again. "I'm sorry, Elffin, but standing back is exactly what you have to do."

"Get off me!" The hurt blended stronger with the anger in his face and it was now directed at me. I saw he thought I had betrayed him. So much for our budding friendship. "I'll teach you not to meddle with my affairs!" he snarled.

"These are not just your affairs, Elffin," I told him patiently. The young prince shook his head and in a moment of his fury, he drew his blade. "I want to help," I said hastily as Prince Elffin raised the sword in my direction. This was his own metal blade, not the wooden ones we practised with earlier.

"How you behave affects the whole kingdom," I went on. "It is true you stand to inherit all of this." I gestured my hands around the castle grounds. "Yet how do you expect your people to listen to your rule, if you confront your father? You need to be careful because of Princess Thaney, too," I pointed out. "Her father, King Lot, is a powerful man and a much-needed ally."

"I don't care," Elffin snarled. He had pointed his blade to the path, but here he raised it again. "I don't care about King Lot," he repeated. "He would hardly approve of her antics. You have no right to stop me, King Bryce." He glared at me.

With that, he made to move past me. In a flourish, I unsheathed my blade and stepped forwards to block him. Wielding my sword against him was the last thing I wanted to do, but I could not let Elffin do this. He gave me little other choice.

"You dare to challenge me?" the young prince breathed. His eyes were wide with shock and rage. His voice was dangerously soft, again reminding me of King Urien. It would take nothing now for the lad to strike me. I had to be careful.

"Why not?" I kept my voice urgent, but even. "You dare to challenge your father. Don't you see?" I lowered my sword, hoping he would understand. "If you confront your king, you will set others to do the same. What would stop others attacking you, when you come to take the throne? If you do this, your rule would never be secure." I lowered my blade still further.

"I'm not without sympathy with you, truly, but this is not the way." Elffin's gaze was still hard, but thankfully, a seed of doubt now crossed his features. Presently he leant forward, peering around the corner again.

"Well, the opportunity is gone. They have left," he snarled. I thought this just as well, but did not tell him this, lest I provoked him. "What is the way, King Bryce? How would you deal with this?" Elffin's voice was rife with scorn, but at least here he put away his sword.

"Well, having a friend wouldn't hurt," I pointed out. The metal clinked as I sheathed my own blade. Prince Elffin only snorted softly, as he folded his arms and looked away. I frowned, surprised by his obnoxious, sullen countenance. Where had his maturity gone? Perhaps it was just his hurt coming out, I told myself. Being heir to the throne would be pressure enough, without his father's affair.

"As I said, King Lot is powerful," I said. "Even if he would agree with you about your father, he would not tolerate you confronting them, or speaking out against his daughter."

"I don't care who her father is," Elffin sniped. He was looking at the ground now, moving his foot to scuff loose pebbles about. His appearance was so sullen my patience began to wane.

"Aye, you do." My voice was rough and blunt now. "Like it or not, we need Gododdin in the fight if we are to survive this war with the Angles. King Owain is being foolish," I admitted. At this, Elffin's head shot up, his sullenness replaced with sheer surprise.

"I bid you keep that to yourself, lest he takes the head from my shoulders," I told him. The young prince smirked. "You yourself said the whole of Rheged likely knows about this," I pointed out. "It won't be long before word reaches King Lot. He might have heard about it already. Bide your time," I suggested. "Stay out of it, lad. I suspect King Lot will put a stop to it himself soon. King Owain will soon face the consequences of his folly without your help."

"Aye, I suppose." Elffin's arms were still folded. I hid a sigh. This was probably all the gratitude I would receive from stopping him potentially ruining his reign, before he even claimed the title of king. "So, I am to just bear this injury to my mother?" he asked, clearly frustrated.

"Aye, perhaps, for the time being." I folded my arms as I thought. Elffin glanced down, scratching distractedly at the stubble on his chin. "If this is merely an infatuation, then it will pass in time," I thought aloud. "However, even if your father really has fallen in love with Princess Thaney, then it will not be too long until King Lot intervenes."

"Do you think my father could lose King Lot as his ally, if he finds out?" Prince Elffin asked now, frowning with renewed interest. I was glad to see the rage beginning to fade from his features.

"I doubt it," I answered him ere long. "Gododdin is as threatened by Bernicia as Rheged. King Lot knows his chances of survival are much greater if the treaty with your father stands. Though, I do not believe either of them will count the other as a great friend."

"Aye." Prince Elffin smiled wryly once more. "Though part of me longs for King Lot to confront him, I know it will not be good for Rheged." He sighed again as he resumed his walking. "You're different from other royals I've met, King Bryce," Elffin told me now.

"I'll take that as a compliment," I chuckled. Elffin smirked again. Now King Owain and Princess Thaney had gone, we took up our walk again. "My road to being a royal of Rheged was far from unconventional," I said. It was rather an understatement.

"Aye, of course." Elffin's eyes flickered with interest and recognition. "My father told me the story, of how you and Aunt Sarah were King Cedric's long-lost niece and nephew. Weren't you a soldier, before learning the truth?"

"In Gaeson's army." I nodded. "I did not even know Sarah was my sister until I discovered the truth." A faint smile crossed my features. "We were adopted separately," I added, at the surprise on Elffin's face. "It's a long story."

"So, you did not even know each other?" I smiled, more than happy to accept the change of subject. Anything to take his mind off the foolish actions of his father.

"Actually, we grew up as neighbours." Even now, the fragrant smell of her father's rolls from the bakery a little further down the street from our houses drifted through my mind. The warm scent of fresh bread was almost tangible.

"We were found together," I explained. "In the snow, by my mother and Sarah's mother. My father who raised me in Gaeson was a soldier and he had overheard talk of what had happened in Klumeck. They knew who we were, but they had to keep us a secret, in case King Reghan found out."

Prince Elffin nodded here. The lack of surprise on his features told me he already knew most of the account, of how most of my kin had been murdered that night by the Wolf. We knew now that this had been done by the orders of King Morgant. For a moment I was lost again, seeing the swirl of the blizzard and the overturned carriage. The weather today was a pleasant sort of cold, but suddenly I shivered, remembering the chill frozen deep in our bones.

"Sarah and I would have died that night, if not for our mothers," I resumed, tugging myself back to the present. "After a few years passed, Sarah moved next door. It was too much a risk to tell us the truth, but I suppose they did not want us to be separated. There was a connection between us immediately, so we grew up as close friends. It was almost twenty years later that we discovered the truth."

"I see." Prince Elffin folded his arms. "You are right, about my father." He sighed. "I apologise," he said, more formally. "It's just that my father vexes me so."

"At the risk of further impertinence to His Majesty, I can certainly understand why." Elffin smirked again. Then, as our footsteps continued crunching on the path, his expression turned thoughtful.

"What you said before, about me ruling all of this one day…" he trailed off and sighed. "How do you find being a king?" I glanced at him, seeing the weight of his inheritance heavy on his shoulders.

"I'm not sure I'm the right person to ask," I admitted. "As you know, King Cedric was dispossessed as the king of Klumeck by the Bernicians, over six years ago now. They captured my uncle's kingdom only a few short weeks after my identity was discovered."

"Oh, of course," said Elffin. "I'm sorry." I sent him a wry smile as the short path evened out into one of Caer Ligualid's smaller courtyards.

"Not to worry. I know my sister leads well the Klumeck citizens that remained here. Many of my people moved to Gaeson after our uncle's death, so in some sense I am leading them, but…" I sighed.

"It is a strange thing, to be a king without a kingdom," I admitted now. "Stranger still to learn I would not reign from Klumeck itself, so soon after discovering who I really was. Only the Lord knows how my uncle felt about it. He kept much of his grief to himself."

"You tried to retake Klumeck a few years ago, didn't you?" Prince Elffin asked, as we left the small courtyard behind and continued on the gravel path.

"Aye, four years the summer just gone." I did not even have to close my eyes to witness again the scenes of that night. "We had outlined the strategy in secret for months," I told Elffin. "At first, everything went well." I was reliving it, then. The archers and I had swiftly taken down the few guards patrolling Klumeck's walls.

"We had barely a casualty, but then…" The rest of my sentence trailed away, remembering how the Bernician horn had suddenly blasted. "The Bernicians were spilling over the hill, at the top of Klumeck. We barely had time to plunge back into the trees." I shook my head.

"It was only because we sent out soldiers with lanterns as a decoy, going in a different direction, that we escaped. It was after that we first suspected there might be a spy in Gaeson." We passed near Caer Ligualid's stables now, far grander than the ones in Gaeson.

Hay was strewn haphazardly across the cobbled path outside. The sun had parted through the fog of cloud, gleaming on the uncovered cobbles. It was a crisp, sunny autumn day. However, neither the strong familiar aroma of the horses, nor the pleasing weather — which was just the kind I loved — could take my mind from the Wolf.

"Aye." Elffin's tone was dark. How he spoke that one word told me he knew just who the spy had been and how much harm he had caused Rheged. "I'm glad you killed him," he said again, taking us back to the start of our conversation.

"It almost wasn't a choice, to take his life," I reflected heavily. "My daughter would never have been safe with him alive." Elffin nodded.

"My father taught me that is often the way of things, with our enemies," the young prince agreed. "The nature of war is to either kill or be killed."

"Indeed. That's why violence will not be a good solution to your father's affair," I pointed out. "King Owain is ever ready to test his blade. I don't believe he would use it against his own son and heir, but no good will come of provoking him."

"Aye, I know." He sighed again, then suddenly glanced my way. "Daniel is the name your parents gave you in Gaeson, isn't it?" I nodded. "Which should I call you?" I smiled.

"Daniel is fine. Bryce is the name my parents in Klumeck gave me," I told him. "I use it now as my royal title, the same as Sarah does with Lynette. I still mainly go by the name of Daniel," I clarified. He nodded. We now came upon the small courtyard where, perhaps half an hour before, Elffin had been practising his swordplay.

"If you'll excuse me," he said now, "I think I shall visit my mother." He suddenly broke into a sheepish grin. "Thank you, Daniel, for stopping my rash actions earlier. I see the folly of them now."

"You're welcome, Elffin. A good day to you." After giving me a final nod, the heir of Caer Ligualid headed off to see his mother. As I watched his departure, a little frown settled on my features. The lad had done well not to confront King Owain — even though it had taken my own blade to stop him. Had my father behaved as despicably whilst my mother lay ill, I was not at all sure I would have held my temper. I hoped indeed King Owain's folly would end soon, if there was not to be a feud between father and son.

***

"Have you heard?" I froze on the ornate staircase, my hand paused on the banister. A servant had whispered the question, far more loudly and carelessly than he had meant to. From his tone, right away I knew something had happened. I took another cautious step down the staircase. After taking another, a servant leaning against a doorway came into view. His arms were folded, facing away from me. Two servants were partially visible on the other side of the threshold.

It was two mornings after practising combat with Elffin in one of the castle's courtyards. The final banquet the previous evening had passed in much the same way as the others. In truth, I was glad to see the back of the indulgent affairs.

"Prince Elffin marched out of breakfast this morning, looking for King Owain," the servant rushed on. "Do you think at last he will confront him about his father?"

"May I ask what you are talking about?" My frosty voice boomed down the stairs, echoing around the corridor below. All the servants jumped. The one who had spoken leapt in my direction, face stricken as he immediately bent his head. The other two servants darted forwards, bowing hastily and a little clumsily.

"Do tell me what you've heard." My voice was quieter but still cold as I walked down the stairs. "I am most interested."

"Most apologies, Y-Your Majesty," the first servant stammered. "I only heard that His Highness Prince Elffin has gone to speak with His Majesty King Owain in the garden."

"I see. It is hardly for you to gossip about," I pointed out, folding my arms. "Perhaps you had better spend less time on idle talk and more time on your duties?"

"Apologies, Your Majesty. Of course." The servants hastily bowed again, obviously flustered. I smirked as I watched them bustle out of sight, but then my brow furrowed as I headed to the palace gardens, where I had walked with Prince Elffin.

From the servants' gossip, I feared the worst. Was the lad really going to challenge his father? I sighed. Had he only been able to hold onto his temper for two days? I broke into a run as I passed through a door leading outside. As much as I empathised with Elffin, I knew I had to stop him before it was too late.

"Your Majesty, I bid you wait!" Sure enough, as I came to one of the gardens, I heard Elffin's furious call to his father. He stood on the loose pebble path with his back to me, fists clenched. "Your deeds are too much."

"Take care, Your Highness," I whispered, hurrying to Elffin's side. King Owain had stopped a little further along the path, glowering at his son. They were a few paces apart, but at any moment the king might bridge the gap to challenge his son.

"There are witnesses," I bid him urgently, my gaze flickering around the palace garden. Servants, guards and even a few court nobles had begun to gather to view the spectacle before them.

"I don't care," Elffin protested loudly. "Why should I care who sees me? He clearly doesn't." My eyes widened at his blatant accusation of his father. What had happened in the last day or two, I wondered, to make him dare to defy his father so openly?

"You should listen to King Bryce, boy." King Owain's voice was quiet, but we heard him clearly enough. All had gone silent for his words. It was folly to think so, but even the birds seemed to have quietened their morning chorus.

"Do not say something you will regret," the king said icily. "I won't tolerate your disrespect any further." His hand moved, ever so calmly, to the hilt of his blade.

"What of the way you disrespect my mother?" Elffin countered, but a thread of uncertainty entered his voice. King Owain's hand flexed almost invisibly upon the hilt of his blade.

"Do not vex him," I whispered desperately to Elffin. "No good can come of this." Mercifully, King Owain had not drawn his sword yet. I hoped it was an empty threat. I prayed I could convince Elffin to back down before we had to find out.

"Follow King Bryce's wisdom, my son." King Owain's voice was almost soft, yet it punctuated the morning air like a blade. "Do not attempt to meddle in my affairs, even if they displease you." Prince Elffin only snorted, shaking his head.

"Aye, you are a prince, but you are also barely a man," King Owain said now. Elffin's countenance grew in rage. He expelled air noisily through gritted teeth. I stared at the king. How could it help to provoke his son further?

"I am the King of Caer Ligualid, the Supreme Ruler of Rheged." King Owain parted his sword just a little from his sheath. The revealed portion of blade gleamed in the morning sunshine. "Do you really wish to challenge me? In view of all these people?" he glanced around the palace garden.

"Back down, Elffin." My murmur came even more urgently. "Apologise and walk away." I lowered my voice to a whisper. "You don't want to do this, lad."

"Don't I?" Elffin challenged, turning back to me. His eyes were full of rage, but they were calmer than I expected. "Is this the life of a king, Daniel? To do whatever you wish, never caring about who you hurt? Is this the life I am to inherit?"

"It need not be," I whispered back swiftly. His conflicted gaze bore into mine. "It's up to you what you make of the throne. You can be a much better king than your father, Elffin," I pointed out quietly. "However, if you persist in challenging him, you might not get that chance."

"Well, boy?" King Owain's voice was slow, deliberately rife with sarcasm. He sneered, then, a gesture uncannily familiar to that snake, Aldred. It seemed even from the grave, that foul wretch's twisted smile could still haunt me. I swallowed hard.

"Are you going to challenge me this day?" King Owain prompted darkly. His hand was still upon his sword hilt. "Or do you see fit to tolerate my rule a little longer?" Suddenly, the king grinned. I got the distinct impression he was enjoying humiliating his son like this.

"We haven't got all day, Elffin." King Owain's voice was flat. "Will you challenge, or will you yield?" he ended impatiently, when his son still did not reply.

"I..." Elffin paused. It seemed the whole of their bond, linked by blood as they were, hung in the balance of this moment. Would the young prince remain the king's son and heir if he did this? Elffin glanced at me. I shook my head, my gaze begging him a final time. Suddenly Elffin sighed, his shoulders slumping. He took a step backwards and lowered his head.

"I yield, my lord the king," Elffin answered his father at last. His voice was cold, but at least he had said it. I held my breath. King Owain stared hard at his son for a moment, before he nodded, sliding his sword fully back into his sheath.

"Good. I'm glad that's settled." The king held onto the hilt of his blade a moment longer, before at last his hand relaxed, leaving the hilt of his blade. It seemed he would forgive his son, even if Elffin had yielded coldly, through gritted teeth.

"Just as well." King Owain gave a short laugh that was utterly devoid of humour. "I would hate for your blood to be spilled all over the path. It has only lately been tended." He turned away.

"Oh…" the king said casually, after taking a few strides away. His hand was back on the hilt of his blade again. "Mind you never attempt to challenge me again, boy." King Owain's voice was suddenly sharp, cutting through the garden to reach us. "I might not be in such a merciful mood, next time."

"I'm not a boy," Prince Elffin muttered, careful to keep his voice so low only I could hear them. For a few moments, the world was still and silent, the only sound being King Owain's boots as they crunched upon the loose gravel.

"What were you thinking, Elffin?" I whispered. At last, the people began to disperse. I felt as though I could breathe fully again. "What happened?" The young prince was quiet for a moment.

"I should have stood my ground," Elffin muttered angrily. He clenched his fists in frustration, staring hard at the spot where his father had vanished. "Now my weakness has been clear for all to see." He looked up then, his gaze flickering to where the guards, servants and nobles were heading back to their duties. "I am a fool."

He walked on a few paces, then sat abruptly on a nearby bench. I approached him, suddenly aware the birds were singing again. Had they really quietened for the king, or had I just stopped noticing them?

"Do you wish for me to carry on walking?" I knew the lad might well want to be alone. After a moment Elffin shook his head, his face bent to the grass at his feet. I moved to join him, sitting on the other side of the bench.

"You are no fool, Elffin," I told him quietly. "There are times when it takes courage, wisdom, even strength not to fight. Today was one of those days. You did the right thing." Prince Elffin only sighed; his head bowed to the ground again.

"No one will think less of you because you did not challenge your father. Besides, I doubt very much he wanted to fight you, deep down. He had to answer you publicly." Elffin snorted softly, shaking his head. King Owain's sneer came to mind. Suddenly I wasn't sure whether King Owain would have minded challenging his own son.

"I did not mean for it to come to this." Elffin shook his head, still staring at the ground. Everyone else had gone, leaving us alone in the palace garden.

"Two days ago, you agreed not to challenge him," I pointed out, folding my arms. "What happened?" I prompted again. With that, Elffin at last raised his head to look at me.

"My mother has been too ill to leave her chamber most mornings." Elffin sniffed the cold morning air and wiped his nose with the back of his hand. "When I came to breakfast today, Princess Thaney was sitting next to my father, in my mother's place." My eyes widened as I nodded slowly. That certainly would have been enough to send the lad over the edge.

"The rest of my family ate with them, without saying a word. As if my mother had never even existed." I heard the heat returning to Elffin's words. "I could not tolerate my mother being treated this way, even if she was well."

"Defending your mother's honour is a noble intention," I said quietly. "However, she would not want you to jeopardise your position for her sake."

"Aye, I know." Elffin sniffed again, leaning back on the bench now. "There was another reason why I was so vexed. My father is the one who is a fool," he burst out. "It won't be long before the scandal makes us the whole laughing-stock of Rheged. Our alliance with Gododdin itself might be threatened once King Lot finds out." He glanced to me. "Princess Thaney is with child."

"What? Truly?" I asked, eyebrow raised. Elffin merely shrugged.

"Surely, though, King Lot will take her back to his lands, once this reaches him," I said, frowning. "Why not bid your tongue a little longer, lad, if you knew this?"

"I could not bear it, Daniel." Elffin's outburst was miserable as he shook his head. "The thought that she is with child, taking my mother's place in our family, giving him a new child…"

"The anger at injustice is no easy thing to bear," I said gently. In my mind's eye I was in King Reghan's cell after he had abdicated, filled with fresh rage that he had been the one to order the death of my kin. I knew how easy it was to lose control, for it was only the thought of Evelyn that had stayed my hand from slicing his throat.

"It is not only anger at my father," Elffin now admitted with a sigh. He spoke nothing further for a moment. The birds chattered above us and the guards thudded into the gravel path as they took patrol.

"I hate their affair, but when she leaves… that is a brother or a sister I likely will never meet." Regret filled his words. I looked at the prince. Despite the passionate outburst to his father, I knew he was still hiding a lot of emotion. I could only imagine how torn his heart was.

"I'm so sorry, Elffin," I murmured simply. I threaded my hands together as I sat back upon the bench. "King Lot's temper may cool in future months," I pointed out. "Perhaps in time, when the child is born, you could request a meeting?"

"Perhaps," the young prince echoed. There was a faint thread of sarcasm in his voice. I could well understand it, for King Lot did not seem to be the most forgiving, like King Owain in that respect. "I wish for peace, Daniel, for our people to be safe," Elffin said flatly. "If what my father has done threatens the alliance with Gododdin…"

"It won't, lad," I answered simply. "Even if King Lot hates your father, their alliance must stand. Gododdin needs us, as much as we need them."

"Aye, I hope you're right. There is another matter." Elffin hunched forwards again, his fingers drumming listlessly on the seat of the bench. "My mother is affected by my father's actions much more than it appears," he admitted. "I fear she is growing worse again." His tone was rough, his speech disjointed.

"Only a few weeks ago the surgeon said her health was stronger, but these past few days… I have never seen her like this before. It's not just her body that suffers, Daniel. I don't know what will happen," he ended shortly.

"I'm sorry to hear that," I told him, my hand reaching to his shoulder. "I will pray Her Majesty improves," I said quietly, suddenly thinking of my mother in Gaeson. Enid had always been a physically strong woman, but some of the fire in her faded the day she learned my father was dead.

"My mother is unwell, also," I murmured. "Almost since my father died fifteen years ago, there has been barely a day where she has left her bed. I can only imagine what you are going through, lad, but you need not face it alone."

"You have my thanks, Daniel." He sent me a quick smile again as my hand left his shoulder. "Thank you, again, for stopping me doing something foolish. I have had training, to guard my emotions, but you wouldn't know it," he ended bitterly.

"You are still human, Elffin," I told him. "Some things in life can never truly be prepared for. Emotions are not a bad thing; you just need to work on what to do when the rage hits you. As do we all." The young prince returned my smirk as he nodded. I think he understood.

"Aye." He stood from the bench. "I think I will be alone, for a while." His countenance changed and I saw the walls coming down his face, shutting out his emotions. "Good day to you, King Bryce." The lad was taking comfort in formalities, as I had done so often.

"Good day to you as well, Prince Elffin," I said, standing. With that the lad left, heading through the palace garden in the opposite direction to his father. I folded my arms, frowning as I watched him. Inside, I was cursing King Owain for his folly. How could he expect his son to bear it? Did he not care about the pain he was causing to his kin?

Standing there alone in the palace garden, I prayed that Elffin would not challenge his father again. Hopefully, the lad would keep his mouth shut and King Lot would soon take his daughter back to Gododdin, for the sake of a unified kingdom. After all, with the war with Bernicia looming closer than ever, the last thing Rheged needed was the royal house divided.

Chapter Four

The air felt restless as I wandered along Caer Ligualid's corridors a couple of days later. It was my last night in this kingdom, before returning to Gaeson tomorrow. Ideally, I would have liked to stay longer with Sarah and my new nephew, but the duty of the crown bid us home.

I stretched my listless arms. The disquiet was almost palpable, lingering within Caer Ligualid's ancient stone walls. Was this why I couldn't sleep? I tried to ignore this feeling of hidden tension lurking somewhere. I headed for the ramparts, as I often did if sleep wouldn't come. Presently I stepped out onto one of the higher balconies. I lifted my eyes to the sky, but thick cloud covered the canvas above me, concealing any stars.

Abruptly, my instincts, sharpened by over a decade of warfare, told me I was not alone on this balcony. Though I had no evidence to say it would not be a friend, my hand quickly went to the hilt of my blade as I peered through the darkness.

"Evening, King Bryce." A voice greeted me, just as I perceived a dim outline to my left. My hand left my sword, instantly recognising him.

"Your Majesty King Owain." I bent my head in a swift bow. "I hope the evening finds you well, sire." To my surprise, the great king gave a soft snort.

"About as well as can be expected." His tone was glum, ending his speech in a weary sigh. My brow creased slightly as I took a step closer to him.

"My lord?" I questioned. He glanced to me. Much of his countenance was in darkness, but I could sense his stony stare. Was this why Caer Ligualid was so ill at ease? Had this tension somehow reached all the way to my chambers and woken me from my sleep?

"Princess Thaney has gone," King Owain said heavily. My eyebrows rose. "Away into the night with barely a word. Only this note." He held up his hand. I heard the unmistakable crumpling of paper.

"I see, sire." My reply sounded so trite and feeble, but I knew not what else to say. I wanted to empathise with my king, yet I could not condone his affair.

"Aye, you see." He sniggered softly into the darkness. "Soon all of Rheged will see, also, how their king has made a fool of himself," he ended bitterly. He glanced at me again. In the dim light, I had never seen King Owain's face more sombre and resigned. "She is with child, Daniel."

"I…" I trailed off, unsure what to say. He would have already noticed my lack of shock. "I'm sorry, sire," I murmured. Whatever I thought of his affair, I was sorry to see him in pain.

"Aye, well." His voice was flat. "That is the way of things." He sighed again, looking away. "I do not know whether I shall see her again, or meet the child." His tone was even, yet I could imagine the agony lurking beneath his speech.

"Does Her Majesty Queen Penarwen know?" I asked after a moment. I was hesitant to mention her name, but it felt more wrong not to do so.

"She knew of Thaney almost from the beginning, Daniel. Do you think it pains her?" He gave a short, humourless laugh. "Have you not heard the rumours of her own infidelity?" Such gossip had reached my ears, but I said nothing.

"Penarwen and I fell out of love many moons ago." His tone was reflective. Was that regret in his voice? Did he have remorse for how his heart had changed towards his queen?

"She has long looked elsewhere for comfort, as I have. Yet…" I heard the merest trace of sadness spilling over in him. "I have never truly loved again, until now." He suddenly jerked his head in my direction. "You love Queen Evelyn very deeply, don't you?"

"Aye," I answered instantly. I could see why King Owain had asked me that, for I did not want to imagine even a little of the pain I might feel if Evelyn were wrenched away from me.

"I loved Penarwen like that too, when we were first wed." He sounded far away now. "I didn't realise the love had faded for the longest time. Then, I began to notice little things." King Owain sighed. "I no longer cared when royal duty kept us apart, for a week or more. I realised

I found her company tiresome." He drummed his fingers absently on the rampart wall. "In truth," he said flatly, "I cannot remember when I last felt love for her."

"I'm sorry," I said again. I could not imagine my love for Evelyn ever fading. Perhaps King Owain had felt like that about his love for Queen Penarwen. Once, many years ago. The two of us were quiet for a few moments, while the slight breeze ruffled through the otherwise still night. "What will you do, my lord?" I asked at last.

"The same thing I have done for the last ten years." He sighed heavily again. "Penarwen and I will be civil with each other, so at least sometimes, there will be companionship. This is nothing, though, to what I have now known with Thaney…" he trailed off again.

"Still." He coughed. "Doubtless all of Caer Ligualid will know of it by the morning. At least King Lot is still going to stand with us against the Angles."

"That is certainly something, sire," I agreed. It would have been entirely possible for the King of Gododdin to call off the alliance altogether, given the affair. "I was wondering, my lord. Is King Morgant still out there?" I could not help but ask.

"For now." His voice grew hard at once. "He dares me to go to him, Daniel. It takes everything in me not to succumb and ride out there this very moment. I know you must have been tempted, too." He glanced my way again. "I have not forgotten it was your kin he killed, as well as mine."

"Aye," I agreed hotly. I was there again on that ridge, my bow willing me to place upon it the arrow that would end his wretched life. "There are bigger things in this war than our vengeance." I felt like I had spoken those words for the both of us.

"Indeed. So, mind you don't stray from your path home tomorrow, tempting as it may be." He gave the wall a final tap. "I'll say goodnight, Daniel."

"Goodnight, my king." The greeting had barely left my lips before King Owain left me alone on the balcony, my thoughts full of his affair.

King Owain was right. By morning, the whole castle would know. The servants would discover Princess Thaney's sudden departure. One of the kitchen staff might mention it as they brought in fresh produce from the market. By the end of tomorrow, it would have spread through the entire kingdom.

For now, though, the knowledge was limited to King Owain and myself, or perhaps one or two others who had witnessed her ride out into the night. I wondered if Prince Elffin knew she was gone. I frowned, staring into the blackness of the night. I truly felt for the lad, with his unwell mother, his father's affair and a sibling he may never get to meet.

Though King Owain did not seem to care much for his wife and son, I did feel some sympathy that he, too, might never know the child Princess Thaney would bear him. Despite this, I felt it was best she was gone, for the security of the kingdom. At least the alliance with Gododdin would stand. If the war with the Angles was not looming, the friendship between the kingdoms could have ended.

How long would it be, I wondered, before the final march against Bernicia? My thoughts darkened as I stared into the night. Was I facing the direction of King Morgant's camp, that Pasgent and I had discovered not ten days earlier? Vengeance swelled through me, as hot and swift as blood.

"One day." My words were quiet, but not without conviction behind them. "How you mock and tempt us, King Morgant, but we will not yield. We will not give you the satisfaction." My eyes narrowed.

"Yet one day, justice will be done. I will hold you to account for the harm you have done to my family. A sword of Rheged will slit your throat." My hands clenched at my sides. "I pray when the time comes, God permits that blade be mine." With that vow made I turned from the rampart, hoping I would be able to sleep. I was pleased to think that in two days' time, I would be back in my own bed in Gaeson.

***

"Grandmother!" Imogen bounded up to my mother. It was the day after we had returned to Gaeson. I had kept my word and not strayed from the road, so it had been an uneventful journey home. It had been a battle not to let resentment build with every moment Epos had taken me away from King Morgant. One day, I would make do on the oath I had made. One day, my enemy would breathe his last.

“Hello, Immy, my darling.” My mother’s voice tugged me away from my dark thoughts. My daughter climbed onto the bed to kiss her grandmother’s cheek. “Did you see Sarah’s new baby?”

“Aye.” Immy was beaming. “Aunt Sarah had a baby boy. She called him Gilroy because of his red hair. Father said it was the same colour as his other mother.” Imogen smiled.

“Ah, I see.” My mother slowly raised her eyes to meet mine. Her voice was just cool enough for me to notice. I fought not to cringe as I held her gaze. Imogen and I had not visited her for a while and now that we had, it was only moments before my birth mother was mentioned.

“Well, what else?” Enid prompted after a moment, darting her eyes back to her granddaughter as though nothing amiss had been said. “Did he arrive big, or small?”

“He was so small!” Imogen imitated the size with her hands, thankfully oblivious. I was grateful for my mother’s tact. Even if she were irritated, she would not press the matter in front of my daughter.

I ran a hand haphazardly through my hair. Watching my mother and my child, the thought of Imogen meeting Morwenna shot through me. Is this how Enid felt, I wondered, when I spoke of my birth mother? Did she wonder who I truly belonged to? Did she feel discomfort, or even pain? I brushed the thought away, instead trying to join the conversation.

Perhaps about an hour later, I heard the front door open and close. There were the murmured voices of Rachel and her daughters, followed by a scuffling of feet. There was barely the sound of running up the stairs before there came a knock at the door.

“Come in, girls.” My mother’s voice was warm as she called to the corridor outside. Her eyes sparkled with good humour.

Rachel’s two daughters, Alena and Ruth, rushed into the chamber. It had been some months since I had last seen them. Often when Imogen and I visited Enid the girls were away, helping their mother with the seamstress business. I got to my feet, hiding my relief that the dynamic of the room had changed.

“Alena, Ruth,” I greeted them back with a warm smile. “Imogen has just returned from Caer Ligualid. I’m sure she would like to tell you about her new cousin.” Imogen nodded, beaming. In the next moment, she ran out of the chamber with them. I smiled. Rachel’s daughters were wonderful with her, despite them now being nowhere near her in age. I guessed they were now thirteen and fifteen.

"They are fond of her," my mother said, as the three of them left. We heard their laughter echoing through the rest of the house. "Sit, my son." She gestured to the chair next to her bed.

"Aye, thank you." I tried to ignore the slightly strained atmosphere. My mother did not speak for a moment. I drummed my hands on my legs. Was she waiting for me to talk first?

"It is good to see you, Mother." Deliberately, I reached for her hand, wanting to be rid of the awkwardness. "You are looking well."

"You as well, Daniel." Though my mother did not move away, neither did she place her hand on top of mine, like she usually did. "It has been too long." The merest rebuke was on her tongue, but now there was no chattering Imogen to distract us.

"It's been a busy few months." This was true, but it still seemed a feeble excuse to my ears. My mother pursed her lips together slightly. "I haven't seen Alena and Ruth for a while," I said, striving for a more neutral topic. "They seem much grown. I take it Rachel is well?"

"Aye, she is. Children do grow," she said, her countenance softening. "You've done so well for them, Daniel. They are so far away from the day we met them." I nodded slowly.

"He would be twenty, now." I sank back a little into the chair, already thinking of Joshua. The lad had been the eldest of Rachel's children. It was strange to think that if Ruth was thirteen, she was the same age he had been. Joshua would be two years older than Prince Elffin.

Only weeks before I discovered the truth about my royal blood, he had died in battle, over a year younger than the conscription age. Joshua had been terrified and had spoken out about the battle, almost costing him his life before we drew swords with the enemy. I had promised Joshua that should anything happen to him, I would provide for his family. This had given the lad the courage to stand fast.

I saw Joshua once during the skirmish of blades and bones and blood. At some point during the battle, he struck down an enemy soldier and saved my life. By the time the battle stopped, as dawn broke over that bloodied field, the lad was dead. Even now his ashen skin came to mind, in sharp contrast to the bruises and gore that covered face. His blond hair, stained with filth, keenly from the earth that had become his grave. It was a sight I would never forget.

"The boy's colour." End's mutter reached me, snapping me back to the present. I sat a little straighter, glancing to my mother. Her eyes were soft and concerned, as if she knew what memory she had just pulled me from. Presently her gaze flickered to the top of my head. "It is redder than yours?" she asked. It took me a moment to realise she was talking about Gilroy.

"It is," I replied simply. "The most vivid I've ever seen. Almost…" I hesitated, but I had already begun the sentence and she would already know its end. "Almost as red as when I dream of her."

"Do you?" My mother pressed. "Do you still dream of her?" Her voice had that edge to it again. I hid a sigh. She was not exactly helping to make things easier between us.

"Sometimes," I kept my answer vague. "Over the years more memories have come to the surface, since discovering my royal blood."

"Aye, each day she occupies more of your thoughts, it seems." My mother's reply cut out at me. Her bitterness surprised me, as she twisted the bedclothes in her hands. "So much so, you did not even hesitate to name your daughter Imogen, rather than Enid." The hard edge to her voice left, with only a trace of sadness in its wake.

My gaze fell to the floor. Once, in the last four years, she had admitted that this bothered her. Indeed, it brought me shame that when I first held little Immy in my arms, I did not truly consider how my daughter's name might affect the woman now opposite me. The one who had raised me.

"I barely remember her, Mother," I pointed out quietly. "Calling my daughter by that name was just my way of trying to keep her alive, to keep her in my life."

"Aye, I know." She sighed heavily, leaning back against the pillows. "I'm sorry, my son." She stared into the middle of her chamber. "I'm older, Daniel," she told me frankly, as she reached again for my hand. "I do not think I am as strong as I once was. Things bother me that never used to."

"I understand." I squeezed her hand back in return. "I'm sorry if I grieve you, Mother." Suddenly, my words were a rough tumble from my lips. "Aye, I'm curious about the woman who brought me into this world. She was gone before I could fully know her. All I remember is snatched fragments that fade before I can truly grab hold of them." I sighed.

"However, she could never take your place in my heart," I said now, desperate for her to understand. "I am sorry if I sometimes take you for granted, because you are always there. You are the one who has cared for me, since you found me in the snow that day."

"Thank you, Daniel." Her voice was a little rough, but no longer with anger. My gaze had fallen to our joined hands and looking up again, I saw tears sparking in my mother's eyes. "I'm sorry," she said now. "It is normal and right for you to be curious. Old age is making me cantankerous, that is all."

"Truly?" I met her eyes. They glistened only a little. "Truly, Mother, you are all right with me thinking of her? You do not feel neglected?"

"No, my son." Her answer was firm as she smiled apologetically. "I just need to remember that no matter what happens, your love for me will not change."

"Never." I squeezed her hand again. "Actually, I can understand how you feel," I admitted. I sat back in the chair and sighed. "Imogen wants to meet Morwenna."

"Ah." She gave me a small smile, full of understanding. "The curiosity is natural, just as it is for you. Especially since Morwenna is still living," she pointed out. "How does Queen Evelyn feel about it?"

"The same as me, I think," I murmured. "We know Imogen meeting Morwenna is the right thing to do, but…" I sighed again. "What if Immy will prefer her birth mother? What if her view of us will change? What should we do?" At this I looked back to my mother. She nodded knowingly.

"It is difficult, my son, but I will always regret hiding the truth from you." Her voice was hoarse. "Kellen and I did it to save your life, for King Reghan may have killed you if you had been discovered. Still, we hated the deception. We nearly told you once, you know." My gaze shot up to hers in surprise.

"You were fifteen, talking to John about enlisting. We believed you should know the truth." Her voice was quiet, fragile. "You were about to follow in Kellen's footsteps, pledging your sword to the king who had ordered your parents' deaths. We were going to tell you once he came back from the war, but then—" Her voice caught.

"I understand," I rasped. If my father had not died in the battle and come home, would I have known the truth then? Would I have escaped Gaeson and gone to Klumeck, whilst King Reghan and King Cedric were still at war?

"So many times, since his death," my mother went on, "I nearly told you, but every time I did, I thought of Kellen. He would have had the words to tell you, to answer your questions, but I did not." She twisted her bedclothes in her hands as she spoke.

"I feared you would lose your father even more if you knew the truth. That it would taint his memory. I also kept telling myself it would be too dangerous if King Reghan found out." She looked away and wiped the few stray tears that had fallen. "I thought I was sparing you pain, but perhaps it was simply cowardice," she concluded bitterly.

I watched her for a moment, my throat tightening. It was a little over fifteen years since his death, but her grief was as sharp and keen as ever. In that moment, I feared the agony I would feel, if something were to happen to Evelyn.

"Do not make my mistake, Daniel." My mother's voice was strong and passionate now as she glanced up to me. "You have told Imogen the truth about her mother. It is more than I ever did."

"My daughter's birth mother is a maid in Gaeson," I pointed out, "not a princess who was murdered. There would be some scandal if people found out about Morwenna, but there would be no risk to Imogen's life. You and Bridget did what you had to do, to keep us safe. I only lived that night I returned to Gaeson because Evelyn confronted King Reghan," I told her. "If I had not gained her trust, then I would have been executed for treason that night and we could still be at war with Klumeck."

"Ah, perhaps you're right. I thank you, Daniel." She sniffed, then shot me a rueful smile. "Still, I could have told you the truth when you were older. I feared losing you." She reached again for my hand. "Do not hold things back from Imogen. She loves you and Queen Evelyn." My mother smiled again, but this time it was without regret. "There is nothing you could do to change her love for you."

"The same as my love for you will never change," I told her quietly. Her smile widened as she nodded. As we sat there, hands still joined, I suddenly noticed, as if for the first time, that she was older. The lines were deeper on her face, with more white streaks to her hair. There was a frailty to her that was unsettling. How much had I taken this woman for granted? Then I remembered the way her eyes had sparkled when chattering away with her granddaughter. It gave me hope she had plenty of life in her yet.

"The day is getting on, Mother," I told her, after another hour or so in her company. "You are stronger than you know," I told her as I stood, then stooped to kiss her forehead. "I'll arrange for Imogen to meet Morwenna."

"Good." Her smile widened again. She reached out to give my hand a final squeeze. "Try not to leave quite as long before you visit again."

"Aye, I'm sorry. We'll see you soon," I promised. "Farewell, Mother," I bade her, before leaving her chamber and heading back downstairs.

Downstairs, Imogen sat on a chair far too big for her. She seemed delighted with this, swinging her legs back and forth as she chattered happily to Rachel, Alena and Ruth.

"Your Majesty." Rachel stood to curtsey, as did her two girls, though they were hardly girls any longer. Alena was on the brink of womanhood and Ruth would be fully grown soon.

"Good evening. Rachel, good to see you. I hope you are well?" Rachel smiled and dipped her head. "Come on, love, time to go home," I said, turning to Imogen. I could see the disappointment in her eyes, but she still stood obediently from the chair.

"Aye, Father. Thank you for having me," she added to Rachel. I smiled. My daughter's manners were ever improving. We left the house that had been my childhood home.

As we stepped onto the street outside, the familiar scent of straw reached my nostrils. I had sometimes kept Epos in the yard out the back. The smell lingered and I heard the scuffing of hooves upon the ground. Perhaps Rachel was keeping a horse there or renting the yard to another.

"Come on." I took Imogen's small hand in mine as we set off for the castle. The sun was dipping low in the sky, casting streaming golden light onto patches of stone. As usual, passers-by stopped to bow or curtsey as they saw us. I gave a nod at them in return. After six years, I had grown used to the attention a royal received when walking through Gaeson. Imogen, beside me, dipped her head, her skirts swishing slightly. I assumed one of her tutors had given her that instruction.

I glanced at Imogen, then, as we neared the castle. Words poured from her mouth as she talked about one thing or another. Her voice was like a constant steam, like a babbling brook. I tried to listen and offer a reply or two when she gave my way, but soon her speech faded into the background. I was looking ahead to when Imogen would meet her birth mother.

So it was, then, that after confirming that Evelyn was of a similar mind, I slipped out that evening to visit my friend Leigh, the surgeon. Leigh had overseen Morwenna's pregnancy with the utmost discretion and care. If I could trust anyone in Gaeson to get a message to Morwenna, it was him.

***

The next morning, just at the end of breakfast, there came a knock at the door. At once, I guessed who it would be. Morwenna would have been given a legitimate reason to come to our chambers, so that no one in Gaeson could guess the true nature of the meeting.

I stood, wiping my mouth with a cloth before I let it fall silently back to the table. I glanced to my wife, trying to ignore the pounding of my heart in my chest. Evelyn gave me a nod before heading to the door. It seemed to take an age for her to reach it. As I fought the urge to bite my lip, I felt a small hand slip into mine. I glanced to my daughter, to see a little anxiety in her gaze. My wife and I had battled with whether or not to tell her the meeting was coming, but it seemed worse not to inform her.

"It'll be all right, love." I smiled down at her, swallowing my own foolish nerves. "She is a kind lady who wants the best for you. Besides, your mother and I are right here. We won't leave your side."

"You wanted to see me, Your Majesty." I glanced to the doorway to see Morwenna standing there. Her hands were clasped in front of her, with her head currently bowed. I imagined it took all her strength to keep her gaze fixed at the rug at her feet, rather than looking straight at Imogen.

"Thank you, Morwenna, do come in." Evelyn's words were a little stiff, but they were warm enough. My child's birth mother stepped into the chamber. My queen closed the door quietly behind her.

"Your Majesty." Morwenna bowed to me, then, at last, her gaze turned to Imogen. Her features lit up at once, a warm smile curving across her face.

"It's so very good to meet you, Your Highness," Morwenna murmured faintly. Imogen stayed by my side for a moment, before taking a step forward. I tried to ignore the absence I felt, with her hand no longer in mine.

"Nice… to meet you," my daughter said. The maid's faint smile broadened. Evelyn said nothing. We both knew that this was their moment. It was not for us to intervene.

"I have seen you sometimes, around the castle, my lady." Morwenna inclined her head as she spoke to my daughter. "Walking to the throne chamber, or out skipping in the garden. It gives me great pleasure to see the wonderful little girl you are becoming." She was trying not to let her voice catch.

"I… thank you," Imogen answered quietly, lowering her head to look at her shoes. I saw my daughter's movements only in my peripheral vision, however, for my gaze was still directed at Morwenna. Different emotions battled to surface, so blended they were almost indistinguishable. Love and joy, as well as pride. Her eyes burned strongly with something wistful… was it as strong as regret?

"Thank you, Your Majesties." Morwenna inclined her head to us a third time, her voice hoarse. "I will never be able to repay you for raising her. Even at a distance, it is the greatest joy to behold her, to see her living day after day." Her voice wavered, ever threatening to crack.

"We will never be able to repay you, for giving her to us." Evelyn's smile was truly warm now. "So perhaps we can consider both debts cancelled."

"Aye, my lady, quite so." A faint smile crossed her features. The maid's gaze drew back to her child that, in another, perhaps fairer world, could have remained hers to raise. "Might I draw nearer to her, sire?" Imogen had taken but one step forward.

"Of course." My reply was quick, as I squashed the slight apprehension that still lingered. Morwenna crossed a few steps into the middle of the room. "Go on, love," I encouraged Imogen. At my nod, my daughter walked towards Morwenna.

Watching them, my bubble of anxiety fought to rise again. The resemblance between them was obvious. They both had the same small eyes, the same dimples in their cheeks. Morwenna's tied back hair was the same fine, honey-golden hair that belonged to my daughter.

"I pray for you every night, Your Highness." Morwenna crouched down so that her face was level with Imogen's. She held out her hand but did not touch her. After a moment, Immy put her hand shyly in it. My own hands had never felt so empty and listless, but I pushed the thought aside.

"I wish nothing but the best for you, my little lady." Her voice was soft, affectionate. "I pray God will grant you joy for today and wisdom for tomorrow."

"Thank you." Imogen's voice sounded a little stronger. A moment later Morwenna stepped back, the brief contact between them broken.

"I must return to my duties, Your Highness. Perhaps I will see you around the castle, from time to time." She gave Imogen a final smile, then stood, bowing to both of us again.

"Thank you, Your Majesties." Wetness was beginning to pool in her eyes; I suspected she wished to depart before the first tears fell.

"You're most welcome, Morwenna. We will let you know when Imogen may wish to see you again," Evelyn bade her formally. A broad smile flickered across her face. With her head still bent slightly, Morwenna retreated backwards towards the door.

A moment later and she was gone, leaving the three of us in our chamber once more. Imogen turned back to us, the usual cheerful smile on her features.

"You were right, Father. She was a nice lady." My daughter sniffed and glanced back to the table. "Is there any toasted bread left?"

"A little," Evelyn said, chuckling. "Better be quick though, you do not wish to be late for your lessons." As Imogen shoved her last few mouthfuls of breakfast, I felt my anxiety melt away. My mother had been right. Imogen would always remain my child, just as Enid would always view me as hers.

For no matter how many times she spoke with Morwenna, or how closely she befriended her, there was a bond of love between the three of us that nothing could ever replace. She was our kin. It was a fact, as sure and as constant as the sun. I offered up a silent prayer, then, that Imogen would know this love the whole of our lives. That nothing would ever harm or threaten the kinship we had.

Part Two

Chapter Five

One night, two weeks after our return to Gaeson, I dreamt of my mother. She came before my mind's eye, with her soft laughter and her vivid auburn hair. I drifted awake with her calling me by the name she had given me.

As I woke, my birth name ringing in my ears, I knew at once my soldier's instinct had woken me. All was not right. Like the night seven years ago, when my thirst had led me to see Klumeck marching against Gaeson's gates, I was glad that I happened to be awake. I frowned into the darkness. What was it?

A moment later and I heard it. The smallest, barely audible shift of a tread upon the rug. There was someone else in the chamber. I feigned a sigh of sleep, rolling onto my side to face where the intruder would be coming from. I slipped my hand under the pillow. The softest padding came again as they stepped closer. I guessed they were barefoot.

The only other discernible noise was of Evelyn, sound asleep beside me. I dared to slide my hand upwards to the top of the pillow. My fingers brushed against the cold reassurance of my dagger's hilt. I tightened my hand around it as I breathed slowly and steadily. Yet my whole being was completely alert.

Then I couldn't hear them anymore. Evelyn's breath slightly tickled my right ear. My queen slept on, utterly oblivious to the danger we were in. I suspected that for the second time in my life, someone waited to kill me while I slept. I opened my eyes into darkness, trying to judge their location.

Then I pounced, dagger in hand. Evelyn gave a cry of surprise as I leapt off the bed, crashing into the assailant. We both landed hard on the rug and rolled. Before the intruder could fight back, my metal dagger found its home, the metal point just kissing their neck.

"You were not quite silent enough, friend," I muttered. "Move again and you will breathe your last. Evelyn, the lamp," I called. The assailant's weight shifted under me as they tried to get away. I pressed the dagger closer, to the point of breaking their skin. They stilled immediately.

A moment later and dim, amber light from the oil lamp flooded the chamber. It was a man underneath me, his lip bleeding a little. He was clad in Bernician armour. His eyebrows were thickly knotted, his skin flushed. The skin was pink around where my dagger had almost pierced his flesh. He knew how easy it would be for me to rob him of his life.

Evelyn now rose from the bed, pulling a cloak over her nightclothes. She retrieved her sword before dashing for the door.

"The guard out here is dead," Evelyn said. My heart lurched, my hand tightening on the hilt of my dagger. At my wife's words the intruder sneered, despite splitting even further. My loathing of him grew. It took all my being not to flick the knife up to remove the foul expression from his face.

"Guards!" my queen shouted. Her sudden voice punctuated the otherwise still night, echoing down the corridor. I tried to think. How many soldiers might he have killed?

"Why are you here?" I hissed to him. My captive made no reply. Thankfully, then, I heard boots clunking in the corridor. The routine of the night watch meant there would always be someone to hear a cry. Moments later two soldiers came in, swords already drawn.

"Sound the horn," I ordered, standing as they stepped towards the intruder. "Take him to the dungeons and alert the captain. The whole castle and the town must be searched at once."

"My lord." They bent their heads before hauling the assailant to his feet and escorted him roughly from the chamber. Hurriedly, I reached for my trousers. As I buckled my belt and stuffed my feet into boots, I heard a scream. My heart leapt.

"Imogen!" Evelyn cried, as we both ran for the door. Dread clamoured in our stomachs as we thundered down the corridor towards her chamber. We had almost reached it when three enemies, clad in Bernician armour, rushed out of it.

"Mother! Father!" Imogen screamed. She was held by one of them, writhing her arms and legs against the guard's shoulder.

"Imogen!" I yelled. We sprinted after them as though nothing on earth could stop us. As if all the wild beasts that dwelt upon the earth were after our flesh. I kept my gaze on Imogen as we chased after them. It was a sight I would never forget.

Where were the guards? My heart plummeted. I realised there should have been far more sentry, far more to stop them from capturing Imogen.

"Careful!" my wife called. I looked down, leaping to the side just in time to avoid tripping over a helmet, then jumped over another. Had these guards been taken down as the intruders made their way through the castle? Were any of these soldiers even alive?

We raced down a spiral staircase to the next floor of the castle, leaping down the last few slabs of stone.

"Imogen!" I shouted in anguish, as we crashed into a group of Bernician soldiers, ready to ambush us. I tried to fight them off, but they already had their hands on my arms and legs.

"No!" Evelyn cried in despair. We struggled to break ourselves free, but it was no use. There were far too many of them. My stomach tightened as the guard carrying Imogen disappeared.

"Attack!" I heard John cry. Relief coursed through me as swiftly as the blood pumping through my veins. My friend appeared, leaping with our forces into the fray. The ones who held us were swiftly put to the blade. As soon as I was free from the enemy's fold, I raced forwards. It had only been a few seconds, I told myself. I had to cling to whatever remnant of hope remained.

I dashed to the end of the corridor and turned left. The door to the outside courtyard was open. As I sprinted across to it, the image of Captain Bredon came to mind, where his blood had been spilled upon these very cobbles five years before.

My mind snapped back to the present. I ducked and weaved past two Bernician guards, which blurred into the distance as I left the courtyard behind. I was entirely fixed on my goal. I would reclaim my daughter, whatever the cost.

I could still hear the thudding of boots ahead as I pressed on. As the portcullis came into view, I gasped to see it raised. How long had my enemies schemed to kidnap my daughter? Questions fled my mind as the soldiers raced under the portcullis. From the flickering of the torches suspended by the raised metal gate, I saw a soldier on horseback.

"Your horse!" I shouted, rushing forwards. If the guard was

surprised, then she didn't show it.

"My lord the king!" she called at once, pulling sharply on the reins. She swung down from her horse, her feet touching the ground only a moment later.

I leapt up into the saddle, gathering the reins in one hand. The soldier offered me her lantern and I only had time to grab it from her before I kicked the horse into a gallop. As the horse began at great speed down Gaeson's hill, my heart leapt again as I caught sight of the lanterns marking the Bernicians. They thundered through the wooden barricade that surrounded Gaeson.

My horse sped through the barricade a few seconds later. My blood froze as all turned to blackness, not a lantern in sight. They must have extinguished them upon reaching the treeline. We had used a similar trick four years ago in our escape from our failed recapture of Klumeck. Now I was the one desperate to see any glimmer of light, any sign of where they were.

The night sky offered no consolation. Above me stretched thick clouds, cruelly concealing the moon or any stars that might have guided my way. I stretched out my lantern as far to my side as I could. My eyes strained through the darkness, but there was nothing.

"Imogen!" I shouted, all my breath going into that one, loud cry. "Imogen!" My voice pierced the night air again, but there was no response. My daughter's lungs and voice were strong, but I heard no scream back. Inhaled sharply, my stomach tightening further. Had they quietened her by force?

By the light of the lantern, the gnarled, twisted shapes of the forest loomed into view. I plunged the horse headlong into the thick of the woodland, knowing it would be almost impossible for me to find her like this. Cold settled deep into my heart. Had I failed?

In despair, I pulled the horse up sharply by my reins. I shushed him sharply as he neighed his protest. Then I listened, in the hope that I might hear something, anything, but there was nothing. Then abruptly, there was the approaching gallop of a horse behind me.

"Your Majesty!" John called. I distractedly turned around in my saddle, holding the lantern out in his direction. He pulled to a stop beside me. "Anything, my lord?" His words were urgent.

The ball of despair clutched deeper over my heart as I shook my head. Had the Bernicians slowed their horses to a walk, perhaps even dismounted? I strained my ears, but I couldn't hear anything over the humming of nightlife. I imagined a rough hand clamped over my daughter's mouth, ensuring her silence. My stomach lurched. I pushed away the repulsive thought, dismounting.

I touched the damp leaves with a soft thud and stepped further into the woodland. I stooped down, lantern pointing at the floor. In the near darkness, I could not make out any tracks.

"Nothing." I managed the single hoarse word as I straightened again. My friend only nodded. The lantern glowing upon his features showed he was as distraught as I was. "They disappeared into the forest," I muttered needlessly, for surely it was obvious to my captain what had happened.

"We will find her, sire." My brother's voice was as strong and as steadfast as ever, but that didn't stop the hollow numbness seeping through me. Even if she had been kidnapped by Bernicians, I had still broken my vow, the promise I had made to keep my daughter safe, from the first moment I held her.

"Report, Captain," I said grimly, glancing back at him. "Is the queen all right? Is Gaeson secure?" I turned to hand him the lantern.

"Aye, my king," John replied. "Her Majesty is safe, our people already in the caves. A couple of the intruders were captured alive, but most have been put to the sword," he then informed me swiftly. "The soldiers are searching for any that remain as we speak."

"There won't be." My voice was final and not quite my own. "There is no need for them to stay, John. Their mission was a success. They got what they wanted." Each syllable ground out mechanically. Was history to be repeated? I wondered, standing there with John at the start of the forest surrounding Gaeson. Was this how my uncle felt when his family was half-destroyed?

"Sire," John began after a moment, "there is nothing more we can do for her this night. We would only confuse the tracks."

"Aye," I said heavily. I knew he was right. I turned away from the treeline and walked back towards the horse; the heaviest steps I had ever taken. "We will be away with the dawn," I said.

“I’m so sorry, Daniel,” my brother said suddenly, his hand clasping my shoulder. “They took her for a reason, brother. Had they wanted to put her to the sword, they would have done so.”

“Aye,” I murmured. John dropped his hand back to his side. “Let’s get back to the castle,” I ordered wearily, as we remounted our horses. “I must speak with my wife.”

“My lord,” John said simply. As we returned to Gaeson, I clung to the hope that they wished to ransom her; that therefore they would not want to do her harm. Such thinking was frail, like the last flame in all the world, about to join the darkness. Yet the fragile hope remained, inching its way into my veins.

All the adrenaline of chasing the Bernicians had dissipated. I was left feeling wearier in my bones than ever before. I clenched and twisted the reins absently in my hands. There was nothing more either of us could say. My daughter was in the hands of the enemy and we were powerless to aid her. This night belonged to them.

Our horses’ hooves clunked loudly as we passed once more under the portcullis. There were several soldiers, swords in hand, waiting. As soon as we had crossed through Gaeson’s walls, the portcullis slammed back down. I held back a scoffing laugh. It was far too late for our defences to be working now. The danger was gone and so was Imogen.

“John, send a messenger to Caer Ligualid right away,” I said, dismounting the horse. “They may be after Sarah and Gilroy also.” At once I sent up a silent prayer, that my sister and her husband had not suffered a similar heartbreak.

“Aye, sire,” John answered rapidly. Presently the soldier who owned the horse I had borrowed stepped forward, dipping her head. I gave her back the reins with a curt nod, then started the weary walk back to Evelyn, to tell her I had failed.

“My lord.” I glanced to John. Both of us stood alone in the courtyard, apart from a single guard keeping watch. The air was so silent, I could almost believe that these last few awful minutes had not happened. Yet the image of the soldier who had captured Imogen was too sharp, too fresh.

“I am sorry I did not stop them taking her.” My eyes widened in surprise when my friend next spoke. Surely, he did not blame himself. “I am your captain, Daniel. It is my responsibility to serve you and ensure your house is safe."

"You have not failed in any aspect of your service, brother," I told him earnestly, trying to dispel the thread of guilt I heard in his voice. John only bent his head.

"It looks about four hours or so till first light," I said, glancing briefly to the sky. "We must make haste and ensure all preparations are done whilst it is still night. I will need you and Aife with me," I told him. "Gather our best soldiers."

"At once, my lord the king," my captain answered formally. He dipped his head one last time, then marched away to carry out my orders. For a moment I stood still in the almost empty courtyard. There was nothing left to do, but to tell Evelyn I had failed. My stomach twisted again. What if we found her body with the dawn, left somewhere in the woods?

I bit my lip hard in defiance of the thought, so hard I almost made it bleed. I tried to cling to the hope that since they had taken Imogen, it made no sense for them to kill her now. Much more likely, they were transporting her to whoever they were working for — I assumed King Morgant. Yet, this logic did not stop the coldness settling on my heart. My fists clenched at my sides as I walked. Whatever reason they had to keep my daughter alive, it did not guarantee her safety.

I turned the corner of a corridor and stopped abruptly as I saw Evelyn standing there, surrounded by several guards. I knew she was desperate to know what had happened, but in my weakness and folly, my words failed me.

"Well?" Evelyn prompted, crossing the distance between us when still I said nothing. My silence was enough, as grief twisted the urgency on her features.

"I lost them," I said finally, my words hollow. "We pursued them to the forest, but then…" the knot in my stomach tightened further. "I swear," I told her, reaching out suddenly to grasp her hands in mine. "I will do all I can to bring her back to you. I must prepare now—"

"You are quite mistaken if you think you are going alone, my husband," Evelyn said roughly, her voice cutting across mine. "I am your queen as well as your wife. I am coming with you to reclaim our daughter. There is nothing you can do to stop me."

"Aye, very well," I relented after a moment, for she was right. There was nothing I could do to prevent my queen's will. More than that, I had no right to suggest she remain here. "We must make haste, then," I murmured. Evelyn nodded.

"A servant has already packed our belongings," she said, as we rushed back towards our chambers. "I prepared for the worst," she added grimly, seeing my surprise. "I must speak with Lord Melvyn, as soon as our people return from the caves."

I nodded as I swapped my nightshirt for my tunic. Lord Melvyn was the steward of the queen, the one who would carry out her duties while we were away. For my own folly, I had once believed him to be the Wolf. At the time, Aldred had always appeared so amiable, whilst Lord Melvyn seemed so suspicious. However, I had been watching the wrong man.

"I'll head to the dungeons," I told her, buttoning up my tunic. "I'll try to get as much information as I can." She nodded, turning for the door.

"Evelyn," I burst out, my hand going to her arm. I swallowed hard, without any notion of the rest of my sentence.

"I know." Evelyn's voice was rough. She took a single step and pressed her forehead against mine. Her raven curls brushed my left ear as we broke apart again and left our chambers.

A few minutes later, I was heading down the dank corridor of the dungeons. The only source of light came from torches on the walls, softly illuminating the cold stone. Somewhere nearby, water trickled faintly. The stench of blood and human odour filled my nostrils, but I ignored this as best I could.

This was not a place I enjoyed visiting. These dark walls always brought unpleasant memories to mind. Seven years ago, I had been held in one of these cells, the night before my supposed execution. I had been branded a traitor by King Reghan, Evelyn's father. This was just after discovering the truth about my royal blood in Caer Ligualid. I had been beaten senseless by the brutal interrogator (later revealed to be a Bernician spy) who had not even asked me a single question.

Then, sometime later, I had almost killed King Reghan in one of these cells, after discovering he had been the one to order the assassination of half my kin, all those years ago. I had nearly slain him in cold blood because of it. Indeed, only the thought of Evelyn had stayed my hand.

I shook my head. This was why I hardly ever ventured down here. The last time I came here was when I interrogated Cara, the recruit who, after only a few months, I revealed to be working with the Wolf. I pushed down the memories that still threatened to disturb me. Perhaps these thoughts would have troubled me a lot more if all my being was not taken up with Imogen's kidnapping.

A guard advised me where the assailant who had been in my chamber was. I walked swiftly past the rows of adjoining cells, before at last coming to the cell door. I nodded to the guard posted outside. A slight clinking of metal sounded as he turned the key into the lock, then I entered the cell itself.

I inhaled sharply at the sight of the prisoner, then immediately regretted it. The putrid stench permeating everywhere invaded my senses. I clamped a hand over my mouth as I stepped closer, glaring at the man through the metal bars.

A sole flickering torch on the wall lit his pitiful features. His body was slumped back against the stone wall, his hands suspended by thick chains above his head. He seemed barely aware of my presence at first, but then he raised his head. He attempted to smirk, but the expression was somewhat lost between the cut to his lip and the dried blood about his nose.

I remembered the lip was my handiwork, but even in this light I could see the guards had given him a severe beating. Given his crimes this night of attempted murder and kidnapping, I didn't mind the injuries inflicted upon him in the slightest.

"Your Majesty." Although his voice was hoarse with pain, the sarcasm was still rife. "Are you missing your daughter already?"

"How dare you!" I roared, my anger ricocheting around the cell walls. I drew my sword. "Say one more word out of turn and I'll slit your throat," I threatened. At this, he wheezed out a laugh.

"You can't though, can you, my lord?" His scornful tone sounded almost jovial. "I am the only one who knows where your little princess was taken."

"You are a Bernician," I retorted. "It is not difficult to assume you serve King Morgant. Perhaps I do not need you at all." I pointed the tip of my blade at him, sorely wishing to make good on my threat to put an end to his miserable life.

"Bernicia is a vast land, sire." My prisoner's answer was smooth as he held my gaze steadily. "You could search for years and never find her." At this he craned his neck to spit blood.

"Then tell me," I almost growled. The man only sneered again. At this, I replaced my sword with a clunk. I crossed the few paces between us and crouched down to his level. While one hand grabbed his hair tightly, the other retrieved my dagger from my boot.

"Remember this?" I asked softly. I pressed the point of my dagger against his neck. "I may not be able to kill you yet, but that does not mean I cannot cause you pain," I hissed. The prisoner raised his eyebrows. The mocking was all gone from his expression. Now he looked interested, almost impressed.

"I heard the mighty King Bryce was a good man," he muttered. "I suspect you are too soft-hearted for torture."

"Oh?" I breathed. He flinched a little as I carefully pierced his neck. A single drop of blood blossomed from the cut. "Your people marched upon my home, killing my guards, almost killing my wife and kidnapping my daughter. Do you really think this is a good time to test my mercy?" I challenged him.

"Very well, I yield," he murmured. He flinched back, but he had nowhere to go between my dagger and the cold stone wall behind him.

"I value my own skin more than my lord. If you spare my life, I will tell you all I know." I regarded him a moment, then nodded.

"Very well. It is spared, providing your information proves useful." I removed my dagger from his throat. "Well? Where is my daughter?"

"It was on King Morgant's orders," the prisoner admitted. He sniffed loudly, presumably clearing whatever blood remained congealed in his nostrils. "They are taking her deep within Bernicia."

"You told me yourself how vast Bernicia is. You'll have to do better than that." I raised the dagger again. The flicker of the torch gleamed on the small blade, the tip now stained with crimson. "Whereabouts, specifically?"

"I know it is a few days' travel to the north-east." His eyes moved to my dagger, then back to me again. "That is all I know, I swear. I'm a common soldier, my lord. I knew little beyond my mission."

"Your mission to murder me," I seethed. The hint of a smirk returned. I glared as I straightened a moment, folding my arms. Had I really spared him for such little new information?

"I told you all I know, my lord, as was our bargain," The soldier said, as if reading my thoughts. There was a hardened edge to his speech, as if daring me to break my word.

"I will keep to it," I said, taking a step back. "If you tell me why King Morgant sent you to murder my wife and I and kidnap my daughter." He wheezed out a laugh again.

"Other than him being your enemy, sire?" he scoffed. "I promise you, I do not know," he said hastily, as I took a step closer to him again, still holding my dagger. I regarded him another long moment.

"Very well. Get used to your accommodation." I stooped to slide my dagger back into my boot. "You may never again see the light of day." I gave a single knock on the cell door.

"King Morgant seeks to destroy what you love, piece by piece," the prisoner told me, as the guard unlocked the door again. "He would see Gaeson torn down."

"Then as long as I have breath in my body, I will try to stop him." I gave him one final glance before I left the cell, only too glad to be leaving the dungeons.

The clear night air filled my lungs, helping to dispel the putrid smell. Those dank cells were even worse than the battlefield, for at least there, death was fresh. Unlike the sickly-sweet smell of rotting flesh that always seemed to linger, no matter how vigorously everything was scrubbed.

I could not return to my chamber while Imogen was going further away with every single hoofbeat. I therefore made my way up to the highest rampart, where I could study the sky. Clouds still stretched as thick as ever, giving no hint that the dawn would ever come.

The one consolation was that it had not rained. If it stayed dry, there was every hope the Bernician trail would be clear to follow the next morning. We knew the general direction of Imogen's captors, but without the tracks, the chances of finding her were slim indeed.

Though I stood still, my mouth was ever moving. Almost

meaningless mutters tumbled from my lips as I lifted my daughter up in prayer. I vowed again and again that as long as breath was still within me, I would try to find her.

There was hardly any wind, not even the slightest breeze that ruffled my hair. I could not remember a night as still as this one. Were these foul clouds ever going to move? The sky had never seemed so cruel. Had there been any sighting of the moon there could have been a chance to leave now, if the tracks were clear enough. Or, at least, tracing the silver orb through the sky would give me some notion of time passing. As it was, it seemed as though the night would last forever.

Finally, though, the sky paled. About an hour before dawn, enough bleak light filtered through the cinereal clouds to show our path. I headed swiftly for the armoury, then met Evelyn outside the portcullis. It was time at last to pursue those who had taken our daughter.

"Here, Your Majesties. Refreshment from the kitchen." I turned at the hoarse voice and my breath caught in my throat. Stood before me was Morwenna, features torn with anxiety. She held out a tray bearing tea made with stewed herbs and round hot cakes made with honey.

"You will need your strength, my lord, and lady," she whispered. The tray rattled only a little in her hands as she spoke.

"I am so sorry, Morwenna," Evelyn muttered. My heart tightened. Surely Imogen's birth mother feared her daughter's loss as much as we did.

"I will do all I can to find her. I give you my word," I said, the vow spilling once more from my lips. "I will bring her home or die trying."

"I know, sire." Already fresh pools were gathering in her eyes. "I see daily how you and Her Majesty love her." Her gaze fell as a tear spilled down her cheek. "Please eat, my lord."

"Aye, thank you." My voice was hoarse as I took the tea in one hand and the cake in the other. Evelyn did the same beside me. "I advise you to speak to Leigh, if you wish." The surgeon was the only other person who knew she was Imogen's birth mother, aside from John and Aife, who were coming with us. Morwenna curtsied swiftly.

"May God be with you both, Your Majesties," she said, her voice cracking. In the next moment she hurried away from the tray, her feet rushing across the courtyard cobbles.

"You promised you would not return home without her," Evelyn murmured quietly. I nodded, taking a large bite of the cake. She held my gaze as the delicate honey sponge filled my mouth.

"It is time," Evelyn said, choosing not to comment further. I stuffed the last of the honey cake into my mouth and reached for Epos' reins.

"Come, my girl," I murmured as I swung up into the saddle. "We must ride as swiftly as the lightening hits the earth." My horse darted her head. I took it as a sign of agreement. Evelyn drew up beside me on her own horse.

"I leave the kingdom in your hands, Lord Melvyn," Evelyn called, glancing to her steward. Lord Melvyn's eyes were sombre, his moustache twitching only slightly as he bent his head in obedience.

"Farewell," I said, nodding to him briefly. In different circumstances many townspeople would have gathered, to bid their royals farewell, but not this day. They had only lately been given the signal they could leave the caves. Our people were already home, catching whatever sleep they could before the busyness of the new day. Life had to go on, despite the horror of this night.

"When I next return, Imogen," I muttered to myself, tightening my hands on the reins. "You will be by my side. We will bring you home."

"We depart!" Evelyn called out her order. At my queen's command I spurred Epos into a gallop. We bolted through the portcullis and through the wooden barricade. Evelyn rode parallel to me as we swiftly left Gaeson behind. John, Aife and a few other riders brought up the rear. Abruptly then we slowed to a walk, as once more we came to the woodland surrounding Gaeson's hill.

"There, Your Majesties," Aife called after a few moments. She had dismounted and was stooping near the ground, searching for the Bernician trail. The briefest of smiles creased my face. I was glad my friend was with us. If anyone could spot the tracks leading to Imogen, it was her.

"Lead on, Aife." My wife ground out the three words tightly. We already knew their path would be east, for that was where Bernicia lay. "We must make haste whenever we can."

"Aye, Your Majesty," she muttered back. She swung back onto her horse quickly. Aife set the pace at a trot at the front of the party, keeping her sharp gaze to the ground. Yet again, I was thankful the night had been dry. The hooves of the enemy's horses were cracked well into the earth.

Soon, though, progress gave way to frustration. Though for a while we had been following a clear path, now the tracks of the horses began to separate. They would fork off into different directions, before coming together again. Some of them even formed small loops around the trees.

"They are playing games with us," Evelyn ground out through gritted teeth. I nodded, my jaw locking. The Bernicians had known we would not be able to follow them until dawn, so had taken the liberty to make their tracks all the harder to follow. They may even have thought they could lose us altogether, before we even cleared the woodland.

However, they had not counted on Aife's piercing sight. Somehow, my friend seemed to know which path was genuine. Our pace was slow, yes, but I hoped it was sure. The dense forest air and the quiet hum of wildlife gave my soul only a little solace as we weaved our horses behind Aife.

Eventually, we finally broke free of the woodland. Thanks to Aife, we had managed not to lose the Bernician tracks. Now we were out in the open, the dent of enemy hooves upon the grass was obvious. We sped our horses to a trot, then onto a canter.

The terrain began to climb. I sensed the great lake was far below to our west somewhere. I suspected we were not too far from the route to Caer Ligualid. Despite now following much easier tracks across open fields, the tightening in my chest did not dissipate. The only thing that kept me calm was that with each stretch of trodden grass that appeared on the horizon, we did not find Imogen's body strewn across it.

The rest of the day passed in a blur as we climbed steadily higher. I expected the path to turn further east towards Bernician lands, but for now our course remained north. When at last we stopped to make the camp, I saw I was right. As the lakeland fell away beneath us, the great lake could be glimpsed. At this distance, it was little more than a sliver of deep blue.

We had ridden for most of the day, spending a frustrating amount of time in Gaeson's forests. Evelyn and I managed to catch a little sleep that night, mostly due to pure exhaustion. In the morning I longed to speak with her but could not find the right words. It seemed the grief of being separated from Imogen had created a distance between us. I was not quite sure how to cross it.

An hour or so into the second day of our journey, the Bernician route turned sharply right. We were finally going on a more easterly course. Briefly, my heart lightened that the trail might take us straight to Bernician lands, but then we turned another bend in the path.

"Another forest," Evelyn sighed, as we pulled to a stop. The chilly wind blew past. I blinked rapidly to try to prevent the air biting into my eyes.

"They must want to lose us in there, too." My voice was thick with frustration as I rubbed my smarting nose. This cold air was a sure sign that winter was almost upon us.

"Aye," Evelyn muttered. "Well, there's nothing else for it. Into the woodland!" she called sharply. Aife moved to the front of our party again as we headed for the trees.

"We're going the wrong way," I hissed through gritted teeth, after we had been twisting through the trees for what had felt like hours. I glanced up again at the sun again, just visible beyond the dense canopy of leaves. "Why are we heading west again?"

"I don't know," Evelyn muttered from beside me. "We have little other choice but to follow the tracks," she said, keeping her voice low. "Perhaps the Bernicians have reason to go west." I nodded, but my jaw was still tight. I was sure it was simply another chance for them to lose us again.

It was at least another hour before we finally stopped winding through the woodland. Again, it was only thanks to Aife's sharp eyesight that we still had tracks to follow. We climbed higher again, heading for the heart of the lakeland hills. The sun had already sunk below the horizon and all around us was bleak and grey. Soon we were forced to make camp on a high plain, on a stretch of field overlooking one of the smaller lakes.

"Another day of mostly north, with a bit of west thrown in," I said hotly, as I dismounted Epos. "It makes me wonder if they are even going to Bernicia at all."

"Perhaps she will be kept right on the edge of their northern border," Evelyn suggested flatly. Her words just sounded as hollow as my own had been since Imogen was taken from us.

A soldier took our horses away to be fed and watered. I was still uncertain how to cross the gap between us. I glanced instead to the small lake, as the ever-encroaching dusk transformed it to darker hues of navy.

The familiarity of it tugged at me.

Then, as I spotted a cliff jutting out over the water, I inhaled sharply in recognition. It was the same lake that Aldred had ordered me thrown from. I had almost drowned, but Evelyn had dived in after me and saved my life.

"You remember it too?" my wife asked. I turned to see her stood beside me. A few stray curls that had come loose billowed behind her in the breeze as her quiet question hung in the air.

"Aye." My tone was a little curt. It was not a comforting memory. Her features were equally grim. Would there be another night of no talk between us? I longed to bring her some small measure of comfort. Yet what could I offer her, except empty promises and meaningless platitudes?

"Sorry to disturb you, Your Majesties," John said from my right. "I was going to report, sire," he said as I turned to him. "The watch is already organised."

"Very good, Captain," I answered mechanically, still in a voice not quite my own. Suddenly I sensed Evelyn was gone. I looked up to see her a few feet away, wandering listlessly through the camp.

"How is Her Majesty faring?" John asked quietly. I turned back to him, saying nothing. "A foolish question." He sighed. "I'm so sorry." I only nodded.

"There's a stew nearly ready, sire," my captain said, then took a few steps closer. "You should both try to eat something, brother," he added gently.

"Thank you, John," I murmured with a final nod. He dipped his head in a bow as I turned back to the lake. I heard his footfall fading across the camp. I knew he was as genuine as ever as he offered this condolence, but currently I just wished to be alone.

The stew was ready about the same time as the camp was fully prepared, but there was no sign of Evelyn. Assuming she had gone to our tent, I fetched two bowls of stew before making my way to join her.

"Evelyn?" She was there, laying on her side and facing the tent wall. She gave me no reply. I sat, not speaking again for a moment while I removed my boots. Metal clunked dully to the tent floor as I took off each piece of armour.

"You should try to eat something," I murmured, repeating John's advice as I put her bowl of food near her. "It's good," I offered inanely, taking my first mouthful.

"As if that matters," Evelyn hissed harshly. "How can you even think of eating? She may not have any food at all." My queen's rough voice told me she had recently wept.

"The more we eat, the more strength we have," I told her quietly. "So, the better chance we have of bringing Immy home." I pushed another spoonful of stew to my mouth. While I chewed, my hand moved to her ankle. Whilst she did not turn towards my touch, she did not kick me away, either.

"I…" My voice trailed as I swallowed a lump of meat and vegetables. It was time to say the words I had been trying to find since we left Gaeson. "I'm so sorry I failed both of you."

"What?" Her feet moved as she suddenly sat up, her countenance surprised. "Daniel, none of this is your doing. You did all you could—"

"That matters not!" I cut her off roughly. I wiped away a stray carrot from my lip with the back of my hand. "I vowed to protect her, the moment she was placed in my arms," I muttered brokenly. "Whether it was possible to stop them or not, I still failed in my duty." My queen was quiet a moment, her arms folded as she regarded me.

"Then the fault lies with me also," Evelyn said at last. "I could not even make it past the courtyard. At least you pursued her to the forest," she added bitterly.

"We were ambushed," I replied quickly. "You did all you could, you were surrounded by the enemy." My wife laid a gentle hand on my arm.

"As were you, my husband," she murmured. "Either neither of us are to blame, or both of us are." I said nothing to this, but I reluctantly saw her point.

"You should still try to eat," I told her. Evelyn shifted closer, her head resting on my shoulders. I put my bowl on the floor and both my arms encircled her. Her raven curls brushed my cheek.

Then I felt her begin to shake. I held her as she wept as tears trailed down my own face. Grief and despair at what could have happened to our daughter threatened to choke us both. We clung to the other, as if a vicious tempest were swirling all around us. Only by the refuge of our embrace could we be saved.

The candle was burning low when at last my love's breathing

slowed. My queen stirred only a little as I lowered her to the bed, her head resting on the pillow. She turned, falling promptly back asleep. I was glad of this, for I hoped she could find some respite from the pain she endured while awake.

I blew the candle out and lay down, stretching out my tired limbs. My lovely daughter came to mind, with her honey-golden curls and deep blue eyes. That small nose and infectious smile. I could almost hear her laugh floating around the tent. Then suddenly Immy's image morphed, her features now terrified as she kicked and squirmed in the Bernician's arms.

My hands clenched into fists at what King Morgant had done. My would-be assassin was right. It was just a cruel irony, an attempt to repeat history. The foul wretch of a king was trying to destroy all the royals of Rheged, one at a time. That way, we would be doomed to fail when the final reckoning of Rheged came.

Eventually, I did fall into a fitful slumber, but nothing about it was comforting. I was visited by the disturbing dreams of wandering in the snow in the forest outside Gaeson. Now, though, there was a cruel twist. I was not a child searching for my parents.

This time it was Imogen who was lost, staggering half-frozen in the icy elements. My feet sank though snow as I scrambled towards her, but each time I drew near she slipped from my grasp. Then the blizzard rose and whirled her far away, leaving me alone. Cold and dread gnawed at my bones, with the terrible thought I might never hold my daughter again.

Chapter Six

My eyes jolted open to the sounds outside my tent. Slowly, I relaxed again. It was only the scampering of a bird, darting and pecking the grass outside. I forced myself to uncurl my fingers from around the hilt of my dagger. I lay in bed another few moments, staring at the darkened canvas above me. Somewhere beyond the rustling bird came the muted talk of the guards on watch.

I stood and stretched, then opened the door of the tent a little. It was still night, but the earlier wind had dissipated the wall of cloud, leaving the sky clear. A little sliver of moonlight filtered through the flap into the tent. My eyes followed its beam, to where it landed near Evelyn's sleeping features.

Evelyn's raven locks were tousled about her head. Her expression was clear, devoid of the apprehension she now bore whenever she was awake. A half-eaten bowl of congealed stew sat on the floor near her shoulder. The merest ghost of a smile twitched my lip. At least she had eaten something.

I was still exhausted, but I knew I would sleep no further this night. At least my body seemed a little refreshed from the slumber, even if it had only been a few hours. I exchanged my night-shirt for my tunic and trousers, then pulled on my armour as silently as I could. Evelyn did not wake. At last, I buckled on my belt and threw on my cloak.

The cold air hit me bracingly, but the cloak warded off its deepest bite. I was glad of the icy elements. They shook away the remnants of my dark dreams, imagining Imogen lost and frozen in the snow. The rough breeze danced about my hair as I glanced skyward. The bright moon and the infinite array of glittering skies meant it would not snow. The longer it stayed dry, the longer we could follow the Bernician tracks.

It would still be a few hours before the dawn. I looked away from the sky now and rubbed my face, running a hand through my unkempt hair. With my left hand loosely holding the hilt of my blade, I trudged up the slight incline towards the main fire.

As I approached it, the chill that lingered in my bones began to fade. Not even the warmth of these flames, however, could shake the weariness of my soul caused by my dreams. Did others have dark dreams because of dark events? I wondered absently. Or was that only my curse?

A lone cloaked figure sat on watch by the fire. A bow and quiver were slung on their back. As I further neared the fire, I recognised the unique arrows as belonging to Aife.

"Your Majesty." My friend stood and looked my way, dipping her head to me in a swift bow. "Here, sire, have some tea." She crossed to the fire and stooped to a nearby pan. "Did you get any sleep?"

"A little, I think." I was touched by her concern. "Perhaps three or four hours. Thank you," I added, taking the proffered goblet from her. "How about you?"

"Aye, I've had a few hours, my lord. I haven't been on watch long." I nodded, sipping at the concoction of bitter herbs, with a touch of honey. "The dawn is still far off," Aife said, glancing up. "I believe the nights are almost at their full length."

"The snow will start any day now," I agreed grimly. Once the snow began it would last a month, perhaps two. Then the endless weeks of rain would follow, that dreariness between frost and spring, when the earth finally came alive again.

"Is Her Majesty able to sleep?" Though she was relatively near me, Aife's question sounded faraway. I swallowed another mouthful of tea.

"Aye, she was asleep when I left." I curled my fingers around the goblet's base, trying to warm my fingers a little. For a while, neither of us spoke, but it was a comfortable quiet, as it always was with Aife. My ears filled with the crackling of fire and the cold breeze as it whistled through my hair. My gaze was on the flames, watching the dance of ferocious amber in contrast to the deep darkness beyond.

"I believe we will find her, brother," Aife murmured over the gently roaring flames. "There is every reason to hope." I tore my gaze from the fire to look at her. The flickering golden light illuminated her features, weary yet determined.

"Aye, I know," I replied heavily. I took another gulp of the brew. The logic that they must be keeping her alive for a reason was the mantra I had constantly repeated to myself in the last two days. It was the smallest consolation I could cling to.

"If I can do anything, Daniel..." Aife's voice came louder. "Anything at all." I glanced back to my friend. In the dancing auburn glow, her loyalty looked almost fierce.

"I know that, too." My mouth turned slightly, a hollow imitation of a smile. "There is something you can do, actually," I said. "You're relieved, go and get some rest. I'll keep watch until the dawn."

"Are you sure, my lord?" Aife asked. I lifted the cup to swallow the dregs of my tea, ignoring the slight scorching to the back of my throat. "I haven't been on the watch very long..."

"Aye," I assured, lowering the cup again. "It would ease me to know you are refreshed. You need to rest those eyes of yours," I quipped.

"Very well, sire." The corner of her mouth lifted slightly as Aife stood, dipping her head to me in a swift bow. As she passed me, she placed a gentle hand on my shoulder. The contact only lasted a moment, but it brought me a small measure of comfort.

As my friend's boots crunched back down the hill, I poured some more tea and moved to Aife's spot on the rock. From here, almost all the camp could be seen. A rough border of dry twigs and rocks lay a few feet behind me. Hopefully, I would hear an intruder long before they tried to ambush me.

Sitting a little way from the fire again, the cold gnawed at me. My hands wrapped around the goblet again. I took a few more occasional sips, but I had poured myself another more for warmth than nourishment. I was alone, with only the crackling fire for company.

"Keep trusting in God, Immy," I whispered, my words slipping away into the night. "We will find you. We will see each other again." It was fantasy, but I clung to the desperate notion that somehow my child could hear me.

At last, as I sat keeping watch, the dark canopy above paled. The stars faded and the moon's brightness dimmed, blending with the sky's vast blueness. The landscape became visible, with its rugged rolling hills and high peaks. The birds began their cheerful chatter, celebrating the coming dawn. Gradually the sounds of murmured talk grew louder as the camp woke as one.

“Your Majesty.” I stood, nodding at the two soldiers who bowed. Pans were in their hands, having come to the fire to prepare a hasty breakfast before we departed.

I strode quickly back to my tent, anxious to be on our way. More soldiers piled out of their tents already clothed in their armour. Some of them were beginning to take down the camp.

“Love.” My voice was a murmur as I stooped to touch Evelyn’s shoulder. She stirred awake, blinking. It was only a moment before the tension filled her features again. “It’s recently dawn,” I told her. “We’ll be leaving soon.”

“Good… how long have you been awake?” The question mumbled from her lips as she rubbed her face. Then she dropped her hands to regard me. “You’ve been up half the night, haven’t you?”

“Not quite, I did get some sleep. I took Aife’s place on watch duty for a while.” I didn’t tell her about my nightmares. There was no need to burden her with these as well. “I’ll go get us some breakfast.”

By the time I returned, two bowls of boiled wheat in my hand, Evelyn stood outside, clad in her armour. With a true warrior’s instinct, she turned to me before I reached her, finishing tying her hair into its bun.

“Here.” My boots ground to a halt. The merest smile touched her face as she accepted it. We ate wordlessly, even though the wheat could have been boiled parchment. It gave us our energy and strength for the day ahead, which was all I cared about.

“Let us depart,” Evelyn called to John a few minutes later, after we had hastily finished the breakfast. “We’ll not find her loitering here,” she muttered bitterly.

“Aye. I’ll go get our horses.” Any of the soldiers would do this for us, but preparing the horses would give me something to do while we waited for the last of the camp to be dismantled.

“Hello there, old girl,” I murmured a couple of minutes later, having found her at the temporary stables. My hands rested on her neck. My faithful friend was as sure and steadfast as ever.

“How did it come to this?” I sighed. Epos shifted her head from side to side a little. Clearly, she didn’t know the answers any more than I did. I made Epos and Evelyn’s steed ready, then took the reins and walked them over to where our party gathered.

When we finally set off, it was with great relief that the path turned eastward again. Our route stayed on this course for most of the morning, at we traversed around the hills and lakes. The Bernicians really had been playing games with us, attempting to lose us with winding their trail through dense woodland.

Thanks to Aife, though, we were still following the tracks. As the glorious golden sunshine melted the grass stiffened by frost, my heart eased slightly. It appeared we were finally getting close to Bernician lands. I wondered if Evelyn was right. Perhaps they held Imogen right on the edge of Bernicia's northern border.

The day turned into early afternoon and we left some of the highest peaks behind us, still heading east. I was just wondering how far south Klumeck might be, when I sensed something different in the air. Looking around, I detected nothing out of place. We were in a narrow path, with grass knolls either side.

I glanced to Evelyn and John to see their features narrowed, brows drawn tight. Obviously, I was not the only one who suspected all was not right. Further ahead Aife too had slowed, the tension obvious in her shoulders. None of us had seen any trouble, but the sense of foreboding lingered. I shifted my grip on my reins. Epos twitched at the almost imperceptible movement.

"Easy, girl," I whispered to her as we neared Aife, who had stopped up ahead, just before a bend in the path. I drew up alongside her.

The landscape gave way before us, plains vivid with green from the rain a few days before Imogen was taken. A wide river cut through the fields, rushing fiercely. Sparse trees adorned its banks, their branches shivering in the wind.

"There," Aife said in a low voice. I jerked my head to her as she slipped her bow from her shoulders. With one hand, she silently pointed towards the sparse trees. I followed her gaze, in time to see a figure moving from behind the trees.

"They appear to be alone," Aife murmured. She reached for an arrow and set it on her bow, pulling the string tight. "I have them in my sights, Your Majesties. Ready to fire on your command."

"Very well," Evelyn said, from the other side of me. "Aife, on my mark, fire a warning into the trees. The rest of us will ride directly east, in case they shoot back," she instructed. "We will ride directly at them before they can fire their arrows again. Be ready to fight, all of you."

We gave a quiet chorus of obedience to our queen's commands. I drew my sword and grabbed a fistful of reins. Epos pawed the ground.

"Hold," Evelyn murmured. The adrenaline pooled within me. I tried to ignore the roar of hope building in my heart. What if this was the Bernician soldiers? Could we finally have caught up with them?

"Hold…" Evelyn repeated. Aife raised her arrow high, pointing just to the left of where we had seen the figure move. I took a deep breath and exhaled slowly, taking in the last calm moment.

"Let fly!" Evelyn shouted. Aife released her arrow. It whizzed off towards the river whilst the rest of us galloped to the east along the field. I swivelled my head towards the trees at the riverbank, but nobody moved. No enemies plunging from the trees, nor shots fired from archers.

Evelyn turned our trajectory to the north, towards the stream. I held my sword high, spurring Epos on faster. Still, no Bernician soldiers charged us. I wondered whether the figure was alone after all.

As we approached the trees, the single cloaked person stepped out from behind a tree. My hands jerked the reins back, pulling Epos up short. The figure removed their hood. My eyes widened, jaw locking at the familiar face. Two others now appeared. All of them had swords, but their hands were empty.

"I mean you no harm, Your Majesties." Cara took a single step forward tentatively. "Neither do these, also with me." She glanced back briefly at her two companions. I swung down from the saddle.

"Forgive me if that is hard to believe," I said evenly, swallowing my disappointment that the ones who had taken Imogen were not here. "Your intention was less than peaceful when we last met."

"When last we met, sire, I saved your life," Cara pointed out. My gaze narrowed. She spoke of the hairpin she had given Evelyn, the day Aldred threw me into the lake. It was because of the pin that my wife had freed herself from her chains and dived in after me, saving me from drowning.

"My lady." Cara dipped her head to Evelyn. "I regret to bring you bad tidings. King Morgant is marching against Gaeson as we speak."

"What?" my queen challenged, swinging down from her horse also.

Then her features hardened. “We only have your word this is so. Do you think we will trust it?”

“I hope and pray that you will. He marches with most of his army, Your Majesties,” Cara warned. I kept my gaze on my former soldier, who had betrayed us all four years ago. At least her hands were nowhere near her sword. It seemed at least for now, there would be no bloodshed between us. “It is enough to threaten our people—”

“Why are you here?” I cut across her loudly. “You speak of our people, but those are the ones you betrayed, remember, when you aided the Wolf. For all we know, you could wish them all dead.”

“On the contrary, my lord.” Cara shook her head, her eyes meeting mine. “I do not wish the Bernicians to tear Gaeson apart, nor any other part of Rheged. Your Majesties,” she added suddenly, “I know where your daughter is.”

“Where is she?” Evelyn asked at once, while I stepped forward, boots treading on the damp grass. Cara opened her mouth to reply.

“Your Majesties!” Aife shouted. I turned sharply to where my chief archer stood a little way off, looking behind her. I rose my eyes higher, to see a line of Bernician soldiers standing tall. Where had they come from? I jerked back to Cara.

“I did not know about them,” she said immediately. My eyes narrowed. “They must have followed me. I apologise.” She drew her sword, eyes already looking beyond me. In reflex I rose mine a little higher. Did she mean to use her blade against us, or them?

“Our swords are with you, Your Majesties,” Cara said, voice rife with determination. “We have enough to defeat them, if we join together.” I frowned. Could I ever trust her again? Just then, I heard a whizzing sound. An arrow pierced the grass, narrowly missing my left leg.

“Take cover! Head for the trees!” Evelyn shouted. I leapt forwards, giving Epos a rough pat on the rear. My faithful companion immediately took off, galloping out of range.

Ironically, we sprinted for the trees, taking refuge in the very things we thought might conceal an ambush. I ground to a halt, slinging my bow from my shoulder. I plucked an arrow from my quiver, set it on my bow and took a deep breath.

"Fire when ready!" I shouted, just as the enemy riders gave the cry to charge. My eyes roved to my first target. A moment later my fingers released. My arrow raced through the sky, bearing down on the fourth from the left. It pierced a gap in his armour, embedding itself in tendon and bone. In the next instant he fell from his horse.

I jerked back behind the tree, just before I heard an arrow thud into bark. I took a deep breath in its wake. My eyes shut briefly as I reached for another arrow. Setting it on my bow, I whipped back out behind the tree, found another enemy and fired.

As I dived back behind the refuge and leaves, an arrow landed inches from me, hacking again into bark. My breath caught in my throat. A moment earlier and it would have landed in my cheek, beneath my helmet. Killing me instantly.

My gaze darted left at nearby rustling, as Evelyn ducked behind a tree near me. Her wide eyes bore into mine. In that moment, I knew she had seen how close to death I had been. I nodded to her, telling her I was well. She nodded back, her countenance hardening. We both knew we could fall today.

The vow I had made when I was eight years old suddenly came to me, just after meeting her in the snow all those years ago. It had been my promise to love and protect her, until my last breath came. Remembering my oath gave me renewed hope. Yielding my life for my queen was worth it more than ever.

I reached for another arrow. Time seemed to speed up as I placed it on my bow. I breathed out, exhilarated and liberated, knowing these could be my last few moments. I inhaled sharply, leaving the cover of the tree once more.

My arrow pierced another Bernician's flesh, but the enemy were too close for arrows now. I slung my bow onto my back, then swiftly drew my sword. The first rider raced towards me, his horse thundering its hooves upon the ground.

I lifted my blade high, poised for combat. Waiting for the moment to strike. The thick mass of dark curls atop his head shook with his movements. The intense zeal in his eyes to put me to the sword became clearer. I slightly tightened the grip on my hilt.

At the last instant, I leapt to the side. His sword cut through the air cleanly, almost as closely as the arrow that had almost pierced my cheek. I slashed my sword, clanging against his armour. His horse grunted angrily, nostrils flaring. I leapt backwards, lest it tried to kick me. The warrior's angry shout roared through the air. He turned his horse around again. I only had time for a breath before our swords thrashed again.

This time, our blades met. The force of his blew me off my feet; the force of mine almost knocked him from his horse. I rolled to my right to avoid agitated hooves. Scrambling up from the ground, I lifted and clutched my sword ever tighter. My opponent struggled to reach his reins, half bent out of the saddle.

Seeing my opportunity, I darted further to the side. I reached for my bow. My foe galloped towards me, brandishing his sword. I had to be as rapid as lightening, yet as careful as if I had all the time in the world. In the moment before his sword crashed down upon me, I released my arrow.

His horse barrelled into me, flinging me backwards. I landed hard on the frost-stiffened grass. Dazed, I remained on my back a moment, my eyes full of the brilliant blue sky. The sharp winter sun glared down so strong it hurt to look at it. I blinked, trying to remember what had happened. I thought that I had pierced the soldier's arm, but it had happened so quickly.

I heard a rush of footsteps, but I did not know whether they belonged to friend or foe. The sounds of battle blurred together. I tried to move, but it was far too late to defend myself. Briefly, I wondered if my life was spent.

"Daniel!" My lovely wife's face came into view, eyes full of concern. "Are you all right, my husband?" Her hand rested on my cheek.

"Aye, I think so." I sat up slowly. My gaze roved beyond her as the world came into sharper focus. "I — behind you!" I shouted in warning.

Instantly, Evelyn leapt to the side. The soldier I had pierced slashed his sword, narrowly missing her. The armour plates below his shoulder were stained deep crimson. Between them was the top of half of my arrow, protruding from his flesh.

He staggered towards me, his featured a pained, frenzied fury. I still felt winded, but gritted my teeth against the pain in my side. I slammed against him, pushing him away. The Bernician staggered backwards, the tip of his blade kissing the earth. The fight was mostly out of him. I knew his end was near. I opened my mouth to tell him I would spare his life if he surrendered.

Abruptly the soldier growled like a wild animal before I had the chance to speak. He lunged forwards. So be it. As I twisted to avoid him, I slashed my blade across his abdomen, catching him just underneath his breastplate. My enemy sank to the floor, writhing as blood poured forth from his wound. Then he took a deep shuddering breath and was still. It was over.

Panting slightly, I rose my weary gaze to the trees and riverbanks that had become a battlefield. John was fighting another soldier, while Aife shot an arrow into the thigh of a soldier running towards her. Evelyn, too, was in battle, but just then she thrust her sword into a gap at the Bernician's side. My quick, grim smile vanished. Three foes were rushing towards my queen, swords drawn.

"There!" I shouted, rushing towards her. My wife spun around to battle one of the soldiers, just as I took on the second warrior. He was at full strength, far swifter than the soldier with my arrow on his shoulder. I gritted my teeth, parrying his relentless strikes.

His face was full of the flush of youth, his mouth was parted in a slight smirk. I leapt to the side, avoiding his latest attempt to put me to the sword. I wondered if his arrogance would lead to his downfall.

Just then, he misjudged his strike, swinging his blade far too high through the air. I parried him easily then pivoted, stooping to draw my blade against his right thigh. He stumbled to the ground, horror filling his gaze. One hand clutched his thigh, stemming the flow of blood.

I pointed the crimson-stained tip of my sword at his throat. My foe immediately stilled, the fear intensifying in his eyes. He muttered something. I frowned. I knew a little of the Bernician tongue, but not enough to understand him. More words sputtered desperately from his lips.

"Yield and I will spare you," I told him calmly, my voice only a little laboured. Maybe this soldier would relent, unlike my previous foe. "Yield," I repeated. The warrior's expression cleared. I knew we understood each other, warrior to warrior. He nodded quickly, his breathing quick and shallow. Slowly, I lowered my sword away from his neck.

The young soldier staggered away, as fast as the injury to his leg would allow. My gaze moved beyond him to see Evelyn was still fighting her opponent, but two more Bernicians were advancing on her.

"Behind you!" she cried as I sprinted towards her. I kept running. My gaze moved past her, to my next opponent. Evelyn's expression flickered in understanding.

She took off towards me, a hand outstretched. I copied her, sprinting hard across the grass. A moment later and we grasped each other's arms firmly, using the force to propel us onwards. My blade hit the sword of my opponent, while she fought mine.

"Yield!" I cried again to my latest opponent, but he did not relent. A moment later he fell to the blood-soaked grass, dead. I kept my eyes on the last four enemy soldiers. Aife stilled, her spear about to pierce a Bernician's stomach. In the wake of our weapons halting, I quickly surveyed the scene. Of the twelve Bernician soldiers, three were uninjured with another two wounded, including the young lad with the cut I had given his knee. The other seven were dead. The three remaining warriors threw their hands up in hasty surrender.

"Where is my daughter?" Evelyn shouted. I at last lowered my sword, ignoring the beads of sweat cooling rapidly on my forehead in the icy air. My queen glared at them. "I know you can understand me. Where is she? Tell me, or we will show you no mercy."

"We do not know." One of them stepped forwards. I assumed he was their commander; I noticed now his armour was a little brighter than theirs. "King Morgant ordered us to wait here until you came. He said you would follow his path here, if you did not lose the trail in the woods. Kill us all if you must," he said heavily, "But we cannot tell you where your daughter is."

"Very well." Evelyn sheathed her blade. "Leave now and we will not pursue you. Stay to fight and we will cut you all down. This one chance I will offer you."

The Bernician soldier in the brightest armour stared back at her, conflicted. Clearly, he had understood every word. Would he take the bargain?

Abruptly he nodded, then uttered a single word in his Bernician tongue. I assumed it was the order to retreat, for immediately they sheathed their swords. They began to walk away, the wounded leaning onto those injured.

The Bernician commander gazed at us a moment longer, the frustration dancing upon his face. I rose my blade again, just a little, enough for it to be a warning against any kind of trap. At last, with a final nod, he turned to follow his men to their scattered horses.

"Aife, keep your eyes on them," I said. I looked away myself, to survey the damage to our party. Three soldiers were dead, with another injured.

My jaw locked, air escaping my nostrils sharply as I searched for Cara. She was right by the river's edge, crouching beside the water. I kept my blade unsheathed as I walked towards her. Coming nearer, I realised she was beside her two companions.

"Both dead, Your Majesty," Cara muttered bitterly. She glanced to me as she stood, features torn. A bird squawked from somewhere, flying through the trees, utterly oblivious to the blood that had just been spilled.

"That Bernician said they had been waiting for us," I said at last, my voice harsh. "Did you know they were coming? Were you stalling, until they could ambush us?"

"No, my lord," Cara answered immediately. "I did not know they were waiting. I thought perhaps they had followed me." My eyes narrowed in suspicion.

"I have no reason to trust you," I said, raising the point of my blade. As I spoke, Evelyn and the rest of our party joined us. "Take one wrong move and you will see the last of this world." At this Cara shook her head, smiling faintly.

"Why would I come here, sire?" Notes of anger and incredulity escaped her mouth, already lost to the quickening breeze. "What reason would I have to fight those Bernicians? My friends just gave their lives to you, my lord." She glanced back to their bodies, lying neatly next to the river. "They were from Gaeson, too."

"They were?" Evelyn questioned sharply. I glanced down at the dead soldiers. When I was a soldier in Gaeson's army, had I fought with them? Resided with them in the barracks? Could I have led them into battle before they left Gaeson? "Why are you here, Cara?" my wife asked now.

"As I said, Your Majesty," Cara returned evenly. "I came to warn you that King Morgant is marching against Gaeson, as we speak. I overheard one of his spies say he has poisoned your steward, Lord Melvyn. I do not know whether he lives."

"What? If that's true, there may not be a ruler in my stead. King Bryce, I bid we talk." I turned to her, to see she had sheathed her sword.

"Aye, my lady." I dipped my head to her. "Aife, keep your arrow trained upon her," I ordered quietly. "Shoot, if she gives you cause to."

"Aye, sire," Aife muttered shortly in reply. She stretched her bow taut. Cara met my friend's gaze steadily, looking not in the least surprised. With that, my queen and I walked away from the party for a few metres, up a gradual slope to the south.

"What say you, Evelyn?" I muttered, still staring at the spot where we had fought, where four of our party had died. Six, I corrected myself, counting Cara's companions.

"I do not know." My queen gave a long sigh. "I long for Imogen with every breath." Raw pain flashed across her features. "However, I cannot ignore this threat from King Morgant. If he truly marches against us, if Lord Melvyn has been poisoned…"

"This could all be deceit," I said. "The only thing we have is her word. Remember where it took us, the last time we trusted her." I noticed a red bruise swelling on the side of her cheek.

"Would she really have come here if she was not speaking the truth? If she truly served Bernicia, she would not have given me the hairpin that saved our lives," she pointed out. "She would have simply let those riders kill us. Would her two companions have died for a lie?"

"It is unlikely, but not impossible." I sighed. "It depends how much she wants to feed us false information. Perhaps she has some greater goal."

"Maybe. If… look!" Evelyn's cry stilled her words as she pointed. Over the ridge behind the woodland, several riders were heading straight for us. The sound of galloping filled our ears.

"They must have had reinforcements waiting!" I yelled out needlessly as we broke into a run. The party below were already drawing their weapons, looking for the source of the galloping.

"Retreat!" John shouted the order as we reached the others. The

Bernician riders were almost deafening now as we rushed towards our horses. Only Aife and Cara remained still in the whirlwind of chaos around us, with Aife's arrow still trained upon her.

"Aife, Cara, get to your horses!" I shouted. At my command Aife lowered her bow. She slipped it onto her back as both women ran to their horses. The throng of hoofbeats fiercely struck the earth, drowning out all other sound.

Within seconds, I reached Epos and placed my foot in the stirrup. My queen reached her steed as I pulled myself up into the saddle.

"Retreat!" Evelyn shouted the order again. Both of us glanced behind us just as the first riders emerged, to ensure nobody was being left behind.

"This way!" Cara shouted now, mounting her steed. "We can lose them in woods not far from here!" As she gathered her reins and turned her horse around, an arrow struck the ground near her.

"Very well!" our queen shouted. We had little other choice. Cara set off and a moment later I kicked Epos into a gallop. My stomach knotted that we were again running from the enemy, but Evelyn and I had seen how many riders there were. They would have all too easily overpowered us. I glanced back to the treeline by the river, to glimpse the second wave of Bernician riders appearing.

My stomach tightened further to see them trampling among the six dead Gaeson soldiers, assuming Cara spoke the truth about her two companions. Even if she was lying, the two soldiers had fought and died fighting the Bernicians.

As more arrows whizzed past, I jerked my head forwards. My hands gripped the reins tighter, the tips of my boots spurring Epos on. The grass blurred below, a sea of tiny blades rushing past us.

"Your Majesties!" Cara steered her horse abruptly to come alongside us. I shot her a glance, unable to help my gaze narrowing. How would I ever be able to trust her? At the crest of the slope ahead, I saw the woodland she had spoken of emerge before us.

"I suggest we split up, my lady," Cara said now. "They're after me, as much as they're after you." I glanced to her in surprise. "They see me as the traitor, my lord," she explained. "King Morgant has put a high price on my head. That's why they were following me." Her words came swiftly, in between rushed breaths.

"I know where your daughter is, Your Majesties," Cara called out, as the three of us stormed towards the line of trees, the rest of our party thundering behind us. "If you want to see her again, you must trust me." I looked at her sharply at that.

"Sire, do you see that tree?" She brandished an arm in an easterly direction. I followed her gaze, to a sole dead oak standing tall.

"If you believe me, then meet me at that tree in early morning. I will take you to her, sire, I swear." I frowned, studying her features as she gathered the reins in her hands.

"Yah!" With that she tugged her reins sharply to change course. I kept my eye on her as she steered her horse away from the woodland.

I snapped my head forwards again as we headed for the woods. Abruptly I heard the whizzing of an arrow, landing close to us. The question of whether we could trust Cara fled from mind. For now, the most pressing concern was whether we would survive long enough for me to meet her, or not.

"They're slowing down, Your Majesties!" John suddenly called. I swivelled back. Their horses looked as exhausted as their riders. How long had these Bernicians followed us? There must have been two parties, I realised. One that had been waiting amongst the trees by the river, possibly waiting for some time, maybe even before Imogen was even taken.

This second party, though, must have travelled far, given the state of them. If they had come from a Bernician camp, it must be at least a day or two's ride from here.

"Look!" I shouted over the din of our own horses, as almost two thirds of the party changed direction, following the course Cara had taken.

"Perhaps Cara was right," Evelyn called back. "Maybe these are the ones who had followed her." I nodded. Was it possible she had betrayed the Bernicians? Were these riders trying to stop her, and had then run into us?

Even without the riders who had left to chase Cara, we were still outnumbered. We plunged into the treeline. We weaved in and out of thin, tall trees, densely packed. It took all my effort to keep Epos moving rather than crashing into the woodland.

I craned my head back to look behind me, but there was nothing. Looking forwards again, my teeth gritted. The trees were growing sparser. Dappled sunlight shone in broader patches along the earth. The woodland stretched wide, but it was thin. If we were to lose them, it must be now.

"Turn right!" I shouted. Miraculously, my order sounded over the din of the galloping. The horses whinnied sharply in protest at the change of course. We thundered along, the light fading again as we turned away from the edge of the woodland.

"Aye!" Evelyn called from beside me, only a little breathlessly. "At this speed, they won't be looking for our tracks. They'll think we've gone straight ahead."

Together, we led our party through the darkening woodland, but even that did not last forever. As we finally broke from the trees at the western end, I hoped the soldiers had pelted straight ahead, only to think they had lost us in the plains beyond.

"There, that rise up ahead." Evelyn pointed, as we slowed our horses to a gentle trot. We heard no galloping behind us now. We headed quietly up the hill, where large rocks carved into the grass would hide us from view. It was a satisfying thought, to picture the enemy sprawled out only a couple of miles away, wondering how we had vanished.

Chapter Seven

A few hours later we at last stopped to make camp, just after the last of the sun's rays had dipped below the horizon. We had stayed for a while hidden in the hill, but the riders had not found us. Then we dared to move, riding carefully out of the hill's shelter. We deliberately kept to the western edge of the plains, away from where the Bernicians could still be looking for us.

"Here, sit, Your Majesties." John gestured a fallen log. Soldiers set down armfuls of firewood nearby as we accepted our captain's invitation. Soon the crackle of the fire started. The air filled with the scent of smoke.

Evelyn and I sat there silently for a while, watching the flames and the tendrils of smoke that unfurled to the sky as dusk turned to darkness. The soldiers talked little as pots and pans began to clunk. I watched absently as a stew was hastily prepared. Somewhere on the other side of the firelight, a soldier laughed.

"Look, Daniel." Evelyn pointed to the sky, her voice heavy. I followed her gaze to see flecks descending, just visible in the amber light before they melted into the fire. Others joined them, far heavier and slower than rain.

"You know what this means," she muttered soberly. Beside her, I only nodded. The first snow had come at last. It would cover these lands long before morning. I had hoped we would be able to find our way back to the river, but these frozen clumps dashed any thought of finding the Bernician trail we had been following so far. Our last hope of finding our daughter now lay solely at Cara's feet.

"We have no choice," Evelyn said. I did not answer at first; instead, I merely stared absently at a darkened patch of moss lit dimly by the firelight.

"I know," I said eventually. The wind blew past us. As the snow fell ever thicker, I reached for my wife's hand. We sat there together in the dark, the weight of inevitability settling down upon us. There was movement around us for a while, as soldiers bent their heads to us as they retrieved their stew. Soon all our party had gathered food and retired back to their tents, apart from those on watch duty. We were left alone, still staring into the crackling fire.

"I don't want to part from you," Evelyn said. "I want to be with you, to find our daughter." I heard her sniff and wipe at her face.

"I know that too," I murmured inanely. We both knew that she had to go back to Gaeson. She could not risk ignoring Cara's warning. Especially if Lord Melvyn really had been poisoned.

I wished I knew the words to comfort her, but I was so lost myself I hardly knew how. I heard her breathing catch. I suspected tears had come, now there was no one else to hear them but me. Her hand gripped mine tighter.

"I hate this!" Her words shook slightly. "Not only have I had to part with Imogen, but now I wonder whether I will ever see you again." She sniffed loudly.

"I believe we will," I told her solemnly. I turned my head from the flames to look at my wife fully. She wept quietly, her eyes dancing with frustration in the firelight.

"All three of us will be together again," I promised, as my free hand roved gently over her cheeks, wiping away her tears. "I swear, Evelyn. I will—"

"I know," Evelyn said, her tone far gentler as she cut off my speech. "I know what you would say. You were going to vow again that you would not come home without her. That you will never stop searching. Daniel, I—" her voice cracked. She turned away to look back to the fire for a moment. I squeezed her hand, waiting.

"There is another oath I would have you make." Her words came thickly. "Should the worst happen, if you cannot come back with Imogen…" She took a long halting breath.

"Promise me you will still come home. I will still need you, especially if I am to be without her. Promise me, my husband," she bid me fiercely. "Do not make me grieve her alone."

"I promise," I told her quietly, even as my heart threatened to break at the thought of losing Imogen, or my wife. We regarded each other then, in the firelight. Throughout the six years we had been married, we had grown better at being vulnerable to the other, of letting the cracks in our armour show. Evelyn leant in, coming to rest against my cheek. I let go of her hands to embrace her.

"I have asked you for that promise," Evelyn said, her voice stronger and a little more formal as she pulled away. "There is an order I bid you follow, also."

"Aye, of course." I sat up straighter. Evelyn briefly rubbed her face. "What would you have me do, my queen?" I asked quietly. I would strive to obey her will, wherever it would lead me.

"If you find Imogen," Evelyn said, "do not take her directly back to Gaeson. Every bone in my body longs for her," she muttered. "But I cannot risk bringing her home if there is danger." She wiped at her eyes again, but they were dry now.

"Ride instead for Caer Ligualid," Evelyn ordered. "I will send word if we successfully defend Gaeson, or if there was no danger to begin with." Her hands found mine. "Will you do this, husband?"

I hesitated. I knew she sensed it, as the crackling of the fire filled the pause between us. I longed to fight with her, to serve her in what could be the battle for our home. I wondered if my eight-year-old self would consider my vow broken. I knew, though, that she was right. It would not be safe to take Imogen home unless I knew my queen still reigned there.

"Aye." My voice came, barely louder than a whisper. I moved a hand from hers to idly play with the curls that fell about her cheek, watching the amber glow glimmer across her features.

"Aye, my lady," I said, more firmly. "I will do as you ask." My wife held my gaze a moment before nodding. She leant forwards and I drew my arms around her again. The fire's crackling was the only sound, but in that moment, I imagined I could hear the snap of both our hearts, also.

"I miss her," Evelyn said at last. Her breath came rough on my cheek. I nodded; my throat suddenly too tight to speak. My head brushed her loose curls, rustling against my temple.

"You'd better return to me, my boy from the snow," she murmured ere long. A smile glimpsed our features. It had become a tradition between us, this phrase she used whenever we were forced to part.

I wished to find the words to bring her more comfort, but all such words were already spoken. Instead, the undeniable truth rested in the quiet between us. Despite how fiercely I promised otherwise, this could be the last we saw of each other. I closed my eyes briefly, taking in a moment to feel the way her cheek felt against my mouth, how, this near, the sound of her breathing could be heard over the fire.

"Come," Evelyn sighed eventually. "We will both need our strength." Suddenly she stood. Without another word we walked towards our tent, hearts heavy.

The only thread of hope for finding Imogen now lay with Cara. Perhaps, she could lead me to our daughter after all. As my wife and I lay down in our tent, I allowed my imagination to wander. Maybe, on some bright day in the future, I could bring Imogen home to a Gaeson where my queen and people were safe and well. Perhaps, then, I might even see Evelyn smile again.

***

I collapsed gratefully under the tree, leaning my head against the panels of the dead bark. Just for a few moments, I allowed myself the luxury of removing my helmet. The cold air whistled through my russet hair. I ran my fingers through its wayward clumps, separating strands long ago matted with sweat.

Soon the icy wind became too bracing. It took all my energy to heave my helmet back on. I tilted my head against the tree. The ghost of a smile traced my features as the air cooled my skin, still hot from riding. Epos shifted her head beside me, neighing quietly. I knew she was as thankful to rest as I was. I reached out a hand to pat her damp coat, knowing the last few days had been tough for her.

"I'm sorry, old girl," I murmured, raising my head a little to survey the landscape before me. The circle at the base of the tree was frosted grass, but beyond that, the world was a thick blanket of white.

I thought of the party heading back to Gaeson. John and Aife had both expressed a desire to join me, as had a few other soldiers, but I had refused. Gaeson needed their captain and chief archer and if King Morgant truly was marching against our home, then no soldier could be spared.

I reached down to pluck a single blade of grass. Though it was hardly the season for it, I popped the tiny reed in my mouth. My lips tingled slightly as I rolled the blade of grass over them. I stretched my stiff arms above my head, relaxing slightly as the tension began to lessen in my limbs.

Even this physical reprieve, however, could not fully ease my soul. Not whilst Imogen was still missing. These sprawling white fields gave no hint of her location. How I wished I were more than merely human. I yearned not to need slumber, to leap from the ground and fly like a bird. Soaring through the endless grey canvas above, I would somehow find her. Then, I would simply dive down and pluck her from danger, carrying her safely home.

Suddenly, there was a scuffle to my right. I jerked my head down, my hand already on the hilt of my blade. A particularly brave squirrel landed deftly upon the grass. It must have been scampering up the oak tree. I smiled faintly at the swift ball of red and brown fur. For a moment it stilled completely, then darted off out of sight. My gut churned. Immy loved squirrels.

A sharp gust of wind blew past. It began to snow again. The frozen flakes fell fast and heavy and my stomach tightened. I guessed a blizzard was on its way. Then the striking of hooves crunching upon snow filled my ears. Epos raised her head warily at the stranger's presence. I did not bother. I knew who it would be.

"Your Majesty," Cara greeted me simply, her boots sinking into snow with an unmistakable thump. "You must still trust me in part, sire," she said. Her footsteps approached the tree. "I could have easily shot you from afar."

At last, I turned to regard her. Despite the slight smirk on her face, her eyes were as guarded as ever. Cara came to a stop, a few feet away.

"Aye," I answered steadily. "If you wanted me dead, though, you would have killed me long ago. Or you wouldn't have given Queen Evelyn the hairpin that day," I pointed out. I got to my feet. "Either way, you certainly wouldn't have helped us at the riverbank."

"True, my lord," Cara conceded, inclining her head. Then she straightened, our gazes locking again. "You could have killed me yesterday. Why didn't you?"

"Because of the hairpin," I replied simply. Cara nodded.

Understanding, as well as the snow, fell between us. We formed our reluctant pact, based only on the trust we would not kill each other. A fragile alliance indeed.

"Also, you said yesterday, you know where my daughter is," I said. At this Cara turned, looking behind her. I frowned. Did she really believe we might be overheard in this field, in this weather?

"Aye, my lord." Cara turned back to me as hope burned anew in my chest. "Princess Imogen is kept in an abandoned village, on the other side of the high hills. The distance is not great, but with the snow…" Her gaze flickered upwards.

"We must go quickly, sire, before the blizzard thickens. First, we journey to the edge of the hills, then it will take two days to pass over them." She half-turned to her horse.

"Wait," I said suddenly. She looked back. "Have you seen her?" Hope swelled strong, threatening to burst altogether.

"Only three days ago, sire. She has not been harmed." Relief shot through me, as thick and fast as the blood pumping through my veins. Almost dizzy, I leant back against the tree a moment. If only Evelyn had heard this before we parted.

"That's wonderful." I managed to rasp out. Then I grinned, euphoric. The muscles in my cheek felt strange, as if I hadn't smiled fully in years. As if I had almost forgotten how. My joy must have been infectious, for even Cara smiled briefly.

"I was already at the village, when the soldiers arrived," Cara said. I was only there a few hours before I left to find you, my lord. Princess Imogen seems a lovely little girl." A faint smile graced her features again.

I nodded, rapt with attention. The world had stilled and was closing in, blocking all else, even the snow still falling around us. The only thing I knew was that Imogen was alive. My greatest hope had been confirmed, for if Imogen had survived thus far, they must have a purpose.

"We should get moving, sire." At her words, the world abruptly expanded again. "We head north-east." She turned back to her horse again. "We must try to reach the forest at the foot of the hills, before the blizzard really hits us."

"One final point." My words came quickly as I crossed the snow to her. "If you lead me wrong, or into the hands of the enemy, I will not hesitate to kill you." Cara's eyes widened, but she said nothing.

"I'm not a king right now, Cara," I pointed out. "I'm a man searching for my daughter. Only the good Lord knows what I will do to anyone who gets in my way." My eyes hardened further. "Tell me you understand this."

"Aye." Cara murmured the single word quietly as she held my gaze. "I understand, Your Majesty," she said, inclining her head.

"Good." At last, I swung up onto Epos. My gloves, already damp with the snow and the cold, tightened on the reins. "Lead the way."

We set off at a hard trot, speaking little to one another. Hooves sank rather than struck upon the earth as the thick white blanket grew beneath them. The sky transformed to the lightest grey, so it was difficult to see the snow, blending with the ashen canvas beyond. Winter was upon us at last.

"Why?" I shouted to Cara a little later. The snowfall had thickened, but the storm had not come upon us yet. "Why have they kept her alive?" I expounded at her frown. I shifted my reins in my hands. "Why take her at all?"

"That, I do not know, sire." Cara shook her head. "King Morgant did not reveal his schemes to me," she called back, face impassive. My eyes narrowed at the mention of my greatest foe.

"I see." I nudged Epos slightly nearer to Cara, so our voices could be heard better. The icy air bit into me, forcing me to keep my head bowed.

"I doubt you are doing this purely out of the goodness of your heart," I said a few moments later, when the wind had died down a little. "What's in it for you?" Cara did not answer for a moment, turning her torn gaze to the white world ahead of us.

"I do not know," she finally admitted, then sighed. "That night you interrogated me, I told you I was already dead." Cara's tone was wistful, laced with remorse. Did she regret her treason?

"Aye, I remember," I replied tightly, as the unwanted memory came to mind. It was four-and-a-half-years ago, the night before Gaeson's parade was due to start. The next day, while people cheered and waved their flags, Cara betrayed Gaeson, when the Veiled Wolf was revealed to be Aldred.

"The Wolf's guards broke into my cell, after you left," Cara said. Her voice was audible, but suddenly faraway. I glanced to Cara, still looking straight ahead of her. If I had taken her warning more seriously that night, would she still have betrayed us?

"Ewan—" His name cracked with pain from her lips. "He didn't know that the other guard watching over me that night was one of the Wolf's agents. I knew," she added suddenly, voice bitter.

"We take the higher path," she said then, as a forked path appeared ahead of us. Epos shifted slightly as we turned our course further east, getting used to the road after frozen fields and damp earth.

"So," I began at last, unable to hold back the question any longer. "Why didn't you warn Ewan, about the other guard in the cell?" I raised my voice at the last word as the storm kicked up again.

"I had no choice." Cara's gaze was fixed on the road again as she shook her head. "The other guard was there the whole time. There was no time to warn him. There were only minutes before the Wolf's men entered my cell to break free." Her words were faster now. "I knew Ewan would try to fight for me, to try to stop them. My only thought was to spare Ewan's life," she added rapidly. "So, I—"

"What?" The shocked word sprang from my lips. Cara glanced to me, her eyes blended with pain and regret. "You struck Ewan." She did not deny it. "You could have killed him, Cara," I said, not bothering to hide my disgust.

"No, my lord!" She shook her head wildly, her objection desperate. "Ewan refused to leave my cell. They would have killed him easily, sire. I couldn't let them." Her eyes danced in the grey world around us, begging me to understand, ignoring the frozen flakes that fell on her face.

"I knew how Ewan loved me." Cara lowered her gaze. "I don't know how much I returned those feelings, but I cared for him. He would have fought them all, to try to save me," she burst out bitterly. "I was trying to save him."

I barely heard her final whisper. A moment later Cara turned away, but not before I caught a tear slide down her face. Or was it a snowflake, melting on her cheek? Was this repentance genuine?

"Do you hope for redemption, then?" My question came direct, even harsh. Watching her battle through her feelings did not diminish my anger. The woman beside me had still betrayed us all.

"I doubt I could ever achieve that, sire," she muttered bitterly. The thickening snow forced us to slow to a trot, Epos straining with effort to keep going. I sighed, staring at the swirling storm around us. The lack of trust between us was growing tiresome. The unspoken pledge we would not kill each other was the best we could do, for now.

"I was expecting Lord Aldred's goons to kill me in that cell." Cara's words broke into the sounds of the snow a few minutes later, almost startling. Her voice was resigned now. Emotionless. "Then, I found myself alive. The Wolf said he had a further use for me."

"Which was for you to train your arrow upon your queen," I said flatly, unable to keep a little accusation from entering my tone. That day in the palace hall came to my mind's eye, when the Wolf had been unveiled. When I realised what a monster Aldred, whom I had once called my friend, really was.

"Aye." Cara bent her head. Her face gave no indication of whether she regretted her actions. "It was a strange feeling, being spared. I was still imprisoned by him, even after I escaped the dungeons," Cara said. "The only option I had was to stay alive."

Suddenly, the blizzard kicked up viciously, rendering further talk almost impossible. The road was still just about visible, but soon it would be too dangerous to go on any further. Epos had little strength left.

"There!" Cara's call came to me across the storm a few minutes later. I could just see where her hand was pointing. Following her arm, I caught sight of the outline of dense trees.

"Well done!" I called back, the icy air whistling through my teeth. Even if I couldn't trust her, her exceptional navigation had got us here, despite the blizzard raging all around us.

Without Cara as my guide, I could easily have been lost, perhaps freezing to death before the storm even died down.

After tense minutes of slow riding, we eventually reached the treeline. Branches knitted together above and around us, protecting us from the devastating force of the blizzard. The air was not much warmer, but the wind no longer roared in my ears.

Epos snorted softly. The noise was almost loud in the sudden stillness. I leant forward, brushing the snow from her parchment coat.

She shook her neck this way and that, clearly as glad to be out of the open as I was. The further our horses walked into the forest, the quieter it became. Even though the ashen sky was blocked by most of the treetops, it was not much darker, for each of the higher branches were coated with white.

"This will do." I broke the quiet abruptly as we reached a clearing in between the trees. In the centre of it, the snow fell a little more, but nothing like the blizzard on the road.

"I'll gather wood, my lord," Cara said a little shortly, dismounting from her steed. While I set about seeing to the horses, she walked around the edge of the clearing. The air filled with boots trudging through snow and branches snapping. Though the higher branches were damp with snow, some of the lower ones were dry. Hopefully, they would burn well.

I spoke quietly to Epos and the other horse, taking off their gear. I threw long rugs over both of them, knowing they needed as much warmth and protection as they could get. I gave them each a few oats, but I would not give them water until it had warmed through a little.

"The fire will start soon, sire," Cara said from behind me. She was arranging the wood in the middle of the clearing, having carefully set it with stones so that the fire wouldn't travel to the trees.

"Thank you." I was confident in her skills in making the fire. Even if she still planned to betray me, it would not profit to have us both burn to death in the middle of the night.

I turned my back to the horses. Soon, I heard the tell-tale scraping of two sharp rocks. By the time I had made the horses as comfortable as possible, the sparks from the rocks had caught.

The still forest was permeated by the crackling fire, snapping in the air like dry twigs. Vivid and amber yellow hues flickered, licking the air. I swallowed hard. Suddenly the image came of watching the fire with Evelyn the previous night. I could almost feel her head, resting once more on my shoulder. My heart panged as I turned away.

When I next looked back, my former soldier was placing a pan of water near the fire. Then Cara straightened, rubbing her hands, extending them towards the flames. I stretched out my own limbs, suddenly exhausted.

"Rest if you wish, my lord," Cara said, glancing over to me. I gave a nod. A little way from her I sank down, resting my head against the tree bark. The fire's warmth just about reached me. I pulled my cloak a little tighter.

I lifted a heavy arm to wipe the sweat from my forehead, long since chilled in this weather. My eyes drifted shut, listening to the gentle roar of the fire. At the sound of Cara's footsteps approaching, my eyes snapped open.

"Relax, my lord." Cara smirked faintly, her words carrying more warmth than I expected. "As we said, if we wished to kill each other, we would have tried to do so already." The corner of my own mouth turned slightly as I nodded.

I kept my eyes open, though, watching as she went to one of the saddlebags and retrieved a tightly bound cloth. My stomach rumbled as she unwrapped it to reveal several cubes of cut red meat.

"A hare I caught yesterday," Cara said quietly, answering my unspoken question. "I'm sorry there isn't much," she added, sticking the cubes onto the end of two long, sharp sticks.

"I'm grateful for whatever there is." After the long day of riding, it would be good to line my stomach with something. The small bowl of boiled wheat this morning felt like a lifetime ago. I licked my dry lips and reached for my waterskin.

Cara settled by the fire, occasionally turning the sticks with the meat on them. The smell of hare cooking reached my nostrils. Then I raised my head, to the section of sky visible from the woodland clearing. The last of daylight was ebbing away. The smoke blended, fading into the canvas above as night truly began.

"I have to know," I said at last. Cara looked up, her eyes meeting mine over the fire. "Why did you give Queen Evelyn the hairpin, that day? Why not just let Aldred kill us?"

"Because I never wished to harm you, my lord," Cara said calmly over the gently roaring fire. "I trained that arrow upon my queen because it was the only way to survive. I never wanted to hurt her, or you." She shook her head, staring back into the fire. "I don't want us to be enemies, my lord the king. I did what I had to survive, that's all."

"That's all?" I echoed softly. "What if I had not yielded, when the Wolf ordered you to shoot my wife?" I asked pointedly. "Would you have killed her?"

"I have seen the way you love Her Majesty, my lord," Cara answered quietly. Her eyes flickered down to the meat. "I knew you would do nothing to bring her harm."

"It was still a risk to her life," I pointed out bluntly. "You made a promise when you enlisted. As I did, so many moons ago. You are supposed to risk your life, as a soldier. It is not the other way around!" I said hotly.

"You broke your vow long ago, Cara," I told her, shaking my head as the disgust crept back into my words. "You're nothing but a coward."

"I know," Cara admitted heavily, turning the sticks over again. I clenched my hands into fists. Rage, once abated, coursed through me anew. Was that all the reply she would give me?

It seemed she would say nothing more. Cara stood, crossing to the saddlebag again. She retrieved a cloth filled with chunks of bread and a few greens to add to the cubes of hare meat. She separated the food onto two separate cloths.

"Here, my lord," Cara said, carrying one of the bundles of food over to me. The smell from the meal was tantalising, but my insides were churning anew.

"You committed treason against, us, more than once." My voice was hoarse, yet ire punctuated each syllable. Cara's hands stilled, her gaze locked with mine. She knew I still carried my sword. How easy it would be to draw it and slit her throat.

"Aye, my lord." Her voice trembled only slightly. "Sire, you told me you are no longer a king, but a man searching for your daughter." I glared. Was she using Imogen to gain my trust?

"I know where the princess is, sire," Cara said. She squatted down to me. "I know I did you great wrong that day, my lord. The memory of it has plagued my mind ever since." She put the cloth of food onto the snow near my food.

"That is why I gave Her Majesty the hairpin," she murmured, at last answering my question. "That's why I'm trying to help you now. I know it will never be enough, but I am trying to put it right." Cara stood, her arms dropping to her sides.

"You should try to eat something, my lord." She walked back to the fire. My eyes followed her a moment longer before they fell to the pile of food at my feet.

I lunged for the cloth as my stomach growled fiercely. Popping the first cube of the meat in my mouth, my eyes drifted shut. The taste of the tender, succulent hare briefly overwhelmed my senses. The greens added a refreshing flavour and the bread, although a little stale, made the meal more substantial.

I tried not to eat too quickly, but I was famished. The meal was finished within moments. My eyes closed again as I relaxed against the trunk of the tree. My stomach was not quite full, but it was immensely happy I had filled it with something.

Cara's movements opened my eyes again. She was bent over the fire, heating another small pan of water close to the flames. She held a small pouch in her hand. I sat up straighter, frowning, as she sprinkled something into the water.

"Herbs for the tea, my lord." My eyebrows rose. How did she know I was even watching her? Cara poured the metal cups and brought one over to me.

"Thank you." My fingers curled around the mug, enjoying the warmth. Cara picked up her cup and settled down against another tree.

"It is about time I thanked you for something else, also," I said. She glanced up at me. "You did betray us all, but you also risked your life to give Queen Evelyn the hairpin. If you hadn't, my wife and I would be dead," I said bluntly. "I would have no child to search for and Aldred would have carried out his awful scheme against Rheged. For that, you have my gratitude."

Cara inclined her head to me. When she looked up again, her eyes had softened, a small smile glimpsing her face. I wondered when the last time she had fully smiled was.

Gradually, I realised the sweat from my riding was ever cooling my skin. The fire's heat reached me, but the cold of my metal was drawing out any hope of warming me. Reluctantly I put down my tea and peeled off the metal plates. I would much rather receive a quick death from a Bernician blade, or even Cara, than slowly freeze to death.

The wind chilled my tunic and other garments, but I felt a lot lighter. I drew my thick cloak tighter, then reached to pull up the hood. At once

I noticed the difference. My body would soon grow warm again. However, it was not just the flames that gave me comfort. It was the thought that my companion had seen my daughter alive, not four days ago. I savoured the solace this gave me, as tangible as the fire, or the tea I was drinking.

I made the most of my newfound comfort, letting the tea slide gratefully down my throat. It had no honey, but I was used to the bitter taste now. I watched the snow continue to fall into the clearing, a fine dust that barely disturbed the fire. My eyes grew heavy. Despite what little sleep I'd gotten, I automatically resisted it.

"You should get some sleep, sire, I will keep watch." My eyes opened fully to see Cara sitting nearer to the flames. She held her bow loosely in her hand, her gaze already trained to spot movement.

"I slept well last night," she pointed out. "I suspect you have not slept well in days and you will need your strength for passing over the hills tomorrow. Besides, my lord, if I wanted to kill you, I would have just put poison in your tea."

"Aye, I suppose." The corner of my mouth lifted at the thread of humour in her dark voice. I tugged the hood a little further about my head. Somewhat confident that Cara would not kill me, I succumbed to slumber within moments.

Through the darkness, a familiar laughter began. It floated towards me, like a cool breeze on a midsummer morning. Recognition swept through me as a warm embrace. My mother who had borne me appeared, with her vivid auburn hair and sweet smile. Contentment seeped into my bones.

Abruptly, the laughter stopped. The joy from my mother's eyes vanished as horror filled her face. My mother laughed again, but now as a high-pitched screech, almost a scream. She howled as if fear had made her lose her mind.

I tried to look away, but my dream held me captive to the terrified orbs of her soul, staring back at me. I was trapped, helpless to do anything but watch. I would have jabbed hard at my skin, but I was formless. This twisted figure of my mother was the only thing punctuating the darkness.

Abruptly, the perverse laughter died away. Relief coursed through me, but then a new sound reached my ears. Something even more painful to hear, though a moment ago I would not have thought that possible.

My daughter called to me, her voice wracked with fear and pain. I yearned to look for her, but I was still trapped, simply to watch whatever was in front of me. My mother's form was still before me, her gaze more terrified than ever. Cold spread through me with the realisation that my mother was not looking at me. Rather her gaze pointed through me to whatever was beyond. That was the true horror.

Suddenly, the scene in front of me shifted. The nightmare panned away from the horror writ large on my mother's features. I knew I was about to confront this unspoken terror.

Though in the last two or three days, I had longed to look upon Immy more than anything else, abruptly I yearned to somehow close my eyes or turn away, to block whatever this hellish vision wanted me to see. The dream ignored me, shifting the image in front of me with a tangible tug, as if someone were turning my head.

Then, abruptly, there was Imogen, sat some distance away in the darkness. There was nothing immediately grotesque about her appearance. In the moment of seeing her, my mother's terrified screeching fled from my mind. I almost forgot I was dreaming. I just wanted to hold my daughter.

Imogen's small legs were tightly pressed together, her arms wrapped tightly around her knees. Her head was bent, buried in her wrists, but I caught the muffled sound of her sobs. I yearned to comfort her, but I had neither arms nor hands to do so. The vision brought the huddled figure of Imogen closer.

Dread flooded my being, waiting to see why my mother had been screaming. There was something wrong with this vision of Imogen, but I could not see what yet. Fear churned through me. I was at the mercy of this nightmare.

Then, when Imogen's knees and arms and face seemed only inches away, she rose her head. My mother began her screams again, because my daughter wasn't looking at me. She wasn't seeing anything at all.

Instead of her face, her eyes, little nose and chin and cheeks that I loved so dearly, there was nothing. There was a huge chasm in the centre of her, matching the blackness beyond.

The chasm where her features should have been, grew. Pressure from somewhere behind me pushed me further towards the horrifying image. The black space stretched wider and wider, until it was ready to swallow me whole. My mother's screams filled my ears. Then I was jerked forwards, my stomach lurching as I fell through nothingness.

I snapped awake, breaths heavy. I was drenched in cold sweat, not good at all for the icy weather. Somewhere to my right was a rustling movement. I jerked upright, looking around.

"It's only a fox, sire." Cara's calm voice reached me. I glanced to her, still sat by the fire. I nodded, still trying to even my breathing. Lowering the cloak of my hood I rubbed my face, trying to shake off the remnants of the dream.

Cara was not looking at me, but at a cluster of trees off to my right. She held her bow in her hand, with an arrow set upon the string, but not pulled taught. Her features were concentrated, but untroubled.

"There," she murmured. Her eyes flickered to me, then back to the spot in the trees. Slowly I parted my cloak. The chilly breeze bit my clothes, still damp with the sweat from my dream. Moving as if I had all the time in the world, I reached to the dagger in my boot, in case the creature attacked.

Only then did I finally look to my right. I glimpsed something moving at the edge of the clearing, weaving in and out of the trees. A moment later, the animal stepped brazenly into the space around us. Its body was sleek and long, its paws padding silently into the snow.

Then it stopped and looked at us. Its vivid orange coat danced and burned in the firelight. The fox parted its mouth, snarling just a little. My gaze travelled to Cara, but though she was watching it intently, her bowstring was still not tensed.

"Move along," her murmur came. My eyebrows rose, watching her. "Move along," she repeated, her voice calm and steady. "Don't make any trouble and neither will we." Cara sounded confident, with something almost ethereal about her tone. My hand gripped the hilt of the dagger.

Abruptly, the fox bent its head. It sniffed the snow once, then twice. Then it moved, slinking back the way it had come, until it blended with the trees and the night.

"Bad dream, my lord?" I glanced to see Cara watching me, a thoughtful frown across her features. I swallowed hard as my nightmare came to mind.

"It is nothing." I slipped my dagger back into my foot. I stretched out my slightly cramped legs. "How did you do that, with the fox?" I did not wish to dwell on the darkness of that dream.

"I've been told I have a sense with animals." Cara shrugged. "I first noticed it when my father would camp sometimes, in the woodland around Gaeson."

"Your father was a soldier?" I guessed. Most of the men in Gaeson were, at least for a time. "Does he still serve?"

"No, my lord. He died four years ago, when the Bernicians breached the courtyard in Gaeson." She looked away as I nodded. Soldiers knew they could die in battle — but it did not make it any easier.

"You wouldn't have known this, sire," Cara said, then stopped again. Her eyes, holding a little sadness, searched mine. "Captain Bredon was my father."

"What?" My eyebrows shot up, my nightmare forgotten. My thoughts fled to my old captain, whose last breath I had witnessed. Whose blood stained the cobbles of Gaeson's courtyard, my hands with it. This was Cara's father?

"I didn't know he was married, or had any children," I said slowly. "He didn't seem to even know you, when you were in recruitment training." My mind went further back, to the day I had first met Cara and Ewan, during their assessments.

"My father didn't want the other soldiers treating me differently." That same shadow of a smile crossed her face. "I did not know him well, my lord. He spent most of his time in the barracks." I shook my head slowly, trying to make sense of it. I glanced back to Cara, studying her anew in the firelight. There was something resembling her father in her eyes, perhaps, but not much else to show that she was kin.

"I take far more after my mother," Cara said, as if reading my mind. "It proved useful when my father told me he didn't want the soldiers knowing who I was." She turned away from me, then, glancing to the fire.

"I was almost glad, the day he died in the courtyard. I know that sounds awful," she rushed on. "But the Wolf had already begun to poison my mind. Had he known then that I had betrayed Gaeson… I think that knowledge would have hurt him far more than the blade that killed him."

"I was sorry, the day Bredon died." It was an understatement. "He was a good captain and a good friend. He knew my father, too." Cara only nodded.

"Bredon knew Aldred was the Wolf," I said almost to myself, suddenly remembering my friend's last words to me. "Was he a friend of your father's?"

"Aye, sire." I heard the rough crack of her words, her face still pointed to the firelight. "That's how he knew me. I had been in the army only a few weeks when he suggested we meet. He was a friend, at first, flattering my skill with a sword. After my father died," she continued haltingly, "he had a drink with me in one of the taverns. He told me how sorry he was, how he would have been proud. He wanted me to do a few favours for him." I saw Cara raise a hand to wipe her eyes. "By the time I knew what a monster he was… it was too late."

"I'm sorry," I said quietly. If Cara spoke the truth, then she was far more of a victim to the Wolf than I had realised. I turned my gaze upwards. The sky had lightened a little, beginning to illuminate the looming gnarled branches above me.

"I believe it is about two hours before dawn, my lord," Cara said now. I nodded, stretching my limbs again. I was still warm — Cara had done well to keep the fire going.

By its amber glow, I saw that the dusting of snow in the clearing had thickened considerably. It would still be nothing compared to what it would be like outside these woods. I frowned, thinking of Epos and Cara's steed trudging through the stuff. We would have to slow our progress and checking on the horses regularly. I sighed. Time was an indulgence we could not allow ourselves.

"I'm awake now, if you want to get some sleep," I offered, ignoring my stiff muscles as I stood. My mind was far too full of my recent nightmare to sleep now.

"Aye sire, thank you." We made to swap places. "Here, my lord." As she passed me, she held out a skin of something into my hands.

"I see." I took a sip. It was wine. "I hope you have not been partaking whilst keeping the watch." Cara returned my smirk.

"Only a few sips to take the chill away, I assure you." She settled down by the same tree, trying to retain whatever warmth I had left there.

"There's something else I've been meaning to tell you, my lord," she muttered. I glanced over the fire to her. "I knew Joshua."

My eyes widened in surprise. Though, when I thought about it, it made sense. Joshua, had he lived, would have been her age now, perhaps a year younger. At once his pale features came before me, covered in blood. The fear in his eyes had never left me.

"He was a friend from my childhood," Cara said quietly. "We lived on the same street. I even saw you that day, sire, when you moved Joshua's mother and sisters out of her house. I guessed then that Joshua was dead." She looked again to the flames.

"Thank you, for your kindness to Joshua's family that day," Cara muttered, suddenly dragging me back to the present. "My whole street remembered it, when Gaeson discovered who you were."

"It was all I could do. He was a year before conscription age." My voice sounded tight and strange. Cara nodded, her face full of knowing sadness. I swallowed hard.

"Did Captain Bredon know Joshua, then?" I asked suddenly, just as Cara leant her head back against the tree. She blinked at me for a moment, considering.

"No, my lord, I don't think so. He spent most of the time in the barracks," she reiterated. "I went to Joshua's house, not the other way around. He was usually watching his sisters."

"I see," I murmured. "I'll let you sleep. I'll wake you at first light, then we'll get moving," I told her. Cara inclined her head, then leant it back against the tree again. Her eyes slipped shut.

I took a couple of swigs from the skin of wine. The sweet spice swirled around my tongue before sliding gratefully down to my stomach. I gazed around the clearing, picking up my bow. I tried to concentrate on the watch, but my previous conversations with Cara lapped around my mind.

Cara was Captain Bredon's daughter. Cara had been childhood friends with Joshua. Would Bredon have treated the lad differently that night, had he known Cara was his friend? Would he have rebuked him so harshly, for speaking out against the war? I suspected he probably would have, seeing as he had hidden the fact Cara was his daughter. It wasn't until after I learned of my royal blood that I even knew my captain's name.

My blood chilled a little. Captain Bredon had known the Wolf, as had my father, Kellen. Had the three of them been friends? Had Aldred always been filled with deceit? I thought of the close bonds I had with John and Aife. What pain it would have caused Bredon, to discover his friend's true nature.

Perhaps Cara was right, I thought presently. Perhaps Bredon had been better off, never knowing how Aldred had manipulated his daughter. I looked at her now, her expression clear as she slept. If the Wolf had already known her, perhaps Clara had never had much chance to resist him. After all, for a time I believed I could wholeheartedly trust Aldred.

Had I been too harsh with her? I wondered now, taking another sip of the wine. There was right and there was wrong, but God had also given us forgiveness and grace. Cara had trained her arrow upon Evelyn that day, but she had also given Evelyn that hairpin. Watching her today, it was clear that she regretted her actions deeply, unless she was even more skilled in deception than I first thought.

She seemed a shadow of her former self, I thought now. Where was that fierce young recruit, filled with care that ran to the infirmary after Ewan's nose was broken? If my former soldier sought redemption, did I have the right to stop her? If Bredon were here now, he would want me to forgive Cara's crimes. Perhaps, if Cara led me safely to my daughter, it would be time to pardon her.

Eventually, birdsong began, proclaiming the coming dawn. At first it was quiet and sparse, but soon there was the collective chorus, altogether producing an almighty racket. I glanced to Cara to see she slept soundly through it. Like the thousands of soldiers before her, she had the warrior's instinct. The almighty din of birds would not wake her, but the single footstep of an intruder would.

There was still plenty of wine left. My sips, like hers, had been sparing. Enough to fortify me against the cold, but not so much it dulled my senses. I stood, beginning to heat fresh water for the tea, then turned to wake Cara. The sooner we were on our way, the better.

Chapter Eight

"The village is just over that hill, sire. I recognise that tree." Cara pointed a few feet up ahead of me. We were both on foot, our horses tethered to a cluster of trees not far away.

"Good," I said simply. A smile flashed across my face at the thought of seeing Immy again. It had been three days now, climbing over the tall hills with the woman I now knew was Bredon's daughter. Snow, ice and wind had blasted at us from several directions. At times, we had been forced to stop altogether and wait for the blizzard to die down.

In that time, I had begun noticing little mannerisms that reminded me of her father. I saw him in the way she frowned when trying to keep her horse on the road, almost indistinguishable from the blanket of snow either side. Or the conflict in her eyes the rare times Aldred was mentioned. I hadn't recognised it before, but now I knew it was the same fierce, complicated gaze I had seen in my old captain when he heard Joshua was dead, or after King Reghan had branded me a traitor.

The crunching of Cara's boots against snow and loose stones brought me back to the present. I watched her begin the steep incline, then glanced at her. We had left the high hills behind us and we rode across the frozen fields. The world was unrelentingly white. Not for the first time, I wondered how Cara knew exactly where she was going. As much as I wanted to deny it, one inevitable truth deepened in my mind.

"You know this terrain very well," I said, making no attempt to hide the edge in my voice. Cara stilled on the hillside. I closed the few yards between us.

"Aye, sire," she replied neutrally. "I've been here a few times." Cara held my gaze steadily, with no surprise in her eyes. Perhaps she had been waiting for me to ask her.

"You said you were already in the village when the Bernicians with my daughter arrived," I said. My hand was already on the hilt of my sword. It had not snowed yet this morning, so my words pierced the still air around us. "That does not mean you weren't complicit in her abduction. Did you know what they would do? Did you aid them?"

"Aye," she admitted heavily. My temper erupted. I pulled my blade free the same moment she unleashed hers, obviously expecting my attack. Metal clanged together as our swords locked. The early sunshine glinted off our blades.

"So," I ground out through gritted teeth. "This is who you really are." Cara's gaze hardened. I saw my words had hit their mark. In that moment, I no longer cared that Bredon was her father. She had showed she was like my old friend. If I had the chance, would I kill her? I could not tell.

"You do not understand, my lord." Cara tried to keep her voice steady, but it trembled. With fear, or anger? I could not understand her at all. To my surprise, her gaze softened. "Please listen," she whispered, but my resolve only hardened.

"I've heard enough of your lies," I seethed. "How could I ever trust another word you say?" Cara's face paled, but then she nodded.

"I know. So much I've done." Heavy regret laced through her words again. "So many crimes I've committed, telling myself survival was the only thing that mattered. My father would be so ashamed." A tear crawled down her face.

Abruptly Cara jerked to the side, breaking the contact with our blades. I staggered a moment, but I kept my balance on the hill. There was a single thud as Cara dropped her sword onto the frozen hillside. She took a step back, her palms outstretched towards mine.

"No more." Cara shook her head. "I don't want to kill you, my king. I never did." Her words were a soft whisper as she sank to bended knee. "I know the fate I deserve," she muttered, another tear trailing down her features. "Justice demands my life be taken." Cara bent her head. "Go ahead, my lord. I only ask you make it quick."

A slight breeze picked up, tickling the neat bun of hair atop Cara's head. My sword was still in my hand as I pondered. She was a traitor to Gaeson and to Rheged, having trained an arrow upon my wife and being involved with Imogen's kidnapping. Yet, she had also given Evelyn the hairpin and run away from King Morgant and helped me rescue my daughter.

It would only take the flick of my sword to end her life. For a moment I imagined it. The fresh, hot blood spilling from her skin, splashing over my hands. My anger dissipated. I had made the vow to spare life whenever I could. Cara had surrendered and I could not murder a warrior in cold blood. Besides, if I did so, I would never be able to think of Bredon without also remembering how I had killed his daughter.

I slid my blade back into the sheath. At the sound, Cara looked up, her expression unreadable. The few tear marks had already frozen on her face.

"You may rise," I told her. "Reclaim your sword." Cara inclined her head and got to her feet. "How did you know I wouldn't kill you?" The ghost of a smile flittered across her face.

"I didn't, sire," she answered simply. "I knew you had the right to take my life, but I know you are also a merciful king. I finally realised that even if you would never trust me again, I could entrust myself to your justice." A stronger breeze blew past us. Something in my shoulders lessened. It was as if imagining killing Cara had made me stare into a black, bottomless abyss, but I had turned away. I remained in the light.

"King Morgant had his dagger pressed to my throat, the day he ordered me to arrange the supplies for the kidnapping of Princess Imogen," Cara admitted now. "I was not there, that night, but I was involved in the crime." She rubbed her fingers together for a moment.

"Not a day has gone by, sire," she said, "that I don't regret taking his dagger and doing it myself." Fresh tears welled in her eyes, but they didn't fall. "As soon as I saw Princess Imogen, crying and cold and hungry—" she looked away. "I knew then that survival is not always worth it."

Mercy and forgiveness. The two concepts I had thought about that night in the forest rolled around in my head. I still had the power to pardon her, or to have her executed for her treason. I might not have slain her now, but if we both made it back to Gaeson, what then? Would I pass judgement on her?

"If I might suggest, sire," Cara said now, breaking into my thoughts. "We should get moving." The day's first snowfall had begun, as tiny flakes melted into my gloves.

"Aye." The two of us set off in silence up the hill, crunching upon snow and hard earth. As we reached the peak, the sun peeked through ashen clouds. It cast sporadic light onto the endless white snow, shimmering in arbitrary patches of gold.

"That is the village," Cara said. I glanced to see where she was pointing. There was a sparse gathering of trees and beyond that, a few houses and buildings clustered together.

"What happened here?" Upon closer inspection, most of the buildings were charred remains. This village wasn't just abandoned. It looked as though life had never entered the place at all.

"Part of the Bernician campaign, my lord," Cara answered quietly. "Some places are rebuilt but most, like this, are just left. I think most of the villagers survived, at the time. Princess Imogen is in the village hall," she said, pointing. "The tallest building, in the centre."

I nodded, my heart quickening. Suddenly, after the last few days of searching and clinging to hope amidst despair, I was on the brink of seeing her again.

"Thank you, Cara." My words were quiet as I glanced to her. "You know you did her a great wrong, but you risked your life, coming across the mountains to tell me. Your father would be proud." Cara smiled genuinely, then, far more than the fleeting expression I had seen so far.

"I live to find favour in your sight once more, my lord the king." Cara bowed her head. I smiled, putting my hand on her shoulder.

"That you have already done," I told her. Her breath hitched. It struck me how long she had been hoping to hear those words. "Cara, you kept our bargain. I would appreciate your help, but it is not an order. You need do no more."

"Aye, I do," Cara muttered fiercely, as she stood. "This I do for myself, sire, as well as to serve you, that I might once again have honour." I held her gaze for a moment.

"Very well. You have my thanks." We both turned our heads to the village that lay before us, to the hall where Imogen was being kept. "Let's go."

The two of us broke into a swift, silent run down the hill. Though I concentrated on where I put my feet, I couldn't help but smile again at the thought of seeing Imogen. We raced towards the few trees that stood between us and the village.

“My lord!” Cara’s cry cracked the sky. She was pointing to my right. Turning, I saw a Bernician archer. He was pulling back his bowstring, arrow pointed straight towards me.

“No!” Before I could even think, Cara dove towards me. The full force of her weight toppled me down the hill. The world spun as I tumbled down the short incline, coming to a stop just short of a sharp rock. Dizzy, I put my hand to my head. Motion was difficult; the world was still blurred.

“Go, sire!” At Cara’s third cry, the world came keenly into focus. She was lying against the hill a few feet above me. Her abdomen was covered in blood from the arrow impaled into her side. At the sight of it, time sped back to normal.

“Cara, hang on!” I scrambled back up towards her, my hands full of snow and loose stones. She gave a grunt of pain as I reached her, pulling her to her feet.

“Lean on me!” I shouted. Another arrow landed at my right foot. We set off as quickly as possible, but we only made it a few metres before she stumbled.

“Leave me!” Cara shouted in frustration. She pulled firmly away from me, landing hard in the snow. I reached to her, but my hands stilled, seeing several Bernician soldiers racing towards us.

“Go, sire.” I glanced to see her crawling to take shelter near a nearby rock. She retrieved her bow and reached for an arrow. Despite the pain in her countenance, her face was almost peaceful.

“I can’t leave you here,” I said helplessly. Suddenly, she looked very much like her father. My hands were stained with her blood. Just like they had been stained with his, the last time I spoke with him.

I glanced to the hillside, reaching for my own bow. My crimson fingers set an arrow. I found my first target and let fly. We worked silently, quickly shooting down the Bernician soldiers.

“No.” Cara’s voice came steady when I turned to take her arm again. “Sire, the village is heavily guarded. More reinforcements will be here at any moment.” Her words were tighter now, punctuated by pain. “If you’re captured now, they may well kill her,” she said bluntly. Cara turned her head to spit. Brilliant crimson shot into the snow.

"If that happens, I will have died for nothing. Your only chance is to run for the treeline. Go," she repeated haltingly. "I'll follow you." Cara's hand reached out to clutch mine tightly. The strength of her grip gave me hope she might survive.

"It's like we said," she murmured. "Some things are not worth surviving." She breathed tightly as she smiled again. The expression reached her eyes, despite her pain. She looked liberated, I realised. Free at last from King Morgant's shadow. "God be with you, my king," she whispered.

"Now go!" She pushed me away. Far away, I heard boots crashing through snow. I thought of my daughter. It was impossible not to obey.

"I hope to see you again, Cara. Gaeson will welcome you if you make it back home." I squeezed her hand. "God be with you as well."

Then I was off, running down the hillside. I had to reach the treeline before the next wave of Bernician soldiers emerged, if I had any hope of making it to the village alive. I sprinted to the left, a different direction to where the Bernicians had come from. Every footstep I took was closer to my daughter, but further away from the dying comrade I had just abandoned.

Soon, the ground beneath me became level. I sped across the field; eyes trained on nothing but those sparse trees ahead of me. I heard shouts. Glancing behind, I saw eight soldiers pursuing me.

A moment later, one of the soldiers fell, Cara's arrow embedded into the flesh in their side. A magnificent shot. I turned back forwards as the soldiers cried out in confusion. My legs sank as I ran, swallowing me halfway up my shins with each step. Running in my cloak was hard, but several of my enemies were cloaked also. I hoped the terrain was as difficult for them.

I heard the dim thud of arrows, landing in the snow nearby. Deliberately I weaved as I ran. I thought of Imogen, of her honey hair, of the quizzical turning of her head that was so akin to Evelyn. Her gentle laugh that reminded me of my birth mother, though that should be impossible. No, I had to survive this.

At last, I reached the few stray trees, far too sparse to be called a wood. I darted in and out of the first few before coming to a stop. The shouts of the Bernician soldiers sounded much nearer now. I did not have long. I threw off my cloak and reached for my bow.

The fingers of my right hand were stiff from the cold, even through my gloves. I set an arrow on the bow. I took a couple of deep breaths to try to steady myself, then inhaled deeply. I swirled around the shelter of the tree and aimed at my first target.

My arrow sailed through the air to puncture the bare skin at the soldier's neck. I heard his anguished shout and the soft thud of his body hitting the snow as I whirled back around the tree. In the moment before I shot the arrow, I had counted my enemies — four. Three left, now.

An enemy arrow landed in the snow, inches away from the tree. I took a moment to stem a bead of sweat crawling down my right temple. I guessed Cara would have taken down another soldier before the Bernician soldiers spotted her. It was likely they had split in half — the other three would have raced up that hill towards my comrade. I swallowed hard, pushing down the ball of dread forming at my stomach, for it was even less likely she would survive.

I reached behind me for another arrow. I gritted my teeth in frustration, realising I was running low. Just then, I realised how quiet everything had become. I strained my ears, but any boots crunching upon snow had stopped. They had regrouped and now the world had become still, which was far deadlier than their angry shouts. Somewhere a bird chirped noisily, oblivious to the slaughter it was about to witness.

For a few seconds, I did nothing, just listened. They were as silent as I was. The bird did not help, still squawking away. They knew exactly what tree I was behind, but I had no idea where they were. Drastic action was required. I placed my bow on my back, bundled my cloak under my arm and took a deep breath, before jerking out my free hand.

I just snatched my arm back before the enemy arrow sailed past. It landed with a swift thud into bark. In the next moment, I ran. There was a loud whizzing as another arrow narrowly missed my ear. I ignored it, concentrating on weaving in and out of the trees. They were my only allies now.

I skidded through the snow to land behind another tree. I frowned as I caught my breath, considering the angle of the arrows that had missed me. From that, I could roughly judge where the enemy soldiers were. My cloak fell to the floor as I reached for my bow and set another arrow. I pulled the bowstring taut. Inhaling deeply, I swerved around.

As I had hoped, one of the Bernician soldiers had left their cover slightly to see where I had run. An instant later and my arrow was soaring towards him. I whipped back behind the tree, just as an arrow from another archer sailed past my head. The first Bernician soldier cried out, telling me I had not missed. I hadn't heard anyone else, so now there were only two enemies separating me from the village.

Adrenaline coursed through me as I breathed deeply. My gaze searched and found the arrow that had just missed me. From where it punctured the snow, I could work out where the archer was. I imagined the arc of their arrow, trailing backwards somewhere to my left. I needed them to shoot again to be sure.

I thrust my arm out into the open and jerked it back again. The air was quiet and still. Despite my immediate danger, I smirked. This soldier was obviously shrewder, or perhaps they had simply learned from their fallen comrade. My expression cleared, deciding to wait for my foe to move first. At least in my new position, I couldn't hear that bird anymore.

I took a moment to rest my head against the bark, but I remained fully alert. My ears strained for any movement while my breathing steadied. My fingers flexed on the bowstring.

A soft scraping sounded in the snow. Was it one of the soldiers, or simply wildlife? I could not tell. The sound, barely audible, came again. No, that was definitely a boot. The corner of my mouth turned again. Their impatience would be their downfall. The next time they moved, I would strike. Distantly, I realised I was chewing my lip.

The unmistakable shuffling sounded, faster now. I whipped around the tree. The Bernician soldier ran towards me, bow in hand. Anger and shock danced on his face, time slowing as he raised his bow. I shifted my angle and fired.

The arrow hit his leg, forcing his bow down. His own arrow sailed harmlessly through the air for a couple of metres. The archer hit the snow hard, rolling and writhing. The crisp white around him turned vivid crimson as he clutched his leg, right where his flesh was pierced. Slowly, I breathed out.

I slung my bow onto my back, gathered my cloak and sprinted through the snow towards the fallen soldier. I expected to have to avoid further arrows, but there was nothing. Perhaps my final opponent was not an archer. My foe's expression contorted in fear as well as agony as I reached him.

In desperation he reached for his dagger, but I trod firmly on his wrist. He grunted as he dropped his last defence. I grabbed the dagger and hurled it away. His expression cleared, seeming to accept his fate, but I shook my head. Instead, I took him by the shoulders and hauled him towards the protection of a nearby tree, ignoring his grunts of pain, leaving a crimson smear through the snow in his wake.

I now reached my dagger, then cut a small piece from the bottom of my cloak. I wrapped it around the wound, stopping the flow of the blood, but left the arrow in his flesh in case this was keeping him alive. His eyes looked greatly confused as I moved his hand to put pressure on the wound. This man might be my enemy, who had tried to kill me — but I still wished to spare life where I could. The village was probably not even a mile away, so he should live long enough to get help.

That done, I pulled him to his side. He groaned a little, but I ignored him as I retrieved the five arrows from his quiver, adding it to my remaining two.

"Thank you, friend," I muttered, straightening. The Bernician soldier frowned, but he was now more curious than anything else. "You never know, we might meet each other again." The soldier frowned further, clearly unable to understand me.

Then, in my peripheral vision, I caught movement. Instinctively, I spun around, drawing my sword. The third soldier was rushing towards me.

"Come on, then." My words were dark and quiet as I raised my blade. I stepped away from the tree the wounded archer rested against. Absently, I noticed I had been right. The third soldier had no bow.

"The great King of Klumeck," the soldier taunted, coming to a stop a few yards away. "You come to reclaim your daughter?" His use of my tongue was coarse.

"Aye," I called back, my voice reaching him easily over the fine dust of snow and the slight breeze ruffling through my hair. "I come to bring her home. If you yield, I will spare your life." I lowered my sword a little as I spoke. "It will be forfeit if you try to stop me. The choice is yours."

"I hear it is thanks to that traitor, Cara, that you come here." He spat out her name, then grinned, a sneer that showed the yellow of his teeth. "No matter. We gave her a fond welcome home."

"She is no traitor," I told him evenly, thinking of her final, sacrificial act. I knew then that if I survived this, if I returned Imogen to a safe Gaeson and all was well, Evelyn and I would pardon her publicly. All Rheged would know of her bravery and what she had done for our daughter. "What is your decision?" I asked. The soldier grinned wider.

"You are weak, from your journey through mountains and snow." The soldier brandished his sword. The metal of his blade looked dull, compared with the bright snow around us. "I think I will take this chance," the Bernician said. "King Morgant will honour me, when you are dead."

"Very well." I gripped the hilt of my blade tightly. My other hand raised my shield into position. My opponent had already made his first mistake. Aye, I was exhausted, but my determination to find Imogen was powerful, giving me strength in my weakness.

My enemy gave a cry as he leapt forward. I saw it coming and parried him. Our blades crashed into each other, piercing the stillness of the sparse woods. I pivoted, butting the right side of my body into him. The soldier staggered backwards but remained upright. All traces of the sneer had vanished from his face.

The snow fell heavier now. Thick clumps drifted thick through the air as we circled each other, slightly obscuring my vision. He lashed out, but I ducked. He too leapt back as my sword sliced towards his arm.

"You have some skill of your own." My praise was genuine, albeit begrudging. The Bernician soldier's mouth turned, his smile matching the iciness around us. Twice now, our blades had tasted nothing but air. Had I underestimated him?

I kept my face impassive. This could be a long fight and I did not have time for it. I considered simply running from him, but I remembered my exhaustion. This soldier had doubtless just come from the village and his youthful legs would catch up with me in seconds. If he did, he would show me no mercy. Only one of us was going to survive. If I had any chance of freeing Imogen, I needed to kill him.

"Come, then," I invited, straightening. I brandished the tip of my sword in his direction. "As God is our witness, let us see what we are made of, you and I."

A single breath left my lungs, my boots crashing through the snow as I rushed at him. He saw me coming, parrying me easily. He moved to strike his sword against a gap in my shoulder. I swivelled to block him. Our blades danced fiercely again and again, with neither of us yielding. I pushed against my gnawing frustration, for if it got the better of me, it could easily lead to my downfall.

I leapt back once more, using all my training to keep my countenance even. If it was to be a long fight, it was better to accept it, I told myself sternly. I would be no help to my daughter if I was killed here, alone amongst snow and trees.

I took a few paces back, breathing deeply as we circled one another again. The puffs of my hot breath vanished into the icy air. The Bernician soldier suddenly grinned. Perhaps he suspected I was near my end, that it was simply a matter of finishing me off. I would use his arrogance to my advantage.

The clumps of snow fell faster still as I waited. I suspected a blizzard was on the way. The wind began to howl between the trees. My boots crunched with every step.

The Bernician soldier charged, his grin gone. I saw my opening — I had to be quick. I dropped my shield. My opponent frowned slightly, but the confidence was still in his eyes. I ran forwards to meet him.

At the last moment I leapt forward, ducking down into a roll. As my helmet bashed the snow, I saw his features upside down, surprise filling his face. In the next moment I thrust my sword out behind me, slicing deep against the back of his knee.

He cried out and twisted away. Somehow, he managed to stay upright, hobbling on his good leg. Blood spurted out onto the snow, transforming pure white to hot, vivid crimson. I straightened, the tip of my blade dripping red.

"A good move," he admitted, reluctantly. He would have almost sounded amused, if not for the agony punctuating his breaths. I was impressed he was still on his feet.

"Yield," I repeated to him calmly. His face stopped contorting a moment, enough to look me in the eye. "I will spare you." For a moment, his face was still as he considered. Would he surrender? Then, with his features torn in fury, he leapt forward. His last desperate effort was both pathetic and admirable.

I dodged to the side, thrusting my sword in reflex. It found its home in his abdomen. He took one staggering step forwards, but then fell. By the time he hit the snow, blood was pooling at his mouth. I knew the wound was fatal. I yanked my blade free. The Bernician writhed with wild eyes. Then he was still. It was over.

My breaths came heavy as I lowered my sword. I didn't bother to clean my blade. There was no time and I reasoned soon it would be bathed in blood once more. I trudged through the snow to pick up my shield, slinging it onto my back. There was a metal clink as I sheathed my sword and picked up my cloak, bundling it under one arm. Then I turned towards the village and ran.

That unmistakable crunching accompanied every footstep. The wind whirled huge snowflakes into my face, freezing my cheeks underneath my helmet At least the blizzard made my approach to the village almost invisible. If anyone still pursued me, hopefully I would lose them in the storm.

Those sparse trees, once my refuge as I weaved through them, now seemed imposing. I was glad to leave them behind. Soon, I was scrambling up a steep incline. I remembered seeing the ground rise before the village earlier, back when I stood on the hill with Cara Hopefully, I remained on course.

Was Cara still alive? I swallowed hard and though it disgusted me to do so, I pushed the thought away. I had no choice but to focus only on reaching the village. The image from my terrifying nightmare a few nights ago came to mind, unbidden. I shook my head slightly as I reached the top of the short hill.

With the swirl of the blizzard all around me, I could just about make out the looming outlines of buildings up ahead. Swiftly, I shook out my cloak and threw it on, then I fell to the ground, rolling this way and that. I hoped the snow would stick, leaving me hidden in the storm.

I pulled the cloak of my hood closer around me. Peering through the swirls of ice and snow, I surveyed the village. All the wooden buildings were in obvious decay, barely standing. Whatever structures remained still carried the black stains of smoke. There was a hint of something acrid in the air. I suspected no amount of snow would fully eradicate the fire and smoke that had once enveloped this village.

My teeth gritted. Suddenly this scene was too familiar to Klumeck. The first time I saw the kingdom that was my inheritance, almost seven years ago, was just after it had been set ablaze. I swallowed hard. At least Cara had said most of the villagers had escaped the inferno in time.

I breathed as slowly as a hunter as I dragged my mind from the villagers who had once lived here. My eyes travelled, searching for movement. Though my sight was not as sharp as Aife's, soon I had spied no less than ten soldiers in patrol of the area. Still more were probably inside some of the buildings.

For a minute or two I simply watched them, studying their routines. Most of them marched around the village in pairs, others alone. With each movement, their heads looked in every direction, searching for any intruders. Searching for me. It would be almost impossible to move past them, even in this snow.

"Are you here, King Bryce, oh mighty one?" I froze to the spot at the sound of his voice. He sounded only a few yards to my left. His loud, sarcastic challenge gave me hope I had not been detected. Silently, I turned my head. He stood away from me, his feet only a yard away. The soldier could see me at any moment. Slowly I reached for my dagger. My hand curled around the comforting reassurance of the small blade's hilt.

I leapt up. Before he could even turn around, my left hand clamped over his mouth. In the next moment, I sliced the dagger across his throat. Warm blood spurted over my glove. I guided him to land softly in the snow, already dead.

I slid the dagger back into my boot. Looking at his corpse for a moment, an idea came to mind. My hands, already numb with the cold that had long ago seeped through my gloves, scooped snow onto the Bernician's armour, cleaning it as best I could. The icy chill threatened to devour me whole as I stripped from my own armour. I pulled on the Bernician's breastplate and helmet.

I bundled my own armour in my cloak. It was with great reluctance that I stowed my bow, shield and quiver there also, for the Bernician soldier I had just killed was not an archer. I couldn't risk being discovered just because I did not want to part with my arrows. I did however keep my sword, as it would be sheathed until I needed it. The Bernicians would probably not notice any difference, especially in this weather. I left the bundle against a nearby tree.

I straightened, shaking the snow from my gloves. Resisting the temptation to run, I set out with an even soldier's tread towards the village. As I marched, I set up a swift prayer to God that my strategy would work. As I clambered down the hill, the blizzard eased a little, leaving me thankful for my disguise.

Three soldiers came into view, talking quietly with one another. I could make out some words, for I had tried to learn some of their tongue in the last few years. I pulled the Bernician helmet a little further down my head, then made myself walk casually past. I told myself they had no reason to suspect me. Hope tightened in my chest. Every step was a step closer to my daughter. Not long now, Immy love, I thought. Not long now.

I kept the soldier's even march as the storm died down, as quickly as it had arisen. I passed the few buildings on the outskirts of the village, then at last the village hall came into view. I kept it at the centre of my sights, ignoring my quickening heart rate. Imogen was in there.

"I know you are out there somewhere, King Bryce!" A large guard strode out of the hall, his deep scornful bellow cutting through what little remained of the wind. It took all my years as a soldier not to react. "I do hope so, for the sake of your daughter. After all," he added almost gleefully, "it would not be suitable for Her Highness to stay out here for long."

It took everything in me to keep my pace even. Inside the Bernician armour, my blood boiled. Had they simply left her to freeze somewhere? I thought quickly. The fact that both guards had been taunting me meant they suspected I was near. Maybe one of the soldiers had run back from the trees to give a report.

"We will consider keeping her warm, if you surrender," her captor continued. Every muscle in my body screamed for me to race the final distance to the hall. I would do anything, if only protect the hairs on her head. I clung to the hope that the guard was bluffing. It would make no sense to take Imogen all the way here only to kill her. I had to believe Imogen was still inside the hall.

"You, where are you going?" The soldier who had taunted me asked abruptly in his Bernician tongue. I stopped short, coming to attention. It was strange, forming this posture as if he was my commanding officer. I had not done so since discovering the truth about my identity.

"A guard on patrol asked me to report, to you, sire," I answered, in the best dialect I could muster. I inclined my head to him. "There is still no sign of King Bryce. Cara, that traitor, has disappeared." My foe's gazed hardened.

"I know that, you fool," he grunted back angrily. "Otherwise, we would have seen him. Get back to your post! He could be here any moment."

"Yes, sire, only…" I paused, breathing a little easier now that my disguise had passed its first hurdle. "He also asked me to report back to him on the status of the prisoner," I continued evenly. "Might I check on her welfare, sire?"

"No, you may not," Imogen's captor grunted, eyes flashing dangerously. "Who gave you that order? Tell me this instant!" I held his gaze a moment, knowing I had no answer. In that moment, I knew I could not talk my way into seeing my daughter. I had only one chance.

"Of course, sire," I answered hastily, whilst my mind stilled on the decision I had made. My hand gripped tighter on the hilt of my sword. "It was only that—"

Still mid-sentence, I leapt at him. He gave a strangled cry as I banged him into the door behind him. As we fell through the air into the porch beyond, my hand scrambled for the dagger at his belt. I retrieved it, just as he pushed him off me.

"King Bryce, I presume," he growled, launching forwards. His right hand smashed into my jaw. I staggered backwards, crashing into the porch floor with searing pain.

"His Majesty King Morgant will be pleased, once I tell him you have been finally dealt with." He sneered as I stood, but he had not seen I had his dagger. The soldier took a moment to draw his sword, his eyes gleaming with triumph. I let him revel in his supposed victory. I stepped backwards as he revelled, as if flinching from him. I waited for him to fall into my trap. He stepped forwards.

At the last moment, I stepped to the side, with a flick of hand I thrust the dagger deep into his side. He gave a loud cry, just before I crashed the metal plates of my arm into his temple. He emitted a single, low moan as he sank to the floor.

"You're right." I straightened from his unconscious body. "I have come for my daughter. Not you, nor any other foe, will keep me from her," I muttered darkly.

Someone behind me yelled. I spun around, drawing my sword just in time to block my latest opponent. From the ire in his gaze, I wondered if I had just knocked out his captain. The thought brought me more than a little satisfaction.

My latest opponent charged forwards again. Even though I again parried, the force of him crashing into me sent me backwards, clattering against the porch floor. My gaze flickered to the door to the main chamber. Would this soldier stop me from seeing her, after I had come all this way?

"No." The cold, simple answer came from deep within, as the Bernician leapt forwards again. I would never give in. The soldier slashed with his sword, but I rolled to the right. I brought my sword up. My blade sliced across his side. My enemy grunted. I tried to move away, but he landed too quickly.

He writhed and scrambled half on top of me, with agony permeating his frustration. I cursed to see my sword just out of reach. My fingers stretched and curled. I nudged the sword hilt further out of reach, cursing. The Bernician suddenly let out a wheeze. A laugh laboured with pain. I tried to wriggle against him, but it was helpless.

I stilled, letting my mind clear, trying to think. I could not yield now, not with Imogen so close. I realised the Bernician was attempting to reach for his own sword. I waited until he shifted again.

I heaved with all my might when he reached for his sword. Mercifully, because he was off balance, he toppled away. As he landed with a heavy thud, I rolled to my left. My fingers clutched the hilt of my blade. His agonised eyes flickered in alarm, then stilled in horror as my sword pierced his neck.

I rose unsteadily, panting. Had anyone else heard the scuffle of the fight, or the first guard's cry? It was impossible to tell. I didn't wait to find out. I simply shoved the entrance to the porch door shut, then rushed to the inner door and hurled it open. This was it. The hope I had been clinging to all this time would be finally answered.

Part Three

Chapter Nine

I dashed across the threshold. Instinctively, I kept my blade raised, but no guards leapt out to pounce me. Nor could I hear the shouts from Bernicians outside. I probably only had minutes, not even that, before the guards spotted their captain was missing.

I caught my breath a little, stepping further into the darkness of the chamber. My eyes danced wildly about the room. For a moment despair slammed into me. Was this hall truly empty? Had I come all the way here, for nothing? No, I remembered — the captain outside had spoken of guarding Imogen. She had to be here somewhere. Then a flicker of movement caught my eye.

I forgot all else as I raced across the chamber. It was here, in the corner of this abandoned village hall, that I glimpsed my daughter for the first time in a week. She wore thin rags that broke my heart. Her little arms shook with the cold. Her hands were tightly bound with thick rope to a large table nearby.

"Imogen." My voice croaked out her name as I knelt beside my daughter in the dust. "Immy, can you hear me?" Her face was still bent to the wooden floor. Was she even conscious? I reached for the dagger in my boot, slicing through the rope that bound her.

"Imogen," I called a little louder, catching her in my arms as she fell forward. How long had she been tied up like this? Her skin was like ice. Terror stole into me. Was I going to lose her to the cold, so soon after finding her? I looked around, helpless.

My eyes found a large cloak neatly folded in half at the other end of the large table. What cruelty to keep comfort and warmth so close, yet so far from her icy hands. I guided Immy to the floor for a moment, then leapt towards the cloak.

"Imogen? It's your father," I muttered, pulling the cloak over her body. As I pushed her head through the opening, I saw her eyes were dim slits, barely open, with no flicker of recognition. The cloak was far too large, so I bundled it up in front of her, raising it almost level with her chin. I took my knife and hacked at a piece of rope, then tied that around the bundle of cloak. I hoped it would add a vital level of protection to her front.

My head jerked up at the loud talk of the Bernician soldiers. They sounded confused. I slid my dagger back into my boot and gathered Immy into my arms. The outside door creaked open, then I heard loud shouts. I dashed for the window, at the other side of the chamber.

Swerving Imogen out of the way, I bashed the full force of my weight into the window. Its wooden door yielded instantly. We both toppled out, landing in the snow. In the next moment I was up, sprinting as fast as I could, carefully holding Imogen over one shoulder.

I heard boots dashing across wood and stone behind me, then giving way to the swift crunch of snow. More shouts. I prayed I was out of arrow range. I kept running, my eyes on the bank up ahead, where I knew my quiver lay. If I could get to my bow before they caught me, we had a chance.

Somehow, I cleared the village unscathed. The Bernicians were still rushing behind me, but they sounded fainter. I remembered from watching them on the ridge that several of them had been wearing cloaks. Good. I hoped their outer garments were tripping them up, slowing them down.

My eyes found and stayed at the tree where I had placed my old cloak, carrying my normal armour, my shield and my quiver. The terrain changed as I ran uphill again, my free gloved hand digging into the snow as I scrambled, my boots nearly giving way as the loose stones rolled underneath.

I skidded to a halt at the tree, sending clumps of snow flying. I had precious few seconds. Finding the bundle of my cloak and armour, I shook everything loose. Grabbing my bow and an arrow, I spun around to see three Bernician soldiers scrambling up the hill, only metres away. Their faces were grave, their gazes cast just ahead of them as they concentrated on the hillside.

I had time for one stilling breath. Despite the numbness in my fingers, I let an arrow fly into the arm of the first soldier. He shouted as the force sent him backwards, tumbling back down the hill. The other two soldiers stopped in alarm, their faces jerking up.

I fumbled behind me to pluck another arrow from my quiver. My fingers brushed feather briefly as I set it upon my bow. I pulled the string taut, aiming at the second Bernician. My arrow pierced their side and crimson spurted against the brilliant white as his body rolled down the hill.

A minute later, just before he was too close to shoot, my arrow found the neck of my final opponent, killing him instantly. As the corpse collapsed into the snow, my gaze was looking below to see six or seven Bernicians leaving the village. They would be here in less than a minute.

I cursed under my breath, slinging my shield, quiver and bow onto my back. I would have loved the chance to change back into my own armour, but there was no time. I gathered Imogen, still only half-conscious in her bundle of cloak, into my arms. Grabbing my own cloak as well, I took one last look at the soldiers to see that the first of them had reached the bottom of the hill. Then I turned and ran.

I half-sprinted, half-slid down the hill to level ground again, then raced back through the sparse trees. The second hill came into view. My heart lurched. Would I find her dead? Four Bernicians lay scattered across the hill, one quite close to where Cara had set her bow upon the rock.

My boots thundered into the snow as I raced past the Bernicians Cara had cut down. I came to the rock, then my eyes widened. Cara wasn't there. The wound had looked fatal, but had I misjudged it? Was she alive somewhere? Or had she fallen and died somewhere half-covered in snow?

I reached the peak of the hill. Once again, I half-slid, half-raced to the bottom. Relief escaped my lungs as I saw the woodland ahead, where hopefully I could lose my pursuers. In a clearing in the small wood, the horses were waiting. We had piled the fire high with logs, but the blizzard could have doused it, even with the shelter of the trees. Probably less than half an hour had passed since Cara and I had left them. I hoped that the horses were still warm.

"Only a little further, Immy," I muttered. I dashed into the wood. It was open woodland; I could already see the horses. Epos jerked her head up and snorted angrily. Of course, I realised. I was wearing Bernician armour.

"It's me, old girl," I told her. By now, she had already recognised my scent as well as my voice. She darted her head in cheerful recognition. I was glad I had left her saddled, ready for my return.

"I'm sorry, my friend," I said to Cara's steed, clearly looking around for his owner. I slashed my sword to cut the rope that tethered Epos to the tree and swung up onto her. I placed my feet into the stirrups, moving my daughter into position between me and the reins. The Bernician soldiers were louder again. They had reached the woodland.

"Don't worry," I called to Cara's horse. "They'll take care of you, I hope." I kicked Epos into a gallop. At once my mare thundered off, her hooves pounding into the snow beneath her feet. We cleared the woodland in seconds. As we emerged onto the plain, the blizzard picked up again. This was a blessing and a curse, for it would aid our escape, but it would not help my daughter's half-frozen state.

Epos crashed through the thick snow covering the open fields. My eyes fixed on the tall hills Cara and I had spent the last days travelling through. The paths were treacherous, but I knew of nowhere else to go, for this was the route out of Bernicia. Perhaps when we got close to the hills, we would find one of the caves Cara and I had sheltered in on the way here.

Immy bounced in the saddle in time with Epos' hooves thundering beneath us. I pressed Imogen even tighter to me, not wanting to crash her head against my breastplate. I glanced back and could see no one pursuing us. The world was an endless white, swirls of ever thickening snow blasting through the wind.

"Whoa." I called to Epos across the growing blizzard, slowing her to a stop. "Good girl," I murmured, leaning forward to pat her coat, slick with sweat and melted snow. I let go of the reins a moment while I shook out my cloak, still stiff and frozen from where it had buried under the tree. It had been inconvenient to run with it under my arm, especially while also holding Imogen, but I was glad of it now. I threw the cloak over both me and Imogen. The fabric was heavy and cold, but at least it would help to stop the icy wind cutting through me. I pulled up my hood and set off Epos at a trot.

I looked around and strained my ears as I rode, but there was nothing, apart from the whirlwind of the blizzard and the slushing of Epos as she trudged through the snow. I kept my eyes peeled ahead, but soon I could see nothing, the snowstorm causing the tops of the tall hills to fade from view. Even with trying to keep Epos on as straight a course as possible, it was ridiculously easy to get lost.

"Keep us steady, girl," I murmured, clinging to the faith that Epos' trotting was taking us closer to the tall hills. From there, I could find my way back to Rheged. Back to home.

"Home." I murmured the simple word aloud, tasting it. No notion had ever seemed as sweet. My stomach tightened and the flavour soured, however, as I imagined Gaeson in ruin. Had my queen been able to return to her kingdom in time to defend it? Was the enemy already at Gaeson's gates? Had she defeated King Morgant? I bit my lip. I did not even know if Evelyn was alive.

As Epos trudged on, the adrenaline of finding Imogen, our escape and riding at full pelt faded fast. I realised, more than ever, the acute danger we were in. My daughter and I could easily die here from the cold.

"Can you hear me, love? Immy, please speak." I had seen her chest moving in the village hall, seen her eyes just about flicker, even though there had been no focus in them. How long could Imogen survive out here? This was painfully like how I had been left in thin rags in the snow, with nobody expect Sarah, holding my hand limply. Imogen was only a year older than I had been and just as cold.

"History won't be repeated, Immy," I whispered to her, making yet another promise I prayed I could keep. A tear or two fell from my eyes, only to freeze on their journey down my chin. "You won't be left in the snow, because I'm here," I murmured. "I've found you."

Epos slogged through the snow faithfully, but I knew how tired my horse was. She had been resting since dawn, but the gallop through the snow would have cut away any strength she had rebuilt. Even now my faithful companion was slowing to a walk, her stamina fading fast in this fierce storm. The icy temperature seeped through the cloak and into my armour, further chilling the sweat that had run during my escape with Imogen.

Perhaps I should have risked my chances staying to fight the

Bernicians in the village, but there had been so many of them. Death had seemed far quicker with them, than this blizzard.

The chill bit further into my bones. Soon I could no longer feel the reins. A few more tears fell, freezing to icicles on my face. Had I really endured so much to find my daughter, only for us to die in the snow like this? Was that nightmare about Imogen, so empty and lost and leading me to oblivion, about to come true?

Gradually, though, I lost the sense of the cold. My mind took me away, to a realm where I had kept my vows to return Imogen home. I was in a comfortable chamber in Gaeson, where King Morgant's threats had come to nothing. A fire crackled in my hearth and Imogen had fallen asleep in her mother's arms.

Evelyn met my eyes across the chamber, with a smile that reached her eyes, truly happy again. John and Aife sat nearby. The four of us laughed and talked, drinking wine as if none of this had ever happened.

Then, suddenly, the cold blew me awake, startling my senses. I wasn't at home, having kept my promise. I was outside in the middle of a growing blizzard, in a sea of frozen, endless white. It brought a sudden, agonising clarity. I was going to die out here. My time had finally come.

"I'm so sorry, Immy, my love." I cradled Immy closer with what little strength I had remaining. I was lost in the snow again, about to lose another little one I could not protect. It was ironic, that I had survived the snow over twenty-five years ago, only for this piercing cold to claim me now.

With my last thoughts I prayed to God that He would keep her safe, already having claimed me. That she would somehow find my wife; that the two would live happy, love-filled lives in safety, until I met them again. Perhaps even if I died, she might survive.

"Lynny." I was almost four years old again, helpless to do anything but to hold my little sister's hand to the blizzard around us. Then her hand was gone. Where was she? I didn't know, I didn't have the strength to look for her. "Mother," I mumbled desperately. "Father."

My grip of Epos' reins slackened as I lost hold of reality. I slid from Epos still holding Imogen, barely aware of the soft thump as I landed into the snow. I kept falling, sliding into oblivion, in the dreadful knowledge that I would never wake again and that my daughter may well join me. I had not protected her. I had not brought her home. My last thought was to know how miserably I had failed.

***

I seemed to be having a rather pleasant dream. I felt luxuriously warm, as if all the horrors and hardships of the last week had simply melted away. I could hear the gentle crackle of a fire nearby. Presently, I detected a delicious aroma lingering through the air. Was it beef? No, hare, I corrected lazily. Someone was making stew. Perhaps there would be a nice goblet of wine to go with it.

What had happened? My thoughts were far away. I struggled to keep hold of my senses, my thoughts crawling through mud. A slipperiness wanted to claim me, to let me drift until I could no longer think at all, just floating and sliding merrily through all eternity. I let it flow over me, content to drift forever.

Then, there was a sharp tug, a prod in my mind, almost painful. Not all was right. Something stopped me drifting, something important, like an itch I could not scratch. What was it?

"Imogen." Her name tumbled from my lips as I woke. Her unknown fate had stopped me drifting into death. My eyes opened blearily to see I had not entirely been dreaming. Warm blankets covered me. A fire crackled gently nearby.

I was lying in a large cave. The flickering light of the flames cast shadows that danced on the rocks. Epos was tethered in a corner. She shifted her head in my direction. The smell of hare came even stronger now and my stomach growled its way to life. I ignored it as I sat up, looking further around. The Bernician armour and my weapons were propped against the cave wall.

"Imogen!" My daughter was lying on blankets nearer to the fire. I left the luxurious mass of blankets to crawl across the hard cave floor.

"Immy," I murmured. Hope and euphoria soared through me, upon seeing her little chest fall and rise. Her body was warm, but a touch to her forehead showed no signs of fever. She was alive. I took a halting breath. My eyes slipped shut as tears welled.

The sound of crunching footsteps across snow reached my ears. I blinked rapidly, listening. They were some distance away, but whoever it was, they were heading our way. My eyes found my sword, still propped up against the wall. Logic told me they meant no harm, because of the fire and the stew and the blankets, but whoever was in the snow now might not be the one who had showed us such kindness. After all I had been through to get Imogen, I could not take the risk.

I rushed to my sword and shield. It was mightily reassuring to wrap my fingers around my blade's hilt. Then I waited, as a single figure hooded in a thick cloak entered the cave. They were hunched over, both hands holding onto a bucket.

The figure suddenly straightened as they saw me. They slowly lowered the bucket to the floor. The snow shook from their cape as they removed their hood, to reveal a middle-aged man with a clean face and a balding hairline. The stranger raised both his hands, with palms outstretched. A sign of peace.

"Friend." The man gestured to himself. He gave a small smile. "Friend," he repeated. "I mean no harm." There was a strangeness to his accent. His features were sharp, but with a kindness in his eyes.

"My daughter," I said simply, lowering my weapons. I pointed at Imogen. The stranger seemed to understand, for he nodded enthusiastically.

"Yes, she…" He paused, grasping for the words, confirming my suspicion that my tongue was unfamiliar to him. "Tonic," he said now, his face clearing a little. "She sleeps, then she is better."

"You gave her something?" There was an edge to my words. I glanced to Imogen again. "A tonic? What have you done to her?"

"Only sleep. Make her warm," he said. He seemed unfazed by my sword, or the harshness of my tone. "I made stew. Friend," he said a third time. He pointed to the flames. "Please, sit. Rest." He pointed to the mound of blankets where I had woken up.

I considered for a moment. The man seemed friendly enough. I reminded myself that, if not for him, Imogen and I would have frozen to death in the blizzard. I crossed to the wall and dropped my shield. Rather than leaving my sword there, I buckled on my belt and sheathed my blade. Then, at last, I made my way back to the pile of blankets.

"Stew will be ready soon." The man smiled again. I glanced to

Imogen. When I found her in that hall, her skin had been ice. Now she was warm, with strong signs of life. My gaze travelled back to the man. He sat on the cave floor, using a small rock to shove snow from the bucket into a pan by the fire.

"You are not a Briton," I said bluntly. The man looked up, hands stilling at the bucket. "Neither are you a Bernician. Where do you come from?"

"Ah," the man said, then smiled and pointed at himself. "I am from Rome." My eyebrows rose in surprise. "Here, water." He handed me a cup of freshly melted snow. I had not appreciated how weak I was, for the hot water revived me almost instantly. I gulped noisily, ignoring the almost scalding heat, the warmth shaking me into wakefulness.

"A Roman?" I echoed, lowering the empty goblet. Those from Rome had left Briton after their empire across the sea collapsed, over a hundred and fifty years ago. At least, that was what my father, Kellen, had told me. "What are you doing here?" The man smiled again, sitting back.

"I am a priest." He put his hands together and slightly bent his head. "I come to tell the Angles — the Bernicians," he said. "About God."

I frowned, for this made the stranger complicated. If he was an ally of my enemy, then I did not know whether I could trust him. As a priest, though, he would not be any threat. Besides, he had acted to save my daughter's life.

"Why are you here? Were you in the village?" My words sounded harsher than intended as the priest looked up again. "Were you with those who took my daughter?" Priest or not, I could not regard him as a friend if he was involved in her capture. Though, that was what I thought about Cara, I remembered suddenly.

"I was far south, with King Ethelbert," the priest answered, a little vaguely. I nodded. I had heard of him. King Ethelbert was a king of the Angles in the kingdom of Kent, far to the southeast.

"I came here the day before yesterday, to visit King Ethelfrith." My jaw tightened at the mention of the Bernician king. "King Ethelfrith then sent me to meet King Morgant."

"You met King Morgant?" Weak as I was, bitterness still sharpened my words. Venom churned anew in my stomach. "He is my enemy," I told him, as evenly as I could. "He ordered my daughter be taken from me."

"I was most… upset," he said, after searching for the word. "When I saw your child there, I asked King Morgant to let her go, but he would not. I am sorry," he added. "But I am a priest."

"I understand," I told him, my suspicion disappearing as quickly as it had arisen. The man in front of me was no warrior. "How did you find us? How did we get here?" I gestured the cave around us.

"I was due to return south this morning," the priest answered. I nodded. That explained why he was so well supplied. "I was about to leave, to meet others on the road, when I heard shouting. I saw you run from the village with the child."

"They took my daughter from me," I said again. My throat was a little tight; I cleared my throat. "I was taking her back." The priest only nodded, with no judgement in his gaze.

"I followed behind the men who were chasing you," the priest told me. "They were surprised to see me, but I said I was meeting friends. They did not stop me. The storm came," he said. "So I did not see you at first. But then the snow eased. I saw you in the snow, holding your child."

"Then you took us to this cave?" I guessed. The priest nodded. "Thank you," I told him sincerely. There was still a sense of uneasiness, but I knew now it was not because of this man. Shame filled me — and I knew well why. I suddenly remembered my last thought, falling from Epos to crash in the snow. I had failed to protect my daughter.

"I'm glad you found us." My voice was quiet as the priest brought the stew to his mouth to taste it. "I'm only sorry you had to help us." He looked over to me, confused. "I should have stayed awake, to help her," I said. "I failed her." Bitterness escaped my voice.

"No, my lord," came his immediate answer, shaking his head, eyes wide and serious. "You look like you have been travelling for many days," he said. "Your soul was strong, but your body was weak. No shame." He shook his head.

I looked at him. I could see his point. Perhaps I wasn't to blame for my body not being invincible. After all, there was no shame in accepting the kindness of another.

Imogen stirred suddenly. I jerked my head towards her, but she only gave a little sigh before her breathing deepened again. Her slumber was so normal, I could have been checking in on her chamber in Gaeson. The euphoria hit me again as I smiled fully. My jaw felt strange, the muscles unused to such movement.

Had it only been a week since we had separated? Her absence had been so painful, it seemed so much longer than that. As I gazed at my little daughter, my smile faded. I was beginning to notice the changes in her. Her honey hair, usually so soft, was matted together with dirt and grease.

I pushed away my rage. I had found Imogen and she was alive, but would she be my same smiling child? She looked so familiar as she slept, but when she next woke, how changed would she be?

"Some bread, my lord?" I glanced back up to my new companion, blinking at him. In all my anxiety about Imogen I had almost forgotten he was there. "I am sorry, to disturb you." He held out the bread to me.

"Not at all. Thank you," I returned gruffly. I knew he would have seen the raw emotion on my face. I looked down to my roll, turning it over in my hands, to try to hide my embarrassment. I tore a chunk of the roll and stuffed it in my mouth.

"There is nothing weak, to care for your child," the priest told me, just as I began chewing. The bread was fresh and slightly warmed by the fire. It tasted wonderful, compared to the dry husk that remained in my supplies.

"It is not best, for me to show weakness," I said, after swallowing. The priest gave a small frown, but then his expression cleared as he nodded.

"Because you are a king." My eyebrows lifted in surprise. "You are a king, yes? King Bryce," he greeted formally, inclining his head. "I heard the soldiers shouting your name."

"Of course." I nodded. "Call me Daniel," I said. The priest looked a little surprised, but he nodded. For some reason, I was keen for this stranger not to assume the usual formalities.

"Daniel," the priest said slowly. I nodded. "Daniel," he repeated, then pointed to my daughter. "What name?" he asked simply. I gave a small smile.

"Imogen." Her name sounded strange on my lips suddenly, as though her name burned somewhere deep on my tongue. "Immy, for short."

"Imogen," the priest said. "A beautiful name. She will be well," he said firmly. I only nodded again. It seemed that finding Imogen and the blizzard had cut away any capacity for me to hide my emotions.

"Imogen was my mother's name." The priest smiled again in understanding as my birth mother's crimson hair and soft laughter came to mind. A moment later, a pang of guilt shot through me. Once again, Enid, the mother who had raised me, had come to my mind second. I pushed the feeling away, for explaining why I had two mothers seemed too complicated to explain.

"Here, it is ready." The priest began to ladle hot contents into the bowl. "Soon," he murmured, nodding at Imogen. "She will wake soon." I nodded, giving him a small smile. I felt finally able to relax a little. At last, I could believe my daughter was alive and would be well. It was all thanks to this priest.

"Thank you." I took the bowl of stew from him. I glanced again to my daughter. Now I was reunited with her, I couldn't tear my eyes away, in case somehow, we were separated again.

"I too know of God," I told my new friend as he handed me a wooden spoon. "You are like the man from Samaria, who came to the man in need," I told him. My mother had told me that story as a child, of the religious men who had passed by the man in need, then the stranger who helped.

"I am glad to help," he said simply, his accent as prominent as ever. "Please, eat," he invited. The aroma from the stew was heavenly.

We had almost run out of food by the time Cara and I had reached the village. I was ravenous. The sight of the meal reminded me how physically weak I was. I doubted I would have survived even going to the Bernician village without Cara.

My new friend could clearly cook. The hare meat was so tender it melted in my mouth and the stew was seasoned well with herbs and spices. The burst of energy it gave me was almost shocking, as the warmth of it spread throughout my body.

Although the stew was so hot it almost burned, I couldn't help but wolf the food down. I almost forgot about the priest's presence, compared to finally eating a full meal. The bits of hare Cara had given me the night before we began to cross the mountains, was probably the last time I had eaten anything hot, apart from the odd bowl of boiled wheat I had scrounged from my supplies.

I looked up to see the priest smiling at me. He was eating a much smaller portion, with rather more composure than me. He reached for the loaf and tore off another piece.

"Thank you," I repeated, taking the hunk of bread, which I used to mop up the gravy. "Very good," I told him, indicating the bowl. The priest smiled and inclined his head. I swallowed the last stew-soaked morsel. Imogen stirred. My gaze jerked to her as she half-murmured something. Though it was unintelligible and probably to do with her dreams, I rejoiced. It was the first time I had heard her voice since the night she was taken away.

"How did you first learn about God?" the priest asked me. I turned to look at him, wiping my mouth with the back of my hand.

"From my parents." This time Kellen and Enid, who had raised me in Gaeson, who came to mind. "Thanks to their care, I have never known a day without God. They taught me the stories, from the Scriptures. Daniel," I added, pointing at myself. "From the story of Daniel." The priest smiled and nodded

"How about you? What made you devote your life to God?" The priest frowned and I remembered he was not fluent in my tongue. "Priest," I said simply. "Why?"

"Ah." The priest smiled again. "I was…" He paused here, as he searched for the right word. "I was the head, of where monks learn," he said. I gave a nod. It seemed the priest had overseen a monastery. I curled my hands around the goblet of warm water. With this in my hands, my belly full at last and the roaring fire nearby, I could have been back in Gaeson.

"The Pope, he told me to come here. King Ethelbert also invited me," the priest said. "To tell the Angles about God. Your people know of God from the Romans who came before?"

"Aye." The Romans had often talked about Christ and shared the story of the Scriptures with the Britons. I glanced to Imogen as she stirred. My daughter was still half-asleep, but her little hands curled and relaxed into fists as she yawned.

“She will wake.” The priest smiled as he stood. “I shall fetch more snow for the fire.” I gave a small smile as he picked up the bucket, still mostly full. I was thankful for his tact in giving us space. His boots clattered as he walked through the cave.

“Immy?” I spoke gently, crossing to her side as she finally began to wake. “Immy, love, can you hear me?” My voice was raw.

“Ah,” my daughter mumbled. Already, distress marked her features. She shifted her arms, loosening them from the blankets. My heart broke at the sight of the red lines at her wrists, where her cords had been.

“Immy, be still, it’s all right. It’s me,” I muttered, desperate for her to recognise me. Immediately her arms stilled in my hands. She opened her eyes fully and they met mine.

“Father?” That single word nearly undid me. It came quiet and frail, wrought with uncertainty — but she had spoken it. My daughter still knew who I was.

“Aye, my darling.” Tears were welling fast, for I had feared I might never hear her call me that again. “It’s me,” I repeated. Those few words burned in my throat again.

“Father!” With that cry she leapt into my arms, with a strength that surprised me. Any other thoughts were lost, compared with holding her in my arms again. Her honey hair nestled against my shoulders, a few strands tickling my neck.

“I have you, my child,” I whispered, my tears still falling. I took a shuddering breath. “I have you.” Thanks to the kindness of the priest, my child was not dead. I had found her and kept my vow.

“Father, Father, Father.” She kept mumbling my name. I heard her little sobs and felt the moisture of her tears on my neck. Her warm breath was in my ear.

“Immy.” I said her name again, a little stronger. A few stray tears still slid down my bruised cheeks. For a minute, then, we were both quiet. I listened to the roaring fire and her breath in my ear.

“How did you find me, Father?” Imogen asked after a while. I raised my head, moving a little apart from her. I glanced to the cave entrance, but the priest had not yet returned. I hoped he was safe.

“I looked for you, Immy.” My answer was simple as I rose a hand to gently wipe the tears from her eyes. “I kept searching until I found you.

I never would have stopped."

"I know, Father," she answered, with complete certainty. Her absolute trust in me nearly undid me all over again. "What's that smell?" She suddenly sniffed and sat up straighter. "Is that stew?"

"Aye." Gently, I disentangled her from me and crossed to the fire, putting what was left in the pan into a bowl and set it on the cave floor.

"We'll just wait for it to cool a bit," I said, coming back to her. "It's a little too hot now." Imogen nodded, but her eyes looked half-starved. I swallowed hard. When would she have last eaten? Would they have starved her? Rage tightened the knot in my stomach to see the matted mess of her curls, the dirt on her face. She had been so poorly treated. When had my child last been washed? I longed to ask her what she had been through but stopped myself. She was safe.

"Where is Mother? Is she here?" Imogen asked, as I drew a blanket closer around her. I hesitated only a moment before smiling down at her.

"Your mother was looking for you too, with me." I paused to brush one of her curls away from her eyes. "She had to go back home, love." A little confusion and disappointment flashed across her eyes. "The important thing is that she misses you terribly. She will be so happy to see you again." Imogen smiled at that. The expression stole my breath away.

"What about my friend, is she here?" she asked. I frowned. "A woman, she was there when I arrived. She held my hand and told me she would come find you."

"Cara," I realised. "Aye, she is my friend too." My voice grew tight again. "She found your mother and me looking for you. She took me to the village. We got separated," was all I said. "Here, I think your stew is ready."

Her countenance brightened immediately at the prospect of food. Yet her eyes remained a little dim, as if there were a flame inside her not fully lit. I handed the bowl to Imogen and she fell upon the bowl as if she had not eaten in days. I looked away, knowing this could well be the case.

"Try not to eat it too quickly," I cautioned her lightly. As Immy devoured her meal, I heard footsteps trudging through the snow. Unlike last time, I was relieved, for I had begun to worry something had happened to the priest. As he stepped into the threshold of the cave, bearing the bucket full of snow ready to be melted, Imogen jerked her head up. She gasped, her spoon clattering back into the bowl.

"It's all right, love." Already she had moved half-behind me, her arms clutching my leg. "He's a friend. He's the one who brought us to the cave and made this food."

"Hello, Imogen." The priest's voice was kind and warm. Imogen slowly raised her head. "Are you enjoying the stew?" Imogen glanced to me, as though she wanted to check she was truly safe. I nodded.

"Aye, thank you." Her voice was small and quiet. Hunger overtook her caution, then, for she reached forward for her bowl, but she stayed close, leaning against my leg.

As Imogen finished her meal, the priest brought out a block of wood and a little knife. I watched as he began to carve the wood into something. Presently, he began to whistle as he whittled, mostly turned away from us. At once I understood his actions and was thankful for it. Not only was he giving us privacy, but his quiet whistle might be the most normal sounds she had heard in a week.

A while later, Immy was as clean as I was ever going to get her with the hot water from the fire. She had complained only a little, when I had tried to undo the matted mass of dirt and grease which was her hair. Still, it was a lot better than it had been. I bundled her up again in the cloak I had taken her from the village in and settled her back upon the priest's pile of blankets which was her bed.

"I'm sorry it isn't very comfortable, sweetheart," I murmured. The blankets could not help to soften the rocks she was lying on. She was so exhausted, I imagined she would fall asleep before realising how uncomfortable she was. I sat next to Imogen, with my knees drawn up in front of me.

"Tell me a story, Father," Immy bid me, in a half-slumbering murmur. She rolled towards me, then, with one hand reaching to curl round my lower leg.

"All right." My hand reached to her damp, tousled curls as the corner of my mouth turned. "Which story would you like?" I enquired.

"Tell me the one about Mother in the snow and the cloth, please," she mumbled back. My smile broadened as my free hand reached into my tunic.

"Very well." I retrieved the cloth I still carried in every tunic. My mind immediately turned to Evelyn. At this very moment, she could be battling King Morgant and his raiders in Gaeson.

"I carry this cloth everywhere." My voice came calm and quiet, hoping the rehearsed tale would send her to sleep. "I used to sew pockets on the inside of my tunic, just so I could keep it with me." I shifted a little on the floor to get as comfortable as I could upon the rocks, then leant my head back against the cave wall.

"One day, when it was snowing, much like it is today," I continued, "I was in the stables where I used to work with my father." Then the words tumbled out of me, describing how I had been crying, how Evelyn had come upon me. How her voice had been so sweet and how we had thrown snowballs at each other. I was only four years older than Imogen was now, I realised.

"What happened next?" Imogen murmured, noticing I had paused after telling her how I had helped Evelyn climb through the library window. I swallowed hard, for tonight, I did not want to dwell on this part of the story.

"I stood there in the snow, thinking about how beautiful and kind Princess Evelyn had been. I already knew I loved her," I told her hoarsely. "Then and there, I made a vow in the snow." Suddenly I was no longer simply telling my daughter a story. I was reliving myself in the snow, making my oath.

"I promised…" my voice was barely more than a whisper. Imogen murmured something beside me. I thought she might be falling asleep again. "I promised I would always serve her and protect her, no matter the cost. I would fight with her and for her, until my dying breath." Immy's breathing deepened and I knew I was now talking only to myself.

"When I joined the army," I muttered, "I was doing so in my father's footsteps, with his sword. It was not only for my father, though. I joined the army for her."

I glanced down to see my child asleep in the blankets. I was glad. The fragile dam upon my emotions, already wrecked by the events of this past week, was beginning to snap entirely. Swiftly I stood, stooping to retrieve my cloak and gloves, now dry and warm. I pulled them on hurriedly as I rushed past the fire, ignoring the priest's confusion and the way Epos startled, jerking her head towards me.

I ran out into the icy night air. The storm had passed, the snowfall now slow and gentle. I staggered through the snow, before dropping to my knees a few metres from the cave. I clenched my fists, ignoring the cold and wet seeping through my legs.

Was my promise now broken? I wondered. Evelyn was still my queen. She had ordered me to go on alone while she went back to Gaeson. It had been right for me to go on and search for Imogen and I rejoiced that she was alive and safe.

Yet still my heart broke. Had I failed my queen, my wife, my love? What would I do if I arrived at Caer Ligualid to hear word that Gaeson was lost, that Evelyn was dead?

"Please let her live, God." The desperate plea tumbled from my lips, already lost to the wind, the swirl of snow already thickening again. "Have I failed her?" I shouted, knowing nobody would hear, nobody could give an answer. Frustrated, I bent, punching the frozen blanket beneath me. I attacked the snow again and again, my fierce cries lost to the storm.

"Daniel? King Bryce?" Dimly, I heard the priest coming alongside me. I rubbed my icy gloves roughly over my features. "I bid you come inside, my lord," he urged. I gave no reply, as my hands dropped listlessly to my sides.

"Come," he repeated. I heard the worry in his voice. Slowly I staggered to my feet. Wordlessly, I let him steer me back towards the cave.

"Sit, please." He gestured to the fire. I sank to the floor next to it. I peeled off my gloves to find my fingers red and raw underneath. I kicked off my boots, then reached towards the fire.

"What happened?" he asked, eyes wide with alarm. I glanced to Imogen as a fresh bout of weakness and shame shot through me. She had slumbered on, oblivious.

"My wife." I heard the pain crack through my words and swallowed hard. "My wife, Evelyn, is Queen of Gaeson, my home," I said, turning to my new friend. "She was with me, looking for Imogen. We heard word that King Morgant was coming to Gaeson, with a raid. She had to leave, to defend our home. I stayed here to look for our daughter."

"It was right, for you both, to protect your child," the priest said, his face awash with understanding. I gave a single nod.

"Aye," I told him roughly. "Queen Evelyn's last order to me was to take Imogen to our capital city, Caer Ligualid, because Gaeson may no longer be safe."

"You wish to fight for your home, alongside those you love," the priest summarised simply. I nodded. "This is natural, but you chose well." His calm, certain words helped. "It may be well, at your home," he added. "But if not, it is right you stay away."

"Aye, I know." I sighed, stretching my tired muscles. I scooted back a bit, to lean against the cave wall. I folded my arms, glancing to the priest. "What is your name?" I felt foolish that I had not asked this earlier, but he only smiled.

"I am Augustine, at your service." He inclined his head. I raised my brow slightly at the sound of the foreign name, but then it might be a popular choice in Rome. "I do not think I will ever be able to repay your kindness," I told him now.

"You are welcome. Kindness does not always need to be repaid." A small smile crossed my face, my emotions continued to settle. I still feared for my wife and home, but the despair was not as raw now. Imogen stirred nearby, still sleeping.

"She ate all her meal tonight." I glanced to Imogen again as she slept on. "I hope she will be strong enough to travel by the morning." I yawned and stretched my arms over my head. "What are your plans?" My hands dropped back to my sides.

"In the morning I will head back south, for I will already be one day late to return to King Ethelbert. My companions await me in a town." I nodded.

"The king will wonder why I was delayed. I will try to think of a way to tell him without having to lie. He would not like me helping his enemy." He grinned suddenly, revealing a gap in his teeth. "I shall leave you some, whilst the child recovers." His hand gestured his supplies. I smiled again in thanks.

"Sleep, my friend. You need your strength." Augustine gestured the blankets I had been lying on when I first awoke here. As I glanced at them, I realised how exhausted I still was. I hoped that Imogen would have a little more strength tomorrow, that there might be a little more colour in her cheeks.

I let my eyes slip shut, in thankfulness that God had reunited us. I had found my daughter at last. The nightmare I'd had in the woods came to me, but for the first time it did not tempt me to despair. Thanks to Augustine, that dark dream would not be coming true. Yet I fell into slumber that was still a little fitful, my spirit not truly content. I knew I would not sleep well again, until I knew my wife and home were safe.

Chapter Ten

"Is that what I think it is, Father?" Imogen asked quietly, sat in front of me on the saddle. She had been strong enough to travel and thankfully the blizzard had passed us by.

"Aye." I pulled Epos gently to a stop, then relaxed my hands on the reins. We had spent all yesterday crossing back over the tall hills and mountains, reversing the path I had taken with Cara. Our route had then taken us west and slightly south.

I turned back in the saddle to glimpse the foot of the hills. We had joined with the road from Klumeck and Caer Ligualid, far more south than when I had met Cara a few days ago. Cut into the largest hill, the ruins of Klumeck lay visible. I had not seen it since the attempt to recapture the fortress four years ago. After the spectacular failure of our plan, we first suspected there might be a spy in Gaeson.

Klumeck looked undisturbed. We were so close. A large part of me yearned to take Imogen there, to introduce her to the home I could barely remember. It would be folly, though, for my dispossessed kingdom was now firmly within Bernician lands. There could easily be a legion of soldiers lying in wait.

Staring at the ruins, my mind took me further back, a year before our failed recapture, when Klumeck was first lost to Rheged. Despite the chill in the air, I could almost feel again the intense blaze of the fire. That frenzy of flames that engulfed everything it touched. Once again, the charred bodies strewn across the ground came to mind. Though most of Klumeck's citizens had escaped, a few poor souls had been either cut down by the sword or left to perish in the fire. I swallowed hard.

"Come on." I deliberately steered Epos around again, heading further into the safety of Rheged's borders. What could my life have been like, I wondered, if Klumeck had survived? Would I have still married Evelyn? Would we have ever suspected there was a spy in Gaeson, or uncovered it to be Aldred? Would my uncle, King Cedric, still have died in the battle outside Caer Ligualid? I suspected Sarah would never have married Pasgent, for she would never have come to Caer Ligualid to dwell with the displaced Klumeck citizens living there.

Epos gave a soft snort, sounding happier than she had done all week. In the distance, the first of Rheged's lakeland hills had come into view. At this, we joined the road heading north. We were finally on the path to Caer Ligualid.

"Good girl." Immy poked her arm out of her cloak to slide her hand across my mare's damp coat. "She's tired, isn't she, Father?" I caught the thread of concern in her voice.

"Aye, she was racing so fast and hard to come get you." I glanced down to Epos, adjusting the reins to keep her on the road. Or, where I judged it to be, where the layer of snow and ice was slightly thinner. I slowed my faithful friend to a walk. "We'll let her get her strength back, now we've found the road."

"Why are we going to see Aunt Sarah?" My daughter glanced up at me. "Why are we not going home, Father? I want to see Mother." I did not answer for a moment.

"I know you do, darling. So do I." I hesitated. What could I tell my daughter? She was only four years old, far too young to be told the true horrors of war, yet old enough to be aware of the things around her. I knew she would probably remember her ordeal for the rest of her life.

"We're just going to visit Aunt Sarah for a few days, love," I began gently. "Mother and John and Aife went back early, to check everything was safe and well for when we come back."

"I understand," Immy replied quietly. The sad, heavy tone in her voice let me know she probably understood far more than her four years would suggest.

"You will be safe, Immy, as long as you're with me," I told her firmly. Epos trudged along as I spoke, kicking up snow behind her hooves. "If for some reason we cannot go home yet, your mother might even be waiting for us in Caer Ligualid."

Had I said too much? I expected more questions, but Imogen said nothing further. My thoughts turned once more to Evelyn. Had she made it back to Gaeson in time? Would they have defended our home against King Morgant? I set my jaw, brow furrowing. I would not have to wait much longer to find out.

We continued our journey quietly, passing along Rheged's northern hills and mountains. They were the only variant in this world of frozen white. At least, for the moment, the sky was clear. I hoped our calm weather would continue.

Presently, we found the road before us cleared. Rheged citizens had dug up the snow in huge mounds at either side of the road. I was glad, for it would make Epos' journey even easier. Due to our slow pace, the sun was low in the sky when the magnificent city of Caer Ligualid came into view. Rheged's capital kingdom imposed itself splendidly on the surrounding plains, as it always had done.

"There it is, Immy." My whole body sighed in relief at the sight of it. "Caer Ligualid, where King Owain reigns as Supreme Ruler of Rheged. Do you remember the last time we were here?"

"Aye, Father," she returned quietly. "We came when Gilroy was born." I nodded. I was about to speak further, but I sensed her withdrawing again. Today was the most she had talked since we had left the cave yesterday. I knew that reticence was expected after such trauma. I hoped that her exuberant chatty nature would return one day, but I suspected it would not be soon.

The sun had almost dipped below the horizon when we finally reached Caer Ligualid. It turned all the snow around us vivid gold, so it looked like the whole city and surrounding plains were gleaming. After three days on the road, we were finally here.

"It's beautiful, isn't it, Immy? The way the light has caught on the snow," I added. I saw Imogen's head nod, but she didn't reply.

I suddenly remembered I was wearing Bernician armour. I had kept it on in case we met the enemy on the road. Hurriedly, I threw off my helmet and breastplate. They thudded into the snow. I raised a hand to the guards watching from the ramparts. There were shouts. They would not be able to recognise me yet, but without the armour at least they would not be tempted to shoot me on sight.

I heard a louder shout as I caught my name. My face broke into a smile as I heard the tell-tale clink of the portcullis being raised. Imogen and I passed under the extended metal bars and we wound up a paved slope briefly before arriving in Caer Ligualid's courtyard. I had just swung down from the stirrups when my sister raced in.

"Sarah!" Relief shot through my voice as I swung down from Epos. Imogen wore a faint, fragile smile, but her eyes were nervous. She did not move from the saddle.

"Let's get you down, love," I said gently. Imogen let me take her from Epos, who stood as steadfast as ever. A stable boy ran out into the courtyard. "Take good care of her," I directed to him. "She has been riding in this weather for many days."

"At once, my lord." The lad bowed quickly and then led Epos slowly away. I turned to Sarah again, still standing a few feet away.

"Hello, Immy," Sarah began tentatively. She took a single step forward, then another. Her boots slushed in the thin layer of snow; I guessed the courtyard had been recently cleared, but now the snow was beginning to cover the cobbled stone again. My sister crouched down to my daughter's level.

"It's so very good to see you, my dear." Sarah outstretched a hand, searching her niece's face. I hid my relief when cautiously, Imogen stepped forward to take her aunt's hand.

"There, there," Sarah murmured, as my daughter stepped further forward into her arms. "You're safe now, Immy." She stood then, but Imogen stayed at her skirts. Sarah raised her head to me and frowned. "Is that Bernician armour?"

"Aye. I had to infiltrate a Bernician village to find her," I explained. "I wanted to get my old armour back, but there wasn't time. Sarah," I said quickly. "What of Gaeson?"

"Gaeson is safe." She smiled warmly. "As is Evelyn." Relief tore through me. Laughing, I crossed the space between us and embraced my sister.

"Here. Sorry, Immy." Sarah reached into her skirts to retrieve a letter. "We received word from her three days ago."

Hurriedly, I took the letter from her. At first my eyes rushed past the words so fast I almost missed them. I took a deep breath then made myself read the contents slowly.

My dearest Sarah,

I am sending this to you as a matter of urgency. We received word from a messenger that Lord Melvyn had been poisoned and was upon his deathbed. We were told this was orchestrated by King Morgant. He knows Daniel and I are out looking for Imogen along with our captain. Therefore, Gaeson is vulnerable to attack.

While Daniel has stayed to look for Imogen alone, the rest of us raced back to Gaeson as fast as our horses could gallop. Within a few hours of our return, our enemies appeared over the horizon. With the support of the troops who had returned with me and by God's grace, I can say we won the day. Our home is safe once more, for the moment.

I had to stop reading here. Relief and adrenaline coursed through me, so strongly it made my hands shake. I closed my eyes again. Upon opening them once more, I saw Immy watching me apprehensively. I shot a quick smile her way before turning back to my wife's hand.

King Morgant vastly underestimated us. I believe that with Lord Melvyn poisoned, he thought he had the element of surprise on his side and that without a leader, Gaeson would succumb to chaos and confusion. This could well have been the case, if not for the messenger who warned us.

I fear, however, that King Morgant's defeat will only make him a more dangerous foe. He came to Gaeson with a relatively small force, but he will not make that same mistake again. If he comes to challenge Gaeson's throne, it will be with all the troops he has under his command. I can only pray we will be ready to meet him when that day comes.

I looked up again from the page, my relief sobering. For of course, she was right. King Morgant was not about to give up on his campaign to destroy everything Rheged held dear just because he had not won the day. It would make my greatest enemy even more dangerous. Yet, I pushed this dark thought to the background for now. For the moment, Gaeson was safe, Surely, that was all that mattered. I turned to my wife's hand again.

I hope all at Caer Ligualid is well and that Daniel comes to you soon, Imogen with him. God grant us all strength if he does not. With every bone, I want to ride to Caer Ligualid immediately, but duty holds me here. Should my prayers be answered, should my husband and daughter be with you — tell them Gaeson is well. Tell Imogen I cannot wait to see her home soon.

With my love,

Evelyn, Queen of Gaeson.

"You said this came three days ago." I raised my head to my sister. "I had only just found Imogen. If Evelyn had not returned…" I trailed off. What could have happened barely bore thinking about. Cara had not just risked everything to save my daughter's life, but all Gaeson, also.

"We'll stay here a few days, till you get your strength back a bit, then we'll return home." I glanced to Imogen as I spoke, then stretched my arms above my head, cracking a smile at Sarah. "In the meantime, I think we could both do with a wash."

"I was not going to comment, brother, but a bath may suit you well." Sarah chuckled. Another faint smile, slightly stronger than the last, flickered across Immy's features. It gladdened my heart. I hoped it would not be too long before she smiled again fully.

"Come on, love," Sarah murmured, wrapping a gentle arm around her niece again, who had not yet let go of her skirts. "Want to stay with me?"

"Aye," Immy answered in the smallest whisper. As the three of us headed in the direction of the castle, my throat tightened at how much harm King Morgant and his men may have caused my child. With effort, I pushed the thought away. What Imogen needed now was peace and reassurance, not my anger about my enemy.

"We'll see you in my chamber, in a while then," Sarah said. The concern in her gaze let me know she was as concerned about my daughter as I was.

"Of course." I nodded. "See you in a few minutes, Immy," I added gently, as we came to the end of the grand staircase. Imogen shot me an anxious glance, but only pressed tighter to her aunt. I lingered a moment, watching them turn down the corridor, then turned in the other direction.

It was not until I crossed the threshold of the chambers Evelyn and I usually had when we came to Caer Ligualid that I truly began to relax. I heard hot water being poured, a blissful sound. It was with relish and satisfaction that I could finally remove the rest of the Bernician armour. I dumped the metal plates, long stained with blood, into a basket by the door.

I had tried to wash as best I could on the road, but I had not had a proper bathe since Imogen was taken, over a week ago now. All my garments were filthy, the rest stuffed hastily into my saddlebags which would now be sorted and cleaned whilst Epos was attended to.

"Thank you," I told the servant sincerely, as she came out of the bathing chamber. "This is truly a welcome sight."

"Your Majesty." She inclined her head as she curtsied. "Shall I take your sword and your armour to be cleaned, sire?"

"I'll keep my sword with me. The armour…" I frowned, hesitating. "It isn't mine, but perhaps it could be kept in the armoury." After all, Caer Ligualid may discover some use for it.

"Your Majesty." She inclined her head again and left, carrying the basket under one arm. Finally, I was left alone.

I unbuckled my belt and my sword clattered to the floor. Slowly I peeled off my vestments, before at last crossing to the bathing chamber. My feet rejoiced as I stepped into the wooden tub. I sank mercifully into the water. The heat lapped all around me, easing my tired limbs. I closed my eyes, leaning back. A washcloth sat on the side, but I did not reach for it yet.

I rubbed a little hot water over my face, as I heard the main chamber door open. My hands stilled, but a few seconds later, the chamber door closed again. It was probably the maid. As I sank deeper into the water, the images of the last few days began to swim through my mind, as I expected them to. I had not been in an all-out war, but I had seen plenty of bloodshed and broken bones these last few days.

It all started with the skirmish in Gaeson when Imogen was kidnapped. Then the battle by the river, just after we met Cara. Finally, then, there were the soldiers in the village. My fists clenched, seeing Imogen again in the thick cords. That cloak cruelly out of reach.

That last image of Cara came to mind now, the fierce determination amidst the agony plain on her face. The pure white of snow transformed to deep crimson from the blood flowing from her side. Then seeing her horse when Immy and I passed that way, fully expecting to see her owner. I swallowed hard. Was Cara dead? Had King Morgant's men found her? I was not looking forward to telling Ewan. He would be in despair to have missed seeing her, especially now her fate was unknown.

I took a deep breath, slowly uncurling my hands. There was nothing

I could do to help Cara now. By the grace of God Imogen was safe, thanks to her sacrifice and the actions of Augustine the priest. We would have been dead, frozen in the snow that day without his aid. I splashed a little water on my face, praying that the priest was safely on his way south, with King Morgant none the wiser of how he had helped us.

How long would it be before I faced my greatest enemy? The one who had sent the Wolf into Gaeson's midst to poison the ear of King Reghan. The one who had sent the Wolf to murder half my kin. As much as I wanted peace to endure, I could not deny how much I craved to confront him.

I sat up straighter, sending a little water spilling out of the tub as I seized the washcloth. I scrubbed myself clean, but too hard. My skin was red and raw by the time I was done. I stood from the tub, dried myself and pulled on a simple robe. I ran my hand through my damp hair, revelling how good it felt not to be clogged up with dirt, sweat or blood. My hands rubbed over my face again. My journey to find Imogen had left me relatively unscathed, but I could feel the mark of recent cuts and scratches.

Leaving the bathing chamber, I smiled to see a pile of fresh clothes on the bed and my dirty garments were nowhere in sight. The only thing that remained was my sword, stained on the floor where I left it. I carried my belt, sword still in its sheath, back to the tub. Reaching for the wash rag again, I ran the cloth over my blade again and again until the metal gleamed.

With myself as well as my sword at last clean and dry, I slipped my feet into softer, indoor shoes. The boots I had worn on the road would be being cleaned. Invigorated, I at last left the chamber to see how Imogen was faring.

"Your Majesty." I turned at the voice to see Taliesin entering the small hall interconnecting my corridor. He bowed low as his small cape swept behind him.

"Good day to you." My tone was civil as he straightened. In truth, I still had mixed feelings for Caer Ligualid's foremost bard. I had distrusted him for years, but then he had proved his loyalty in helping us identify Aldred as the poisonous traitor he was. Since his recent 'prophecy' about my daughter, however, my feelings towards him had cooled considerably.

"I am pleased to see you safe and well, my lord," Taliesin continued, as I made to continue to walk past him. I stopped at his words, turning back to where he stood next to the entrance of a spiral staircase. "I was sorry to hear about Her Highness," the bard continued.

"I thank you." My voice was only a little stiff. I was sure he was about to mention his prophecy, but he simply bent his head. Perhaps I had misjudged him. I turned away, heading down the corridor.

"I told you I had the sight, my lord," the bard called out. I hid a sigh, as I turned around. Perhaps I had judged him accurately, after all. "I foresaw harm would come to her, sire. Will you therefore grant me that the rest of my vision might come true?"

"Certainly not." I strove to keep my voice even. "You made my daughter upset, the night Prince Gilroy was born."

"My intention was not to distress her, my lord." Taliesin inclined his head as he walked towards me. "I believe it to be a gift from God, my king, for the good of Rheged. It was this sight that led me to suspect Lord Aldred's true character, when all others thought him good."

"I see." I folded my arms. A little curiosity was rising, to blend with my annoyance. "I don't suppose this sight of yours warned you that King Morgant would betray us at Ynys Metcaut? Or that His Majesty King Urien would fall that day in battle?" My words picked up their pace.

"Where was your gift, bard, when my uncle died?" I challenged him, unable to keep the heat rising in my voice. "Why were you not foretold about the ambush at Klumeck four years ago? Or when my parents were murdered in their beds?"

"Great tragedies, all." Taliesin was quiet and calm. I took a deep breath. It seemed that after this last week, I needed to retrain in keeping my anger at bay. I frowned at him, wondering whether his comment held genuine sympathy, or whether he merely wanted to pacify me.

"I deeply lamented my sight did not warn me about these deaths, particularly His Majesty King Urien's demise," Taliesin said solemnly. "It is a gift, sire, not an ability. Not always a pleasant one, at that," he pointed out. "I cannot control its occurrences, much as I would wish to."

"How convenient," I said flatly. "King Morgant is at war with us. His desire to destroy the royals of Rheged has been known, ever since he had King Urien assassinated. He already orchestrated the murder of half my kin.

"It is not difficult to assume King Morgant would come after us again or kidnap my daughter. You will, therefore, perhaps grant me my cynicism," I said, striving for a more civil tone. "Furthermore, please distance yourself from my daughter. She is in a fragile state."

"As you wish, of course, Your Majesty." He inclined his head in assent. "You have made your disapproval clear, my lord," he told me as he straightened. "However, know that I am here, should you require my service. Whatever else you may believe, I am loyal to Rheged," he concluded firmly. I regarded the poet for a moment, then nodded.

"Thank you, Taliesin. I do believe that. Forgive my temper." A reluctant smile crossed my features. "It has been a rather tiring time."

"Of course, sire. I bid you a good day. I pray the princess recovers soon." With a final bow he walked away down the corridor, his cloak swishing behind him.

I proceeded towards Imogen's chambers, just down the corridor from my own. My brow was still furrowed. I found the idea of Taliesin's 'gift' most disturbing. Could it even be true? I shook my head a little, trying to put these thoughts to the back of my mind. I quietly entered Imogen's rooms.

As I approached the bed, I was pleased to see Imogen at last looked a little peaceful. She looked fresh and clean after her bathing, clothed in a simple shift. I could not help but reach out a hand, gently brushing away a strand of hair that had fallen across her cheek. Imogen stirred slightly. I removed my hand quickly, not wanting to wake her. I sank down into a nearby chair, just as a soft knock came at the door.

"I thought you might be here when I returned." Sarah's voice was warm as she greeted me. Behind her, a maid came in bearing a tray.

"I hope King Owain does not mind me staying up here," I said as the maid set the food gently down upon the table and left again. "I know he would wish us to join them for dinner, but with Imogen the way she is…"

"He understands, of course," Sarah murmured. "It looks as though she will slumber through the night." My sister glanced in Imogen's direction. "She ate all of her dinner, earlier, so this is a good sign." Sarah folded her arms and looked at me. "How does she really fare?"

"I need to confirm with the surgeon, but I don't think she will have lasting physical damage," I said, as Sarah walked to a chair near mine. "Emotionally, however…" I trailed away, averting my gaze as my voice caught. My hands drummed listlessly on my lap.

"I hate King Morgant as much as ever," she burst out bitterly. I looked back; it was rare to see such anger in her gaze. I nodded. It was also her kin he had murdered. Her niece who had been kidnapped.

"We must be sure to love her all the more," she said. Her words were just as strong, but the heat had gone out of them now. Sarah reached across to clutch my hand briefly. I gave her a small smile.

"I do miss you sometimes, Lynny." My sister's eyes widened slightly, then she returned my smile. I rarely used the nickname of her birth name, Lynette. A name that spoke of our parents, of our home in Klumeck. The life that came to me only in stolen fragments. A life she could never remember.

"I miss you too." Sarah gave my hand a single squeeze. Since she had chosen to reside in Caer Ligualid with the Klumeck citizens who still lived here, I had felt her absence keenly. "Dinner?" she suggested, letting go of my hand.

"Aye." Quietly, I moved my chair nearer the table. I sat, as Sarah passed me a plate laden with pie, bread and vegetables. I hadn't seen such a welcome sight since Augustine's stew in the cave.

"Where is Gilroy? How does he fare?" I reached for a knife to cut my pie. Steam escaped as creamy chicken poured from the opening.

"He is well, thank you. He should be asleep for the night, hopefully. My maid will come if he wakes." I nodded and put the first mouthful of pie in my mouth. Delicious.

"I've already sent a note to Evelyn," she told me now. She poured a large helping of wine into my goblet and a small measure into her own. "To let her know you and Imogen have arrived safely."

"Thank you for that," I said with feeling. I would have gone to send a message as soon as the meal was over, for I did not want Evelyn to worry about our welfare a moment longer than she had to.

"Of course." Sarah reached for her wine to take a sip. As she lowered her goblet again, I saw a small frown of concern enter her features. "How are you, Daniel?" her voice was gentle as her free hand touched mine briefly.

"Exhausted." I took a large gulp of wine. "I miss my wife and I'm concerned about Imogen. However, I have my daughter back." I set my wine back on the table. "Evelyn and Gaeson are safe, so I can ask for no more than that. How fares Caer Ligualid?" I stabbed at another piece of meat.

"Queen Penarwen is unwell again." My sister sat back in her chair. "In fact, the surgeon now believes she will soon pass into the next world."

"What?" My head jerked up, a hunk of bread suspended halfway to my mouth. I glanced at Imogen as she stirred, but she simply turned over and continued sleeping. "I'm sorry to hear that," I said.

"Aye," Sarah murmured, her frown deepening. "For a brief time after you returned to Gaeson, she seemed well again, but her health has gone much worse in the last week or two."

"Sad news indeed," I murmured. I tore off another piece of bread and soaked it in the creamy sauce of the pie. "Does King Owain visit her?"

"Not really." Sarah sighed. "Talk of his affair with Princess Thaney spread like fire among the people." I nodded, swallowing my mouthful of bread. "It was a folly of his own doing, but I was sorry for him at the time. Now, though…" She frowned, shaking her head a little. "King Owain seems intent to ignore his wife, even when she lies on her deathbed."

"That is a shame." I reached again for my goblet, my plate now empty. "It'll be hard on Elffin." I took a mouthful of wine. "The last time I saw him, he was convinced his mother was still unwell. I think he suspected this all along."

"Really? Poor lad," Sarah murmured. "He'll make a fine king, but he must be sure not to quarrel with his father too much. I worry sometimes he will end up as hot-headed as his father." I smirked, nodding. "They must keep the peace, if we are to stand against Bernicia." This was a sobering thought. The drums of war were inevitable; they would only get closer. There came a knock on the door.

"Excuse me, Your Majesty, Your Highness." A servant — I presumed another of Sarah's maids — curtseyed low. "My lady, Prince Gilroy has awoken. I tried to ease him back to slumber, but he is most distressed."

"That's all right. I'll come now." Sarah glanced at me with a smile. "I will try to settle him, then bring him back here. It has been some weeks since you last saw your nephew."

"Aye. If Imogen should wake, she would be glad to see her cousin," I said. Sarah left the chamber with the maid, closing the door gently behind them. I glanced at my daughter, reassured by the peaceful expression across her face as she slept. I hoped slumber granted her rest from what plagued her when she was awake. I leant back in my chair and let my eyes close.

"Here he is." My eyes flew open as Sarah came back into the chamber. "Sorry, did I wake you?" I shook my head, rubbing my face a little. In truth, I didn't know whether I had slept or not.

"Hello, little lad," I greeted tenderly, as my sister placed my nephew gently into my arms. "He's grown so much." It had only been a few weeks, but his limbs were all longer and his hair, once only wispy strands, had thickened a little. I was pleased to see the blazing auburn colour had not faded.

"All is well, Gilroy," I murmured, as he began to stir in my arms. The babe quietened again, his gaze transfixed upon me.

"It's been a few weeks since Princess Thaney left," Sarah thought aloud, watching us. "Her pregnancy may well be showing by now."

"A shame that the child will never know their father, or their siblings," I said, then sighed. "At least hopefully she and the child will be safe in Gododdin, even if her father is stern with her." I glanced at Imogen again and scratched my head.

"I'll visit Queen Penarwen, tomorrow, but for now I need to get some sleep, before I fall off this chair." I stood, stretching my tired limbs.

"Of course. I'll watch over Imogen." I smiled in thanks at her kind offer, bade her goodnight and crossed the short distance to my chambers. I was barely awake enough to take off my outer garments. Then for the first time since the nightmare of these past ten days began, I fell asleep in peace, slumber reaching me as soon as my head touched my pillow.

***

"Enter, King Bryce." Her voice called through the door, stronger than I expected. It was the morning after my return to Caer Ligualid and Sarah had taken Imogen and Gilroy for a walk after breakfast. I turned the handle and crossed into the chamber.

"Your Majesty." I inclined my head. Queen Penarwen sat by a gently roaring fire, with a blanket covering her lap.

"It is good to see you well, King Bryce." As she watched me, the corner of her mouth lifted slightly. "Princess Lynette told me last night you would come."

"I was sorry to hear you are unwell, my lady," I said as I approached. Elffin had been right to suspect she had not fully recovered. She looked frailer than ever in the flickering firelight.

"Not to worry." Queen Penarwen spoke a little weaker now. "It is simply my time. Come and sit." I inclined my head again.

"Are you not cold, my lady?" Icy air filtered through the open window, contradicting the roaring fire. Queen Penarwen smiled again, pulling her shawl closer about her.

"My physician says that the fresh air is good for me. I should like to go outside, but I am told I must rest. A shame, really," she murmured, half to herself. "I would have liked to walk among the gardens. I know I shall never again see flowers in bloom." She paused here, fidgeting with her shawl.

"No matter," she said suddenly, her voice almost forcefully cheerful. "I'm so glad Princess Imogen is safe. I did not stop praying for her."

"Thank you, my lady." I clasped my hands loosely together to stop them clenching with the thought of what had happened to her. "It makes my blood boil, to think of how they treated her." I looked away to the crack in the window, a sliver of piercing blue sky.

"Understandable. Revenge is all too human, but it is powerful and seductive." The slight warning to her words drew my gaze back to her.

"Do not be too hasty in desiring it, Daniel. We forget how much destruction it leaves behind." She spoke heavily. Her breaths came quick and shallow now. It seemed talking was difficult for her. "I expect you will be leaving for Gaeson soon," she said, a little lighter.

"Aye, my lady." I nodded. The thought of home lightened my heart considerably. "I'll let Imogen rest here a little longer before the journey.

I hope the good weather holds; I've had enough of blizzards."

"You must be missing your wife," Queen Penarwen suggested. There was an edge of something laced to her words. Was it as strong as regret? "I do not think King Owain will grieve much for me, when I have passed on." She sighed, leaning back. It was like regret but more subdued. Closer to a quiet resignation.

"All of us have our own time to leave this world," she continued, before I could offer further condolences. "Neither ire nor bitterness can slow its coming. I did not realise my time would be so swift." She sent me a wry smile as she leant back in her chair. "It is what the good Lord has ordained."

"He loved me, once," she mused, her eyes slipping shut. "Things began to change sometime after Elffin was born." Her speech sounded faraway. "Owain's love faded so subtly, I hardly noticed it at first."

"How it pained me," she continued, "when I realised his heart was no longer turned to me. Even amidst this sickness, when I am near my deathbed, the king is too grieved over the mistress that bears his child to bid me farewell." Queen Penarwen smiled ruefully, opening her eyes again.

"I think it would be good to depart for the better shores soon. This sickness will be gone and I will no longer be married to a man who no longer loves me."

"I'm sorry," I murmured. From the sadness in her words, I wondered if Queen Penarwen might still love King Owain, even after everything he had done. Even if he no longer loved her, it seemed cold for him not to visit her. "You still have some time, my lady," I pointed out. "Perhaps he will come to you, before the end."

"It is unlikely. As I said, the woman he mourns for is not me." She moved her hands together then, sitting up a little straighter. "I am glad you came, my lord. I had in mind to send for you."

"Oh? What can I do for you, my lady?" Queen Penarwen regarded me for a moment, her gaze suddenly much sharper.

"I know Elffin is fond of you." She lowered her gaze to the blanket as she spoke, one hand pulling idly at a loose thread.

"I thank you, for the good friendship you formed with my son when you were last here. I know war is coming." Queen Penarwen raised her head to meet my eyes again.

"King Owain no longer loves me, but he still loves his people well. I shall pray for him not to fall in battle, while I still have breath left. If, however, the Lord does take his life in this war, Elffin will ascend to the throne." She stopped pulling at the thread in the blanket.

"Should that happen," she said, "I wish you to advise him. His father has not instructed him that well, of late. He has been far too occupied with other matters," she muttered coldly. I nodded.

"Of course, my lady. Though the way I became king was unorthodox, to say the least," I pointed out. "So, I do not know how much I can aid him, but if I can, I will."

"You will be able to empathise more than most," the queen said, her voice a little weaker again. "You were not as young as he is, but kingship was thrust upon you when you too were not ready for it." The memory of my uncle, King Cedric, lying dead outside Caer Ligualid's castle walls shot through me. "If King Owain dies in battle, I fear the same will be true of my son."

"I was certainly unprepared," I agreed, trying to push the image of my fallen uncle away. "I give you my word I will help him if I can, when that time comes."

"For that, you again have my thanks," Queen Penarwen answered. She then leant her head back again. "I must ask you to leave me, for I grow weak. I must rest."

"Of course." I stood. "Good day, Your Majesty." I bent my head. Queen Penarwen did not reply, but nodded slightly, managing a faint smile. I left her chambers, shutting the door quietly behind her. As I headed down the corridor, I pushed away the uncomfortable feeling that this quiet conversation might be the last time I saw her alive.

I had not departed Queen Penarwen's rooms long before coming across King Owain himself. The man who, apparently, would not go visit his dying wife.

"Your Majesty." I dipped my head as we came to a stop in a small hallway. "I thank you for your hospitality towards my daughter and me."

"It is no trouble." He gave a dismissive wave of his hand. "Your usual chambers will always be ready for you here. I am glad the princess is safe."

"As am I," I answered. King Owain began to pass me by, but a surge of boldness overcame me. "I have just come from Queen Penarwen's chambers."

King Owain stopped, the swish of his cloak ceasing behind him a moment later. He fixed a hard stare upon me but said nothing. My resolve hardened in the wake of his silence.

"Her condition had not changed." My tone was even, but I was astonished he did not even ask about the welfare of his wife.

"Aye, I'm aware of her sickness," he replied steadily. His brow had narrowed further. "It is most tragic, I'm sure." I could not fathom him. He was speaking as though Queen Penarwen was a stranger, not the wife he had wedded almost twenty years ago.

"Indeed," I said. King Owain resumed his steps. "I'm sure she would appreciate you visiting her, my lord." He swivelled around quickly, his eyes livid. "I know the love you had for her may long have faded, sire," I said, in my most diplomatic tone. "However, she is still your wife."

King Owain still said nothing for a moment. His glare was almost as furious as his father's had ever been. I resisted biting my lip but instead held my ground, meeting his gaze steadily.

"I thank you for your concern, King Bryce." He almost growled out the words, sounding anything but thankful. "I must ask you, however, to stay out of my personal affairs." I reminded myself I was speaking to the Supreme Ruler of Rheged. Even if we were on friendly terms, I had to be careful.

"Of course, Your Majesty. My apologies." I bowed my head. When I looked up again, he was walking away. I frowned, watching again the swish of his cloak as it trailed regally behind him. Though I was desperate to return home to Gaeson, for the first time I felt uneasy at the prospect of leaving.

How long would Queen Penarwen have left before she departed this world? I wondered. Would the relationship between King Owain and Elffin sour further with her dead, especially if King Owain sent for Princess Thaney? I felt as helpless as Sarah, caught in the middle of it all. My sister understood, however, that my priority had to be to get Imogen home. With that, I headed for the stables to see how Epos was doing. In the next day or two, we would at last make the journey back to

Gaeson.

***

“Do you see it, Immy? It’s home.” My heart threatened to burst from relief and exhilaration to see Gaeson still standing tall. Imogen, secured by my arms as I held the reins, raised her head. She had spoken less during our journey than our entire time in Caer Ligualid. I suspected she was far more anxious on the road.

“Home,” my daughter murmured. I rejoiced to hear some happiness entering her voice. “Will Mother be there?”

“Aye, she is waiting for us. Nearly there, old girl,” I said quietly to Epos. My loyal companion pricked up her ears in anticipation, sensing we were near Gaeson. After such an arduous journey, my faithful friend would be as happy as I was to be home.

Soon, we passed through the wooden barricade and arrived outside the portcullis. The guard from atop the wall gave a loud shout. The corner of my mouth turned as I raised a hand to wave at him. The metal bars with their cruelly extended points slowly extended upwards until they clinked into position. I was very thankful I was now wearing Caer Ligualid armour and would not be mistaken for the enemy.

“Here we are, Immy.” We entered the courtyard. The news of our return was spreading fast, with people already filling the courtyard.

Suddenly, the palace hall doors swung open. There she was, my queen, her gaze wide and raw with emotion. It seemed maintaining her royal composure was as low on her priorities as it was on mine.

“Mother!” My child’s cry was so full of feeling, my heart almost undid right there in the courtyard. I forced myself to keep a little dignity, rather than falling apart in front of the crowd. Gently I reached Imogen and lowered her to the floor.

Evelyn walked slowly, almost uncertainly, down the palace steps. I patted Epos’ neck before a stable boy came and took her away, but my eyes remained fixed on my wife. A few feet away, Evelyn stopped and outstretched her hand.

“Imogen.” My breath caught in my throat as my wife’s voice cracked. It was as if all of Evelyn’s hope and despair, all her soul, all that she was and ever would be, was declared in that one broken word.

“Mother.” This time Imogen was barely audible. The crowd had fallen so silent, however, that I imagined her whisper reaching all the way around the courtyard of stone. In that moment, it was as if a key had unlocked something deep inside of her.

“Mother!” Immy cried out again, breaking into a run. Evelyn just had time to stoop and open her arms before daughter ran into mother. The scene of them finally reuniting was almost more than my battered heart could bear. My vision grew misty, but I blinked the moisture away.

The crowd, standing thick around the edges of the square, began to cheer. I stayed where I was, awaiting my queen’s invitation. I did not have to tarry long as Evelyn straightened. The threat of tears was even larger as a broad grin cracked my Evelyn’s features. At last, I knew my vow was fulfilled. Not only was my daughter home safe, but at last I had seen my wife smile again.

“King Bryce,” Evelyn greeted a little more formally, but joy sparkled through her words. She dipped her head to me. “It is very good to see you well, my husband.”

“Queen Evelyn.” I half-bent into a small bow, only feet away from her. I straightened, once more finding the joy and love in her eyes. Right then, I knew I could not keep to formalities any longer. Careless of the watching crowds, I crossed the gap between us and captured her mouth.

The people went wild, but I hardly heard them, fully taken with the taste of my wife’s kiss. Her hand rested on my cheek. Ere long we broke apart, but then Evelyn bent her head to rest against my neck. One arm slipped around Imogen’s shoulders, the other around my wife’s waist.

“My boy from the snow,” Evelyn murmured into my flesh. The three of us clung together for a few moments, as though nothing in this world could ever break us apart again. Presently, I realised our daughter was trembling. Evelyn noticed at the same time, stepping back from us.

“I shall take her inside,” she said. I nodded. “Come on, my darling.” Gently, my queen led Immy away from the courtyard, where the crowed still cheered.

“Thank you,” I called loudly, raising my arm. Almost instantly, the noise of the people died away. “It is joyous indeed, for the princess and I to be home amongst you once more.” My sentence was greeted by another round of applause.

"However, my daughter has been through a very great ordeal." At this, the people of Gaeson were quieter than ever. Concern and sympathy crossed many of their faces. "Queen Evelyn and I appreciate your love and support, as always. I bid you now to resume your normal lives, in peace and quietness. That is all." I raised my hand again.

There was a general murmuring of support, but no deafening cheers. My people understood the need for sensitivity. As the crowd began to disperse, I turned towards the palace.

I strode through the main double-doors, Evelyn's court officials were leaving out of the side doors. My queen stood near her throne at the far end of the chamber, arms comfortingly wrapped around our daughter. I took a single step in their direction.

"Your Majesties." As the double doors swung again, I turned around, already beaming at two voices I knew and loved.

"It is good to see you and the princess. Forgive the intrusion—" I cut off John's formal speech by stepping close to them and throwing an arm around each of them with a joyful laugh.

"No intrusion at all, my friends. You know that." I smiled again as I stepped back. "Look who it is, Immy!" At her name being mentioned, Imogen peered around Evelyn's skirts.

"It's lovely to have you home safe with us, my lady." John's eyes crinkled, looking upon her with much tenderness. I knew I had never loved my friends more than at this moment.

"Hello, Uncle John, Aunt Aife," Imogen managed to mumble. Evelyn lowered a hand, stroking our child's honey-golden hair briefly.

"No doubt you'll be tired, love. Perhaps you'd like to go rest a while before dinner? I'll stay with you," she said firmly. "I'll leave John and Aife to report to you," she told me. I nodded.

"Aye, please, Mother," Imogen said. She looked very relieved at the prospect of leaving people, even if it was only John and Aife. We had just arrived, I told myself. No doubt Imogen found being back here overwhelming.

"It's a joy to see you are both well," I said, turning back to my old friends as Evelyn gently led Imogen out of the throne room, two guards treading silently behind them.

"Thank you, sire." Aife inclined her head. "It is good to see you in good health as well, my lord. How is Her Highness doing?" Her tone sobered a little. I sighed.

"Physically, she has already recovered a lot, thanks to our stay in Caer Ligualid, but she seems a shadow of her former self." Worry began to work its way even deeper into my bones with the thought. I folded my arms, glancing to the spot where my wife and child had disappeared.

"She has been through a lot, as you told the crowds," John muttered, drawing my gaze back to him. "She may well return to her old self now you are home."

"Aye, I hope so." I dropped my arms as I turned back to them. "Thank you, for escorting our queen home and defending Gaeson. What do you have to report? Does Lord Melvyn live?" In my delight in seeing Evelyn, I had not even asked about this yet. Both of them straightened a little as our talk became more formal.

"Aye, my king, but barely," John returned. I nodded, pleased that Gaeson's steward still breathed. "King Morgant came here with a thousand men," he reported. "We expected the force to be bigger, but he planned to take us by surprise, with our queen away and our steward dead."

"Our captain and chief archer would have been away, too," I pointed out. "We may well have been thrown into confusion and chaos, if not for Cara's warning."

"What happened to Cara, sire?" John asked. "I take it she did lead you to the Bernician village? Could her word be trusted, in the end?"

"Aye," I answered immediately. "I never would have found Imogen without her. She was injured," I told them. "On a hill just outside the village. She shot down several soldiers, allowing me to escape." The image of our hands gripping in the snow, slick with her blood that turned the snow crimson, thrust itself into my mind.

"When I came back that way with Imogen, she was gone. I don't know where Cara went, or if she even survived," I admitted heavily.

"You had no choice, my lord." Aife was quick to confirm what I kept telling myself. "You might never have brought the princess back to us otherwise."

"I know." I rubbed weary hands over my eyes. "There's something else, too." In everything that had happened, I had almost forgotten to tell them. "Cara was Bredon's daughter."

"What?" John and Aife both looked stunned. I gave them a rueful smile, remembering my similar reaction. "Cara is the daughter of Captain Bredon?" John repeated. I nodded. He gave a low whistle.

"Bredon didn't want anyone to know the connection," I said. "What has happened in the days after the raid?" I stretched my hands up, then dropped them back to my sides. "How lies the land?"

"I led a patrol yesterday, sire," Aife answered. "We travelled as far north as the lake and monitored the start of the roads to Klumeck and Caer Ligualid. There was nothing."

"Praise be to God." Relief flowed through my veins here that King Morgant was not on the horizon. We had time to strengthen our defences. "For now," I ordered John, "make sure our army rests and recovers its strength. You never know when we might need it. Keep up the archery drills," I directed Aife.

"Aye, my lord." Aife inclined her head. "Make sure you are also among the rested, brother," she added, as the three of us left the palace hall. I smirked — my friend knew me so well. I was pleased indeed to be back in Gaeson after these two hellish weeks away. As the three of us settled into easy conversation, I prayed peace could last a little longer before war's shadow reached us.

Chapter Eleven

Four months later

When at last the news of war came, it reached us on a day like any other. I was out on the back fields of Gaeson, behind the stables. Imogen played with Alena and Ruth, Rachel's daughters. It was a welcome break after a morning of council meetings and other duties.

My frown burrowed deeper as my I watched Imogen. Of course, she was not really playing. She stood and watched to the side, fidgeting with her hands. The two sisters were far too old to be playing little children's games, so it was entirely for Imogen's benefit, to help her try to interact with the world around her again. Occasionally, Alena and Ruth would succeed in engaging her. A small smile would break across my daughter's features, but she remained withdrawn.

"Your Majesty." I gave a quick nod to John as he came to stand beside me. He moved to lean against the wall. "How is her Highness today?" he asked quietly.

"She has recovered much since she arrived back in Gaeson," I said, then sighed. "I sometimes wonder whether she will ever be as she was. It's hard to see the lingering harm."

"I'm sorry, Daniel," John murmured from beside me. "We must pray that in time, she will recover fully. Princess Imogen is strong," he said.

"Aye, that she is." The thread of fierceness in my voice surprised me. "She has her mother's spirit. Every day I see her smile a little more or speak a little freer. We simply have to take each day as it is." John nodded, briefly touching my shoulder.

The sound of the horn blasted through the air. The peace and quiet Imogen craved cracked like an egg. I leapt back from the low wall, looking around. John already had one hand on the hilt of the sword.

"Girls, hurry!" I shouted, but they were already running towards me. The five of us raced back to the castle. The horn had only been a short blast, which gave me hope, for a longer blast signalled that the enemy was at our gates. Perhaps our people would not even have to go to the caves. What could have caused such commotion?

"You, there!" I skidded to a halt as we came upon two guards nearby. "Escort Her Highness and her friends to her chamber and stand guard outside. Take them to the caves if the order comes."

"At once, Your Majesty," he answered, bending his head. I barely had time to give my daughter's hand a gentle squeeze before the three of them were off, the guards' boots thudding either side of them.

"Your Majesty!" I turned to see Aife running towards us as we rounded the corner, sprinting towards the courtyard. "My lord." She dipped her head as she fell into step beside us. "Apparently there is someone at the gate, sire," she muttered as we ran. "Dressed in Bernician armour."

"On their own?" I frowned as we pounded across the courtyard. The soldiers were clamouring in front, trying to see who it was. "Move aside!" I roared. They split immediately, giving me a clear path to the portcullis.

"Stand guard. Do not fire unless I give the order." I stepped up to the metal bars to the lone soldier, standing beside their horse. Not only that, but they were clutching their reins as if that were the only thing to keep them upright. The other hand was pressed against their side. Whoever they were was barely conscious, not in any condition to fight. Peering closer, I recognised the soldier's eyes, blinking rapidly as they tried to keep a hold of the world.

"Cara!" The soldiers behind me gasped at my shocked cry. "Raise the portcullis!" As the metal spikes swiftly retracted, I ducked my head under.

"Someone, get the surgeon!" I took hold of her shoulders, helping her to dismount before she fell. "Cara," I murmured. Someone took the horse away. "Can you hear me?"

"My king," she whispered. I peeled off her helmet. Her hand still clutched her abdomen. I realised her bloodied hands grasped the tip of an arrow. Cara's mouth moved, her eyes wild and urgent — but no sounds came out.

"Stay with me," I instructed her gently. "Help's coming." I pressed my hand to her wound to try to stop the bleeding. Cara's countenance was pale and a sheen of sweat covered her. My other hand touched her forehead — she was hot to the touch. It was a miracle she had reached our gate alive.

"Cara!" The strangled cry came from Ewan, cracking through the quiet as palpably as the horn had. I glanced up at him as he pushed his way through the lines of soldiers. He had not seen her in four years, but from the agony tangible on his face, I knew he loved her still.

"Ewan…" Cara breathed. Her face was haggard, torn in pain, as she raised one blood smeared hand towards him. Ewan grasped it as he fell to the ground beside her.

"Sire," she rasped, turning back to me. "I bring warning. It's starting, my lord." She panted the words that were torture to speak. "He's… he's coming." Her eyes rolled to the back of her head.

"Cara," Ewan muttered brokenly, one hand at her shoulder as she lost consciousness. For a moment he looked at me, heartbreak plain on his features. His hand desperately moved to the tip of the arrow, still embedded deep into her flesh.

"Do not touch that arrow!" I looked up to see Leigh running past the soldiers. "Bring the stretcher!" he called out behind him, before kneeling between Ewan and me.

"Do not remove that arrow." His voice came low and urgent. "If we remove it, we may cause more damage," he said rapidly. "For all we know, it's what's keeping her alive." His hand moved to her forehead and cursed. Two soldiers arrived, carrying a stretcher.

"Put it down here," Leigh commanded simply. I straightened, but Ewan remained still, bent over her body. "Ewan," Leigh said calmly. "The best thing to do is to get her to the surgery. Help me." Ewan nodded, his face a picture of anguish. Wordlessly, as the surgeon took hold of her ankles, Ewan helped her onto the stretcher.

"Careful," Leigh muttered, as the two soldiers lifted Cara from the floor. "My lord." The surgeon nodded to me almost as an afterthought before he was off, issuing the instructions to the soldiers as he went. I glanced back to Ewan, the despair all to evident on his face.

"Leigh will do his very best." What else could I say, while Cara still had the arrow tip stuck in her side? I clapped a hand on his shoulder. "Come on." The two of us crossed back into the courtyard.

“Lower the portcullis!” I ordered. “Back to your duties,” I said to the soldiers still surveying the scene. At my order, the soldiers saluted and began to disperse.

“Captain, double the watch, for the time being,” I called to John, as the clunking metal of descending metal spikes sounded. “Aife, head to the highest rampart. See if she was followed.”

“My lord!” they both chorused. Ewan and I rushed to the surgery, ignoring the soldiers heading back to their tasks. One of Leigh’s hands was waiting for us.

“Your Majesty.” She gave a bow. “Leigh is currently operating. We cannot admit anyone, lest we give her more sickness.”

“The wound is not clean, then.” I folded my arms. “Not by the look of that fever.” At this Ewan turned away, running a hand distractedly through his hair. I did not tell him that a little blood now smeared his short, dark curls.

“We’ll wait here. Go back and assist Leigh,” I ordered to the physician’s assistant, knowing there was nothing more we could do. She bowed her head and dashed back into the surgery.

I leant against the wall, keeping an eye on the sun through the open window. Though the golden orb did not lower much in the sky, it felt like we were standing outside Leigh’s surgery for hours. Ewan could have worn out the floor with his pacing, though it was made of stone.

At last, Leigh opened the door to his surgery. Ewan whirled around to face him. The physician’s features were urgent. His hands held a bit of cloth, with his fingers, stained crimson.

“Cara still lives,” Leigh said simply. Ewan almost staggered backwards in relief. “She breathes easier, but she won’t wake for some time. I managed to remove the arrow tip.” He began to cleanse his hands with the cloth as he spoke. “A piece of wood near the tip splintered off and remains in her body. That is why she has been touched with sickness.”

“What can we do?” Ewan burst out desperately. Leigh glanced to him as he rubbed his hands on the cloth, sympathy set heavily on his features.

“Pray,” Leigh answered simply. “Pray that the splinter has remained intact, that I am able to retrieve it cleanly and that she will recover. Sire.”

He gave me a swift nod before disappearing again. Ewan inhaled sharply, his hands roving through his hair again. I turned to see John running towards us.

"I've organised the extra watch, my lord." I nodded, then briefly told my captain of Cara's condition. "What did Cara say, sire? It looked like she was telling you something."

"She said that it is starting." I repeated the words lodged in my brain. "That the war is coming." Though I was anxious to hear more from Cara, the warning itself was obvious. "King Morgant and King Ethelfrith must be on the move," I said.

"I must report to Her Majesty." I turned to Ewan. "Don't let anyone except Leigh's hands enter until he says. Let us know if anything changes."

"Be sure to keep Cara's warning to yourself," John said to Ewan. I nodded. The last thing we needed was the rumour of war spreading to every citizen. "We'll be praying for her," John muttered.

"Aye, thank you, sire, Your Majesty." Ewan dipped his head to both of us, revealing the sheen of sweat plastered atop his forehead.

As we left him, we heard his boots thudding as he resumed pacing outside the surgery. My heart tightened, suddenly remembering how helpless I had felt when the interrogator had pierced Evelyn's throat, nearly seven years ago now. Little else matched the despair of a loved one's unknown fate.

"My lord King Bryce, Captain." Our queen greeted us formally as we entered the palace hall, after a guard announced us. John bowed low, whilst Evelyn and I inclined our heads to one another.

"We shall pause the court session here." At our queen's simple command, the councillors stood. They rose as one and departed the chamber.

"The palace guards told me it was Cara at the gate," Evelyn said, walking down the steps to meet us in the middle of the throne room. "How is she?"

"Alive, for now," I answered quickly. "Leigh is operating. He thinks he can save her." Absently, I noticed the blood from Cara's side still stained my hands.

"We must pray for her recovery," Evelyn said swiftly. I rubbed my hands together, but the crimson ingrained in my skin would not easily shift. “How does she come to be here?”

“I don’t know,” I admitted. “She came with a warning, but she only said ‘the war is starting’ before she fell out of consciousness. She was wearing Bernician armour,” I said. “I can only assume the Bernicians captured her after I last saw her.”

“No doubt this is King Morgant’s work,” my wife said darkly. “She must have escaped his clutches, but received a fresh arrow in the process,” she speculated. I nodded.

“The first action is to find out where King Morgant and King Ethelfrith are,” she continued. “If they are amassing their armies, King Owain will have received word of it. I will write to him.” We had not heard much from King Owain in recent weeks, since the passing of Queen Penarwen last month.

“In the meantime, my lady.” John gave another quick bend of his head. “Many soldiers were at the gate when Cara returned. They have gone back to their duties, but doubtless they are discussing it.”

“You can hardly blame them,” I said with a soft snort. “A former warrior-turned-traitor appears at our gates after four years’ disappearance. It is bound to be of interest.”

“Indeed, sire,” John replied, smirking slightly. “What would you like me to tell them?” He glanced between us.

“King Bryce and you are the only ones who heard Cara’s warning.” Evelyn’s brow knit deeper. “Tell the army only that Cara risked her life to save Princess Imogen. We thought she died in battle, but now we assume she was captured by the enemy, then escaped. This is all we know anyway,” she pointed out. “There is no need to add fuel to aimless gossip.”

“At once, Your Majesty.” John dipped his head. “Ewan also knows, but he will keep Cara’s words to himself. I also heard from Aife,” he said. “She says there are no signs of the enemy.”

“Good.” I nodded. “You best go back, love,” I said to Evelyn. For a moment, she simply met my eyes. It seemed only yesterday that Imogen and I had come home. The three of us were only just getting used to living our lives in peace again. We searched the other’s gaze, our countenances conveying what we had no time to say aloud.

“Aye,” Evelyn said slowly, breaking the moment. “The councillors will be wanting to resume the day.” She smiled wryly. Dealing with court business was hardly her favourite task.

“Your Majesty.” John bowed low as Evelyn nodded to the guards to summon back the officials. “I sent a few of the guards to the treelines, sire, to see if they can spot Bernician tracks, in case the enemy are hiding out of sight.” Already as we left, we could hear the murmured talk of the councillors as they re-entered the grand chamber.

“Very good. How goes the daily training?” I asked, as we stepped back out into the courtyard. A little rain was falling. A palace servant was bent near the portcullis, mopping up Cara’s blood.

“Well, my lord.” My captain folded his arms as he turned to me. “They practice three times a day, with particular focus on combat and archery training. All of us knew war was never far away.” His tone grew heavier. “Do you have any change of orders for the army, sire?”

“No, not until we know more,” I replied thoughtfully. “Any change of routine would just fuel their gossip further. There is nothing else for now,” I told him now. “Only let me know the moment surgery finishes. That’s all brother.”

“My king.” John gave a final dip of his head. I stared after him a moment, as he strode away to resume his duties. The rain fell heavier now. The cobbles of the courtyard glistened, reflecting water and light back up to the sky. My open cloak billowed about my shoulders in the wind, as the cool breeze whipped my cheeks. I rose my head to the dreary sky, praying God would spare Cara’s life.

Then, with little else to do to distract myself from waiting until we heard from Leigh, I left the courtyard and took the winding path around the castle, heading towards the stables. A small smile hovered at my face, as I spied the library window that I’d once helped Evelyn climb through, all those years ago.

My shoulders relaxed as I approached the main doors, the comforting musty aroma already reaching my nostrils. I paused in the threshold, catching sight of Aife and my daughter. Imogen stood on a high stool, braiding Epos’ hair.

“Good day, Your Majesty,” Aife greeted, already aware of my presence. She looked up, her hand stilling from brushing my mare’s coat.

“Aife.” I gave her a quick smile as I approached them. “Do you not have a lesson now, my daughter?” Imogen turned to me, a sheepish shy smile breaking through her features.

“After I went to the ramparts, I thought some time in the stables would do her good,” Aife said. I nodded, smiling at the slight sparkle in Imogen’s eyes as she tended to Epos.

It gave me hope, reminding me of the unabated joy she had once had. A lifetime ago, I had wondered whether to start rebuking her for the way she would clap and run about, or barrel into my arms. What I wouldn’t give now for such wild, innocent affection, untouched by pain and fear.

“We came to see how Epos was,” Imogen said, as I crossed the straw-laden floor to them. I slipped an arm around her, planting a kiss to the top of her head. Epos’ ears twitched in enthusiasm as my free hand came to rustle her mane, carefully avoiding Immy’s neat plaits.

“A fine idea.” I was glad Aife had taken Imogen away from the castle at such a time. She had been in her chamber when Cara returned, but the rushing about of the soldiers and servants would have distressed her. It was far better for her to be here, in Epos’ soothing presence.

“Aife taught me how.” Immy nodded towards where the hair at Epos’ mane had been plaited into braids. The shy smile played at my daughter’s mouth again.

“They look wonderful, love.” My hand roved gently over the white patch on Epos’ forehead, lighter than the rest of her tan, the colour of parchment. My horse had been well tended since our return, for her coat was as soft to the touch as it ever had been.

“Is Cara better yet?” My eyes jerked to my daughter at her sudden question. “I heard one of the servants talk about it as we went to the stables.”

“I told Her Highness that Cara had come back today, but she was unwell, so Leigh is tending to her,” Aife said quickly.

“Aye, Leigh is still looking after her,” I answered carefully. I did not want to deceive my daughter, but I did not want to distress her either. It seemed I could never get this balance right.

“I hope she gets better.” Immy’s tone was quiet and thoughtful, her hand once more on Epos’ neck. “She was kind to me.” I raised a hand to the top of my daughter's golden honey hair.

"I know." I knew that without Cara, I probably never would have found Imogen in that village. I still didn't know what King Morgant's vile scheme had been. For all I knew, I might never have seen my daughter again. I swallowed hard, squashing the shame that I had once called Cara my enemy. I could not have been more wrong. She had made mistakes, aye, but she had proven herself to be one of us, once and for all. I prayed my friend would survive, so I could thank her for all she had done.

***

"Your Majesty." I leapt up to my feet at the sound of Leigh's voice as he rapped on the door. I raced across the room, flinging the door wide to admit him. At once my eyes searched his in unspoken question.

"She lives, sire," Leigh revealed at once, a small smile flashing quickly across his weary face. I sighed in relief, stepping back from the threshold. "I thought you would want to know right away."

"You thought right." I gestured him into my study chamber. "Well done, my friend. Come in and sit down. Is she awake yet?" I turned to fetch the flagon of mead I kept under the desk.

"She awoke for a few moments, my lord, before falling into slumber again. I retrieved the splinter of wood," he murmured, sinking gratefully into the chair opposite mine. As he roved a hand through his dark hair, I noticed the sheen of sweat upon his forehead.

"When I matched it with what was left from the arrow at her side, it seemed to be all of it." Relief ran clear through his words. "I've sown up the wound and hopefully it should heal cleanly. When she wakes again," he said, "I pray the sickness will have left her."

"Well done," I told him again. "Here, have a drink." I poured him a generous measure of the mead. "You look like you need it."

"Aye, I will, thank you, my lord," he replied, taking the goblet. "Surgery is thirsty work." He smirked as he lifted the mead to his mouth and took a long drink.

"I don't suppose she said anything while she was awake?" I asked urgently. Leigh shook his head, lowering the goblet again.

“Nothing of any great significance. She seemed to mumble something, but it was mostly incoherent.” Leigh’s frown deepened. “John happened to come by the surgery shortly after she woke, sire, just before I came to you. He asked me the same question.” He took another sip of the mead.

“I’m guessing she holds vital information about the Bernicians,” he said. “But I insist you wait until the morning before trying to speak with her. She is still very weak.”

“Of course.” I took my first taste of mead. “I doubt one night should make much difference, in any case.” I sighed. “Cara came to warn us that war may come upon us sooner than we think. The queen will send a message to King Owain at dawn, to see what word there is of Bernicia.”

“I see, sire.” He supped a little more of the honeyed tonic. “I think you do right not to tell Gaeson this yet. It may be weeks, even months, until the call for battle finally arrives.”

“Aye. There will be an announcement from the balcony when the time comes.” I drummed my free hand absently on the desk for a moment. “I especially do not wish to disturb Imogen, whilst she is still recovering.” I glanced up at him.

“I quite understand, sire.” Leigh inclined his head with a reassuring smile. “Her spirit is strong. I am pleased with her progress.” A small smile crossed my own face, but it did not touch the worry that probably still marked my face. “The princess is doing remarkably well, Daniel.” His tone was gentle as he dropped my title. “It may be a long road yet, but I see no reason why she will not be as full of life and joy as she ever was.” I only nodded, my throat suddenly tight.

“If you’ll excuse me, sire.” He stood, swallowing the dregs of his mead. “I think I will check on Cara and one or two of my other patients, before retiring.”

“Thank you, Leigh. I shall see if Cara is strong enough to speak in the morning.” I also departed my study chamber, bidding him a goodnight in the corridor outside. I headed for my chambers, with the delicate taste of mead still on my tongue. I prayed Cara would be well enough to tell us what she knew when the dawn came.

***

"My lord." I froze at the tired heaviness at Leigh's voice when I reached the surgery doors, almost as soon as dawn broke. I breathed again, however, when I saw the small smile playing on his features. "It was a long night, sire, but Cara's sickness is all but gone."

"Your Majesty," Ewan panted, skidding to a halt beside me. Leigh broke into a grin, clapping his hand onto his shoulder.

"Cara will recover well, as far as I know." The surgeon's words were warm. Ewan exhaled in relief, as if he had not taken a full breath since her return yesterday. Quite possibly, he hadn't. "The slumber has done her much good. I believe the wound will heal cleanly." Ewan's grin was almost giddy.

"Cara is very weak, my lord." Leigh inclined his head to me again. "However, she is awake for the moment. I believe you may speak to her, for a time."

"Good. I am sure it is not in your nature to spread idle rumours," I said, turning to Ewan. "As you know, Cara may well have vital information about the enemy. Should she speak of war, it must not leave this surgery."

"Aye, my lord, I quite understand." Ewan bent his head swiftly. The two of us followed Leigh into a smaller ward of the surgery.

"Your Majesty." Cara rasped her greeting, her eyes widening a little as she saw me. She tried to sit up in the bed, but I raised a hand to stop her.

"Rest, please, do not trouble yourself." Cara lay back. She breathed quick and shallow. Her gaze, though a little pained, was clear. I sat in the chair near the end of her bed. "It is good to see you, Cara," I told her warmly. "How do you feel?"

"I feel a little weak, my lord. I am only glad to find myself alive," she muttered wryly. Then her eyes flickered to the man who had continued to love her these last four years. "Ewan." His name was a whisper as she outstretched her hand to his.

"Cara." Her name on his lips was laboured, full of feeling. He reached forwards to take her hand. The two of them said nothing else, the heavy quietness almost tangible between them.

"I do not wish to cause you any distress," I began. "I wondered, if you could tell us about the warning you gave us."

"Aye, my lord." Cara's gaze returned to mine. Ewan dropped his hand from hers, stepping back. The spell between them was broken again, for now.

"What do you know?" I sat forward a little. "Take your time, please," I said, as she made to sit up again. Ewan helped her, rearranging the pillows behind her back.

"I overheard King Morgant talking, sire." Her voice was calmer as the pain subsided a little. "Well, he made no effort to lower his voice," she said. "I believe he meant to mock me with his plans for Rheged. I do not believe he would have been as free with his tongue had he known I would escape."

"Likely not," I murmured. Cara shifted a little, then winced and clutched her side. I wondered if the fever leaving her brought the pain into sharper focus.

"He and King Ethelfrith are readying their armies for Catraeth, sire," Cara said, words falling swiftly now. "That is where the final battle will take place. Not only that, my lord, but King Morgant said he and King Ethelfrith have joined with Deira. They are fighting as one."

"I see." Mouth dry, I sat back a little in my chair. Deira was an enemy Anglian kingdom to the south of Bernicia. Catraeth itself was a settlement deep within Deira, a few days' ride from Gaeson. My frown deepened. The armies of our enemies would be vast indeed. Could Rheged defeat the Angles, even if we were allied with Gododdin and Strathclyde?

Cara sank back a little further against the pillows and motioned Ewan to pass her some water. Though she was still in pain, the urgency had gone from her features. Her task of warning Rheged was done.

"What happened to you, Cara?" I asked quietly. "When I came back past that spot on the hill, you were gone."

"I ran out of arrows, that day in the snow," Cara muttered. "I managed to shoot several of those following you, sire." I nodded. Only a few Bernicians had pursued me into the trees.

"Three remained to capture me." She ground each syllable out, as if every word took extreme effort. "They took me back to that same village hall. Two guards were dead in the hallway, I think you had only just gone.

King Morgant came back to the village about an hour after you left. He was most displeased to find the princess gone." A wry smile crossed her face.

"King Morgant came back so soon?" I echoed, sitting back again. It sounded like the three guards escorting Cara would have come upon me and Immy only minutes later. We would have been captured by King Morgant also — we could well have died in that village.

"King Morgant had me beaten," Cara said flatly. "I was kept in that village hall in the dark for…" she frowned. "I lost track of the days. I think it was weeks, perhaps months."

"I'm so sorry," I rasped. In effect, she had traded places with Imogen. One hostage for another. Cara shook her head.

"You could have done nothing else, my lord. I was pleased to serve you. I—" Pain cut off her words as she shifted again. "At first, I thought I might die from the wound in my side, but they treated me just enough to keep me alive. King Morgant said I had betrayed Bernicia," Cara went on. I glanced to Ewan. His eyes were narrow, his countenance hardened in a silent broth of rage and pain.

"He always said he would kill me, but that it would be slow," Cara said. "He enjoyed watching me lose sense of time and place. King Morgant told me he would keep me alive just long enough to see Rheged fall apart. I nearly lost my mind, but the hope of coming home to warn you kept me alive."

"I'm so sorry, Cara," I muttered again. I remembered that dank, dark cell with the interrogator all those years ago, when King Reghan had ordered me executed. I was almost driven to despair then, but that was only one night. This was months.

"One day, one of my guards came in drunk." Her voice came a little stronger now. "I talked him into giving me some of his skin of wine. I don't believe he thought I would be strong enough to be a threat. When he came near, I struck him and overpowered him." She took a little more water.

"Then you escaped," I guessed, as she caught her breath again. My friend nodded and then winced, as if the very movement caused her pain. "How did you get your injury?" I asked her now.

"I was on the road to Gaeson, my lord, when I came across a

Bernician patrol. I think they were looking for me and spying out the land. My horse rode like the wind, but it was not fast enough to lose them. Many arrows flew past me.

"I thought I would die when this one pierced me. When I realised it would not kill me quickly, I made for Gaeson. It was all I could do to stay conscious upon my horse," she ended.

"We thank God you did," I replied. Ewan nodded, reaching to take hold of her hand again. "Is there anything else you can tell me?" I prompted. Cara shook her head a little.

"Very well," I said. "Thank you for all you have told me." I reached forward to take her hand. "Thank you for all you have risked, Cara. It is because of you my daughter is still alive. Any past crimes against you are pardoned," I told her earnestly. "You are part of Rheged. Welcome home." She managed to smile, despite the pain in her features.

"Thank you, my king," Cara rasped. Then she glanced to Ewan. "I need to rest, but we will talk again soon."

"Of course. There is no rush," he told her quietly. We stood. I let go of her hand, but Ewan bent, pressing a kiss quietly to her palm. Ewan and I departed the infirmary together. After telling him to go and rest before he resumed his duties, I leant my head against the wall. I listened to Ewan's boots fading in the distance. The cold of the stone helped to calm my whirling thoughts.

I had no reason to doubt any of Cara's account, given all she had risked in what she had done for my daughter and coming back to warn us. My mouth went dry again. I could hardly imagine the size of the force that could be waiting for us. Even with our own alliances, this could be the beginning of the end for Gaeson, even for Rheged itself.

Still, even if defeat were inevitable, even if we were doomed, we would still fight this war with all we had. It would not do to simply loiter in this corridor. With that thought, I swiftly made way to report to Evelyn. The time to prepare for war had come upon us at last.

Chapter Twelve

"Your Majesty!" One of the palace guards dropped into a swift bow at the threshold of my study chambers. Her helmet was tucked under one arm and her forehead glistened a little with sweat underneath her blonde plaits. "Her Majesty requests your presence in the throne room, my lord."

"Very well." From the grim urgency in her features and the quickness of her breath, I knew at once it was not good news. We rushed to the palace hall.

"Queen Evelyn." My greeting was formal and swift as I burst into the throne room. Imogen, Alena, and Ruth were playing quietly in the corner. Absently, I remembered Immy's morning governess had been taken ill the night before. I flashed my daughter a quick smile as I approached the throne, then I focused my gaze straight ahead of me.

"What news, my lady?" The question sprang from my lips as I bent my head to her. Evelyn stepped clear from the senior advisors of her court as she dipped her head back to me. I guessed the letter in her hand had just arrived, not long before my queen was to meet with her court.

"King Bryce." My wife nodded to me. "I have just received word from King Owain." Her voice was as sober as her countenance.

"Your Majesties." Just then there were footsteps as John rushed into the chamber, bowing to us. Evelyn's eyes were cold as her gaze flickered down to the parchment in her hands.

"King Owain confirms Cara's reports," our queen said heavily. "Prince Pasgent's scouts followed King Morgant's troops heading towards the Deiran border."

"So, the Bernicians are indeed amassing at Catraeth," I murmured, my features hardening. The reckoning of Rheged had come at last. It was time to face our final destiny, whatever that may be.

"King Owain says King Ethelfrith has written to him," Evelyn continued. "A challenge for Rheged to meet them in Catraeth." She looked up darkly from her letter. "We must prepare for war." She sighed then, her eyes clouding.

"However, King Owain also writes of another matter." Her tone was carefully even. I wondered if Evelyn was hiding disapproval. "It seems that after the death of Queen Penarwen, King Owain sent for Princess Thaney. He invites us to their wedding next month."

"So soon?" My eyes widened. His late wife was still so fresh in the ground. "I suppose he wishes to wed her and meet his child, before we face the enemy."

"Indeed," Evelyn muttered. "He writes that the child was born a few days after she arrived. They have a son, named Kentigern," she said. "King Owain's wedding is to take place three weeks before we march to Catraeth."

I inhaled sharply, then forced the air to escape evenly through my nostrils. I knew this final stand was to be expected, but still the reality of it still stunned me somehow.

"There is a final note of good news regarding a war, which is no doubt another reason for a hasty wedding." I raised my eyebrows. Could there be a hopeful edge to such sombre tidings? "Gododdin is to march with Rheged."

"That is a comforting thought." I folded my arms. King Lot, Princess Thaney's father, must have forgiven King Owain for everything that had happened to his daughter. Either that, or he was tolerating his prospective son-in-law for the sake of peace across Briton. "What are your orders, my lady?"

"King Owain's strategy is that he and the force from Gododdin will travel southeast," my queen answered. "We will join them on the road and march to war. Prepare the army, Captain," Evelyn commanded, shifting her gaze to John. "I will make an announcement soon to the people but until then, I trust you to use your discretion. There is still no need for undue panic."

"Very good, Your Majesty." John bowed. "I will await my lady's announcement. My lord," he directed to me, before inclining his head once more to us.

"We will take a small escort for the wedding, in case any of King Morgant's raids attack us on the road," Evelyn said now, as John left the throne room. "I'm sure his dark shadow is still stretched over Rheged, even as he goes to Catraeth." She sighed, meeting my eyes. "We will then return home and then three weeks later, depart for war," she said grimly.

We were alone, save the two guards standing next to the door and Rachel's daughters playing quietly in the far corner with Imogen. Evelyn let her guard drop a little, enough to show the resignation playing on her face. I took a step closer, raising my hand briefly to her curls. I was sure that my expression mirrored hers.

"You know what I would say," I told her quietly. "For the sake of Gaeson as well as for Imogen." Evelyn only nodded. In previous battles, I had gone to war whilst Evelyn remained behind to lead the defence of our people and our home.

As with all things, though, the final choice was up to her. The quiet drew out until we were almost drowning in it. My fingers traced the length of her loose raven locks.

"I will do whatever my queen commands," I murmured. My hand dropped limply back to my side. Evelyn regarded me a moment longer before nodding.

"Very well." My wife sighed, as though taking in all the air in this grand chamber. Then her gaze hardened slightly as the shield slid further down her features.

"King Bryce of Klumeck," Evelyn said formally. "The Bernicians call for war. Rheged is to march against them at Catraeth. As commander of our army, I must ask you to lead them into battle on that fateful day. Will you do this?" She already knew my answer. I gazed at this strong, wise woman whom I had always loved.

"Aye, my lady," I returned, bowing my head. With my head still bent, I reached to take her hand and swiftly kissed it. As I straightened, I saw the merest hint of sorrow flickering in her eyes.

"So be it." Evelyn took a deep breath. "I will stay here to defend our walls and our home. Our good Lord knows we are never more vulnerable to raids than when most of our army has gone." I nodded slowly, both helpless in the face of inevitability. It was simply the way of war.

"Wait for me, Ruth!" Both of us swivelled round, snapped out of sadness by the most glorious sound. One I feared I would never hear again. Had it been my imagination? No, there it was again. Immy was giggling, laughing along with Rachel's two daughters.

I broke into a wide grin. I glanced back to Evelyn to see a large smile upon her features. I certainly would not have expected such happiness, so soon after hearing I would be marching off to war.

"I must inform the council." Any levity abruptly disappeared, vanishing as quickly as it had arisen. "Then I must plan how to announce it to our people."

"Aye, of course." I nodded. "I'll take Imogen to her next governess, then I'll return in time for the meeting." Evelyn gave a small smile. "Come on, Immy love," I called, turning away from my wife.

"Must I stop? Aye, Father," she added quickly, as I raised an eyebrow. I quashed a hint of sadness that I had to halt her play when she was enjoying herself so much, for the first time in so long. Immy ran to take my hand. We began to leave the palace hall, Alena and Ruth walking behind us.

"Your Majesty, might I speak with you for a moment?" Just after we re-entered the courtyard, I turned to see Alena had stilled her steps, biting her lip.

"Of course. Just go on a bit further ahead, you two," I directed to the younger girls, not wanting them to overhear the conversation. "What is it, Alena?" I glanced back to her. Alena seemed to hesitate. "You heard," I guessed, in a quiet murmur.

"I didn't mean to, my lord," she said immediately. "Only, there was a moment where Imogen ran down the throne room with Ruth and…" Her voice trailed away. "Will we really go to war, sire?"

"Aye, sadly. I know you didn't mean to overhear such grim news," I assured her. "Please do not mention this to anyone." We resumed walking, following Ruth and Imogen as they turned down a corridor to another area of the castle. "Her Majesty will announce it to our people soon."

"Of course, my lord." Alena dipped her head as we walked. Then, as she straightened, I saw determination in her gaze. "Sire, I wanted to tell you… I think I wish to fight," she said at last. My eyebrows rose.

"I know how," Rachel's eldest daughter continued quickly. "Her Highness Princess Lynette taught me a few lessons before she left for Caer Ligualid and I have practised every day since. I considered enlisting last year, but I knew my mother needed my help with her trade. However, if we were to march to war… I wish to pledge my sword, my lord."

"I see." I folded my arms as we walked along Gaeson's corridors to Imogen's next governess. "I would not doubt your skill. I will not tell you not to, Alena. I am sure Gaeson — all Rheged — would be grateful to have your sword. However, I will say what the captain says to every recruit — be sure," I told her. "There is nothing like the reality of war. You should think about your mother, too," I murmured.

"My mother is also why I did not enlist last year, after I became of age," Alena admitted, inclining her head again. "I know she still grieves Joshua, my lord."

"Indeed." The image of his corpse suddenly came to mind. All the seven years since that dreadful day had not softened that sight. The sharpness of his pale skin against the blood that covered him, the terror struck in his gaze — it would stay with me till my grave. "Do you remember him much?"

"Aye, my lord," Alena answered. "He used to tell such terrible jokes." A small smile briefly crossed her features. "I know my mother would not wish for me to fight and that it would cause her pain if I did." A frown replaced her smile. "Still, sire, it feels right, to do battle in his name."

"Well, there's no rush," I said, as we approached the chamber where Imogen would have her mid-morning lessons. "Think upon the matter further. Is that all?"

"There was something else, sire…" She hesitated. Immy and Ruth were up ahead, waiting, as Alena came to a stop for a moment.

"I still remember the day you came to our old house, to tell my mother Joshua was dead." The words rushed out of her, with her face still cast to the ground. "I was only nine — it is only now, as an adult, I can fully understand how you saved our lives on his account." Alena raised her head again. The first sign of tears sparked in her eyes.

"I wanted to thank you, Your Majesty. You gave us our livelihood that day. Our business, my mother's health, the very house we live in… it is all due to your kindness. I will be grateful to you, my lord, until the day I die." She bent her head quickly to kiss my hand.

"You're most welcome, Alena," I told her, giving her a little smile as she straightened again. "It was the best I could do, for Joshua. He was afraid of battle, but… he was very brave, in the end."

"I think so, too," she murmured, sounding far away, then she quickly curtseyed. "Your Majesty." At my nod, she hurried away.

"Go on in, Imogen. Ruth, you had better catch up to your sister." Ruth's eyes widened, not realising Alena had already gone. She gave a slightly flustered curtsey before rushing off to join her sister.

"Enjoy your lesson, Immy," I bade my daughter, before she disappeared through the door. Alone in the corridor, I sighed as I made my way back to the throne room, restless with the memory of Joshua.

I needed some air, so I went out of a side door and took the slightly longer path through the castle gardens. How long would we remain here? I thought, for once yielding to my anxieties about war. Could we stand against Bernicia and Deira, even with the help of Gododdin? There must still be hope, I thought stubbornly. I passed by rows of neat hedges and trees, not far from where I had asked Evelyn for her hand in marriage, almost seven years ago now. We would cling to the hope of peace until the last.

***

"I thought I might find you up here." I nodded but did not turn around at the voice I loved so well. I continued to look down at the rest of Gaeson, staring at the home I was not at all sure I could protect.

"I knew you would," I said at last. Evelyn often knew my thoughts before I had them myself. It was two weeks later, the night before my queen and I were to journey to Caer Ligualid. I sensed her coming to stand beside me. The two of us stood there for a few moments in the summer breeze. My hands gripped the balcony wall tightly.

"Do you remember when we stood on this very balcony, seven years ago?" my wife asked now, as the sun continued to embrace us in its warmth. Her hand moved to rest atop one of mine.

"Every moment of it." I shifted my hand so that our fingers interlaced. Then I turned to her and tried to smile, but the expression didn't feel quite right.

That night was the second time King Cedric had led Klumeck's army against Gaeson's gates, long before I knew he was my uncle. I had come up here to find Captain Bredon, to question him about why we were fighting against them, when they should be our allies. It also marked the first time I had spoken to Evelyn since meeting her as a child.

"Later that night, you took me to the forest." Evelyn's voice sounded far away. "That's when I realised you were the boy I met in the snow. The next day you fell from that cliff. When I finally saw you again, alive, I knew I had already given you, my heart." My queen moved her hand from mine to place it upon my chest. "You will have my heart, always," she whispered.

"I know, love." I smiled fully this time, despite the ever-beckoning shroud of war. "You know you have mine also. I will keep it forever and cherish it," I said softly. "All the days of my life, so help me God." Evelyn broke into a true smile, her solemnity receding again.

"I'm pleased you remember your vows," she muttered. Her mouth lifted into a smirk. "Seven years, nearly, since we were wed." I glanced down to her left hand upon my chest, to the gold band around her finger. The metal had only slightly dulled with time.

"I will never forget that day, not for as long as I live," I told her, almost fiercely. Evelyn moved to rest her hand in the nape of my neck and I wound my arms around her.

"I know what you would promise me," she muttered into my skin, warming it with her breath. "That you will return, that we will see one another again. I pray to God you can keep your vow, as you have kept so many others."

"You know how much I will strive to." My voice was quiet and a little grim as I stepped back from her, turning to survey our homeland once more. "You will need to be ready, if we lose this fight."

"I know. King Morgant won't be satisfied, even if Rheged formally surrenders. He means to destroy us, doesn't he? Piece by piece. Kidnapping Imogen showed us that," she muttered bitterly. Her raven curls blew back a little with the wind.

"Aye. No doubt he has ordered raids to come in his stead." I shook my head, snorting softly through my nose. "It seems such folly to be going to Caer Ligualid tomorrow, with all that is about to befall us."

"Perhaps that's why King Owain is doing it now. None of us know who will return." Evelyn reached out to take my hand again. "He wishes to enjoy more time in the sun before the night comes." She sighed here, folding her arms, then glanced to me. "Is our army ready?"

"Aye. We have been preparing for war from the moment Imogen and I returned to Gaeson, as you know," I assured her. "I have regular reports from John on their training, especially of the recent recruits. They'll be ready," I said, almost forcefully. We could not afford for them not to be so. "Does King Owain say whether any other of the old alliances will stand?"

"I have not heard from him since his letter, so I only know of Gododdin and maybe Strathclyde," Evelyn answered, coming to lean on the balcony wall again. "I think the feud between King Rhydderch and King Gwollag is still ongoing," she said. They were two of the kings that had stood with us at Ynys Metcaut.

"So much for the Coalition of Kings," I sighed. It was such folly to let such petty differences keep them apart, with so much of North Briton at stake. Of course, we could not count on the other two kings in that alliance. King Urien was dead, and King Morgant had long ago revealed himself to be the cruel traitor that he was.

"It may only be King Lot, then," I muttered. "He does have a vast army at his command," I murmured. "He has ties to several different kingdoms to the north. He might still bring some from Strathclyde with him." I sighed. "Perhaps, with his help, we might win the day yet."

"Indeed. Come," Evelyn added presently, stretching her arms above her head briefly before stepping back from the balcony. "It is time we prepared. Our alliance with King Owain would not benefit if we were late for his wedding."

"Aye, true enough." I smirked. With that we descended for the balcony, preparing to attend what would probably be the most pompous celebration I had ever witnessed.

***

"Look at the people, husband." Evelyn's voice was grim, quiet. I glanced at her, confused, before peering out of the carriage window. It was three days later. Having travelled to Caer Ligualid, Evelyn and I were riding in one the most splendid carriages I had ever seen, heading for the wooden church building where King Owain and Princess Thaney were to wed. “What do you see?” she asked.

“Caer Ligualid have gathered for the wedding,” I answered. Sure enough, people were lining the streets, waving flags bearing Caer Ligualid’s seal. If I had thought my wedding to Evelyn was a splendid occasion, it now seemed rather modest in the light of King Owain’s forthcoming nuptials. I had never seen so much grandeur, not even in the late King Urien’s most flourishing speeches.

“Look harder,” Evelyn said. We raised our hands to wave out of the window. “Study their countenances.” I frowned as I did as she asked, paying closer attention to the expressions of Caer Ligualid’s citizens. It only took me a few more moments to notice it.

“You have a sharp eye,” I told my queen, glancing back to her. “They cannot pretend fully. Not when they know war is coming.” Evelyn nodded as I looked back out of the carriage window. Now my wife had remarked upon it, the real mood of the people was obvious. For although on the surface they seemed full of jubilation, their hard eyes and forced smiles were all too plain.

“King Owain will have announced the war some days ago, I assume,” Evelyn muttered. The carriage slowly trundled its way through the city, towards the church. “How can King Owain expect his people to rejoice when they know their loved ones are soon to march for war?”

“Perhaps they find it easier, to pretend to themselves,” I suggested. The carriage at last drew to a stop outside the steps of the wooden church building. The clamour of the crowd grew. Although in the last seven years of royalty I had grown used to such noise, the forced nature of it made my stomach tighten. Still, with little other options, I fixed the same smile onto my own features as I raised a hand to wave.

“Come on, love,” Evelyn murmured to Imogen, who had spent most of the ride looking out of the window, but without really seeing anything.

Although in the last four months or so our daughter had recovered somewhat, she was still very withdrawn. Indeed, I hadn’t heard her laugh since the day she had been playing with Ruth and Alena. Imogen could probably sense the ever-threatening doom of war. Leigh was still optimistic, but how could Immy laugh and smile, with so many marching off to war and when her home could be torn apart?

The three of us walked into the church and headed up the aisle to take our seats near the front. As we did so, I realised my mind was already ahead, to the days after this wedding. King Owain and his new bride would hardly have time to be together before he would leave for war. Indeed, after a day or two in Caer Ligualid, we would barely be home again before I left with most of our army, heading for Catraeth.

I tried to forget the war that was coming as I got gratefully to my feet from the hard, wooden seating. After all, surely today of all days was meant for most people to escape the harsh reality of war. As King Owain and Princess Thaney began their slow walk towards one another from across the church, the same way Evelyn and I had done so seven years ago, I reached for her hand. A small smile touched my face as I felt my wife's fingers curl around mine.

We stood and sat through the various elements of the service. It seemed to last hours longer than my wedding to Evelyn had done. Then, in the middle of the ceremony, Taliesin came to stand in front of us all. He began what seemed like the longest ode he had ever penned. Though the bard's words were engaging, my attention started to drift.

It wasn't until near its end that I understood why the service was so long. This was perhaps the last royal act before we departed for war. No wonder they wanted the moment to last as long as possible. It was also no wonder that the townspeople saw straight through the pompous celebrations. With war about to touch us all, how could the citizens of Caer Ligualid see King Owain's grin as anything other than false?

At last, the service ended, much to my relief. King Owain and Princess — now Queen — Thaney were wed. She had her hand tucked under his arm as the two of them proceeded out. A girl behind them threw little petals from a basket. Just then, the image of the late Queen Penarwen flashed through my mind, sitting by the fire with the shawl around her shoulders. My eyes travelled to Prince Elffin, looking utterly impassive. I could only imagine what torture he was going through, seeing his father remarry when his mother had only been buried barely more than a month ago.

As the church doors opened, the crowd roared. Although it almost deafened us, somehow there was almost something hollow to it. It was as if no matter how hard Caer Ligualid tried, the falseness of the day could not be ignored.

King Owain and his bride turned back to the congregation, giving a final wave before departing the church. In the smallest fraction of a moment, I glimpsed the hardening of his features before he broke into a large smile. The tenseness of his jaw, gone an instant later, told me that he, too, had sensed the real mood of the people. I wondered how angry the Supreme Ruler of Rheged might be, knowing that after all the extravagance and pomposity of the day, the enthusiasm of his people was still less than heartfelt.

So it was, again, that later that day Evelyn and I stood with smiles fixed onto our countenances, making polite chatter with royalty, politicians, and nobles alike. I was longing for the day to be over. I felt that it was far better to accept the inevitability of night coming, rather than be those who still pretended it was day long after the sun set.

The tone of utter extravagance and pomposity continued. The splendour of the feasts following Gilroy's birth seemed almost frugal in comparison. I did not even get a chance to speak to Sarah, but the few meaningful glances I exchanged with my sister across the grand banquet chamber told me she enjoyed the so-called festivities as much as I did. As much as I detested the mingling when Gilroy was born, I suddenly wished I were there. For at least then, war did loom just over the horizon.

"Thank goodness," I muttered, arriving in our chambers much later. I sat on the bed and roved a hand through my hair. "I do believe King Owain tried to make that feast last forever."

"He will have precious few days with his new bride before he leaves for war," Evelyn murmured as she turned from the dressing table. "It will be harder than ever, watching you ride away for battle. I know we agreed I would stay in Gaeson, but…" She moved to sit beside me on the bed.

"Aye." I moved my head to briefly kiss the top of hers. "Knowing it is right does not make the parting easier to bear."

"You will leave three days after we come home." Her gaze flickered down to where our hands were still joined. "It was so different the last time we were both here," she reflected now. "Gilroy was just born. War felt so far away still."

"Aye. I worry for Imogen, too," I admitted. "Imogen was only just beginning to feel safe again." I sighed. "Sometimes I think she is too young to understand any of this, but then with everything that happened to her—"

"She endured things no child should ever have to experience." The anger at the injustice of it all burst through her words. "She seems grown beyond her years. Do you think she will ever return to the child she was?" Her voice sounded small suddenly.

"Maybe, perhaps. All we can do is love her as she is," I murmured. Her head moved against my shoulder as she nodded again. "She has so much strength. We can only pray God enables her to endure all that is coming." Once more I was already there, standing on the battlefield at Catraeth, awaiting destiny. My wife was tangible on the bed beside me and my daughter was in a nearby chamber, but in some ways my mind had already left them. I wished desperately to forget the hell that was coming, though, so I clasped my wife's hand a little tighter.

I let my eyes slip shut, concentrating on the feeling of her touch and the feel of her head against my shoulder. No wonder King Owain wanted to hold onto daylight as much as he could before the inevitable night arrived. Even if my mind had left them, my heart never would. All I could do was pray that God would keep them both safe until, if it was in His will, I could return to them.

Part Four

Chapter Thirteen

I sighed as the sun dipped below the horizon. The last of daylight had ebbed away, leaving the surety of night in its stead. The scent of smoke filled the air as the campfires were lit. It was supposed to be summer, but I couldn't stop rubbing my hands together. Then again, I wasn't sure that this was from the cold.

It was almost two weeks since I had sat with Evelyn in our chamber in Caer Ligualid. Now, at last, on the eve of battle, the reckoning of Rheged had come. It had been a difficult road to war, with twisting paths over hills, south of the mountains I had travelled across with Cara. At least, this time, I hadn't been forced to contend with blizzards.

We had joined with the rest of King Owain's army and with the force from Gododdin on the border of Deira. The kingdom of Deira was as strong an ally to Bernicia as ever. Catraeth, where we would make our last stand as soon as dawn broke, was in the heart of Deiran lands.

"Your Majesty." I glanced to John, to see him bend his head. "I have just heard word from King Owain's captain, sire. His Majesty says King Morgant would like to talk to you."

"What?" I sputtered in astonishment. "He can't wish to negotiate terms of peace, surely." Even in my wildest dreams, I knew King Morgant and King Ethelfrith would not have gathered the whole of their might together, only to stop tomorrow's battle.

"No, my lord." My captain shook his head. "He only reports that King Morgant would like to meet both you and His Majesty King Owain. His Majesty seems eager to accept the invitation, sire."

"I can imagine." I shot John a weary glance as I stood. "Very well, I had better go along before King Owain does something he'll regret, like starting the war tonight." I could not deny that I, too, wished to confront King Morgant before the battle began.

I headed to the clearing where the horses were being kept. It was with some reluctance that I prepared Epos for riding, for she looked settled. I had wished to give her a few hours' respite before the battle began. Somehow, they always knew when their owners were about to fight for their very lives. We would be fighting on foot, but the horses would still be anxious. I murmured comforting words to Epos as I led her outside of the Rheged camp.

"Evening, Your Majesty," I greeted, coming to where the Supreme Ruler of Rheged waited for me atop his horse. He merely nodded back, his face already hard and grim.

I swung up onto Epos, leaving without a word to confront our greatest enemy, the one who had murdered — or ordered the murder — of both our fathers. Suddenly, I feared that the danger of starting the battle early might not be enough to stay King Owain's hand.

We rode fast and silent across the plain before us, coming to a stop at the outskirts of one of the Bernician camps. Two soldiers waited for us. I guessed they were high in rank. They led us to the centre of the camp. A large fire crackled in the centre of the clearing.

"Ah, King Bryce, we meet fully at last." My hand tightened on the hilt of my sword at the low, almost nasal voice. I peered around. At first, I couldn't see him, but then I made him out in the darkness, illuminated by the nearby flames as he approached. His countenance was impassive, with just the slight crease of his brow as he observed us.

"There is no need for your helmets, no harm will come to you as long as you give us no cause," King Morgant said flatly. "Let us speak to each other face to face."

"Very well," I said. The cool of the breeze ruffled through my hair as I tucked my helmet under my arm. I noted King Owain made no move to do the same.

"I have been following your movements with interest," King Morgant said. A glimmer of a smile creased the face of my greatest enemy. I expected a cruel sneer, the way the Wolf's had been. To my surprise, however, the smile, albeit glimpsing, seemed genuine.

"As I have been yours." I answered him as evenly as he had spoken to me. How strange it was to see my foe in flesh and blood, after all this time. The only other time I had spied this man was across the field in Ynys Metcaut. I had known then from my uncle that King Morgant could not be trusted. Little did I know then that he was Aldred's master. The real orchestrator of much of my pain.

"You killed my father," King Owain burst out, standing as tense as ever beside me. Clearly, his strategy was not to match our enemy's nonchalance.

"Aye." King Morgant admitted it easily, almost smoothly, as if the matter were purely academic. He smoothed back the few black curls from his receding hairline and cracked a grin. "I'm afraid if we were all to list the kings we had killed, we would have little time to speak on any other subject."

"How dare you!" King Owain shouted hotly, stepping forward as he drew his sword. "I will have my vengeance!" A circle of Bernician soldiers took one step forward, swords flashing in the firelight.

"Patience, sire," I admonished him quietly, my hand on his shoulder. "There will be plenty of blood to be spilt on the field tomorrow, you can take your vengeance then. Look around you." I gestured to the soldiers, lethal in all their stillness. "If we kill him now, neither of us will leave this camp alive. There is no cause to start the war now." King Owain's eyes flickered to meet mine.

"I see plenty of cause, Daniel. So should you," he growled, still in the heat of his rage. His hardened eyes bore into mine a moment longer before he reluctantly slid his sword back into its sheath.

"A wise decision. King Bryce is right, though." King Morgant held up one finger. With a united clink of armour, the Bernician soldiers took a step back, obscured by shadows once more. "If you lay a finger on me, neither of you will live long enough for the battle tomorrow." King Morgant then tilted his head as he regarded me curiously.

"I had expected such an outburst from you as well, given my crimes against you," Morgant stated. My eyebrows rose, that he should refer to his atrocities so plainly. Had he no shame?

"You have committed great wrongs against me," I agreed, my eyes hardening. "You murdered my parents, my aunt and unborn child. Then, later, you took the life of my uncle." King Morgant still did not react, while I pushed down the rage swirling within. "Killed by your servant Aldred, the Wolf, who was nothing but poison."

"Ah yes, you killed my man," he said. Here, the slightest hint of regret entered his tone. "A shame. He was one of my most faithful servants." Then he cracked another grin. "You see, Daniel, you are not innocent of shedding blood."

"I have never claimed otherwise," I answered swiftly. "The Wolf had to be stopped, before he brought ruin upon all of Rheged at your hands. Then, lastly, you took my daughter away from me."

With these last words, my hatred of him kicked into life. I took a step towards him before managing to control my anger. King Morgant raised another finger and the Bernicians retreated again. In my growing rage, I had not even noticed them advance. My enemy stood there, a small smile of triumph on his lips. King Morgant enjoyed it, I realised. He relished any reaction we gave him.

"Tell me why." My command came loudly. "Why did you take my daughter?" I asked again, making myself calmer. The small smile had gone from Morgant's face.

"To break you," he answered simply, so quickly and cleanly from his lips. "You should have died the night that Princess Imogen was taken." The first spark of anger flashed across his face as the embers danced between us.

"Aldred would have succeeded. You just can't get the assassins these days," he added scornfully, making a wheezing sound that could have been a faint laugh. My eyes widened. I simply could not fathom my enemy. Did he have no humanity left?

"So, kidnapping my daughter was the second-best option," I guessed, trying to get my initial question answered.

"Aye," King Morgant answered shortly. "They had orders to take the princess if you were still alive. The second time you have survived." He gave a mirthless laugh again. "You should have died when Aldred came to Klumeck all those years ago. He would have done if he'd stopped King Cedric's wife from screaming."

"Her name was Angharad," I answered hotly. "She screamed because you sent Aldred to kill her. You didn't just kill her, either. My cousin's life was taken that night also, before they had even taken their first breath in this world." My rage threatened to spiral again.

"Ah, some honest ire at last." King Morgant grinned, then his expression sobered rapidly. "I can see you judging me, even though you try to hide it. You and I are not so different, you know," he murmured.

"Maybe if you knew our similarities, you might understand my actions." His voice suddenly sounded almost imploring. Would this monster now actually attempt to justify his crimes?

"There are no similarities between us." More anger bubbled at the mere thought of it. "I do not kidnap people, nor murder them as they sleep," I pointed out hotly. King Morgant only smiled again.

"True, but there are certain parallels to our past. Or have you forgotten the kingdom of Bernicia was dispossessed from me?" His voice became soft. "You are not the only one who had their family assassinated in the name of war."

"What are you talking about?" My curiosity got the better of me. Beside me, King Owain stood in stony silence. King Morgant stretched out his hands, then joined them together and flexed his fingers back.

"Your parents and your aunt died in their beds when you were three, assassinated on Aldred's instruction," King Morgant began drily. "When I was seven years old, King Ida came to the castle of Bernicia." His voice was almost devoid of emotion as he began the count. "I heard my uncle shouting. I ran to hide in the wardrobe." His gaze was lost, faraway.

"The door to the chamber opened. Through a crack in the wardrobe, I saw it was my mother." His face hardened a little. "Before I could go to her, or even call out, her assassin reached her. He stabbed my mother in the back with a long dagger." His voice quavered slightly; the most humanity in his voice since he had stepped out of the shadows.

"My uncle was King Brad Hen of Bernicia," King Morgant continued in a soft murmur. "He whisked me away in a carriage. As it sped me away, I saw him being killed just outside the castle."

His eyes as well as his voice were still far away. I could tell he was reliving it. Was his kin's murder crueller than mine? My mother's scream haunted my nightmares, but King Morgant had seen his mother slain.

I imagined a terrified little boy, hiding in a wardrobe. I pictured his relief when his mother entered the chamber, only for it to be transformed into the pure terror of seeing her stabbed from behind. I saw him being whisked away through the castle by his uncle, barely able to comprehend what he had witnessed. I almost heard the fast clopping of hooves and the juddering of the carriage as it rode him away to safety, only for him to look back to see his uncle, the king, meet his end. For that, something in me stirred. Despite the pain that he had caused me, I felt some semblance of pity.

"I became the king of a land stolen away from me, at just the age of seven." King Morgant's countenance and tone were again impassive. "Like you, I was raised in another kingdom. I lived in the kingdom of Gododdin for a time." His eyes moved to King Owain suddenly.

"Speaking of which, I heard you recently married King Lot's daughter." He grinned again. "Many congratulations on your recent nuptials. I would love to meet her one day for myself." He bent forward and swept his arm dramatically in a mock bow.

"Halt your words," King Owain ground out, his hand once again the hilt of his blade. "You will not speak of my wife, or you will speak your last. No matter what your men might do," he growled, glaring at the Bernicians who had once more stepped nearer to the fire.

"Save it till tomorrow, sire," I warned, though I was not much better at controlling my anger than he was. I turned back to King Morgant, my curiosity still winning. "Go on. In what other ways are we… similar?" I swallowed my deep distaste at such a notion.

"You sought revenge on Aldred, once you discovered the truth," King Morgant said. I nodded dismally, remembering my battle with the Wolf at King Hussa's permission, reliving the moment where I plunged my sword into Aldred's flesh.

"I did the same," King Morgant continued. "Twelve years after the night I left Bernicia, when I was nineteen, I snuck back into the castle to murder King Ida as he slept."

"You killed King Ida?" King Owain echoed loudly, as though he had not heard right. I was just as astonished as he was. King Hussa was the son of King Ida — they should have been sworn enemies forever. How could they have ever come to an accord?

King Morgant said nothing more for a moment. One of the Bernician soldiers moved forward to place more wood on the fire. The flames roared and crackled, enveloping the wood into its blazing caress. It made my foe's countenance even more visible. King Morgant's eyes were as dark as ever, but the vivid amber hues now showed streaks of grey in his once raven curls.

There were also several lines carved into his features. I could not tell if they had grown with age, or whether I had been too far away to notice them at Ynys Metcaut. From the shadows around his eyes, I saw that King Morgant looked as fatigued of war as I felt.

"What happened then?" King Owain asked abruptly. King Morgant's gaze had been locked with mine, as if he were assessing me as much as I was him. Now, though, my foe glanced lazily towards him, almost as if bored.

"Well, naturally, the Bernicians — they are of course the Angles, but they have occupied my land for so long even I refer to them as that." He smirked. "They wished to avenge their fallen king, so I went into hiding. As I said, I went to Gododdin for a time. I also sought refuge in Strathclyde for a while. It was there that I met Aldred and employed him in my service," King Morgant continued drily.

"While I was in Strathclyde, I heard King Ida's son, Glappa, had been killed in a battle with the Britons. I then met Glappa's brother, Adda, who had taken the Bernician throne." He rose a hand to idly scratch his nose. "I made an alliance with him, to work to weaken the cause of Rheged in exchange for status and power within Bernicia once more."

"How did you do it?" I asked him, astonishment replacing my anger for a moment. "How did you sign an alliance with him, when you had killed his father and he had killed your uncle?"

"All things are permissible in war," King Morgant returned icily. "You yourself were once at war with King Cedric before you knew your true identity. Would you not have killed your own people?"

"That was different," I protested sharply through gritted teeth. "As you say, I didn't know. You and King Adda would have known you had killed each other's kin."

"Aye, but you still managed to put aside those differences for the sake of a greater goal. Klumeck followed you, even though you once fought them as your enemy. You married Queen Evelyn, also, knowing her father, King Reghan, had been manipulated by me to send Aldred to kill your kin. Didn't you nearly kill him, too?"

"Do not mention my wife," I warned him hotly. I realised my fists were clenched and slowly uncurled them. "I did not slay King Reghan, though I longed to," I pointed out. "That is the biggest difference between us."

“Perhaps a weakness, I think,” King Morgant said, tilting his head in thought as he regarded me. “My alliance with King Adda was based upon the notion we were of more use to each other alive than dead. Adda’s father had killed my uncle and so I, in turn, killed Adda’s father. When we first met, we had the choice to kill each other, or work together.” Here he lifted a shoulder in a half-shrug.

“I was not so entranced by the folly of youth to believe I could bring down the whole of the Angles to reclaim my former kingdom,” King Morgant admitted now, with a faint chuckle in his voice at the thought. “So, I joined forces with him.”

“You mutually agreed not to kill the other, that you might serve a greater purpose.” It was uncomfortably like the pact I had made with Cara before I knew whether or not she was my enemy. “What happened next?” I was more curious of King Morgant’s account than I liked to admit.

“We planned a simple strategy,” my greatest enemy said. “We were to weaken Rheged by turning your kings against each other. It was my idea to have Aldred assassinate King Cedric and his kin.”

My eyes widened. It struck me again how calmly he spoke of murdering most of my family. My enemy was so without passion in his discourse, he could have been discussing the weather.

“King Reghan was driven by paranoia, ambition and greed in equal measure,” King Morgant went on. “It was almost too easy for the Wolf to persuade him that King Cedric was mounting an attack. As easy as it was to have your uncle killed in battle four years ago.”

Ire shot through me, so powerful I could barely speak. It took every fibre of my being not to leap forward and batter his skull to the ground, consequences be damned.

“You ordered the assassination of my father, also, when you betrayed the Coalition of Kings at Ynys Metcaut.” King Owain’s voice seethed over the crackling fire.

“Aye.” King Morgant nodded. “King Hussa and I had agreed he had served his purpose.” He grinned again, the firelight catching the glint in his teeth. King Owain drew his blade.

“My father was not your pawn!” he bellowed over the roar of the fire. “He was a better king, a better man, than you have ever been.”

"A shame he is not here to speak of his goodness for himself." King Morgant chuckled, as the circle of soldiers emerged into the firelight again. "King Owain, this is your last warning." His eyes narrowed. "Draw your blade again and I shall have no choice but to declare the battle begun." It seemed to take effort from every fibre in his body for King Owain to slide his sword back in his sheath.

"As for you, King Bryce." King Morgant's gaze snapped back to mine. "It was a beautiful twist of fate that King Cedric's surviving kin came to Gaeson. The thought that you might serve your enemy, that you might even kill your uncle in battle…" He snorted in amusement.

"You are responsible for so many deaths, not just my kin." My hand pressed the hilt of my blade so deeply it was almost painful. Fury, white and hot, sped through my veins as swiftly as blood.

"Your plan with King Adda caused the war between Gaeson and Klumeck," I said hotly. "It lasted for almost twenty years." The image of Joshua swam into mind, then blurred with the many Klumeck soldiers I had killed in battle before learning the truth.

The chill crept into my skin, despite the warmth of the roaring fire. I had taken the life of those who would have been my kin, those who one day I could have ruled. It was all thanks to King Morgant, the monster who stood opposite me.

"Careful, now." King Morgant's eyes danced with humour in the firelight. "Are you really going to draw that blade now, Daniel? One order from me and my army will kill your men as they sleep, or sup wine to give them courage before the battle. Is that what you want?" His tone hardened.

"No." The single word spat from my lips. It was only the thought of John and Aife, of Ewan, of all my people joined together, that my hand left the hilt of my sword. "So, since that day, you have been allied with Bernicia."

"Aye," King Morgant admitted easily, as if he were purely apathetic to his treachery. "The Bernician kings fell swiftly in the next few years. King Adda, King Ethelric, King Theodric, King Frithuwalld, King Hussa and now, finally King Ethelfrith. Each time a new Bernician ascended to the throne, I met with them to tell them of my alliance to Bernicia. Each Bernician king was more than happy to let Lord Aldred and I continue the scheme I had thought of with Adda, decades before."

"The scheme of destroying Rheged," I said darkly. "It was always you, wasn't it?" My voice was soft and at once did not sound like my own. "I've known that for a while now…" I swallowed. "You have been the orchestrator of all my pain." My fingers itched to take the hilt of my blade again.

"I do not understand you," I burst out. "You have told us how your land and your people were taken from you, how your mother and uncle died right before your eyes. What kind of a monster must you be?" I almost whispered, but I knew he heard me, even over the crackling of the fire. "To endure such agony, only to inflict it on others?"

"It is war, King Bryce, nothing more." King Morgant sighed. "For those twelve years, before I killed King Ida, I thought of revenge with every breath. My mother and my uncle haunted my dreams." My mouth tightened, nodding grimly. What he spoke of was uncomfortably familiar. "It was when I made the alliance with King Adda, however, that I finally learned the truth." He sighed again.

"War isn't personal," he said at last. "We are all just pieces in the game, trying to stay alive. What does it matter if I kill your father, or you kill mine? We are all trying to do right by our people."

"You're wrong," I retorted, loud and crisp over the crackling flames. "War is always personal. Every life we take leaves behind grieving kin. I do not understand how you, who know this pain more than many, can call it anything else."

"I have been fighting every day, since my uncle put me into that carriage," King Morgant answered sharply. We stared at each other across the firelight, the dark shadows still flickering and dancing across his countenance.

"It's been a long fifty years of war, Daniel." King Morgant's voice was flat suddenly. My eyebrows rose — I hadn't realised he was as old as that. "Perhaps when you have been fighting fifty years, you will be as fatigued of war as I am. Then, maybe, you will understand the impersonality of war."

"Never." My answer was quiet and calm as I regarded my greatest enemy. "You are nearly double my age, so I grant that your experience of war far surpasses my own," I conceded.

"However," I growled passionately. "I am fatigued of war already, King Morgant. I long now to be able to put away the blade I bear. Even if I lived through five hundred battles of blood and bone, I would never lose sight of their humanity." King Morgant said nothing, but I knew I was right about him.

"You do not see them as people on the battlefield, do you?" I went on. "You do not see the fear in their eyes, nor the hopes and dreams they might have. You do not see if they are male or female, or the rings that might be on their fingers. To you, they are simply animals to be slaughtered."

King Morgant and I did have much grief in common, I reflected. Was this who I could have been? If I had been old enough to know what had happened that night in Klumeck, when Aldred murdered my kin in their beds, would I have spent my childhood harbouring revenge? Was I staring at the monster I might have become, had God not kept my humanity?

"Perhaps you are right, King Bryce." King Morgant's tone became academic again. "Nobody spared a thought for the humanity of my mother when she screamed her last breath, least of all Rheged," he ended bitterly. His eyes were far away again. Was he once more living it, seeing the life leave his mother through his seven-year-old eyes?

"Is that why you made the deal with Adda, all those years ago?" I asked now. "Because of what happened that night?"

"I found out my uncle had written to Rheged, when King Urien had only been on the throne a few years." For the first time in our strange discourse, King Morgant's eyes blazed with ire. "He feared another raid from the Angles. Your father did nothing," he spat. "We were allowed to bleed to the core."

"So, because my father did not aid your uncle," King Owain said slowly, "you've dedicated your life to tearing Rheged apart? Betraying everything the Britons in the North stand for?"

"Aye," King Morgant declared. He sounded almost proud. "King Urien cared nothing for my humanity," he said, turning back to me. "Why should I think of the humanity of anyone else?" he challenged, voice rising with renewed anger.

"Because we have a choice, King Morgant," I said. His brow was furrowed, while the amber glow still danced upon his face. "We can decide not to inflict the horrors we have endured onto others."

"How profound." My foe smirked. "Come then, tell me. What makes you so superior to me, that you have made a better choice?" Staring at him, strangely, my rage began to dissipate. It was replaced with some semblance of the very last thing I expected to feel — pity. Aye, this man was a monster, but the pain and grief he still bore made me think he might have some shred of humanity left in him.

"Heaven knows I would have every right to tear you limb from limb, given all that you have done to me and my kin," I answered him evenly. "Yet still I see your humanity, in all of this. I still see you as a child, seeing your mother die before your very eyes."

"That does not excuse him!" King Owain growled, loudly breaking his silence. I averted my gaze from my foe to glance to Caer Ligualid's ruler.

"I never said it did." I was unsure where my calmness came from. "King Morgant is accountable for all his sins, for all the lives he has so cruelly and needlessly taken. Yet still I see him." I turned back to face my foe. "He is a man, as well as a monster."

"Your pity is your weakness, King Bryce." King Morgant cracked another grin. "Perhaps tomorrow, on the battlefield, we will see if that pity will keep you alive."

"It has done so far," I answered evenly. "I look forward to it." He inclined his head. It seemed our conversation was over. I glanced to King Owain who said nothing; simply glared at our enemy. "Let us leave this place in peace, my lord."

"Very well," he growled, through gritted teeth. King Morgant rose a hand and at his command, two or three Bernician soldiers stepped forward from the circle to escort us to the outskirts of the camp where our horses were waiting. I gave a final nod to King Morgant, who cracked his last grin in return.

With that we left the fire, where my greatest enemy had been so cordial and yet so cruel. I kept my hand on the hilt on my blade, but King Morgant seemed to be keeping his word. Our escort made no move to attack us. As soon as we reached our horses, they turned and disappeared back into the darkness.

"How could you bear him speaking to you like that?" King Owain burst out as we mounted our horses, ready to ride back across the field towards our camp. This time tomorrow this open ground would be full of blood. Corpses would be either burnt or left to be pecked at by birds.

"I don't know," I answered him honestly, gathering Epos' reins in my hands. "It was only the threat of the war starting tonight that stayed my blade."

In truth, I had no idea how I had been able to leave the man who had murdered most of my family so calmly. That strength had not come from me alone. King Owain glanced back to the camp. Though I could only make out the outline of his head in this darkness, I could well guess his thoughts.

"Come away, sire," I bid him quietly. King Owain jerked his head back to me. Though it was early summer, I felt the chill of night settle in now we were away from the flames. "What is one more night in his miserable life? We need to wait only till the dawn, then his life is ours to take." In the darkness, I heard him snort softly.

"Very well," he repeated, but this time there was no growl to his words. We set off at a canter, the hooves of our horses clapping loudly upon the earth. "Then there is but one thing we need to decide." As we rode, the clouds had parted, unveiling the moon.

"What is that, my lord?" I asked. He looked to me. In the moonlight I saw him smirk as he shifted the reins in his hands.

"Which of us should kill him?" His voice came deep, clear over the sounds of riding. Slowly, our camp came into view as hooves thundered across the earth. "Both of us have equal right to."

"Aye, sire," I agreed simply, as we drew nearer to the sparse fires of our camp. "I suppose it depends on who will find him on the battlefield first."

"True." Owain let out a sharp laugh and then grinned. "You never know, we might both be dead long before we face him in battle. Yah!" He cried out suddenly, kicking his horse into a gallop before I could respond. I stared after him, the clopping of his horse piercing the stillness of the night.

"Easy, old girl." I patted Epos' neck, but I knew my faithful companion was perfectly calm. As I set her off at a trot, I knew I had been speaking to her to reassure myself. I wondered how King Owain could laugh and joke about the death that threatened to swallow us all whole. Perhaps that was how he coped with it.

As I faced the prospect of my own fate, I could not be quite so comical. Would this field I now crossed in the dark be my grave? Would I breathe my last on this ground? As soon as the sun rose, this earth would be soaked with blood as well as light.

I entered the camp and dismounted Epos, handing her to a nearby soldier. I removed my helmet and glanced at the moon, its light still shifting and dancing as the clouds sauntered past it. There was one crucial detail I would not know till the dawn. Only when the horror started, when the point of metal might scrape and bite into my flesh, would I know if my blood would also be shed on that field.

***

I sat on the edge of a small stream just outside the main camp. The gentle lapping of the water filled my ears. I had often thought a babbling brook was one of the gentlest lullabies known in nature. Indeed, this tranquil picture was hard to reconcile with what the dawn would bring. I shook my head a little, focussing again on my present task.

Once more, I plunged the cloth into the cold of the stream, before scraping the soaked rag against my blade. My hand was almost numb from the chill of the water. The metal gleamed in a shaft of moonlight, turning it to a metal so pure, surely not a particle of dirt could remain. Yet still I did not stop. No sooner had I wiped the cloth onto my sword, then I plunged into the brook once more.

I knew it was foolish, but over this at least, I still had some meagre measure of control. I did not know if I would survive tomorrow but caring for my own blade brought me a degree of comfort. Plenty of soldiers could have done this task for me, but tonight of all nights, I wanted to do it myself.

"I thought I was alone out here." My head jerked up in surprise to hear Aife's voice. Her figure, mostly shrouded in the night, stood a few hundred yards away along the stream. How long had she been standing there? I straightened, ready to call out in reply.

"I hope I haven't disturbed you?" My words of greeting died in my throat as I realised she was not talking to me. The other speaker was John.

"Not at all. I've only just arrived here myself. I wished for a few moments of peace, before tomorrow," Aife answered. There was a pause in their conversation here. I sheathed my sword, intending to go out and join them. "It's a beautiful night, isn't it?"

"Aye," John replied quietly. The heaviness of his voice froze me in my tracks, just as I was about to announce my presence. Something I could not quite distinguish kept me in the shadows. For a few seconds, all I could hear was the babbling of the stream.

Though they did not speak, I sensed the spell building between them. It reminded me of the few moments before I had asked Evelyn what she felt for me. Suddenly I felt trapped. I sensed the importance to leave them alone, but they both had such sharp hearing. If they noticed my movements, then I could take away the last chance they had to talk of their hearts.

"Do you ever regret it?" Aife asked earnestly, yet her voice sounded soft. They sounded so near, but with the clouds passing over the moon, they remained shadowed outlines.

"Regret what?" John's voice was hoarse, almost fierce. At once, I knew my instinct had been right not to join them.

"What could have been," Aife said simply. She gave a sigh. I heard the movement of footsteps. Then abruptly, I saw her as she stepped into a sliver of moonlight, filtering through the woodland.

"I won't be coy and pretend I don't know your meaning." There was a faint thread of humour in John's voice. I felt shame that I could hear this, but I was sure they would hear me if I tried to slip away.

"Well?" my sister prompted quietly. Her tone matched his gentle teasing. It was John's turn to sigh. Any notion of levity seemed to expire with it.

"When I think of duty, the answer must be no," he began carefully. "Our bond in battle is like none other I have ever known." A slight trace of sadness entered his words now. "I think, perhaps, you know my movements before I do."

"You know I have felt the same, about you," came Aife's reply. "Our paths have been for the good of Gaeson." A brief silence followed. I could not help but imagine all the words that remained unsaid, hanging in the balance between them.

"I do not doubt it," John said. His face was still obscured by shadow, but I imagined a small smile crossing his features. "I'm sure I would have died many years ago, without you beside me."

"Aye, the same as with me," Aife murmured. "It has been worth it, to fight together. Our duty." Her final words were touched with sadness. I saw her figure half-turn away.

"Indeed," John agreed heavily. Was the moment between them gone? Would this be the closest my friends would get to speaking aloud what was so plainly in their hearts?

"If, however…" John began a little tentatively. "Perhaps, just for this moment…" He cleared his throat. "Perhaps, just once, I might answer your question according to my heart."

"Aye," Aife said immediately. "By all means." I watched as John stepped forwards into the shaft of the moonlight. The intensity of his gaze pierced through the silver glow that enveloped them.

"If I were to speak my heart, Aife, rather than duty," John said, his voice faster and stronger now. "Then the answer must be yes. There has never been a single day where I have not regretted what could have been." By the glow of the moon, I saw his hands take hers. I willed myself to look away, but I was transfixed.

"Duty has kept us apart, aye, but that has not stopped my heart." One hand left hers and rose to her cheek. "I have always loved you, Aife," he said roughly. "I always will."

In response to his declaration, Aife's hand rose to his cheek also. John's eyes slipped shut at the contact. The moment between them was so intimate that I looked away, ashamed once more that I could not give them the privacy that they deserved.

"I think I've always known your love for me." Aife spoke quietly now. "As I think perhaps you've always known how very much I love you," she said breathlessly.

My heart both leapt in joy and sank farther into sadness. Joy that Aife's love was returned, yet despair that their duty had prevented them being together.

"Aye," John breathed, his relief all too evident. "I think I have. It is very pleasant to hear you say it, though, at least this once." Aife laughed openly this time; their levity returning along with joy.

"I quite agree." Aife chuckled, but her voice sounded a little thick. She sniffed and cleared her throat. Could my sister be crying? "So, what now?" Aife asked simply.

"Duty." John's voice was heavy with regret. "At least I can take comfort in knowing your love. That, I believe, will give me even greater strength to face what comes with the dawn," he said, his voice still sombre.

"Aye." There was another pause. I could only imagine the raw love writ large upon their features. "After the battle?" she asked, a little uncertainly.

"I suppose…" My brother spoke tentatively again. "If we both survive tomorrow, then we shall discuss what decisions to take." In the moonlight, I saw Aife nod and wipe her eyes.

"Until then, however…" he murmured, his voice trailing away again as he paused. He moved his hand to rest upon her cheek. "If God allows this one night to take for ourselves, then may I kiss you?" he asked earnestly. Aife exhaled a little joyful laughter.

"Aye, John," she answered him breathlessly. Another little laugh escaped into the summer evening. "I thought you'd never ask."

Curiosity made me look at them again. Both of his hands rose to rest on her cheeks, framing her face. Aife's hands lowered to his neck. In the beauty of this intimate moment, I knew I should look away, but I seemed frozen, unable to tear myself away from the scene before me.

Then it was too late to avert my gaze. Abruptly, John bent his head to meet her mouth. Even at this distance I saw how hungry and passioned their kiss was, for this could be all they would ever have of each other. Aife's hands moved closer around his neck as she returned his kiss. They broke for air before their mouths met again.

"I love you." Her words were punctuated by haggard breaths. I saw the sad smile that filled his countenance as he looked at her.

"I love you." He bent his head to kiss her again; a far gentler, lingering embrace. The sadness was still in his features when they stepped apart.

"Do not grieve for us, John," Aife told him gently. "There have been times when I have regretted what could have been. It is tempting to regret it now, most of all," she admitted. "For the most part, however, I have been content to fight alongside you. That I do not regret," she murmured. "Yet now I know what it is to love you in this way, to be yours. I always will belong to you, John."

"I am yours, Aife," John agreed passionately. "I shall always be yours, just as you have said you are always mine. Perhaps that is enough, for now." Aife nodded. John bent his head to press a gentle kiss to her forehead.

"I am content indeed," Aife murmured, then stepped back from him. "I think I shall retire. I think perhaps I can sleep now."

"Of course." He took her hands again. "I will treasure these moments for as long as I live. Whether that be till the dawn, or fifty years from now."

"As will I," she said. John bent his head to close the gap between them; they kissed a final time. Aife turned away, their hands only parting reluctantly. Her footsteps crunched on the loose stones by the edge of the stream. Then, as that faded, the gentle lapping of the brook was the only sound. John raised his head to look at the moon. I wondered if I should try to slip away or wait for him to leave.

"You can come out from behind that tree, now, my king." My eyes widened. I stepped out to see John looking my way, a wry smile on his face.

"I'm so sorry, John," I said earnestly. "I was cleaning my sword. I was about to come and see you both, but then I thought I would be interrupting…"

"I'm very glad you didn't." John broke into a grin. "I might never have forgiven you," he said in mock indignation.

"That's what I thought," I replied. My brother smirked before he sighed and stretched, lifting his arms above his head. My boots crunched against loose stones as I stepped closer. "Are you all right?"

"I'm much better than all right." John broke into another grin as he glanced to me. He dropped his hands back to his sides. "She loves me, Daniel," he told me simply.

"Aye, that she does." I clapped a hand on his shoulder. "I'm glad for you, my friend." I then stepped back from him. "We had both better sleep while we can. Walk back to the camp with me?"

"Of course." The two of us began our journey back, knowing we were that much closer to the inevitable bloodshed starting in a few hours. "How do you fare, brother?" he asked. "How did meeting King Morgant go?"

"He has lost most of his humanity," I told him. "He keeps just enough for me to have a little pity for him, even with what he did to us. King Owain is looking forward to finding him on the battlefield tomorrow." John smirked as we reached the camp, illuminated by sparse fires.

The fear of battle already permeated the very air, seeming to lurk between every tent. A few unfortunate soldiers patrolled, on watch duty on tonight of all nights. The dread intensified further with the fact that nobody spoke of it.

"Do you remember when we were children, John?" I heard the soft thread of nostalgia in my tone. "How we used to play with Sarah? Running, fishing, climbing trees?"

"Aye." His voice came quiet, a faint smiling crossed his face. I wondered if he, like me, was wishing he could be anywhere else but here, on the brink of war with death silently waiting.

"You've always been there for me, John, since the moment we met." Raw emotion was clear in my voice now, but I no longer cared. "I'm glad you are my captain, brother. I'm glad you are with me."

"I could be nowhere else," John said. As we came to my tent, he suddenly stepped forward to clasp my arm. "I am pleased to be beside my lord. I could not ask for a better king, nor a better friend. I am with you to the last."

"Knowing that makes the burden of war so much easier to bear. Goodnight, John," I said. "I'll see you in a few hours."

"Sire." John inclined his head to me, before heading to his tent. I pulled back the flap to enter the threshold. I pulled off my newly cleaned armour, discarding the plates in the corner, ready to put them on again at dawn. I stripped to my long underwear and climbed into the makeshift bed. As my body began to warm again under the covers, I felt in my tunic pocket to carefully retrieve Evelyn's lace cloth.

Having found it I rolled onto my back, tracing the faint pattern of the lace. I imagined her features. First came the raven tresses of her hair, curled locks that when loose descended to just below her shoulders. Then her face, creamy skin in contrast to her hair. Evelyn's kind and wise eyes, sparkling with her goodness. Still to this day, her smile made my heart sing, her kiss sweeter than the finest mead.

I then focused on my daughter, with her golden honey hair and her eyes as deep a blue as the great lake on a clear day. The thought of her warmed my soul, but also sobered it a little. Imogen had made incredible progress after her terrible ordeal, but she still seemed so different to the feisty, joyous child she had once been. Immy had aged, far more than she should have done at being almost five years old. In her eyes I glimpsed an invisible burden, that Evelyn and I could not quite lift.

Although I did not want to, I found my thoughts shifting to King Morgant. His features came before me, illuminated and flickering with firelight at his camp. Whatever pity had arisen was squashed with the pain of what he had done to my daughter, what he had done to my kin. Revenge seeped into my bones. My last thought, before I fell into a nameless sleep, was that if King Owain did not find him first, I would make him pay for what he had done. If I still had breath in my body and God granted it, I would take his life.

Chapter Fourteen

It looked like it would dawn bright when I left my tent the next morning. Currently, the sky was deep blue, with an early morning mist lingering upon the wet earth. It filtered amongst the trees and clung to the woodland floor. Could this beautiful morning really be the start of the horrors that were about to come?

I surveyed the camp. The only talk was the murmuring of those who had taken the last watch and the few who busied themselves making breakfast. For many fighting today, it would be their last meal. I swallowed hard. It was only an hour or so before we marched for war. I hoped those still slumbering could have some last few moments of peace.

"Your Majesty." I turned to see John striding towards me, inclining his head to me briefly. His hands curled around a cup of hot tea. "Sire." He held one out to me.

"Thank you." I took it from him gratefully, taking a cautious sip of the almost scalding concoction of brewed herbs and honey. "It's a beautiful morning."

"Difficult to imagine such peace would be here today." I nodded. I glanced to my brother to see that he had never looked more stoic. It was a sharp contrast to his joy-softened features last night. I turned to the sky's lightest point. By the time the sun rose, we would be on the battlefield.

"Well." I sighed heavily, in between mouthfuls of tea. "Here we are at last." John nodded gravely. We stood there, silent for the most part, as the camp transformed to life. Soldiers amassed from tents, sliding swords into place. Some of them joined the queues for breakfast, but others did not bother partaking what could well be their final meal.

A raw, undulated horror flickered in the eyes of some of the younger soldiers. The last four years had been relatively peaceful, so I felt for those facing their first battle, especially one such as this. In contrast, in the older warriors there was a resigned numbness I knew well.

Hollowness had replaced the desire for revenge and bloodlust I had fallen asleep with last night.

A young soldier approached, bowing before giving us both a bowl of boiled wheat. I placed my cup on the ground and accepted it from him. I ate mechanically, almost forcing it into my mouth. I needed my strength if I were to survive the day. Afterwards, I picked up my tea again and sipped it slowly, watching as the dawn grew inevitably closer. Until, at last, I saw King Owain heading for the battlefield, his army falling in line behind him.

"Let's go." My command came rasped and hoarse, in between sucking air. John gave a nod back, taking the half-empty bowl and cup from me and handing it to a passing-by young soldier. Relief flickered in his eyes as he inclined his head to us. I think the lad appreciated the chance to do something as normal as washing a dish, while he still could.

"My lord." I turned to see Aife beside us. She held her spear, her bow and quiver slung on her back. My sister would be leading the archers from Gaeson on the higher ground, just before the battlefield. In another life, had I not discovered my royal blood, I would have been standing beside her. Instead, I would be marching the whole of Gaeson and Klumeck's armies into battle.

"Aife." John's use of her name would reveal nothing to an outside observer, but I heard the love tracing through that simple word. As if my brother had spent his whole life waiting to speak her name like that. John's eyes had softened briefly, a small smile crossing his features.

Aife's mouth curved in response, a slow smile that lighted in her eyes. Joy, despite what we were about to face. Suddenly, I felt like an intruder again. Their exchange only lasted an instant, but it was enough for my dearest friends to convey all the love they had for each other.

Then the moment was gone. The three of us walked through the camp. I marched at the front, with John and Aife behind to lead the procession. I opened my mouth to give a command, but there was no need. Wordlessly, the armies of Klumeck and Gaeson sensed the reckoning of Rheged had come at last. The soldiers began to amass behind us, their metal armour clinking as they fell into line.

As we walked, the years receded. Though many boots thudded into grass damp with dew behind me, I felt as alone as when my father,

Kellen, had died. Fifteen years old again, barely a man and grieving. I could almost smell the bundles of straw in the hayloft of the stables. The horses below whinnying, almost as if they knew their carer had died.

My hands clenched in determination. I would fight for the memory of my father — as well as Adair, my father in Klumeck that I could barely remember. I would fight for the living, too, for Evelyn and Imogen and Sarah, for John and Aife. I would fight for all I loved most in this world, both past and present.

That blazing passion and pain of humanity — this was what King Morgant was blind to. I had learned from last night that this was the greatest difference between us. He had long ago decided to see people as no more than objects in his path. If King Morgant could not use them for his own power and gain, he would simply destroy them.

As I walked to the battlefield with all my brothers-and-sisters in arms, I knew that we had to put an end to King Morgant's tyrannous reign. Regardless of whether we won the day. I tried to tell my foe last night about the humanity of those we fought, but he did not listen. Perhaps, therefore, I had to show him the power of the soul with the point of my blade. Though I always dreaded war, I found, with some satisfaction, I was looking forward to personally teaching him that lesson.

Soon we reached the start of the field that King Owain and I had crossed the previous night. We stopped on the grass while Gaeson and Klumeck's armies marched to form their ranks, taking one last moment for the three of us to stand together before it started.

"I am ready, Your Majesty," Aife said from beside me, before I turned to talk to her. My jaw locked, praying I would see her again.

"I know," I said, giving her a sad smile. "I have the highest faith in you." My captain's face was impassive, but I could only imagine the pain he felt at parting with her. Yet Aife was my chief archer; she had to leave us for the higher ground. John and I would be on the front lines, ready to plunge into hell.

"Very well, the archers await you," I muttered. For the steady beat of the war drum sounded as loud as ever. We could delay the inevitable no longer. "May God be with you, Aife, my sister." I reached out to grasp her arm.

"May our Lord keep you safe, my king." She stepped forward. "I'll see you soon, Daniel, my brother," she whispered roughly. Our foreheads touched briefly. A well of emotion rose, but I swallowed it back down. I stood back, nodding quickly. Then, before I could turn away to give them one last moment alone, Aife turned to John.

"John," she said quietly, only a little brokenly. They clasped the other's arm. Nobody could have guessed anything different about their embrace, apart from the piercing gaze between them. "I pray we see each other again." They brought their foreheads together, only for a moment. Functionally it was the same embrace Aife and I had just shared, but theirs was so much more.

"Aye," he agreed fiercely. "You are in my very soul, Aife. Now and always." A sad smile softened her face as she nodded. In the next moment she was gone, walking away from us both. We lingered a moment, watching Aife's plaits sway a little in the breeze.

"I suppose it is time, brother," I said. My captain only nodded. Together we made our way to the front of the lines, mud squelching a little underfoot. It hadn't rained, but the early dew had moistened the earth. Soon friends and foes alike would be sliding and scrambling as the blood poured onto the ground.

The steady clink of arms sounded as soldiers turned to face forward after we passed them by. In the wake of their movements, the war drum was louder than ever. I glanced to my right, to where King Owain stood some distance away. Our gazes met for a moment, and he gave me a single, grave nod.

Across the battlefield, the conjoined armies of Bernicia and Deira stood waiting, a wall of metal as far as I could see. It was almost laughable to think that I had once considered the army of Klumeck such a vast force, a sea of lanterns in the dark.

Both the Bernician army that had marched to Caer Ligualid and even the siege of Ynys Metcaut paled in comparison to this. My hand tightened on my sword hilt. My stomach knotted with the dreadful thought that we may not win this war.

"Before we left, I told Evelyn..." The words tumbled out of my mouth quietly as I swallowed down the first lump of fear rising in my throat. "I told her that sometimes I wonder whether I'm a king or a soldier. That perhaps I'm only one, pretending to be the other." I tore my gaze from the sea of metal in front of me. "What do you think, brother?"

"There is no pretence, sire; you are both." My captain gave no hint in his face that he had just said farewell to the woman he loved, perhaps for the last time. "The one thing you are is not false, my lord. You are my king, who I am proud to serve." Here he dipped his head quickly, then his eyes fixed upon me again.

"You are also my brother, whom I fight alongside as I always have done. I do not see two warring selves, Daniel. Only one, the one who is both ready to lead us and give his life for his people. The best man I know," he ended quietly.

"Thank you, John." My answer was barely above a whisper. Looking at him, I saw all the years of our friendship in the solidarity of his features. "The same to you, old friend."

"My lord," he said, a small smile curving at the side of his mouth. With that, we switched our gazes back to the field. Abruptly, the war drums stopped. The eerie silence that followed was almost deafening. My teeth gritted. King Owain and I had attempted negotiations with King Morgant the night before, if we could term it that, so we would not ride out to meet him now.

"This is the furthest most of us have ever travelled." My voice sounded clear over the silent air as I drew my own sword. "We left Rheged many days ago, but home has never been closer to our hearts. Today, we fight not just a distant enemy," I went on. "We fight for our families, our lands, our very way of life. We fight for who are and who we love!" My voice rose yet higher. "May God be with us all!"

A chorus of agreement boomed out as my soldiers drew their swords and thrust them into the air. At last, I slid down the visor of my helmet. I lifted a hand, ready to give the signal to the archers.

I trusted that above us, Aife and her archers would be setting their arrows upon their bows. My head turned, searching for King Owain. As the Supreme Ruler of Rheged, it was at his signal that we would commence the battle. King Owain drew his sword.

We cheered and raised our swords again. My blade glinted in the new dawn. As I met King Owain's eyes a final time, he gave a single nod. I drank my last breath of free air, full of grass and trees and wind.

"Charge!" I bellowed, at the same moment King Owain and King Lot's guttural cries pierced the air. This was it. The reckoning of Rheged had come.

The sea of Bernicians and Deirans tore towards us as one steel wave. Moments flashed by as our boots trampled over mud. Then, all at once, inevitability arrived. They bore down on us, the culmination of a wrathful tide. I thrust my sword at the first man I saw. It pierced his abdomen. He gave a cry as I leapt over him. Then I saw my next opponent.

Already, agonised screams filled the air, blood soaking the earth. The ancient dance of kill or be killed had begun. Metal clanged against metal; blood spilled against blood. Bone broke against bone as war chants transformed into the howls of the wounded and dying.

I grunted as an arrow thudded emptily against my breastplate. I ducked against my foe and parried. My sword found a gap at his armpit. I rose my shield to bash against his head. Charging forwards again, I tried to tear through the wall of metal before me. I knew to stop would be my doom. The only option was to keep going, whatever the cost.

Abruptly, a force knocked my right arm, sending my sword flying. I cursed, dropping to the floor. As I rolled, the enemy who bashed my arm landed on top of me. I gritted my teeth against the weight of their armour. My right hand was trapped as my foe scrambled on top of me, reaching for my throat. My left hand found my dagger from my boot. In the next moment, I plunged it into his neck. Blood spurted forth as I pushed him away. It took considerable effort to pull my dagger back out of his flesh.

I took a moment to breathe while I reached for my sword. As I got to my feet, my right arm ached a little. I could still wield my blade, however. That was all that mattered.

"Protect the King! Protect the King!" I pivoted on the spot as I heard the warning. For a moment I wondered if they were referring to me, but I was not in immediate danger. Then I spied them across the field. King Morgant and King Owain. To my dismay, my greatest enemy had the advantage.

"Protect the King!" The cry sprang from my own lips this time as I raced towards them. King Owain fought valiantly against four or five other Bernician soldiers, as well as King Morgant. I smashed into a soldier, plunging my sword into a gap on his leg, then kept going.

I sprinted towards the Supreme Ruler of Rheged, as I had done to King Urien at Ynys Metcaut. The same way I had run to King Cedric, my uncle, in the battle outside Caer Ligualid. Would I be too late to save a king, for the third time? Would King Owain meet the same fate as them?

I ran towards King Owain, as swiftly as my legs could carry me. Abruptly, Prince Elffin leapt into the fray. My eyes widened in horror and I almost tripped over a fallen Bernician soldier. It was brave of the lad to try to save his father, but if they killed him too, the direct heir would also be lost. My jaw clenched. I simply could not let it happen.

I reached the circle of warriors surrounding father and son the same time as another couple of Briton soldiers did. Together, we sprang into the fray. At the last moment I rolled. My helmet kissed the bloodied earth. As I rose on bended knee, I slashed across the knees of my first foe. Then I leapt to my feet, putting my next two enemies to the sword also.

Cold indifference shot through me. I realised I didn't even care about these enemy soldiers. Though desperate to aid King Owain, I yearned to get close enough to King Morgant, hacking at any enemy flesh. The same way I had longed to kill the Wolf. I could almost imagine the smell of blood that would burst forth from King Morgant's veins.

I was almost there, when one of King Morgant's thugs yanked my shoulder painfully. I turned briefly, forced to put him to the sword first. Then, as I turned back, King Morgant savagely swiped his sword across King Owain's neck.

"No!" I cried, as the body of King Owain crumpled, his soul wrenched from his body.

Yet again, I had dismally failed to save another of Rheged's kings. King Morgant sneered, his blade raised high to strike Prince Elffin, whose gaze was transfixed painfully upon his father's body.

"No!" I took off again towards the monster and leapt forwards. As I sailed through the air, the grieving lad at last turned his stricken face to King Morgant. I saw the shock entering his gaze. Elffin blindly tried to parry him, but far too late to block the fatal blow successfully.

I landed, my sword crashing against King Morgant's blade. The force of it brought our faces only inches apart. King Morgant glared at me with open hatred. I summoned all my rage to return his stare in double, even triple measures. I kept the pressure on my blade, locking us together.

"Ah, King Bryce." His cruel whisper reached me over the din of the battle. His dark eyes were almost black as they bore into mine. "I was starting to think we wouldn't meet today. Which would have been a shame, don't you think?" he sneered softly.

"Aye. I wouldn't have missed this opportunity," I breathed back. All thoughts of God had fled my mind. All I knew was that I wanted to make him suffer.

"Well." I abruptly shoved him so our swords broke contact. He only staggered back a couple of paces, the sneer still fixed on his face. "Let's dance then, you and I." I pointed the tip of my sword in his direction. King Morgant's crooked smile grew, eyes lighting up as he inclined his head.

"Wait!" Elffin challenged. "He just killed my father. I deserve my chance for vengeance." King Morgant grinned fully now, seeming only too happy with this arrangement.

"I ask you to leave this to me. Your Majesty," I said. Elffin blinked at me, as if only just realising he had inherited his father's kingdom. "Your father would want you to live this day, to rule Rheged," I told him. King Morgant snorted softly.

"It is pure fantasy you think there will be anything left of Rheged, after today," he chuckled. The new king of Caer Ligualid stepped forwards, eyes wild with hatred.

"Wait, my lord," I said again, stopping him in his tracks. "Rheged needs their leader." I did not mention how King Morgant had been fighting twenty years longer than Elffin had been alive. Nor did I give reference to how every ounce of my blood thirsted for vengeance.

"Go, encourage your people. Rumours of the king's death will already be spreading. Your people need know someone is still leading them," I pointed out. His eyes hardened. The new king already had his first test. Would he insist on fighting himself, or would he relinquish revenge and lead his people?

"Very well," King Elffin growled. His eyes darted to King Morgant, then he glared at me. "Kill him for me, King Bryce." My shoulders momentarily slackened out of pure relief as he walked away, accompanied by the guards who had tried valiantly to defend King Owain.

"Well, here we are at last, King Bryce." Morgant said, a thread of humour in his voice. My relief faded as I took a stilling breath to centre myself. I already knew I relished the thought of killing him far too much. Once more all thoughts of God fled. I wanted to smash his smirk into the ground until there was nothing of him left.

"You said yourself I have destroyed most of your kin," he taunted. I said nothing, focusing on inhaling and slowly releasing the morning air. It was already sweltering with the stench of blood and death. "Your mother and your father, your aunt and the child that dwelt within her. Then, nearly five years ago, I killed your uncle." King Morgant grinned again.

Once more I forced myself to say nothing. My insides boiled in white-hot fury. He was just trying to provoke me, I told myself, to make me leap forwards in the heat of my rage. The problem was his tactic had begun to work.

"After I have defeated you, then there will only be your sister and her babe and your wife and your child before I have obliterated your line out of existence. I will have accomplished what I wanted to do over twenty-five years ago." He grinned again. "How is your daughter?"

My teeth chewed my bottom lip of their own accord. I mustered every iota of self-control to stop myself from launching forward to cut off his forked tongue.

"Do not worry." King Morgant sneered again, brandishing his sword at me. "After I have dealt with you and your wife, I promise, your daughter will not be an orphan for long."

"No!" I shouted, the last semblance of my restraint snapping. The snake grinned in the moments before I reached him. Too late I realised my error. King Morgant parried me easily, then spun to attack. I dodged, but not fast enough. The brunt of his sword came down upon my arm.

Thankfully, the force of my impact hit my armour. I leapt back, cleanly avoiding King Morgant's second blow. I cursed myself for my folly. My foe's sneer grew as we began to circle one another again.

Calm, I told myself. Be calm. In my peripheral vision, I saw others fighting all around, but I paid them no heed. All the world I knew right now had shrunk to just the two of us.

"Come on, King Bryce." Morgant's tone dripped with sarcasm, but I strove more than ever to ignore him. I would not be provoked again, for it could cost me my life. "Let me send you back to your parents," he taunted.

I willed myself not to reply as we circled each other. Then, just for a moment, his eyes hardened — and that was enough to reveal his scheme. Carefully, I kept my face clear of my realisation. His mockery was also his power over me. If I resisted him, it could be his undoing.

"I shall then do the same to your sister," he seethed. Though King Morgant's words stung, they suddenly seemed empty. His eyes hardened again. I knew I was right. Ignoring his taunts vexed him.

King Morgant's gaze flickered about his surroundings. I kept my countenance impassive. I simply had to wait a little longer. The snake would launch an attack.

"What makes you think you can do it?" I told him, trying to beat him at his own game. "You have failed so many times before."

King Morgant's features transformed into wild rage. He opened his mouth but for a moment, no noise came out. It was an eerie, silent scream.

"I will finish what we started, boy!" King Morgant bellowed. Spit accompanied every syllable that erupted from his foul mouth.

When he charged, I was ready. I had been waiting for this moment for my entire life. From the time this monster had betrayed his fellow Britons and sent Aldred to murder my parents while they slept.

I held my ground, then dodged at the last moment. I swiftly pirouetted to attack. Understanding flashed across his eyes as our swords clashed. He leapt back, then charged again. Our blades sliced through the air to clang together at every turn. Then I spotted a weakness. As his sword hit my breastplate, I used the momentum to drive my blade up, slicing across his armpit.

Blood gushed forth, spattering his armour. He staggered backwards but managed to stay on his feet. He grinned manically, almost as if he enjoyed the pain. For the first time, I wondered if King Morgant might be insane. He charged forwards, grunting, his sword now in his other hand. I dodged him again, batting away his blade. I leapt to strike him again, but he retreated backwards.

"I could have done it, you know," King Morgant rasped. He sucked air between his teeth, his right arm clamped to his side to try to staunch the flow of his blood. "Aldred nearly had you that night, all those years ago." He craned his head to spit, before glaring back up at me.

"If only your aunt had not screamed," he burst out suddenly. He barked out what could have been a laugh, if not for his frustration. "You would have died long ago if your uncle had not put you in that carriage, or if you had not been found in the snow."

"If only your parents had not been murdered that night," I answered. "Then perhaps the monster I see before me would not be here." King Morgant's face contorted into what could have been rage, or perhaps pain — I could not tell. Then abruptly he laughed, tilting his head to the side, as if truly contemplating the idea.

"Aye, perhaps not. I suppose we'll never know what could have been." King Morgant's eyes gleamed with humour. I could not understand him. He had slackened his grip on his sword and his good arm had lowered almost to the floor. He glanced with mild interest at the blood flowing from his armpit.

"That was a good move." King Morgant gave a wry grin. I said nothing. In this absurd moment, I wondered if he might yield. What would I do? Rage and hatred consumed me. Thoughts of God had fled. After all he had done, I did not know whether I would have the strength or the compassion to grant him mercy.

King Morgant straightened, the smile slowly slipping from his features. He rose his sword. From the hardness of his eyes, I knew he would not yield, making my thoughts about mercy redundant. My foe would fight until either my life was spent, or his.

"You can barely stand," I pointed out bluntly, nodding at his injured arm. King Morgant only grinned again. Did he want to die? Did he wish that he'd died the night he saw his mother stabbed?

"Aye, this is probably my end. I would rather die here trying to fulfil my mission than surrender to the likes of you—" He broke off to cough. Both arms moved to his mouth and further blood spattered to the earth as the wound was exposed.

"Why?" The question growled from my throat. "Why did you make such a vow to murder my family? Purely so the King of Bernicia would grant you power?"

"Partly," he groaned, voice hoarse. "I told you last night, Daniel. King Urien gave my uncle no aid, even though he had written to him with his fears about raiders. He cared nothing for Bernicia, even as the Angles took all we had. What could have happened across Briton, had King Urien heeded my uncle's warning? Could he have turned the tide of this war before it even started?"

"That is ludicrous!" I shook my head. "What happened to you was evil, but you do not have the right to show that evil in kind," I pointed out. The sounds of battle still raged on, but suddenly the war seemed far away.

"You could have worked alongside us. You could have been loyal to Rheged. We could have beaten them back fully at Ynys Metcaut, had you not had King Urien assassinated."

"I wanted him to be stabbed in the back, just as my mother was," King Morgant snapped back. "I vowed I would make Rheged pay for their lack of compassion not to aid Bernicia."

"You taking your revenge on King Urien may have doomed all Rheged," I told him. He sneered, seeming to take pride in all the deaths he had caused. "Your thirst for revenge has turned you into a being far worse than the one who killed your kin." I raised my sword. "Do you yield?" King Morgant sneered.

"I do not." My formidable foe straightened to full height. "I would rather perish by your blade than surrender to it," he said flatly. "I hope once I am dead, my men will hack you to pieces."

"We shall see." I tightened my hand on the hilt on my blade. King Morgant half ran, half staggered towards me. I stood still.

Then, at the last possible moment, I leapt out of the way. I span around, the hilt of my sword bashing into his head. He crumpled to the floor. King Morgant reached for his sword, wheezing as blood from his armpit soaked the earth. I reached him and kicked it out of his hand, just as his fingers curled around the hilt.

"This is for all the blood you have so ruthlessly spilt. This is for King Urien, for King Owain and my uncle King Cedric." King Morgant only writhed a little in the prospect of his end. I raised my blade. "Even if

Rheged loses this day, you will not cause them more pain!" I brought my sword down hard, severing his head from his neck.

I did not have any time to relish in the death of my foe. No sooner had the soul gone from King Morgant's body than a loud cry pierced the air. I turned just in time to parry the attack of the Bernician soldiers. Their eyes were wild and frenzied at the death of their king.

I leapt forwards as my fellow Briton soldiers arrived. Together, we crashed into the metal of the enemy. I raised my blade that no longer glinted in the sunlight, long since stained with blood and gore. The makeshift arena quickly dispersed, friend and foe alike scattering to do battle with one another.

"Your Majesty, duck!" At Aife's voice, I threw myself to the ground. My spirit soared to know she still lived. Her spear sailed past to lodge into the skull of my latest enemy. I rolled to crouch behind a rock, hand gripping my sword tightly. I took a moment to breathe, letting the truth of King Morgant's death sink in.

"My lord," Aife panted, as she rolled next to me. I saw her helmet had gone, obviously knocked off by the enemy. She glanced to me and smiled. "It's good to see you in one piece still, brother."

"You as well." I lifted my visor for a moment. "Thank you for that." I briefly touched her arm as I nodded towards her spear. "John," I muttered, as he ducked for cover beside us. I was immensely grateful for one more moment with them.

"King Owain is dead," I told them heavily. "I just killed King Morgant." Aife only nodded, no surprise in her eyes. Perhaps she had been close enough to the skirmish to witness what had happened. Or maybe the rumours of the battle were already spreading. "Report, Captain," I ordered simply.

"Many are dead, sire," John replied grimly. "I'm not sure if we will win the day." I nodded. He confirmed what I had begun to suspect. "That does not mean we will make their victory any easier." He smirked, then it faded as he glanced to Aife.

"I just wondered, my love," he said quietly. His hand glided through a loose strand of her hair. "If we get out of this alive, will you marry me?"

I could not help but crack a grin, even in amidst the blood, violence, and screams of the dying. Aife smiled broadly, jarring only a little with the angry red graze across her forehead and the mud on her cheek.

"Aye," she whispered faintly. She reached for his hand and clasped it tightly. "I will." John grinned underneath his helmet. The two came together for a brief kiss.

"Well, I think that might just give me the strength to stay alive," he quipped. The smile faded from his features. "Shall we?"

"Once more into hell," I muttered grimly. I slid my helmet visor back down. Aife shifted her grip on her spear. A moment later and the three of us left our haven for the massacre all around us.

***

I stopped dead. Dread entered my gut, swift and thick. The groan came again, somehow punctuating louder than all the other howls of the wounded. The second time, it faded away into despair. I turned on the spot, praying it was only imagination.

A sea of chaos, of blood and mud swirled around me. Bones shattered and lives ebbed away into a mist of nothing. How could I have heard such a cry? He must have been close, to cut through the din of clanging metal of axes, spears of swords. Where was he?

For the groan had been from John. The ball of dread knotting in my heart told me what it could mean. Nameless grief for a sorrow still hidden erupted. I span round again, but there was still nothing. I ran forwards a few feet, towards where I thought the sound had come from.

Then, abruptly, I saw them. I stopped dead as the grief tightened still further, desperately hoping my vision was somehow lying, that it was not as awful as it appeared. I ran towards them, barely noticing the two or three Bernicians I cut down along the way for daring to step into my path. The route that separated me from talking to my friend a final time. One of my closest friends, whom I had known for so many years. Was it to be this way, then? I wondered helplessly, skidding to a stop across the earth, fresh and hot with blood. Was this how the time for the three of us on this earth would end?

As I at last came upon them, the ball of grief threatened to be unleashed, but I would not let it. Not until the last moments of life ebbed away. Until that inevitable time came, I was determined to live in the present. To be with my friend to the end, as we had always promised one another.

"Aife." I rasped out the word. My hand reached to grasp hers as I sank to my knees beside my sister. My old friend's breath came quick and shallow. A little blood pooled in the corner of her mouth. An arrow was lodged into her abdomen, blood gushing forth in its wake. The wound was plainly fatal.

"Daniel." Aife's voice sounded so ordinary, her fingers so strong as they clutched my hand, that it almost gave me hope. Aife shifted, gritting her teeth.

"It was a good shot," she wheezed. The slightest thread of humour traced through her tone. My old friend would keep her wit until the last. John shuffled forward beside her, gripping her other hand tightly in both of his. My brother, one of such reserve, showed his heart openly. Were anyone else to look his way, they would see all that he was, in all his complexities.

The sheer helplessness reflected in both of our expressions. How could I tell him anything that could offer any comfort? Our gazes drew back to Aife, this dear friend, who had grown up in the villages outside Gaeson and had learned to shoot since she was four. Who had stolen John's heart long ago and would now take it with her into the next world.

"I love you," came John's desperate declaration. The well of grief could be barred no longer. The first of many tears began, mixing with the sweat and grime. "I will always love you." He spoke rapidly, trying to utter his heart before she passed.

"You are in my very soul." He brought her hand to his lips and swiftly kissed it. The same words he had told her before the battle started. In another world, before the arrow had pierced her flesh. "That is how I have always seen you. You are one half of me."

"Aye," came Aife's rough reply. "As you are of me." Speech already became almost too difficult for her. She could only have a few moments left.

"I'm sorry, John." At her heartbroken murmur, her free hand left mine, rising instead to cup his cheeks. "That half will have go on from here." Her voice weakened further to a whisper, her breathing growing erratic.

"No, don't leave me." Tears rolled down John's features. "How can I go on, my love? Where can I go on if you aren't there?" He inhaled sharply.

"You'll find your way, as we all do." Her index finger stroked gently at the dark stubble on his chin. A smile creased her features, full of her heart. "No regrets, remember? We promised."

"I'll try, Aife," he murmured, pain pierced through every syllable. I watched them, heartbroken and lost for words. "I will cherish forever the moments we shared last night." My brother kissed her hand and took a single, shuddering breath. "I would've married you—" He choked back a half-sob.

"In another life," Aife rasped. "Aye." John hung his head. "I would've liked to have been your wife," she murmured, her voice suddenly clear yet soft. It was ethereal, almost dreamlike. "I'm glad I had your love on this earth." Somehow, even now, a smile curled at Aife's face.

"You will have mine wherever I go from here, until we meet again." John nodded fiercely and bent forwards. I averted my gaze as they shared their last kiss. In all these last few minutes I had been silent, trying to stem the tide of my own grief in respect for theirs. I heard her breathing growing worse.

"Daniel," she muttered, seeming to sense this. I glanced back to her. Agony and distress were dominant features now.

"I'm here, sister." I tried to smile at her as I reached for her free hand. "We're both here." We stayed either side of her. Aife's eyes found the man who would have been her husband. In another life.

"John." My friend uttered his name a final time before her eyes rolled back and the last breath left her body. Aife was dead.

"No…" John's objection came as a mere whisper, almost mistaken for the whistling wind. The two of us remained there, holding onto her limp hands, both clinging to the woman we had loved, each in our own way, since we were fifteen.

Heavily, my free hand reached to John's shoulder as we knelt there in silence. I did not even try to find the words. In this thick, raw grief, nothing could be said. Death's pervasive shroud, an impermeable fog, settled over us.

"Retreat!" I jerked my head up from Aife. A soldier from Caer Ligualid raced across the battlefield, deftly leaping over the fallen bodies. Seeing us, the soldier ground to a halt.

“Your Majesty,” he panted, inclining his head. He clasped his arm to his chest. “King Elffin has given the order to retreat, my lords,” he muttered. “His Majesty is asking for you. He says we must be swift if we are to—”

“Very well.” My voice sounded strange as I cut him off, as foreign to my ears as it had done the day my uncle died. I sniffed, reluctantly letting go of Aife’s hand.

I looked around, to see hardly anyone still fighting. Any Briton soldiers sprinted towards where the remnant of our armies gathered. The Bernicians and Deirans pursued with swords drawn, but it was a slow march. At least we had given it our all. The force before us was much depleted, not strong enough to give us full chase. Still, at the rate they were marching, they would soon be upon us.

“You,” John muttered from beside me, abruptly getting to his feet. “Grab another soldier and come back to carry Aife to safety.” The soldier widened his eyes slightly, averting his gaze to me. I nodded to confirm the order. He darted off to obey at once.

“There’s nothing more we can do for her now, except to take her body back with us,” John murmured, glancing to me. “I’m not leaving her here, Daniel.”

“I know,” I replied quietly. I glanced towards the Bernicians and Deirans, still steadily marching. “Neither am I.” John’s eyes widened.

“No, my lord. You are still our king, our people need you,” he said through gritted teeth. “You must go — now.” He took a step towards me.

“We still have time.” I glanced back to the enemy, still a little distance away. “I’m not leaving you.” A moment later, the soldier returned, along with another. “Be as careful as you can,” I ordered. One of them held her underneath her armpits, the other her legs.

“Let’s go,” I said. The four of us broke into a run, John and I out front. The two soldiers followed, carrying Aife between them. The even tread of my captain’s boots kept in perfect pace with mine, as always. With every step across the battlefield, I felt the snap of my heart breaking again that my dearest friend was dead.

Chapter Fifteen

So many had fallen. We leapt over the dead bodies of friend and foe alike as the Bernicians and Deirans pursued us. King Elffin was up ahead, where the rest of Rheged temporarily gathered. The new king of Caer Ligualid barked orders for a swift retreat. I swallowed hard, utterly helpless to do anything for these warriors. As helpless as I had been to save Aife.

Could she really be dead? A fresh wave of grief tore through me, and I clenched my teeth. Surely, I was wrong. I would see her wry smile up ahead, eyes flashing with her usual wit.

No, she was dead. I had seen the life ebb away from her, witnessed her last breath. Her corpse followed us, being carried by those Caer Ligualid soldiers. I took a faltering gasp of air as I walked. The heavy burden of grief made even the simplest things difficult.

All the fighting had stopped now. The retreated soldiers scurried about ahead, preparing the horses. Two or three Rheged soldiers spotted me and ran in our direction, but there wasn't much need for the extra protection. I glanced over my shoulder to see that the front line of Bernicia and Deira had paused, although their swords were still drawn.

Perhaps King Ethelfrith already showed more mercy than his predecessors. For the time being, we were almost safe. The same expression reflected amongst the Briton soldiers, some collective instinct, something palpable suspended between relief and pain.

"Your Majesty King Elffin." My breath still came a little heavy as I approached him. I removed my helmet, roving my hand through hair still slick with sweat. Beside me, John silently inclined his head. The young King Elffin met my gaze, grief etched onto his features as surely as it was engraved onto mine.

"You are to prioritise her body." I heard John whispering his order behind us. "Transport her with the wounded to Caer Ligualid. She is to be buried there." My breath caught in my throat, remembering that

Gaeson may no longer be safe. Would King Morgant have made good on his threat to send his raiders to my home? Would he fulfil his promise of destruction, even from beyond the grave?

"Here he comes." King Elffin scowled. His eyes were fixed behind me. I turned around to see King Ethelfrith had broken from his front line, marching steadily towards us. Triumph etched all too clearly on his face. My hand tightened on the hilt of my blade. How dare he look so gleeful, when one of my best friends was dead?

"I'll soon put an end to that smirking face," Elffin seethed from beside me, coming to the same conclusion as me. His hand was tight on his sword also.

"Don't." Elffin turned to glare at me at my harsh word. I remembered I spoke to the Supreme Ruler of Rheged now. "That is, Your Majesty," I corrected, inclining my head to him.

"King Ethelfrith may give us this one chance to surrender to him and retreat with our lives," I warned. "If you put him or anyone else to the sword, they will slaughter us all without mercy," I hissed, as King Ethelfrith grew closer. "We must put up with his arrogance, for the sake of our people."

"So be it." Elffin growled out his tolerance, strongly reminiscent of his father. Air escaped out of my lips in relief. It struck me then that out of the three kings that had met the previous night by firelight, I was the only one still alive. At least remembering how I had struck King Morgant dead brought a morsel of consolation and satisfaction against the vast ocean of all we had lost.

"Greetings, King Bryce, King Elffin," said the Bernician king, coming towards us. I tried and failed not to notice how his eyes sparkled with pride.

"Your victory is clear, King Ethelfrith." King Elffin's voice came forcibly neutral, gritting his teeth. "We hereby surrender." The Bernician king gave a single nod.

"A melody to my ears, gentleman. I'm sorry about your father, in a way. I wished to do the deed myself, but King Morgant got there before me." He grinned. King Elffin's eyes grew frenzied with rage, but mercifully, somehow managed not to reach for his blade.

"Well," King Ethelfrith said, sounding almost bored. "Let's discuss the particulars, shall we? It would be tempting to gut every last one of you as you flee, but you put up a good fight. I don't think my men have the strength." He chortled. I looked away, hardly able to stand him. So much for his mercy, but at least he would let us leave alive — even if not through his own choice. I stood, barely hearing the conditions of our surrender to Bernicia. Up ahead, I could already see the soldiers from Gododdin preparing their own retreat.

"Thank you," King Elffin said stiffly, through gritted teeth. King Ethelfrith only grinned. "Please accept my father's sword as the symbol of Rheged's surrender," King Elffin said formally. He took King Owain's sword from his captain and handed it to King Ethelfrith. Bernicia's king smirked faintly as he took it, before handing it to the soldier next to him.

"It is your right to ask for my blade, also, should you wish it," King Elffin pointed out reluctantly. King Ethelfrith's smirk grew a fraction wider.

"You may keep your blade, King Elffin," he replied. "Perhaps we will meet in battle again one day. Maybe you can even use it against me, if fortune smiles upon you."

"You have my thanks." Caer Ligualid's new king nodded again. I glanced at the lad, still only eighteen years of age, dealing with kingship and the death of his father only months after his mother had gone to the grave. I might have felt some sympathy for him, if all my grief was not directed towards Aife.

"I require fifty prisoners of war from your able-bodied men," King Ethelfrith said, waving his hand dismissively, as if this were purely an academic matter. "I'll take them from Caer Ligualid." King Ethelfrith cracked another grin.

"You'll agree this is most strategic, is it not?" he smirked. "Klumeck was destroyed long ago," he added, glancing to me. "As for Gaeson—"

"What of Gaeson?" The question sprang from my lips. King Ethelfrith's smirk grew. Dread clawed anew at my very core. "Tell me, sire," I bid him fiercely. "Did King Morgant send a raid?"

"He sent two hundred men, just before the battle started," King Ethelfrith said, nodding. "I made no objections, seeing as we had so many to spare." He grinned as my eyes shot wide in horror.

"Rheged has surrendered this day." My voice was a harsh whisper.

"Some of my people may still live. My wife and child might still be alive." I clung desperately to the thought. "I bid you let me go back to Gaeson, my lord. To reclaim whatever is left." I stared at him hard, waiting. King Morgant's humanity had long disappeared, but perhaps King Ethelfrith still had some. My hands clenched into fists at their own accord.

"Soon, Gaeson will no longer be any threat to Bernicia," King Ethelfrith murmured in thought, his arms folded by his side. "King Morgant ordered them to burn Gaeson to the ground." The image of Klumeck burning tore through my mind. Would I be too late to save my home, for a second time?

"Why not? You will only take what little remains to Caer Ligualid. You have my leave to recover all that remain," he said, then grinned. "After all, perhaps once my men have rested, we will find you along the road."

"Very well." I nodded. The single shot of relief at his permission was tempered quickly by the threat. Both clamoured for attention against my soul's wearied grief.

"I believe our business is concluded, King Elffin," King Ethelfrith said then. "You may retreat without us pursuing you. At least, not immediately." He flashed us another grin. "Well," he nodded to us, "till we meet again, perhaps on another battlefield." With that, he left us, heading back to his army.

"Sire." I turned at once to King Elffin. "I shall take some soldiers still able to fight, to see what is left in Gaeson. We will then head to Caer Ligualid, to join our people, with your permission."

"Aye, of course. All will be welcome. You had better move swiftly, Daniel," Elffin said darkly. "King Ethelfrith means to chase you." I nodded. "May God be with you."

"Thank you, my lord. You as well." The King of Caer Ligualid gave me a faint smirk as he nodded. With that, I quickly departed his company, breaking into a run as I headed to where the surviving soldiers of Gaeson and Klumeck had gathered. John, as ever, was beside me.

"Captain, give the order to depart, as soon as possible. I don't want to leave any of our dead here, but we have no other choice."

"Aye, my lord." John's bent his head, his voice and expression unreadable. He then swiftly turned back to the remainder of our people, gathered in front of us.

"Anyone still able to fight, we must prepare to leave now. We ride back to Gaeson, where King Morgant has sent a raid." I took in their horrified expressions. "The wounded will wait here to leave with King Elffin and Caer Ligualid. His soldiers will help you. That is all," he said. "Those who can fight, head back to our camp!"

It took almost all the strength we had left to race back across the battlefield, heading towards the camp. It only took a little time to ready the horses, but the dread gathering in my stomach told me we could already be too late. I swung up onto Epos.

"Your Majesty!" I turned to see Ewan running towards us, his arm hastily bandaged. Clearly, he had come from the wounded. He inclined his head. "Sire, I can fight. I bid to join you." I regarded him a moment, knowing exactly the reason why Ewan wanted to come. Cara had left the surgery, but Leigh had told her she was not well enough to fight. If there was any chance that he could help her, he would jump at it.

"Are you sure?" Ewan only nodded, determination burning fiercely in his eyes. "All right then, hurry." I gathered Epos' reins in my hands. "You're wounded, use a horse." I pointed to a young lad on horseback who seemed to have escaped the battle unscathed.

"Thank you, my lord." Ewan ran and immediately swapped places with the young lad. I glanced behind me to check the lines. Then, with one hand on the reins, I drew my sword with the other.

"For Gaeson!" I shouted. Then we were off, hurrying to our homeland. John and I rode at the front, leading our party to Gaeson. Other soldiers were on horseback, with the others running at the rear.

There were one hundred and fifty of us in total; soldiers combined from Gaeson and Klumeck. It would take us a few days to ride home. I could only pray we would get there in time and that I had enough warriors at my command to stop King Morgant's raid. So many had been too injured to fight and would soon be their way to Caer Ligualid.

Desperation churned in my stomach. It was horribly akin to when my uncle and I had ridden to Klumeck to see what remained. However, that pain paled in compassion to the agony felt now. For then, seven years ago, I had been riding to a place I did not know, that I had only just come to see as my own.

This, though, was my home I had always known. The people I had loved all my life. My heart burned at the thought of Gaeson in ruins. Would the castle have the same fire blazing through it as Klumeck had? Would my mother be trapped in her room, with no one to help her escape? The thought made me spur Epos on even faster.

Soon we had left the battlefield behind. We slowed the horses from a gallop to a canter, for they could not last much longer at full speed. I kept my eyes peeled straight ahead, as if somehow, I could make the horizon ever closer.

If King Morgant had indeed sent off his raid at dawn, as the battle was starting, then they would have left hours ago. The sun was now set high in the sky. We were almost at midsummer now, the sun harsh as it beat down upon us. As we rode, the reality of Aife's death hit me again. To my shame, I had to push it down, even though it burnt deep in my throat. I had to force myself to mourn later. For now, I had to keep my attention on the living.

***

"Here's as good a place as any to make camp, my lord," John called to me as the last of daylight began to ebb away. My captain's voice was almost its normal impassiveness, if not for the hollowness I detected underneath it.

"Very good." We pulled our horses to a grateful stop. I patted Epos' mane in thanks. It had been a hard day of riding. Our best efforts had taken us through the plains and gentle slopes of southern Bernicia. By this time tomorrow, I hoped we would cross most of the southern hills separating us from the border to Rheged. Then, the final day would take us to Gaeson itself. It encouraged me to be that much closer to home, but would it be enough? We could only hope.

By the time darkness fell, the tents had been hastily unpacked and erected. A few soldiers prepared a meal. Others gathered in the dim firelight, trying to rest and warm themselves. A few in our party who insisted they could still fight were dealing with minor injuries, like Ewan.

I had space for the first time since Briton had surrendered to assess my own injuries. There was an angry welt on my leg that had been roughly dressed. I just about remembered receiving it, plummeting to the floor. An axe could not be easily dodged. My right hand ached badly from the soldier who had knocked my sword from me. There was also a cut on my neck, from when a splinter of wood had lodged itself there. Presumably when my wooden shield was hacked to pieces. I was bruised and sore, but still standing. That was so much more than I could say for my brothers and sisters in arms. So much more than I could say for Aife.

I lowered my hand from my neck, looking for John. I spotted him alone, leaning his back against a fallen log, sat a little way back from the fire where soldiers hastily prepared an evening meal. After retrieving a full skin of wine from my saddlebag, I headed over to him.

"Here." I held out the wineskin as I slumped down next to him. My brother stared at the flames in front of him, making no movement to take the wine. I tugged out the cap and took a long drink myself. Words to somehow convey my grief and sorrow fell away, trite and hollow. I couldn't imagine his agony. Surely so beyond the raw pain tearing through me.

"It's so wrong!" I burst out. In the corner of my eye, John nodded. I turned to regard him, softly illuminated by the flames. It was the second time in two nights I had watched firelight play on a man's face, but the circumstances could not be more different. Rather than the sneer of my greatest enemy, this was my brother grieving the woman he loved.

His features were dim, but I could make out the dirt and blood that blackened his features. Whiter streaks where tears had long since run cut through the grime, making his appearance even more haggard. I could not fathom how to comfort him. Perhaps silence was better in the face of the unimaginable, rather than the wrong counsel. For a while, the only sounds were the crackling fire and the quiet talk of the soldiers.

"She's still there, Daniel," John murmured. "In my soul. She'll always be there." My friend turned his gaze heavenward. Fresh tears trailed down his cheeks. "Aife was the better half of me… she brought out the best in me." He swiped at his eyes. "I wonder what I'll be, without her."

His grief undid me. My throat burned, my own tears spilling down my cheeks. I reached to grip his shoulder, hoping that the simple act might give him comfort where words failed. I took another gulp of wine before offering it to him again.

"Thank you, brother." This time John accepted it from me. I glanced to the flames up ahead while he took a long drink. I stared dismally at the vivid hues of red and orange.

The three of us had been in this fight, in this life together, ever since John and I had met her on the first day of recruitment training. They had both stood by me, risking their lives for me the night I had been imprisoned for treason by the late King Reghan. Their friendship had transcended the boundaries of rank when I became a prince, then later a king.

What would our friendship be like, without her? I wondered, echoing John's stricken question. Here, John passed the wineskin back to me, before abruptly getting to his feet.

"I have given the soldiers a rota for keeping watch, my lord." His posture had straightened slightly, his countenance again impassive. My brother had become my captain once more. Perhaps duty was how he would survive the next few days. "With your permission, sire, I'll retire."

"You should eat something, first," I muttered. "We're going to need our strength tomorrow. Take some stew to your tent."

"Aye, my lord." He inclined his head before turning, heading for where the food was being prepared. After few moments I stood, knowing I should heed my own advice.

"Here, Your Majesty." I went to join the line of the other soldiers to receive the meal, but of course, one of the soldiers went to give me a portion directly.

"Thank you." I longed to tell him I was no better than he and deserved no such privilege, but another voice in my mind still resembling logic told me it would do no good. I was a king; it seemed to be the way of things. I looked out towards my brothers and sisters.

"We've all lost a lot today." My voice was quiet as I took in their fatigued and sorrowful expressions. "Yet, hope still lives that our people in Gaeson may be spared. Turn in early, all of you. Get some rest while you can."

"Your Majesty." The soldiers chorused their obedience, inclining their heads as one. I gave them a final nod, before heading with the warm bowl of stew back to my own tent. Once inside, I gratefully discarded my armour. One of my troops had thoughtfully left a bowl of water in the corner of my tent. They had also managed to find clean clothes from somewhere.

I slumped down beside it, plunging my hands into the clear liquid. It was warm; it had obviously been warmed by the fire. I longed for a hot bath, but this would do. It would be a lot more than what most of the soldiers would have to make do with. I grabbed a cloth, scrubbing away at my hands and face before attacking my hair.

I peeled off my clothes, seeped in dirt and gore from the battle. I was careful to remove Evelyn's lace cloth from my tunic. It was stained with grime, so I carefully placed it in the water, massaging my thumb over it to get the worst of it off.

My discarded clothes were long since stained with blood. Some of it was from my own cuts and scrapes, but most of the crimson was from the wounds of others. My throat closed at the thought that some of the blood came from Aife.

After cleaning my body as best I could I sat back, dressed only in a fresh pair of long underwear. Wearily I turned my attention to the bowl of stew, until now ignored. The heavy grief of the day staved my appetite. Yet I forced myself to eat the cooling food, hardly noticing the taste.

As soon as I was done eating, I crawled onto the makeshift bed. One hand clutched Evelyn's lace cloth while the other pulled the blanket over me. With nothing else to distract me, the tide of grief swelled within me again. Alone and relatively safe in the privacy of my tent, I was too exhausted to do anything but yield to it. I buried my head in my pillow like a child, letting hot tears flow as I mourned my friend.

***

Two days later, riding along its eastern bank of the great lake, Epos' ears twitched. The spirits of the other horses had picked up that home was near.

"Nearly there, old girl," I murmured. Epos pawed a hoof upon the ground. "I know. It's all right." I patted her coat, attempting to soothe her. The strained mood filtered through the whole of our party. Relief at being almost back in Gaeson was met in equal measure with the fear of what we might find there. Dread rose slowly, unfurling ghastly fingers. Beckoning us to give up our last hope.

In the last moments before it disappeared, I glanced to the lake. The serene water sparkled in the sunshine, beside the deep russet earth of the bank. The trees and vegetation were a deep, velvet green, touched by the hues of summer. The idyllic scene before us jarred with our mood.

"Take courage!" I shouted, almost an hour later. My voice reached to the back of the lines as we plunged into the woodland surrounding Gaeson's hill. We thundered on, hooves interweaving through dense trees, clopping through earth softened with moss. It was darker here, with the gnarled branches twisting overhead. My stomach knotted. The next time we saw daylight fully, we would know Gaeson's fate. My hands tightened on the reins. I would not give up hope, not yet.

Finally, we broke through the treeline and as we ascended the steep incline, we got our first sight of home. My heart dropped to my stomach. Black smoke unfurled atop the stone, stretching out to the sky. The raiders were here.

I cursed silently as my blood ran cold. Perhaps the raid had only just arrived, but the thick wall of smoke continuing to seep out of the castle told me otherwise. Hope was that much harder to cling on to now. John glanced to me; features fierce. I nodded at him.

"Prepare to fight!" John shouted. I drew my sword. I heard the soft scraping as the others in my party followed suit.

"Just a little further," I muttered to Epos. My jaw clenched as we rode through the wooden barricade, now smashed to pieces. It looked like it had been done with a battering ram. Though we had survived the harshest heart of the war, this raid had the power to kill us just as easily as in Catraeth.

The portcullis was raised, two ladders perched on either side. Several Bernician soldiers lay fallen, arrows protruding from gaps in their armour. Yet, obviously, one of the raiders had made it to the top, then had opened the way for the others.

At last, we thundered into the courtyard. Horror shot through me to see warriors of Gaeson strewn across the stone floor. The cobbles that should be gleaming in the summer sunshine were now spattered with blood. It was so akin to the battlefield we had just left. The stench of death churned my stomach.

"They may still be here!" John's voice roared out. "Search for survivors! Put any Bernicians to the sword!" His orders were met with a chorus of obedience as our soldiers scattered.

"Captain, with me!" I cried, his order enough to kick me into action. I unhooked my shield from my back (a replacement had been given to me on the road) and wielded my blade. "We head for the throne room!"

"Aye, sire." John signalled that three others should follow us. The five of us sprinted across the courtyard. As we were halfway there, the large double doors suddenly opened.

"Queen Evelyn!" I shouted in relief to see her alive, but then my heart stopped. She was fighting off four soldiers at once. My wife fended them off excellently so far, but she was vastly outnumbered. "To Her Majesty!" I roared, tearing off once more, willing my queen to survive for a few more seconds. To bear her loss, just after Aife…

I leapt into the fray, slicing my sword into the arm of the first opponent. They had been so focused on fighting Evelyn that they had not noticed us. My foe staggered. I battered my shield into his temple. The Bernician clattered back onto the palace steps, either unconscious or dead.

A moment later, John crashed into another raider. By now, Evelyn had slid her sword across the neck of one soldier and had turned to face the other. Almost before I could blink, she had deftly evaded his attack. She ducked under his wild blow and as she crouched, she pulled her dagger out and slid it across his leg. He grunted in pain, staggering. She plunged her blade into his abdomen at a gap in his armour.

"Daniel!" Evelyn ran down the last of the steps to embrace me. The nearness of her, alive, overwhelmed my senses briefly. I had kept my promise to come back to her.

"Imogen?" I asked simply, as we stepped apart. Evelyn's features softened a little as she stepped back. Her quick nod was enough to keep hope burning alive in my heart.

"She is safe. She is with most of our people, evacuating through our caves as we speak." She glanced around at the soldiers from Klumeck and Gaeson. "Is this all of you?"

"Many are dead. Others are wounded and are on their way to Caer Ligualid. We lost, my lady." Evelyn nodded as the soldiers began to form ranks around us. The knowledge that Evelyn was alive, and our daughter was safe gave me a chance to breathe again.

However, I had not forgotten King Ethelfrith's threat. For all we knew, he was just behind us, ready to make sure Gaeson was left in ruins.

"King Ethelfrith may be coming," I told Evelyn swiftly. "It is not safe here. We must hurry to Caer Ligualid." Instinct told me that this would be the last day I would stand in my home.

"Your Majesties!" I looked up at John's warning. More raiders emerged into the courtyard. Their countenances were blackened with soot, sneers stretching across their faces.

They were determined to slaughter every last one of us, including my queen. I straightened, raising the tip of my blade. I would not let another royal of Rheged be put to the sword, even after King Morgant had been sent to his grave.

"For our people! For Queen Evelyn!" The cry tore from my throat. The raiders charged. We ran forwards as one line, with Evelyn, John and I slightly ahead. Fighting was a blur as we dodged and parried, our blades hacking into whatever flesh we could find under their armour.

The raiding party that remained were few. Clearly, they had not been expecting Gaeson to put up so much of a fight, nor any reinforcements. I ducked out of the way of my final opponent, then sliced my blade across his thigh. As he stumbled, I slammed my arm into his nose. He fell back, blood spurting.

I glanced around to see if there were any others left, but the skirmish had stopped as quickly as it had begun. Evelyn pulled her bade out from where it had pierced a Bernician's abdomen. I ran over to her. A little blood flowed from under a cut on her cheek, where her helmet stopped, but she seemed uninjured.

"I know not if there are any more of them," my wife said, between rasped breaths. We both turned this way and that, looking for any more raiders. By now, the fire had spread to most of the wooden buildings. I could feel the heat of the blaze from the courtyard.

"We must move quickly!" Evelyn ordered. "Do a search of the town." She turned to her personal guard. Most of them had survived.

"Blow the horn if you come across the enemy. A few of you go to the caves. Tell any that remain to head here. I mean not to leave any one behind."

"At once, Your Majesty." John dipped his head and then began barking orders himself. Evelyn and I left the courtyard.

"I split the soldiers that remained here into three parties," my queen said. "Some came out to fight; some guarded the caves and some escorted our people away. I believe most of Gaeson escaped unharmed." I glanced to her. The key word was 'most'. How many of our citizens were dead?

"You did well, my love." My voice was swift and urgent as we left the courtyard, soaked in Gaeson blood. We could do nothing else to help the dead. The fire would soon consume them.

"Did my mother escape? Rachel and the children?" The pained questions came swiftly from my lips as we came to a stop to check in the old wooden church building, where Evelyn and I had married.

"Aye. They're on their way to Caer Ligualid with the others." At this, my eyes closed briefly. At least I could stop imagining my mother burning alive in flames, trapped in her chamber without the strength to leave her bed.

We made our way out of the church again. There had been no one inside that we could tell. Flames already licked its walls. Soon, the ravaging flames would leave nowhere in our home safe.

"We were right to prepare for King Morgant's raid." I did not bother to hide my fury. "It was sent just before the battle started." I rubbed at the grime on my chin as we hurried down a steep street.

"King Morgant killed King Owain," I reported. Evelyn's eyes shot wide. "I killed King Morgant before Prince Elffin met the same fate. King Elffin," I corrected.

"At least one of you were able to stop him." She rose a hand to rub the cut on her cheek. Then she reached for my hand. "Thank you for returning so swiftly. There weren't enough of us to stop them all. If you hadn't arrived when you did…"

"I'm glad we got here in time," I told her quietly. "It's good to see you alive, my love," I murmured. The feel of her hand and her nearness brought me much comfort.

"You, too." The corners of her mouth softened. "John also." Then I saw her frown and step back, looking around. "Daniel…?" she faltered.

I tried not to flinch as I glanced to her, already seeing the question take shape in her eyes. She was going to ask me what I desperately did not want to tell her.

"Come on," I said suddenly, changing the subject. "John is leading a search through Gaeson, but nobody's checking outside the town."

"I need your horse," Evelyn told a nearby soldier trotting past on a steed. He got down at once an Evelyn swung up and gathered the reins. I swung up behind her. "With us!" she called.

"Aye, my lady." They broke into a jog before us while my queen set off the horse at a trot. We soon left the town behind us, winding our way through the back fields around the castle. The thick wall of smoke darkened the morning sky.

I had made no suggestion of where to go, but my wife knew me well. Without a word passing between us, she understood that I needed to see it one last time.

"Oh," Evelyn murmured, pulling up short. The stables were already on fire. The steed we had taken from the soldier pawed the ground. It was ridiculous, but suddenly I was glad Epos was not here, to see her home destroyed. "I'm so sorry, Daniel—"

"It matters not." The words were too forced, too bitter from my lips to hold any truth. "It's just a building." Except it wasn't. It was a thousand memories of my childhood, tending to the horses with my father. It was in these stables that I had helped birth Epos. It was here when I first met Evelyn as a child, when we played in the snow and she gave me her cloth. Where I hid in the hayloft, the day I was told my father had died in battle.

"Daniel…" She turned around in the saddle to look at me. I braced myself, already knowing the question. "I didn't see Aife in the courtyard," she said carefully. "Please, tell me she is with the wounded, on her way to Caer Ligualid."

"I wish I could." My answer was hoarse. A fresh tear slid down my face, cutting through the mixture of sweat and grime. "Aife died in the battle," I told her brokenly.

"Oh, Daniel." Shock and pain entered her face as she grabbed my hand. "I'm so sorry. I knew what a friend she was to you. To both of us."

"Aye." My answer was short as I took my hand from hers, looking away. “Come on,” I said, bitterness rife in my speech. “Let’s get back to the others. If anyone was in the stables, there’s nothing we can do for them now.”

“Very well.” With that, Evelyn steered the horse around, away from my childhood. The two of us rode back to the courtyard in silence. I pushed my grief further down — for Aife and for our home.

“Your Majesties.” John ran over to us and dipped his head. “We saw no other survivors, in the town or in the caves. We checked in the houses, we shouted as we went, but… there was no one. The raiders seem to have gone.” I nodded tightly — of course they had. There was nothing left for them to raid.

“We must leave, now,” I said, swinging down from the steed. “King Ethelfrith’s forces may be rested by now. He could be heading straight for the road to Caer Ligualid, to find the survivors.”

“Very well. Give the order to leave, Captain.” To my queen’s credit, Evelyn gave no indication of the sadness she felt at learning of Aife’s death, or that she had just ordered us away from our home. I ran to swing up onto Epos.

“Aye, my lady. We march!” John called in a loud voice. The soldiers with us had by this time mounted their horses. I reached to absently pat Epos’ mane one more time to try to calm her.

We departed the square, heading through the portcullis and back down the hill through the barricade. Though it broke my heart to leave my home, it was a relief to get away from fire and smoke. I sucked the clean, summer air back into my lungs. Every clap of our hooves took us closer to our people. My stomach tightened that King Ethelfrith might not be far away. Would he meet us on the road?

Ere long we rode back along the great lake. For now, we took the horses at an easy trot, to try to rejuvenate their energy. Hopefully, it would be easier to break into a gallop if the Bernicians suddenly appeared, either ahead or behind. I glanced up to the hills on the other side of the path. It could be the perfect spot for an ambush.

I opened my mouth — then closed it again abruptly. Grief smashed through me as the unsaid words burned in my throat.

“Go and keep an eye out on those hills above us.” John’s voice was rough beside me. My gazed snapped to him, but my captain’s countenance was as guarded as ever. "If the enemy is there, they will be spotted, my lord," he said quietly.

"Very good." I knew I could trust those two archers as much as I had once trusted Aife. Still, I kept my gaze on John for a moment longer. Had he guessed what I had been about to say? That I had been about to speak her name?

"Well?" I called to the two archers as they reached the high ground, slightly adjusting the reins in my hands. "Do you see anything?"

"Nothing yet, Your Majesty," one of the archers replied. This news gave my heart hope. It meant that our people were that much closer to Caer Ligualid.

"Keep your eyes sharp," John called to them. I looked to him again, but he was now facing forwards, his face as impassive as ever. I wondered if John knew how close I had come to speaking Aife's name out of instinct. I sighed as I tightened my grip on the reins. We simply had to find our people.

***

"Your Majesties!" One of the archers called out, about an hour later. "I see our people! We have almost caught up with them, my lady," he added to Evelyn. The relief was all too plain on his features. "They are around the next bend, after we finish crossing the lake."

"Very well." Then she turned to me with a slight frown. "I'm glad we are nearly with our people again," she told me in a low voice. "Yet I ordered them to evacuate a long while ago, when our watchmen first spied the raiding party. I know we have been moving faster than them, but—"

"They should be much further ahead," I said. My brow furrowed. If after all this time, they had only escaped such a short distance from Gaeson, then it meant that our people were weak. Many of them could be injured. It would make them harder to protect. As much as I would be overjoyed to be seeing Imogen again so soon, I had prayed that our people had progressed further than this.

"Captain," Evelyn called, with fresh urgency in her voice. "Give the order," she said. "We must catch up with them."

"Aye, my lady." He inclined his head and gathered his reins tightly. "With me!" my captain called, as the three of us kicked off the group into a gallop, the others following close behind.

"Keep going, girl," I murmured. I knew Epos would not have fully recovered from the hard riding here — but with our people so close, I had little other choice. Together, we turned the bend in the path, our horses thundering along the road. Then, all at once, I saw them in one long line. It eased my heart greatly to see how many had survived.

"Form a perimeter around them!" John ordered. Many of our people heard his cry and turned back. We were close enough to observe their faces. Some smiled in relief, others hardened with dismay. I could tell why. There was a fair contingent on their way to Caer Ligualid, but even so, the losses we had endured was all too plain.

I slowed Epos to a canter, making my way to the front of the lines of people. I knew Imogen would be here somewhere. Evelyn kept a steady pace beside me, our horses moving in harmony. As we rode, a few expressions turned to joy as soldiers were spotted by spouses and children. However, I could hardly bear the terrible grief marking most of Gaeson's survivors.

"Father!" Imogen cried, as at last my gaze found her. A servant lowered her from a carriage. I slowed to Epos to a stop and dismounted as my daughter ran through the crowd. My heart lightened immensely to see the joy in her face. It was the happiest she had looked since her capture. I pulled off my helmet and bent to one knee just as my child dived into my arms.

"Immy!" I wound my arms around her. My reunion with Imogen was as sweet as when she woke in the cave all those months ago. "I'm so glad to see you safe," I murmured, one hand stroking the honey strands of her hair.

"You too, Father. Mother." She reached out with one hand to Evelyn. The three of us clung together tightly. As our embrace ended, Imogen glanced around.

"There's Uncle John." We looked to see him near the back of the lines, still on horseback. Even from hear we could hear his urgent orders.

"Where's everyone else?" Imogen asked. The ball of dread came back. Aife and my daughter had grown closer than ever in the months since her return to us. I remembered Imogen and Aife in the stables, tending to Epos and braiding her mane in the style of Aife's hair. I fought not to bite my lip. How could I begin to tell my daughter that one of her favourite people was dead?

"Some people were wounded in the battle, darling." My wife's gentle voice spared me from answering. "They went straight to Caer Ligualid. They'll be waiting for us there, won't they?"

"Aye, Mother." Imogen's expression cleared as if something had been solved for her. My heart tightened again. Did my daughter believe Aife would be waiting for her? I didn't want to cause my daughter undue pain, but was it better to tell the whole truth now?

"Why not go back now, Immy?" I shot a glance at my queen. Had she sensed my dilemma? "You'll be safer in the carriage, love," Evelyn said, still looking at our daughter.

"Aye, Mother," Imogen answered obediently. My wife then beckoned over a nearby castle servant, who at once came over.

"Please take her back," Evelyn ordered quietly. "We'll stay close." A servant castle escorted Imogen back to the carriage.

"I'm sorry, Daniel." Evelyn sighed as she glanced my way. "I wasn't sure if now was the right time to tell her. Maybe once we're safe in Caer Ligualid."

"I didn't know either," I murmured. The decision was made now, but had we done the right thing? I did not want to deceive my child, but she was still only four years old. She needed our protection, perhaps now more than ever. Aye, it would be better to tell her the truth once we were in Caer Ligualid.

My eyes were still on Imogen as the carriage door opened. My heart leapt to see my mother there, looking relatively comfortable. Her eyes were full of tears as she smiled, then the carriage door was shut again.

I nudged Epos' reins and set her off at a walk. I looked to see how the soldiers had spread out, sparsely scattered down the lines. John had ordered archers to the high ground, where they kept their eyes peeled for any sign of the enemy.

Our pace on the road to Caer Ligualid was slow. Only a few citizens were on horseback and the carts were taken up with the injured. The vast majority walked, more than a few of them limping. Leigh ran amongst the lines with the help of nurses to administer aid to the worst of the wounded.

I smiled then to see Cara alive, sat on the edge of a cart further down the lines. Though one hand lightly rested on the spot where the arrow had pierced her, she looked well on her way to recovery. Ewan walked beside the cart; I guessed he had given his horse to another soldier. I hoped the two of them would have some peace together, if that was what they wanted.

I glanced behind me again. This was irrational, for the archers on the high ground would spot the Bernicians long before I did. My mind raced with King Ethelfrith's threat. Surely, he chased us at this very moment, following the raid King Morgant sent. The only question was whether they would reach us before we arrived at Caer Ligualid. Or, possibly, if they had headed straight for Caer Ligualid, they could be up ahead, ready to block us. That would be even more dangerous.

My heart tightened with the grief that Gaeson would be no more. It was in the hands of the Bernicians now, set ablaze with the same fires that had once engulfed Klumeck. I glanced to my wife to see her features as hardened as ever. I pushed down on my emotions. There would be time to grieve later. The essence of my home was here, traipsing along the lakes and hills of Rheged.

My hand moved to stroke Epos' neck once again. At least moving so slowly gave our horses a chance to recover. I hoped that the horses would soon gather enough strength to meet the Bernicians head on, should they suddenly come into view. I too relished the slow pace after the hard riding. I let my eyes close briefly, trying to make my body relax a little. All my muscles were tense from the battle and the riding and the grief, even in slumber. We were here, I told myself. The beating heart of Gaeson still lived.

I glanced to John, riding his horse at the other side of our people. I wondered if my friend had slept even a wink, whether a morsel of food sat in his belly. Only up close, when I saw that my brother's eyes were a little bloodshot, did he give the merest hint of the torture his soul was going through. John's voice was strong when he barked orders to the soldiers. Even in his grief, my captain was as steadfast as ever.

Later, as twilight hues faded and the sky transformed from turquoise to the deeper colours of night, Evelyn ordered we make camp. The soldiers' tents were given over to the worst of the wounded. Water was collected from a nearby stream and a little food distributed, some having had the foresight to take whatever was in their larders during the evacuation.

"Your Majesties." A soldier held out some food for us, wrapped in cloth. Evelyn and I were sat with our backs against the fallen log. Imogen lay half curled up to my wife's side.

"Thank you," I murmured, not wanting to wake my daughter. The soldier dipped his head and moved on, distributing the food elsewhere.

Evelyn gave a small, tired smile of thanks as I handed her a hunk of bread. Along with the small pieces of bread there was a portion of cheese and a piece of chicken for us each. As I ate, I reached for the skin of wine I had taken again from Epos' saddlebag. I had thought to find John, but he was on the far side of the camp. Between mouthfuls, I took a swift gulp.

"Here." I passed the wine to my queen. Her eyebrows rose slightly, but she did not comment. Evelyn took a long drink before handing it back. The wine was almost empty. I tilted my head back to swallow the remaining dregs.

"Forgive me, about Aife." My wife sighed, raising her gaze skyward. "Imogen witnessed the destruction of her home today. I thought… it was too much to bear."

"I know." I let the empty wineskin fall to the ground. "It may come as a shock, if she is expecting to see…" I still could not speak my friend's name without it burning my throat.

"Aye. At least then we can pray it will be safe to grieve—" My queen's voice caught, the first crack of grief showing through at all we had lost. "I just want to get our people to Caer Ligualid," she muttered, turning her head away.

"We should get some rest," I said quietly. "Try to sleep if we can." My hand reached out until it found Evelyn's. Her fingers wrapped around mine instantly. I leant back again against the log, closing my eyes. The pure exhaustion of the last few days had caught up with me. As I felt the tug of slumber, I barely had the strength to pray that God would bring some comfort and rest to John. Then I yielded to sleep, allowing sweet oblivion to embrace me.

Chapter Sixteen

The warmth of sunlight, gently filtering down onto my face, woke me the next morning. For a moment I was suspended in the world of half-slumber. Comfortable in the blanket and with my wife sleeping beside me, for a moment I almost believed I was at home, in my bed in Gaeson. Then the crackling of fires and the even tread of soldiers reached my ears.

I started fully awake, sniffing the faintly warm air as I looked around. As my senses came to life, my legs became uncomfortable, cramped from sleeping sitting up. I slid from the blanket and got to my feet, careful not to disturb Evelyn and Imogen. Both were fast asleep, huddled together. As I surveyed the camp, I was pleased it was almost midsummer. Had Gaeson been lost during the winter, I wasn't sure the fires and few blankets between us would keep us warm.

"Morning, Your Majesty." A servant passed two cups of something into my hands. It was stewed tea again, water boiled with herbs and a taste of honey. It would do the job of easing my stiff bones. I nodded my thanks at the servant and sipped at the scalding drink.

"Where are we?" The question came from Imogen as I turned to my daughter, rubbing sleep from her eyes. My wife stirred beside her.

"We camped off the road to Caer Ligualid." I blew on the tea before tasting it again. "I hope we arrive there today," I said. Evelyn nodded back, a knowing frown crossing her face. On horseback at a good pace, we would reach Caer Ligualid by the afternoon. However, at the rate our people travelled, it was possible we would need to camp a second night. I could only hope we reached Caer Ligualid before the last of daylight disappeared.

"Thank you," Evelyn said, taking the cup from me after getting to her feet. My queen glanced around the camp. "All looks the same." I nodded. "Here, Immy, have some tea." She stooped to our daughter. "Careful, it's hot." Imogen sat on the log as she sipped cautiously.

"Good morning, Your Majesties, Your Highness." John bowed as he approached. I could tell instantly how little he had slept.

"You go on ahead, you can report to me later," Evelyn said. I gave her a nod before John and I headed off a little way from Imogen, to talk more frankly.

"The watchmen reported nothing out of turn during the night, my lord," my captain began as we came to a stop. "I received word from Leigh at dawn. Four of the worst of the wounded made it through the night. Leigh believes they should recover fully in Caer Ligualid. Two older men have died," he said.

"Damn." I rubbed a hand over my unkempt features. "I'd hoped we'd had enough of death. Let's hope the rest of them survive." I glanced to my friend. "It seems such a foolish question, to ask how you are." John's gaze remained as steady as ever, despite the slight redness in his eyes.

"I am ready to serve, Your Majesty." Then my captain's face softened a little. "She would want me to continue my duty, to see our people safe."

"Aye," I murmured. "I think you could be right." Duty was John's way of surviving. "Then, I suppose, we'd better ready our people for the day."

"My lord." John dipped his head. I watched my friend walk away. It almost doubled my grief for Aife, to see what her death was doing to this man who had loved her so. Who loved her still, as did I.

The morning sunshine rose as we set off once more, our pace steady but slow. Some of the children soon began to move freely between the lines as the warm summer sun soaked their bones. Even Epos began to relax, twitching her ears a little.

We kept our eyes peeled ahead and behind, but King Ethelfrith's force did not appear. My heart began to believe we might make it to Rheged's capital city safely. The terrain flattened out as we left the mountains and lakes behind us. At last, as sun dipped below the horizon and faded to twilight, Caer Ligualid came into view. The magnificent castle with its three spires had never been a more beautiful sight.

"Nearly there, girl." I lowered my hand to pat Epos' neck gently. I glanced behind me, but there was nothing. The archers were further behind, still looking out for enemy movements.

If I might suggest, Your Majesties." John pulled up his horse beside us. "We could send the Gaeson citizens through first, while we form a line of defence."

"Aye, very good," Evelyn answered. Our captain inclined his head. At once, he was trotting his horse down the line, shouting his orders into the clear early evening.

"I bid you to go with them, my love." My voice was urgent as I turned to her in the saddle. "It is your decision," I said. "You are Gaeson's ruler, not me. Your people need you, as does Imogen."

"Your people need you as well, Daniel. As Imogen needs her father," Evelyn murmured softly. She rested her hand on my cheek. The stubble had lengthened since my ride to war.

"The Klumeck citizens are well established here," I pointed out evenly. "They have Sarah to lead them. Gaeson needs you, our queen." She regarded me a moment longer.

"Very well," she said, as the citizens began walking to Caer Ligualid. I took her hand and briefly kissed it. A sad smile flashed across her features as we broke apart.

"I'll see you soon," I told her. My queen nodded and gathered her reins, before heading to the long lines of our people. I knew Evelyn more than matched my skills in battle, having been trained for war since she was a child… but I could not deny how my heart lightened to see her heading for safety.

"Father!" I frowned in surprise, seeing Imogen had somehow left the carriage and had broken from the lines.

"Immy," I called back, quickly dismounting in time to catch her as she ran into me. "What are you doing here? You need to get inside the city, now." A slight rebuke entered my tone. Imogen only shook her head as the sobs started.

"It's much safer in Caer Ligualid, love," I told her, my arms wrapping around her for a moment. "Your mother and Aunt Sarah are waiting for you. I won't be long behind." Imogen only clung tighter to me. I swallowed hard. How could I make my four-year-old understand?

"Imogen, you have to do this." My voice became sterner. "One day, you will learn what it takes to lead these people. I have to think of you and your mother being safe now."

"Take her, quickly," I told the servant who had caught up with her. Imogen was still crying as the servant took hold of her. "I'm sorry," I called to Immy, as the servant ran with my daughter in her arms. I closed my eyes against the tears that threatened to well. I hoped this was not the last time I would see my daughter, in such distress.

"Come on, girl." I swung back up onto my faithful friend. "One last fight." Though there was still nothing but endless plains, my instinct told me the Bernicians were right behind us. I rode Epos at a trot to fall into line, bringing her to a stop beside my captain.

"Is Her Highness all right, my lord?" John enquired in a low voice. My glance flickered to him briefly, before fixing my gaze resolutely again onto the landscape before us.

"Aye. She just…" my voice trailed. "She wants this to be over, as do we all," I finished. "I — do you hear that?" I asked. The sound of galloping grew ever louder.

"This is it," I said. Any moment now, the Bernicians would be spilling onto the plains. I glanced back to Caer Ligualid, still a good distance away. Our people were going as fast as they could, but their pace would be slow with the wounded in their midst.

"Maintain this line of defence!" John's loud call passed over all the soldiers. "We just need to give our people enough time to reach Caer Ligualid!"

Soon, the galloping cracked the air like thunder. My hands flexed a little on the reins. I dreaded the moment when the Bernicians appeared. Yet, I could not deny that some part of me was willing them on, wanting to put to the sword every single one of them. For Aife and all we had lost.

"Archers, prepare to fire!" I shouted. I reached back a hand. My fingers brushed feathers as I counted my arrows. Six. I cursed silently — but six was better than nothing.

The thunder of their galloping worsened. My eyes widened in alarm, as my fingers rested, poised upon my bow. How many of them were there? None of them had spilled over the top of the cliffs yet.

"Your Majesty!" John's voice called abruptly over the din of clopping hooves. My brother pointed behind us. I twisted round in my saddle to follow his gaze. Across the plain, riding down to us were soldiers from Gaeson, Klumeck and Caer Ligualid. Any that could stand

and hold a blade. Even amidst defeat, our unity had never been stronger.

"Captain!" It was my turn to point. The Bernicians came into view at last. They were too far away to make their countenances, but I could imagine King Ethelfrith's frustration that they had not caught up with us before now.

"It looks as though King Ethelfrith did not come with his full army, sire." The Bernician lines came to a swift halt across the plains. "Nor does he have the Deirans fighting with him."

"Aye. He said he had to wait for his army to rest after the battle. Maybe they are not as recovered as he would like," I wondered aloud. In that moment, the swirling rage to smash every Bernician in my path disappeared. All I saw was a sea of battle-weary souls that didn't want to be here. I glanced behind me again to see King Elffin leading his troops, thundering past the line of Gaeson citizens.

"They are just as exhausted as we are," I said. "Ride to King Ethelfrith with me, Captain. Perhaps we can prevent further blood from being shed."

"Your Majesty." John dipped his head. John and I rode out, leaving the wall of soldiers behind. As I draw nearer, I picked out King Ethelfrith, next to the lanterns being sparsely lit by the enemy lines. Surprise entered his features. He had obviously not expected us to have a conversation.

He turned to one of his warriors. We waited to see if he would give us the chance to talk. King Ethelfrith nodded to a soldier in brighter armour. I guessed it was his captain. The two of them began riding out to meet us. The Bernician king's features were hard and worn, his jaw locked.

"Your Majesty King Ethelfrith." I gave him a nod as the two of them joined us, directly in between the lines of battle. "I thought I might see you again soon."

"King Bryce." A faint smile crossed his features as he angled his head. "We chased you all the way from Catraeth. I had to give our people more rest than I thought, but I'm impressed we did not catch up with you before now." His tone held begrudging, reluctant respect.

"Thank you." My voice was a little strange to my ears. I wasn't used to being complimented by my enemies. "I have a proposal for you, sire," I said. "When we last met, you showed me mercy. Allow me to return that mercy in kind."

"Oh?" he asked. "What exactly did you have in mind?" There was a faint thread of sarcasm running through his tone, but his eyes were alit with interest.

"You are here only with a small force, my lord. You thought to defeat us before we reached to Caer Ligualid." King Ethelfrith conceded this point with another tilt of his head.

"Without the army of Deira, we are now almost evenly matched, but I would guess Rheged just outnumbers yours," I went on. "My proposal is this. I offer you the chance to leave here, now. I give you my word you would not be pursued." King Ethelfrith's eyebrows raised.

"My men have just spent the last two days pursuing you," he pointed out. "What makes you think I would leave you now, with all Rheged so close within my grasp?"

"You won the battle at Catraeth," I admitted. "However, with respect, sire, you underestimated our speed in reaching Gaeson and Caer Ligualid. You did not take enough soldiers with you," I told him bluntly. King Ethelfrith's eyes narrowed into a glare, yet he did not contradict me.

"I think we have all had enough blood spilt these last few days," I told him. "All of us will have lost cherished friends in this war and my people are as weary as yours. Fight us if you must, but I offer you this chance to leave without a battle. Let there be no more deaths this day," I said.

"An interesting proposal," he said flatly. At least the Bernician king seemed to be considering it. He frowned, glancing to his captain, who looked as impassive as John had ever done. Then he sighed as he glanced back to me.

"I believe you are right. There has been plenty enough death already. I thank you, King Bryce." King Ethelfrith looked most deflated. "However, if we ever meet again, I will not show you mercy." I nodded at him evenly.

"Aye, I would expect no less. Neither will we." King Ethelfrith smirked, tilting his head to another side nod. Then he took his reins and began shouting orders in his Bernician tongue. As one, the lines turned and began their swift retreat. By the flickering lights of the lanterns, relief was all too plain on the enemy soldiers that there would be no battle today.

"Well, that was easier than it could have been." My shoulders slumped as my posture began to relax, watching King Ethelfrith lead his warriors away.

"Aye, Your Majesty." A trace of a smile briefly flickered across John's features. "King Elffin may be angry that there is no opportunity to put him to the sword," he said. The sparse lanterns accompanying King Ethelfrith's lines faded, leaving us in the gathering darkness of night.

"Aye, well." I sucked in the cool night air, before releasing it out again in a sigh of relief. "Better to face his wrath than to be in another battle. He'll understand. Come on." The two of us rode back to the conjoined armies of Rheged. As we neared them, I saw the relief written as large on their faces as it had been on the Bernicians. In that moment alone, I knew with absolute certainty I had made the right decision to extend King Ethelfrith mercy.

"Where has he gone?" King Elffin roared, features ruddy with anger. John and I came to a stop and dismounted before him.

"He has returned to Bernicia, Your Majesty." I removed my helmet. "We both agreed there had been too much bloodshed these last few days. I gave my word we would not pursue them, my lord."

"I am the Supreme Ruler of Rheged, not you!" King Elffin shouted, nostrils flaring. "What gives you the right to extend mercy, if I do not wish to?" His cold glare reminded me of King Owain and King Urien before him.

"I will gladly speak of this to you, Your Majesty." I bowed my head to him. "Perhaps in your grand throne chamber?" I did not wish to have a dispute in front of all the soldiers standing around. King Elffin's eyes narrowed even further, but then he nodded.

"Very well. You will join me there immediately." His words were closer to a growl. King Elffin wiped his mouth roughly with the back of his hand, then his eyes roved around him. The soldiers were silent, bent on bended knee.

"Dismissed!" His enraged bark pierced the still air. King Elffin turned to walk swiftly back through the gate. The Caer Ligualid soldiers filed in after him, but the armies of Gaeson and Klumeck remained where they were.

"You have fought well, all of you," I said quietly, turning my gaze to them. "May God grant you rest, and time with your loved ones. Dismissed." They too began to walk through the portcullis, onto the Caer Ligualid's courtyard, far grander than the one at Gaeson. As we walked, it hit me again that this was my new home. I might never see the old castle town again.

"Father!" Imogen broke free from Evelyn as I entered the courtyard. I bent down as she ran past the lines of soldiers, finally beginning to break from formation. I stooped down to scoop her up, my arms holding her small form tenderly.

"Hello, Immy." I kissed the top of her head before gently lowering her to her feet, eternally thankful I could see my darling daughter once more.

"I saw what happened." I glanced up to see Evelyn walking towards me, a small smile of relief painted across her features.

"Aye." I bent my head to kiss her briefly. My heart lessened slightly. Finally, it was over. The heavy shroud of mourning was punctuated with the sounds of friends and lovers reuniting. Perhaps, for a time, we could have peace again.

"I have to talk to King Elffin," I told her quietly as we broke apart again. My hand rested momentarily on Immy's shoulder. "I'll see you both soon."

I turned to cross Caer Ligualid's courtyard. Cobbles shimmered with the amber glow from lanterns suspended around the stone walls. Soldiers and citizens stood aside as I headed to King Elffin's throne room. The glimpses of happy reunions soothed me. I knew I had made the right decision, even if I could not persuade Elffin. If I had not shown King Ethelfrith mercy, how many more of us might have died?

The two soldiers standing guard outside the entrance to the palace stood aside to let me in. I held my helmet under one arm. My left hand hastily attempted to smooth the mass of auburn waves that was my hair, matted together with sweat, dirt and dried blood. I ran my hand once or twice over my face, knowing it would do nothing to improve my appearance.

"His Majesty King Bryce, of Klumeck," a guard called, as I

approached the throne. It was a little strange to see King Elffin sitting there, as King Owain and King Urien had done before him.

"Your Majesty, King Elffin, Supreme Ruler of Rheged." I bowed fully as I stopped just short of the palace steps.

"King Bryce." Elffin stood as he spoke my title, his mouth drawn into a thin line. I raised my head to see Elffin's flushed features, his mouth set into a hard line. How different he looked to the young lad I had practiced swordplay with, or who had been hunched on a bench, grieving his mother.

"Leave us!" he barked to the remaining guards. Immediately the rhythmic clunking of boots began, as his guards as one traipsed from the hall. "How dare you? What gave you the right?"

"Forgive me, my lord." I bent my head again. "I was merely attempting to prevent any more bloodshed. There have been enough deaths," I said quietly.

"It is not for you to judge how I deal with the enemy that approaches my gates," King Elffin answered back harshly. "Have you forgotten that King Morgant served King Ethelfrith? That man commanded those who killed my father!" His loud voice boomed around the palace chamber.

"The whole of Rheged is in mourning for King Owain, just as they are mourning for all we have lost. King Ethelfrith showed me mercy, sire," I reminded him. "King Morgant's raid had already destroyed my home, but my wife and child may not be alive if King Ethelfrith had not given me leave to go to Gaeson, to recover any survivors."

"So, you thought to return the same mercy to him. Noble thought," King Elffin scoffed. "Yet, it was my lands and my gates he marched to. The decision was mine, not yours." His voice had lowered, but his eyes were still full of anger. "Had he caught you but half an hour earlier, he would have had no hesitation in killing all of you."

"That is true, my lord. Had that happened, we would have fought until the end, but by God's providence we had already reached Caer Ligualid. I thought we had lost too much on both sides, sire." I sighed, allowing some of my weariness to seep through.

"Think of your people that will have been spared this day, my lord," I said now. "Just now, the courtyard is filled with reunions, with love and hope. Had we fought, we would have torn each other apart, with very little on either side left."

At this, the anger faded just a little from King Elffin's face and it relaxed just a little. He sniffed, wiping his mouth roughly with the back of his hand.

"Very well. I know why you did it, Daniel," he said, dropping my title. "This the last time you take a decision from me at my own doors."

"I am at your service, my lord the king." My answer was swift as I bowed once more. Though his talk had become more informal, I was only too aware of the edge of his words. Perhaps King Elffin would be far more like his father and grandfather than I had thought. King Elffin gave a final nod as he sat back on his throne.

"Your Majesty." I gave a last bow before departing the throne chamber. As I left, the palace guards traipsed back in to attend to their king.

"Daniel!" I turned to see Sarah running towards me. We embraced quickly. "I prayed you would come back alive, brother." As she pulled back from me, I saw the unshed tears in her eyes. "I heard…" she faltered and bit her lip.

"Aye," I said softly. Any relief was smashed away by grief again. "Aife gave her last breath protecting our people," I murmured, my hand on her shoulder. Sarah nodded. "Imogen doesn't know yet." We entered the courtyard together. "She's going to take it hard."

"Immy's been through a lot." My sister glanced at me again, folding her arms. "So Gaeson is truly gone, in the hands of the Bernicians." Sarah sighed. "First Klumeck was lost to us — and now Gaeson. How is Evelyn bearing it?"

"She endures it well." Absently, I ran my hand through my hair again, trying to separate the matted strands. "How does Pasgent fare?"

"My husband was injured in the battle, but he lives and will recover. More than I can say for most of us," Sarah murmured sadly. "I saw King Elffin's face when he came back. He tries to hide it, but I see how much he grieves for his father."

"So soon after the death of Queen Penarwen, too," I muttered. "I think he thirsts too much for Bernician blood. He would have fought them to the last."

"You did the right thing, Daniel." My sister's hand touched my arm.

"I cannot blame King Elffin for his anger, but perhaps in time he will learn to control it. Hopefully, peace will calm him."

"Aye." I stretched my weary arms above my head. "If you'll excuse me, I need a bath." Sarah gave a faint smile as she nodded.

"Of course. I was on my way to visit Pasgent." She gave my hand a final squeeze. I headed for the armoury, where at last, I peeled off my armour. It was almost too light just being in my clothes.

I walked through the castle, heading for the chamber Evelyn and I usually stayed in when we came to Caer Ligualid. I supposed it would be our permanent rooms now. My wife was already there. Without a word, she stepped forward and into my arms.

"I'm still filthy," I protested, for I could see Evelyn was newly washed. My queen let out a little noise somewhere between a sob and a laugh. She couldn't care less about my state.

"I'm so sorry, love," I murmured to her when my wife still did not speak. "I know what it is to lose a kingdom." She gave a small nod, against my shoulder.

"Immy is sleeping in the next chamber," Evelyn said quietly. "I prepared a bath for you." I sensed that she too wished to be alone, to process the battle and all that had happened.

"Thank you." I entered the bath chamber, beginning the familiar routine of remembering all who had fallen during the battle, including those I had killed. Then, when grief stabbed me, I knew today would be different. All my thoughts were filled with Aife.

Friend. Warrior. Archer. Sister. Intelligent, fierce, kind, spirited. These were just a few of the words that rolled in my head that could help describe one of my oldest and closest friends. Each one was woefully inadequate on its own, yet when pieced together could just about glimpse into the beauty of her character.

How was I to live in a world without my friend? I leant back as my sorrow swelled. Finally, without war and the desperation to save Gaeson's citizens from the sword, I could begin to grieve her fully. At last safe, with nothing else to distract me, I wept for my sister.

***

“Queen Widow Thaney.” I dipped my head to her as I met her in one of Caer Ligualid’s small halls. This was her formal title now, a queen all too briefly now King Owain was in the ground. I had long since bathed and rested and was on my way to hear a report from John about how our army was faring.

“King Bryce.” She gave a small curtsey. In her arms she held her baby son, Kentigern, now about six weeks old. “I was sorry to hear about what happened to your people, but I’m pleased most of them arrived safely in Caer Ligualid.”

“I thank you, my lady. I’m sorry for your loss. I know King Owain loved you well.” She did not reply at first, but the faintest glimpse of a smile flittered across her face.

“We must have had one of the shortest marriages in the history of Rheged. Three weeks we were wed,” she said bitterly. “Of those three weeks, we only had a few days before he marched to Catraeth.” All the injustice of war sparked in the queen widow’s eyes.

“Aye, lad, you’re tired.” She shifted her son in her arms as he whimpered. “You’ve not been introduced to him yet, have you?” Her tone was forcefully bright.

“I’ve not had the pleasure.” Her smile grew a fraction wider as she nudged the lad in my direction. I lifted my hand towards his soft, tiny palm. “He’s got a good grip,” I said, as his tiny hand grasped my finger.

“Aye, that he does.” Her smile faded as she glanced back up to me. “I have informed King Elffin of my plans to leave Caer Ligualid.” My eyebrows rose.

“So soon?” I frowned. Kentigern shuffled in the blankets and scrunched up his tiny face again. “Surely you are still welcome here.”

“Aye, officially.” She sighed as she rocked her son in her arms. “I know King Elffin still blames me for his mother’s death. The welcome in his halls is not very warm.”

“Queen Penarwen was seriously ill for months before you even met King Owain,” I pointed out. “King Elffin knows this.”

“Aye, but King Elffin blames me for her deteriorating so rapidly. He believes I sped up her passing.” Queen Widow Thaney sighed, looking away through the open window.

“I’m not too sure he isn’t wrong,” she admitted, sighing. “Besides, as beautiful as this city is, it was King Owain I loved, not Caer Ligualid. There is no home for me here without him." She glanced to me again. "I'm not sure my father would welcome me back," Queen Widow Thaney said, a faint bitter smile crossing her face. "I will go to my uncle in Strathclyde and raise Kentigern there."

"Then I wish you well." My hand brushed Kentigern's head briefly. "Perhaps you will visit, in time. Imogen will want to know him. He is cousin to Gilroy, so you are kin to us, even if it is distant."

"Thank you. Perhaps." She gave me a final, sad smile. "I need to put Kentigern down for his morning sleep. Good day to you, my lord."

"You as well, my lady." As she left, I turned to the large window again, overlooking the legendary spires of Caer Ligualid. Queen Widow Thaney's words ran through my head.

King Lot had barely concealed his anger at his daughter's wedding to King Owain. I wasn't sure if a single word had passed between them since. I hoped that Queen Widow Thaney would find some peace in Strathclyde to raise Kentigern. In time, she might reconcile with her father.

"Good day, Your Majesty." I looked over to see Taliesin the bard standing there, arms folded. I merely gave him a nod in his direction before turning back to the view. I was in no mood for his poetry or riddles. I only hoped he did not want me to give him an account of our recent defeat. I would rather this day be blotted from history than to live forever through his pen.

"I'm deeply sorry for what happened in Gaeson," he said quietly. I glanced to Taliesin, surprised by the sincerity of his speech.

"Thank you." The bard moved to join me by the window. I still needed to see John, but for some reason I did not excuse myself.

"I wonder if my uncle felt as lost as this, when Klumeck was lost to him." The words spilled out, rushed and foolish to my ears. Why in blazes was I confiding in him, of all people?

"I believe he did, sire." Taliesin's answer was quiet. His eyes, usually sharp, seemed kinder than usual. "In time, though, the people in Klumeck healed in the calm splendour of this city. I pray the people of Gaeson will also find their home here."

"Aye." I glanced to the bard again and sighed as curiosity sparked in his face. "Let me guess. You are about to tell me how your prophecy came true." I had not forgotten Taliesin's strange words the night Gilroy was born.

"It is true that I foretold the princess would face dangers, that she would then overcome. Her Highness has a remarkable strength of spirit," Taliesin said.

"King Morgant was determined to destroy the royals of Rheged, one at a time," I pointed out flatly. "It is no surprise he tried to do harm my daughter. It does not mean the rest of your prophecy will come true."

"Perhaps not, my lord king." Taliesin conceded this with a side nod. "However, I choose to believe her Highness may well turn the tide on this war. I suppose only time will tell." He turned his face back to the view of the city before us, with the plains stretching beyond.

"Aye, well. In the meantime, I need to focus on the present. I await a report from my captain. Good day." I gave him a curt nod and left before the bard had straightened from his pompous bow.

***

As dusk fell, Evelyn, John, Sarah and I stood outside, each with a goblet of wine. John had given me his sober report earlier. Though the beating heart of Gaeson's army remained, it had been stripped bare. So many had fallen. Others still lay in Caer Ligualid's surgery, waiting to see if they would last the night. Even if every wounded person fully recovered, our people would not be the same.

We stood around Aife's bow and quiver, lying neatly on the earth at our feet. There would be a general funeral in the next few days to honour all who had fallen in battle, but the four of us had agreed that it was right to gather here, to honour our friend. The wind picked up and billowed past us, carrying the scent of smoke. Though it was summer, the chill of the wind made the hairs on the back of my head stand up a little.

Time crawled on, yet still nobody spoke. All of us were lost in the thoughts of our sister. I glanced at my kin, painfully aware of Aife's absence. The moonlight and the fire illuminated their features. Sarah's eyes were glistening, but she did not weep. John stood as stoic as ever, almost oblivious to the silent trail of tears rolling down his face. Evelyn stood with her head bowed, her expression hidden. With the noise of the wind and the roaring flames, I could not tell whether she wept.

"We gather here to mark the passing of Aife," I began at last, voice hoarse. "All of us loved her well, in our way." I fought not to look at John. None of us would feel this pain as keenly as my brother.

"Aife was too brilliant for me to describe well here." I felt woefully inadequate to pay my fallen friend justice. "Though, a few things do come to mind. Her heart, for her people and her friends." I smiled faintly. "Her gift for compassion, her wit and good humour. Her skill as a warrior, with bow and spear," I said. "There was a fire in her eyes when she fought."

I searched for more to say, but my mind was hollow. Was this it, I wondered? Surely those few phrases were not enough to sum up her character, nor all that she meant to us. Would she soon be forgotten, along with all the rest of us one day?

"Well said, brother." Sarah spoke quietly. Her hand reached out to take mine as it began to rain. "Shall we head back to the castle?"

"Aye." I glanced to John to see his head bowed against the cold of the wind. "You go on ahead, I'll be there in a moment." I trudged a few steps across the sodden grass to stand beside my friend, who stood as unmovable as rock against the gathering storm.

"Might I have a word with you, John?" My voice was loud to reach him over the rain. My brother stood still for a moment longer, moving his hands to rub his face.

"Of course, Your Majesty." I fought not to sigh as he used my title. I wanted to support him as a friend and brother, but perhaps to return to the formality of our roles was his way to survive. John raised his eyes to meet mine.

"I wanted to tell you…" I clasped my hands together as they leaned atop the fence in front of us. "You need no longer serve me as captain, if you do not wish to."

"Sire?" His confusion was palpable as I looked to the dark mass of green at my feet. "Do you wish me to relinquish my duties?"

"No." Perhaps this conversation was not needed, given how much John clung to duty. "I only meant I would understand if you no longer wished to fight. I believe we might have peace, for a time. King Ethelfrith will need to rebuild his forces, if Deira is no longer fighting with him. I would understand if you desired peace," I said.

“I pray you are right, sire, about the enemy’s forces.” John lowered his head. The wind died down again suddenly as he spoke into the darkness.

“For most of my life, I have known two things.” His voice was grim and quiet, yet I heard the strength behind it. “First, that I know how to fight,” he said. “The second is that I love Aife. She is no more, Daniel.” His voice caught as he dropped my title. “I do not think I can stop fighting, just as I cannot stop loving her, just because she is dead,” he admitted bluntly.

“I always knew Aife might die in battle, or me. Or both of us.” He sniffed and wiped his face again, roughly. “Yet I did not know it would cause this much pain.” He raised his head then, to regard me. “If I can no longer fight beside her, then perhaps I can fight for her.” His earnest, pained gaze bore into mine.

“My place is by your side, brother,” John said. “I know of nowhere else to go, no other way to be. My sword will remain yours until I see her again,” he vowed as I nodded slowly, swallowing the knot of grief that rose in my throat.

“There’s nowhere else I’d rather you be, my friend.” My voice was hoarse as I clasped his shoulder. “I’m fighting for her, too,” I said swiftly. “I’ll make sure, as far as God allows, that Aife did not die in vain.”

“I know.” John’s pained gaze tore from mine to look out across the plains to the city borders. Though the view was nigh invisible, my heart took me further, all the way back to Gaeson.

“Do you think we will ever see home again, Daniel?” John asked. Of course, he too had been drawn to thoughts of Gaeson.

“I hope so.” Suddenly, the wind and rain came back at full pelt. I folded my arms, bowed my head. “I’d like to think so, but… Gododdin is a mighty kingdom, yet we could not withstand Bernicia, even with their aid. Maybe one day.” I sighed. Water trickled down my forehead and dripped off my nose.

“We’ve suffered a severe blow, losing Gaeson.” John sighed as he stood back from the fence. “We can be thankful to be here, for the time being.”

“At least we didn’t make it an easy victory for them,” I said now. “Let us pray it takes Bernicia a long time to strengthen their forces against us.” I stretched my hands above my head, then wiped the rain clear from my face.

"Aye," John said, voice still a little heavy. "Come, let's get out of this foul weather." My old friend paused while he retrieved Aife's bow and arrows. We could keep them in safe Caer Ligualid's armoury, as a symbol of hope. A reminder that we were fighting for her and all the others we had lost this day.

John held them carefully under his arm as we trudged back to the castle. Warm fires, mead and wine would be waiting. The people of Gaeson would try to settle here, as Klumeck had done seven years ago. I prayed God would give us a little peace before Bernicia inevitably marched against Caer Ligualid. The reckoning of Rheged had come, yet we had managed to survive it.

One day, the Bernicians would strike again, attacking our very way of life. It could happen in one year, ten, or even longer. It was up to us to make the most of the peace while it lasted. I cast my eyes to the heavens, ignoring the drops of rain hitting my eyes.

"We'll make this time count, Aife." I whispered this promise as I imagined her walking with God, at eternal peace. Free from blood and war and pain.

My thoughts turned to Imogen, probably fast asleep by now. Would she remember Gaeson? Perhaps only a fleeting memory, like I had of living in Klumeck. Immy would grow up here in Caer Ligualid. One day, she might have to take up the sword herself in this awful war.

Taliesin's so-called prophecy came to mind, unbidden. I remembered too when Imogen was born, I believed her birth to be the forging of a blaze that could never be extinguished. Was that flame still lit? Would Imogen be the one to lead the campaign against our foes? Would she succeed where we had failed?

As we came back to the castle, I knew such wonderings were pointless. None of us knew the future, not even Taliesin. Only God knew the darkness that might still lie before us. The only thing we could do was to make the most of living our lives in peace. For as long as we could, we would keep the hope of Rheged alive.